Her Secret Child

She has a secret she must share…

Three passionate novels!

In April 2008 Mills & Boon bring back
two of their classic collections, each
featuring three favourite romances
by our bestselling authors…

HER SECRET CHILD

The Secret Love-Child by Miranda Lee
Her Secret Pregnancy
by Sharon Kendrick
Riccardo's Secret Child
by Cathy Williams

MISTRESS BY PERSUASION

His Pretend Mistress by Jessica Steele
Stand-in Mistress by Lee Wilkinson
The Millionaire's Virgin Mistress
by Robyn Donald

Her Secret Child

THE SECRET LOVE-CHILD
by
Miranda Lee

HER SECRET PREGNANCY
by
Sharon Kendrick

RICCARDO'S
SECRET CHILD
by
Cathy Williams

⊙™ MILLS & BOON®
Pure reading pleasure

*All the characters in this book have no existence outside the
imagination of the author, and have no relation whatsoever to anyone
bearing the same name or names. They are not even distantly inspired
by any individual known or unknown to the author, and all the
incidents are pure invention.*

*Harlequin Mills & Boon Limited,
Eton House, 18-24 Paradise Road, Richmond, Surrey TW9 1SR*

HER SECRET CHILD
© by Harlequin Enterprises II B.V./S.à.r.l 2007

The Secret Love-Child, Her Secret Pregnancy and *Riccardo's
Secret Child* were first published in Great Britain by Harlequin
Mills & Boon Limited in separate, single volumes.

The Secret Love-Child © Miranda Lee 2002
Her Secret Pregnancy © Sharon Kendrick 2000
Riccardo's Secret Child © Cathy Williams 2002

ISBN: 978 0 263 86122 8

05-0408

*Printed and bound in Spain
by Litografia Rosés S.A., Barcelona*

THE SECRET LOVE-CHILD

by

Miranda Lee

100 Reasons to Celebrate

We invite you to join us in celebrating
Mills & Boon's centenary. Gerald Mills and
Charles Boon founded Mills & Boon Limited
in 1908 and opened offices in London's Covent
Garden. Since then, Mills & Boon has become
a hallmark for romantic fiction, recognised
around the world.

We're proud of our 100 years of publishing
excellence, which wouldn't have been achieved
without the loyalty and enthusiasm of our
authors and readers.

Thank you!

Each month throughout the year there will
be something new and exciting to mark the
centenary, so watch for your favourite authors,
captivating new stories, special limited
edition collections…and more!

Miranda Lee is Australian, living near Sydney. Born and raised in the bush, she was boarding-school educated and briefly pursued a career in classical music, before moving to Sydney and embracing the world of computers. Happily married, with three daughters, she began writing when family commitments kept her at home. She likes to create stories that are believable, modern, fast-paced and sexy. Her interests include meaty sagas, doing word puzzles, gambling and going to the movies.

Don't miss Miranda Lee's exciting novel, *The Guardian's Forbidden Mistress,* out in April 2008 from Mills & Boon® Modern™.

CHAPTER ONE

'PLEASE, Rafe. My reputation for reliability is on the line here.'

Rafe sighed. Les had to be really desperate to ask him to do this. His ex-partner knew full well the one job he'd hated when they'd been in the photographic business together was covering weddings. Where Les enjoyed the drama and sentiment of the bride and groom's big day, Rafe found the whole wedding scenario irritating in the extreme. The pre-ceremony nerves got on *his* nerves, as did all the hugging and crying that went on afterwards.

Rafe was not a big fan of women weeping.

On top of that, it was impossible to be seriously creative when the criterion was simply to capture every single moment of the day on film, regardless. Rafe, the perfectionist, had loathed having to work with the possibilities that the weather might be rotten, the settings difficult and the bridal party hopelessly unphotogenic.

As a top-flight fashion and magazine photographer, Rafe now had control over everything. The sets. The lighting. And above all…the models. When you shot a wedding, you had control over very little.

'I presume you can't get anyone else,' Rafe said, resignation in his voice.

'The wedding's on Saturday, exactly a fortnight from

today,' Les explained. 'You know how popular Saturday weddings are. Every decent photographer in Sydney will already be booked.'

'Yeah. Yeah. I understand. Okay, so what do you want me to do?'

'The bride's due at your place at noon today.'

Rafe's eyes flicked to the clock on the wall. It was eleven fifty-three. 'And what if I'd refused?'

'I knew you wouldn't let me down. You might be the very devil with women, but you're a good mate.'

Rafe shook his head at this back-handed compliment. So he'd had quite a few girlfriends over the years. So what? He was thirty-three years old, a better-than-average-looking bachelor who spent his days photographing bevies of beautiful women, a lot of whom were also single. It was inevitable that their ready availability, plus his active libido, would keep the wheels turning where his relationships were concerned.

But he wasn't a womaniser. He had one girlfriend at a time, and he never lied or cheated. He just didn't want marriage. Or children. Was that a crime? It seemed to be in some people's eyes.

Rafe wished his married friends—like Les—would understand that not everyone wanted the same things out of life.

'Just give me some details before the bride actually arrives,' he said a tad impatiently, 'so I won't look a right Charlie.'

'Okay, her name is Isabel Hunt. She's thirtyish, blonde and beautiful.'

'Les, you think *all* your brides are beautiful,' Rafe said drily.

'And so they are. On the day. But this one is beautiful all the time. You're going to enjoy photographing Ms Hunt, I promise you. Or should I say, Mrs Freeman. The lucky girl is marrying Luke Freeman, the only son and heir of Lionel Freeman.'

'Is that supposed to mean something to me? Who the hell is Lionel Freeman, anyway?'

'Truly, Rafe, you're a complete philistine when it comes to subjects other than food, the Phantom and photography. Lionel Freeman was one of Sydney's most awarded architects. Poor chap was killed in a car accident a couple of weeks back, along with his wife, so tread easily with the groom when you finally meet him.'

'Poor bloke. What rotten luck.' Rafe's own father had been killed in a car crash when Rafe had been only eight. It had been a difficult time in his life, one he didn't like dwelling on.

'Oh-oh. I just heard a car pull up outside. The bride-to-be, I gather, and right on time. I hope she's just as punctual on her wedding day. Now what about money, Les? What do you charge for a wedding these days?'

'A lot less than you could command, my friend. But I'm afraid you'll have to settle for my fee. It's already been agreed upon and the full amount paid up front. If you give me your bank account number, I'll…'

'No, don't bother,' Rafe broke in, not caring about the money this once. Les might need it. He wouldn't be running around covering too many weddings with a broken leg. 'You can owe me one. Just don't ask again, buddy. Not where a wedding is concerned. Must go. The doorbell's ringing. I'll call you back after the bride's gone. Let you know what I thought of her.'

Rafe hung up and headed downstairs, then hurried along towards the front door, curious now to see if Les was exaggerating about the bride-to-be's blonde beauty.

She'd have to be something really special to surprise him. After all, he was used to beautiful blondes. He'd photographed hundreds. He'd even fallen madly in love with one once.

He'd been twenty-five at the time, and had just started climbing the fashion photographic ladder. Liz had been an up-and-coming cat walk model. Nineteen, nubile and too nice to be true. Only he hadn't realised that in the beginning. He'd become so besotted with her he'd actually begged her to live with him. Which she had. But only till she'd milked him for everything he was worth, both personally and professionally. Within a year she'd moved on to an older, more influential photographer, leaving an emotionally bruised and embittered Rafe behind.

He was no longer bruised, or bitter. That had all happened years ago. But he hadn't lived with a girlfriend since, no matter how much he might occasionally be tempted to. And he didn't date blondes any more. Experience had taught him blondes often played sweet and vulnerable and not too bright, when they were actually smart as a whip, sneakily manipulative and ruthlessly ambitious.

Photographing them, however, was another question. A blonde was still his model of choice.

Rafe wrenched open the front door to his inner-city terrace home and tried not to stare. Wow! Les hadn't exaggerated one bit.

What a pity she was going to be married, he thought as his male gaze swept over his visitor. Because if ever there was a blonde who might make him reassess his decision never to date one again, she was standing right in front of him.

Talk about exquisite!

Ms Isabel Hunt was the epitome of an Alfred Hitchcock heroine. Classically beautiful and icily blonde, with cheekbones to die for, cool long-lashed blue eyes and what looked like a perfect figure. Though, to be honest, she would have to remove the fawn linen jacket she was wearing over those tailored black trousers for Rafe to be sure.

'Ms Hunt?' he said, smiling warmly at her. What had been an irksome task in his mind now held the prospect of some pleasure. Rafe liked nothing better than photographing truly beautiful women. Of course, only the camera would tell if she was also photogenic. It was perverse that some of the most beautiful women in the flesh didn't always come up so well on film.

'Mr Saint Vincent?' she returned, her own gaze raking over him. With not much approval, he noted. Maybe she didn't like men who hadn't shaved by noon.

She looked the fussy type. Her make-up was perfection and her clothes immaculate. That white shirt she had on underneath her jacket was so dazzlingly white, it could have featured in one of those washing-powder ads.

'The one and only,' he replied, his smile widening. Most women, he'd found, eventually responded to his smile. Rafe liked his photographic subjects to be totally relaxed with him. Being stiff in front of a camera was the kiss of death when it came to getting good results. 'But do call me Rafe.'

'Rafe,' she said obediently, but coolly.

Ms Hunt, Rafe realised ruefully, was not a woman given to being easily charmed. Which perhaps was just as well. She was one gorgeous woman. Those eyes. And that mouth! Perfectly shaped and deliciously full, her lips were provocative enough in repose. How would he react if they ever smiled at him?

Don't smile, lady, he warned her silently. Or we both could be in big trouble!

'Would you object if I called you Isabel?' he said recklessly.

'If you insist.'

Was that contempt he saw flicker in her eyes? Surely not!

Still, Rafe decided to pull right back on the charm for now and get down to tin tacks.

'Les rang me a little while ago with just the barest of details,' he informed her matter-of-factly, 'so why don't you come inside and we can discuss a few things?'

He led her into the front room where he conducted most of his business. It wasn't an office as such, more of a sitting room, simply and sparsely furnished. The walls, however, were covered with his favourite photos, all of women in various states of dress and undress. None actually nude, but some were close, and all were in black and white.

'I don't see any wedding photos,' the bride-to-be noted curtly as he led her over to the nearest sofa.

'I no longer work as a wedding photographer,' he admitted. 'But I was once Les's partner, so don't worry. I know what I'm doing.'

She gave him a long hard look. 'I suspect you're more expensive than Les.'

Rafe sat down on the navy sofa opposite hers and leant back, stretching his arms along the back.

'Usually,' he agreed. 'But not this time. I'm doing this job as a favour to Les.'

'What about the actual photos? Will I have to pay more for them?'

'No.'

She glanced up at the prints on the wall again and almost rolled her eyes. 'You do take coloured snaps, don't you?'

Rafe was not a man easy to rile. He had a very even temper. But she was beginning to annoy him. Coloured snaps, indeed! He wasn't some hack or hobby photographer. He was a professional!

'Of course,' he returned, priding himself on sounding a lot calmer than he was feeling inside. 'I do a lot of fashion photography. And fashion wouldn't be fashion without colour. But wedding photographs do look fabulous in black and white. I think you'd be pleased with the results.'

'Mr Saint Vincent—' she began frostily.

'Rafe, please,' he interrupted, determined not to lose it. My, she was a snooty bitch. Mr Luke Freeman was welcome to her. Rafe wondered if the poor groom knew exactly what type he was getting here. Talk about an Ice Princess!

'The thing is, *Rafe*,' she said in clipped tones, 'I wouldn't have chosen a wine-red gown for my maid of honour if I wanted all the photographs done in black and white, would I?'

Rafe simply ignored her sarcasm. 'What colour is the groom wearing?'

'Black.'

'And yourself?'

'White, of course.'

'Of course,' he repeated drily, his eyes holding hers for much longer than was strictly polite.

She flushed. She actually flushed.

Rafe was startled. She *couldn't* be a virgin. Not at thirty. And not looking like that. It was faintly possible, he supposed. Either that, or sex wasn't her favourite pastime.

Rafe pitied the groom some more. It didn't look as if his wedding night was going to be a ball if his bride was this uptight about sex.

'I'm sorry but I really don't want my wedding photos done in black and white,' she pronounced coldly, despite her pink cheeks. 'If you feel you can't accommodate me on this, then I'll just have to find another photographer.'

'You won't find anyone decent at this late stage,' Rafe told her bluntly.

She looked frustrated and Rafe found some sympathy for her. He *was* being a bit stubborn, even if he *was* right.

'Look, Isabel, would you tell a painter how to paint? Or a surgeon how to operate? I'm a professional photographer. And a top one, even if I say so myself. I know what will look good, and you won't look just *good* shot in black and white. You'll look magnificent.'

She was clearly taken aback by his fulsome compliment. But he'd never had the opportunity to photograph a bride as beautiful as this. No way was he going to let her muck up his creative vision. With the automatic cameras now available, any fool could take colour snaps. But only Rafe Saint Vincent could produce black and white masterpieces!

'There will be any number of guests at your wedding taking coloured snaps, if you want some,' he argued. 'My job, however, is to give you quality photographic memories which will not only be beautiful, but timeless. I guarantee that you'll still be able to show your wedding photographs to your grandchildren with great pride. They won't be considered old-fashioned, or funny, in any way.'

'You're very sure of yourself, aren't you?' she threw at him in almost scornful tones.

'I'm very sure of my abilities. So what do you say?'

'I don't seem to have much choice.'

'You won't be disappointed if you hire me. Trust me on this, Isabel.'

She half rolled her eyes again.

Trust, Rafe realised, was something else Isabel Hunt did not do easily.

'Why don't you look at some of my more conventional black and white portraits?' he suggested, pushing over the album portfolio which lay on the coffee-table between them. 'You might find them reassuring. I confess the shots on my walls are somewhat…avant-garde. Meanwhile, I'm dying for a cup of coffee. I haven't been up all that long. Late night last night,' he added with a wry smile. 'Would you like one yourself? Or something else?'

'No, thank you. I've not long had breakfast.'

'Aah…late night, too?' he couldn't resist saying.

She looked right through him before dropping her beautiful but chilly blue eyes back to the album. She began flicking through it, insulting him with the little time she spent over each page.

He glowered down at the top of her head, and had to battle to control the crazy urge to bend over and wrench the pins out of her oh, so uptight French roll. His hands itched to yank her to her feet and shake her till her hair spilled down over her slender shoulders. He wanted to pull her to him and kiss her till there was fire in her eyes, not ice. He wanted to see that blush back in her cheeks. But not from embarrassment. From passion.

He wanted… He wanted… He wanted *her*!

Rafe reeled with shock. To desire this woman was insane. And stupid. And masochistic.

First, she was going to be married in two weeks. Second, she was a blonde. Third, she didn't even like him!

Three strikes and you're out!

Now go get your coffee, dummy. And when you come back, focus on her simply as a fantastic photographic subject, and not the most challenging woman of the century.

CHAPTER TWO

ISABEL did not look up till she was sure she was alone, shutting the photo album with a snap.

The man was impossible! To hire him as her wedding photographer was impossible! Rafe Saint Vincent might be a brilliant photographer but if he wasn't capable of listening to what *she* wanted, then he could just go jump.

Truly, men like him irritated the death out of her.

And attracted the devil out of her.

Isabel sighed. That was the main problem with him, wasn't it? The fact she found him wickedly sexy.

Isabel closed her eyes and slumped back against the sofa. She'd thought she'd finally cured herself of the futile flaw of fancying men like him. She'd thought since meeting and becoming engaged to Luke that she would never again need what such men had to offer.

Luke was exactly what she'd been looking for in a husband. He was handsome. Successful. Intelligent. And extremely nice. A man who, like her, had come to the conclusion that romantic love was not a sound basis for marriage, that compatibility and common goals were far more reliable. Falling in love, they'd both discovered in the past, made fools of men—and women. Passion might be the stuff poems were written about, but it didn't make you happy in the long run. Mind-blowing sex, Isabel

16

now believed, was not the be-all and end-all when it came to a relationship.

Not that Luke wasn't good in bed. He was. If her mind sometimes strayed to her own private and personal fantasies while he was making love to her, and vice versa, then Isabel hadn't been overly concerned.

Till this moment.

It was one thing to fill her mind with images of some mythical stranger during sex with Luke. Quite another to go to bed with him on her wedding night thinking of the likes of Rafe Saint Vincent.

And she would, if he was around all that day, looking her up and down with those sexy eyes of his.

Isabel shook her head with frustration. She'd always been attracted to the Mr Wrongs of this world. The daredevils and the thrill-seekers. The charmers and the slick, smooth-tongued womanisers who oozed the sort of confidence she found a major turn-on.

Of course, she hadn't known they were Mr Wrongs to begin with. She'd thought they were interesting, exciting men. It had taken several wretched endings—especially the disaster with Hal—to force her to face the fact that her silly heart had no judgement when it came to the opposite sex. It picked losers and liars.

By her late twenties, desperation and despair had forced Isabel's brain to develop a fail-safe warning system. If she was madly attracted to a man, then that was a guarantee he was another Mr Wrong.

So she didn't have to know much about Rafe Saint Vincent to know his character. She only had to take one look at him. Les *had* provided her with some brief details about him—namely that he was a bachelor, and a brilliant photographer—but to be honest, aside from the warning bells going off in Isabel's brain, Mr Saint Vincent's appearance said it all, from his trendy black clothes to his earring and his designer stubble. The fact he lived in a terraced house in Paddington completed the picture of a swinging male single of the new millennium whose priorities were career, pleasure and leisure, and who was never going to buy a cow when he could have cartons of milk for free. Rafe might not be a criminal or a con man, like Hal had been, but he would always be a waste of time for a woman who wanted marriage and children.

Actually, *every* man Isabel had ever fancied had been a waste of time in that regard. Which was why, when she'd found herself staring thirty in the face, still without the home and family of her own she'd always craved, Isabel had decided enough was enough, and set about finding herself a husband with her head, not her heart.

And she had.

Isabel knew she could be happy with Luke. Very happy.

But the last thing she needed around on her wedding day was someone like Rafe Saint Vincent.

Yet she needed a photographer. What excuse could she give her mother for not hiring him? The black and white business wouldn't wash. Her mother just *loved* black and white photographs, a hangover from the days when that was all there was. Her mother was not a young woman. In fact she was seventy, Isabel having been the product of a second honeymoon when Doris Hunt had turned forty.

No, there was nothing for it but to hire Rafe God's-gift-to-women Saint Vincent. Isabel supposed there was no real harm in fantasising about another man while your husband was making love to you, even on your wedding night. Luke would never know if she never told him.

And she wouldn't.

Actually, there were a lot of things about herself she'd never told Luke. And she didn't aim on starting now!

Her eyes opened and lifted to the photographs on the wall again and, this time, with their creator out of the room, Isabel let her gaze linger.

They really were incredibly erotic, his clever use of shadow highly suggestive. Although the subjects were obviously either naked or semi-naked, the lighting was such that most private parts were hidden from view. There was the occasional glimpse of the side of a breast, or the curve of a buttock, but not much more.

Tantalising was the word which came to mind. Isabel could have stared at them for hours. But the sound of footsteps coming down the stairs had her reefing her eyes away and searching for something to do. Anything!

Fishing her mobile phone out of her bag, she punched in her parents' number and was waiting impatiently for her mother to answer when her nemesis of the moment walked back into the room, sipping a steaming mug of coffee.

She pretended she wasn't ogling him, but her eyes

snuck several surreptitious glances as he walked over and sat down in the same spot he'd occupied before. He was gorgeous! Tall and lean, just as she liked them. Not traditionally handsome in the face, but attractive, and oh, so sexy.

'Yes?' her mother finally answered, sounding slightly breathless.

'Me, here, Mum.' No breathlessness on Isabel's part. She sounded wonderfully composed. Yet, inside, her heartbeat had quickened appreciably. Practice *did* make perfect!

'Oh, Isabel, I'm so glad you rang before we left for the club. I was thinking of you. So how did it go with Mr Saint Vincent?'

'Fine. He was fine.'

Isabel saw his dark eyes widen over the rim of his coffee-mug. Clearly, he'd been thinking she wasn't going to hire him.

'As good as Les?' her mother asked. Les had been hired by her parents before, for their recent golden wedding anniversary party.

'Better, I'd say.'

'That's a relief. I've waited a long time to see you married, love. I would like to have some decent photographs of the momentous event.'

Isabel's eyes flicked up to the two most provocative photos on the wall and a decidedly indecent thought popped into her mind. What would it be like to be photographed by him like *that*? To be totally naked before him? To have him arranging filmy curtains or sliding satin sheets over her nude body? To have to stand—or lie—perfectly still in some suggestive pose for ages whilst he shot reel after reel of film, those sexy eyes of his focused only on her?

Just the thought of it sent her heartbeat even higher.

Fortunately, Isabel was not a female whose inner feelings showed readily on her face. She could look at a man and be thinking the hottest thoughts and still look cool. Sometimes, even uninterested. Which perhaps was just as well, or she'd have spent half of her life in bed.

She didn't flirt easily. Neither was she capable of the sort of coy sugary behaviour some men seemed to find both a come-on and a turn-on. Most men found her slightly aloof, even snobbish. They often confused her ice-blonde looks and ladylike manner with being prudish and undersexed. Which perhaps explained why most of her lovers had been men who dared to do what a gentleman wouldn't, men who simply rode roughshod over her seeming uninterest and simply took what they wanted.

Isabel looked at the man sitting opposite her and wondered what kind of lover he'd be.

Not that you're ever going to find out, her conscience reminded her harshly.

'I have to go, Isabel,' her mother was saying. 'Your father and I were just having a bite to eat before we go down the club. When will you be home? Will you be eating with us tonight?'

Isabel had been living with her parents during the last few weeks leading up to the wedding. She'd quit her flat, plus her job as receptionist at the architectural firm where Luke worked, content to become a career wife and home maker after their marriage. She and Luke were going to try for a baby straight away.

'As far as I know,' she told her mother whilst she continued to watch the man opposite with unreadable eyes. 'Unless Luke comes back today and wants to go out somewhere. If he happens to ring, you could ask him. And tell him I'll be back home by one at the latest.'

'Will do. Bye, love.'

'Bye, Mum.'

She clicked off the phone then bent down to tap it against the album on the coffee-table. 'Very impressive,' she said, giving him one of her super cool looks, the ones she fell back on when her thoughts were at their most shocking. Pity she couldn't have rustled one up earlier when his barb about her wearing white at her wedding had sent a most uncharacteristic flush to her cheeks. Still, she was back in control now. Thank heavens.

She put down the phone and opened the album to a page which held a traditional full-length portrait of a woman in an evening gown. 'I liked this portrait very much. If you feel you could reproduce shots like this, then you're hired.'

'I don't ever *reproduce* anything, Isabel,' he returned quite huffily. 'I'm an artist, not a copier.'

Isabel's patience began to wear thin. 'Do you want this job or not?' she threw at him.

'As I said before, I'm doing this as a favour to Les. The question is...do *you* want *me* or not?'

Isabel's eyes met his and she had a struggle to maintain her equilibrium. If only he knew...

'I suppose you'll have to do,' she managed to say.

'Such enthusiasm. When and where?'

How about here and now?

'The wedding is at four o'clock at St Christopher's Church at Burwood, a fortnight from today. And the reception is at a place in Strathfield called Babylon.'

'Sounds exotic.'

It was, actually. Isabel had a secret penchant for the exotic. Though you'd never tell by looking at her. She always dressed very conservatively. But her favourite story as a child had been Aladdin, and she'd often dreamt of being a harem girl, complete with sexy costume and gauzy veils over her face.

'Do you want me to come to your house beforehand?' he asked. 'A lot of brides want that. Though some are too nervous to pose well at that stage. Still, when I was doing weddings regularly, I developed a strategy for relaxing them which helped on some occasions.'

'Oh?' Isabel tried to stop her wicked imagination from taking flight once more, but it was a lost cause.

'I'd give them a good...stiff...drink,' he said between sips of his coffee.

How she kept a straight face, Isabel would never know.

'I don't drink,' she lied.

'Figures,' he muttered, and she almost laughed.

He obviously thought she was a prude.

'Don't worry,' she went on briskly. 'I won't be nervous. And, yes, I'm sure my mother will want you to come to the house beforehand. I'll jot down the address and phone number for you.' She pulled out a pen from her bag, plus a spare business card from her hairdresser, and wrote her parents' details on the back.

'What say you arrive on the day at two?' she suggested as she handed it over to him, then stood up.

He put down his coffee, stared at the card, then stood up also.

'Is this your regular hairdresser?' he asked.

The question startled her. 'Yes, why?'

'Did they do your hair today?'

'No. I did it myself. I only go to a hairdresser when I want a cut. I like to do it myself.' Aside from the money it cost, she wasn't fond of the way some hairdressers had difficulty following instructions.

'So you'll be doing your hair on your wedding day?'

'Yes.'

'Not like that, I hope,' he said as he slipped the card into his shirt pocket.

Isabel bristled. 'What's wrong with it like this?'

'It's far too severe. If you're going to have it up, you need something a little softer, with some pieces hanging around your face. Here. Like this.'

Before she could step away, or object, he was by her side, his fingers tugging at her hair and touching her cheeks, her ears, her neck.

It was one thing to keep her cool whilst she was just

thinking about him, quite another with his hands on her. His fingertips were like brands on her skin, leaving heated imprints in her flesh and sending quivery ripples down her spine.

'Your hair seems quite straight,' he was saying as he stroked several strands down in front her ears. 'Do you have a curling wand?'

'No,' she choked out, knowing she should step back from him but totally unable to. She kept staring at the V of bare skin in his open-necked shirt and wondering what he would look like, naked.

'I suggest you buy one, then. They're cheap enough.'

Her eyes lifted to find he was studying not her hair so much, but her mouth. For one long, horribly exciting moment, Isabel thought he was going to kiss her. She sucked in sharply, her lips falling apart as a shot of excitement zinged through her veins. But he didn't kiss her, and she realised with a degree of self-disgust that she'd just been hoping he would.

But what if he had? came the appalling thought. What if he *had*?

Just the *thought* of risking or ruining what she had with Luke made her feel sick.

'I must go,' she said, and bent to pick up her bag, the action forcing his hands to drop away from her face. By the time she'd straightened he'd stepped back a little. But she had to get out of there. And quickly.

'If I don't hear from you,' she added brusquely, 'then I will expect you to show up at my parents' home at two precisely, a fortnight from today. Please don't be late.'

'I am never late for appointments,' he returned.

'Good. Till then, then?'

He nodded and she swept past him, her bag brushing against him as she did so. She didn't apologise, or look down. She kept going, not drawing breath till she was in her car and on the road home.

Relief was her first emotion once his place was well out of sight. Then anger. At herself; at the Rafe Saint Vincents of this world; and at fate. Why couldn't Les have recommended a photographer like himself, a happily married middle-aged conservative bloke with three kids and a paunch?

When a glance in the rear-vision mirror reminded her she had bits of hair all over the place, courtesy of her Lord and Master, she pulled over to the kerb and pulled the pins out of her French roll, shaking her head till her hair fell down around her face like a curtain.

'Maybe you'd like me to wear it like this!' she stormed as she accelerated away again. 'Lucky for me it isn't longer, or you'd be suggesting I do a Lady Godiva act at my wedding. I could be the first bride ever to be photographed in the nude!'

She ranted and raved about him for a while, then at the traffic when it took her nearly twice as long to get home as it had to drive into the city. She was feeling more than a little stressed by the time she turned into her parents' street, her agitation temporarily giving way to surprise when she spotted Luke's blue car parked outside the house. She slid her navy car in behind it, frowning at Luke who was still sitting behind the wheel. When she climbed out, so did he, throwing her an odd look at her hair as he did so.

She felt herself colouring with guilt, which really annoyed her. She'd done nothing to be guilty about.

'Luke!' she exclaimed, trying not to sound as flustered as she was feeling. 'What on earth are you doing here? I wasn't expecting you. Why didn't you call me?'

'I tried your mobile phone a while back,' he said. 'But you didn't answer.'

'What? Oh, I must have left the blasted thing behind at the studio. I took it out to ring Mum and tell her how long I'd be.'

Isabel wanted to scream. How could she have been so stupid as to leave it behind? Now she'd have to go back for it. And she'd have to see that man again, *before* the wedding.

'Oh, too bad,' she muttered, slamming the car door. 'It can stay there till tomorrow. I'm not going back now.'

She could feel Luke's puzzled eyes on her and knew she wasn't acting like her usual calm self. She shook her head and threw him a pained look. 'You've no idea the dreadful day I've had. The photographer I booked for the wedding's had an accident and he made an appointment for me to meet this other man who's not really suitable at all. Brilliant, but one of those avant-garde types who wants to do everything in black and white. I pointed out that I wouldn't have selected a wine-red gown for my maid of honour if I'd wanted all the shots done in black and white, but would he listen to me? No! He even told me how he wanted me to wear my hair. As if I don't know what suits me best. I've never met such an insufferably opinionated man.'

Isabel knew she was babbling but she couldn't seem to stop.

'Still, what can you expect from someone who fancies himself an *artiste*. You know the type. Struts around like he's God's gift to women. And he wears this earring in the shape of a phantom's head, of all things. What a show pony! Goodness knows what our photographs are going to turn out like, but it's simply too late to get someone else decent. His name's Rafe—did I tell you? Rafe Saint Vincent. It wouldn't be his real name, of course. Just a career move. Nobody is born with a name like Rafe Saint Vincent. Talk about pretentious!'

Isabel finally ran out of steam, only to realise that Luke was not only staring at her as if she'd lost her mind, but that he wasn't looking his usual self, either.

Always well-groomed, Luke was the sort of man who kept 'tall, dark and handsome' at number one on every woman's most wanted list.

'Luke!' she exclaimed. 'You look like you've slept in your clothes. And you haven't even shaved. That's not like you at all.' Unlike other men she would not mention. 'What are you doing here, anyway? I thought you were going to stay in your father's old fishing cabin up on Lake Macquarie for the whole weekend.' And do some proper grieving, Isabel had hoped. The poor darling had to have been through hell this past fortnight since his parents' tragic deaths. Yet he'd been so brave about it all. And so strong.

'The cabin wasn't there any more,' he said. 'It had been torn down a few years before.'

'Oh, what a shame,' she murmured. But it explained why he was looking so disconsolate. 'So where did you stay last night? In a motel? Or a tent?' she added, hoping to jolly him up with a dab of humour.

'No.' He didn't crack even the smallest of smiles. 'Dad had built a brand-new weekender on the same site. I stayed there.'

'But...' Isabel frowned. 'How did you get in? You didn't break in, did you?'

'No. There was a girl staying there for the weekend and she let me in.'

Isabel was taken aback. 'And she let you *sleep* the night?'

Luke sighed. 'It's a long story, Isabel. I think we'd better go inside and sit down while I tell it to you.'

She tried not to panic. 'Luke, you're worrying me.'

When he took her arm and propelled her over to the front gate, she pulled out of his grip and lanced him with alarmed eyes. 'You're not going ahead with the wedding, are you?'

Isabel waited in an agony of anxiety for him to speak.

'No,' he finally answered, his expression grim. 'No, I'm not.'

CHAPTER THREE

Isabel stared at him, aghast. 'Oh, no. No, Luke, don't do this to me!' Bursting into tears, she buried her stricken face in her hands.

'I'm so sorry, Isabel,' Luke said softly as he tried to take her into his arms.

'But why?' she wailed, gripping the lapels of his suit jacket and shaking them.

His eyes held apology. 'I've fallen in love.'

'Fallen in love!' she gasped. 'In less than a *day*?'

'No one is more surprised than me, I can tell you. But it's true. I came back straight away to tell you, and to call our wedding off.'

'But love's no guarantee of happiness, Luke,' she argued in desperation. 'I thought we agreed on that. It traps and tricks you. It really is blind. This girl you've supposedly fallen in love with—how do you know she'll be good for you? How do you know she won't make you miserable? You can't possibly know her real character, not this quickly. She could be playing a part for you, pretending to be something she's not. She might be a really bad person. A gold-digger, perhaps. A…a criminal even!'

'She's not *any* of those things,' he returned, looking

shocked by her arguments. 'She's a good person. I just know it.'

Isabel shook her head. One *day*! One miserable *day*! How could he know anything for sure? 'I would never have believed you could be so naïve,' she pronounced angrily. 'A man like you!'

'I'm not naïve,' he denied. 'Which is why I'm not rushing into anything. But I can't marry you, Isabel, feeling as I do about Celia. Surely you can see that.'

Isabel was not in the mood to see anything of the kind. She wanted to cry some more. And to scream. She'd been so close to having her dream come true. So darned close!

'Maybe I do and maybe I don't,' she grumbled, letting his lapels go. '*I'd* still marry *you*. I haven't much time for the highly overrated state of being in love.'

And she'd thought he felt the same way.

'Maybe that's because you've never really been in love,' Luke said.

Isabel's laugh was tinged with bitterness. 'I'm an expert in the subject. But that's all right. You'll live and learn, Luke Freeman, and when you do, give me a call. Meanwhile, let's go inside, as you said. I need a drink. Not tea or coffee. Something much stronger. Dad still has some of the malt whisky I gave him for his birthday. That should do the trick.'

Isabel let herself into the house, Luke following.

'But you don't drink Scotch,' he pointed out with a frown in his voice.

'Aah, but I do,' she threw over her shoulder at him

as she strode into her parents' lounge room, heading straight for the drinks cabinet in the corner. 'When the occasion calls for it,' she added, pouring herself half a glassful. 'Which is now. Today. This very second.'

She knocked back half of it, steadfastly refusing to shudder like some simpering female fool while it burnt a red-hot path down her throat. 'Ahh,' she said with a lip-smacking sigh of satisfaction once it reached its destination. 'That hits the spot. You want one?' she asked Luke, but he shook his head.

Swirling the amber liquid in her glass, she walked over and settled in one of her mother's large comfy armchairs, her feet curled up under her. Hooking her hair behind her ear with her left hand, she lifted the whisky to her lips and took another deep swallow. She glanced over at Luke, who was still standing near the doorway, looking startled by her behaviour.

Isabel supposed she wasn't living up to the image he obviously had of her. Up till today it had been easy to play the role of the super-serene, super-sensible fiancée who was never fazed or upset by anything he did. Because he'd never done anything to really upset her.

Clearly, he didn't know what to make of her as her real self, instead of Lady Isabel, the unflappable.

But did he honestly think he could roll up and tell her their wedding was off at this late stage with no trouble at all? Did he imagine she wouldn't be hurt by his obviously being unfaithful to her last night?

The realisation that she had been mentally unfaithful to *him* today tempered her inner fury somewhat, and brought some sympathy and understanding for Luke's actions. Marriages made with the head and not the heart might have worked in the past, she appreciated. But in this modern day and age, with all the abounding sexual temptations, such a union was a disaster waiting to happen.

Still, she would be surprised if it was true love compelling Luke to do this. More likely that good deceiver *lust*!

'I suppose she's beautiful, this Celia,' she said drily.

'I think so.' Luke finally sat down as well.

'What does she do?'

'She's a physiotherapist.'

A physiotherapist. Not only beautiful but clever and educated as well.

Isabel hadn't embraced tertiary studies after leaving high school. Her exam results hadn't been good enough. Oh, she wasn't dumb, just not focused on her school work. She'd been far too interested in boys at the time, much to her parents' dismay.

She had managed a brief receptionist course at tech. That, combined with her looks, had meant she'd been rarely out of a job. Over the years she'd become a top receptionist, computer literate and very competent.

Yet she'd never really been interested in a career as such. She'd always wanted marriage and motherhood. It irked Isabel that this Celia, however innocently, had stolen the one man who might have given her both.

'And what was she doing, staying in your father's weekender? Did he rent it out?'

'No. She's his mistress's daughter.'

'His *what*?' Isabel's feet shot out from under her as she snapped forward on the chair.

'Dad's mistress's daughter,' Luke repeated drily.

Isabel gaped. 'No! I don't believe you. Not *your* dad. With a *mistress*? That's impossible. He was one of the best husbands and fathers I've ever met. He was one of the reasons I wanted to marry you. Because I believed you'd be just as good a family man.'

'As I said…it's a long story.'

'And a fascinating one, I'm sure,' Isabel mused. 'It seems the Freeman men have a dark side I don't know about.'

'Could be,' Luke agreed ruefully.

'I wish I'd known about it sooner,' she muttered, and swigged back the last of the whisky in her glass.

Luke shot her a puzzled look. 'What do you mean by that?'

'Oh, nothing. Just a private joke. I have this perverse sense of humour sometimes. Come on, tell me all the naughty details.'

'I hope you won't be too shocked.'

She chuckled. 'Oh, dear, that's funny. Me, shocked? Trust me, darling. I can never be seriously shocked by anything sexual.'

Luke frowned at her. 'Did I ever really know you, Isabel?'

'Did I ever really know *you*?' she countered saucily.

Their eyes met and they smiled together.

'You'll find someone else, Isabel,' Luke said with total confidence.

'I dare say I will. But not quite like you, darling. You were one in a million. Your Celia is one lucky girl. I hope you'll be very happy together.' Privately, she didn't think they would be, but who knew? Maybe Luke was a better picker than herself when it came to falling in love. *If* he was really in love, that was.

'Thanks, Isabel. That's very generous of you. But we won't be rushing to the altar. Which reminds me. I will, of course, be footing the bill for any expenses your parents have encountered with the wedding. I'll send them a cheque which should cover everything, and with some left over. And I'll be doing the right thing by you, too.'

She shook her head, then slipped the solitaire-diamond engagement ring off her finger. 'No, Luke. I wasn't marrying you for your money. I know you might have thought I was, but I wasn't. I was just pleased you were successful and stable. I wanted that security for my children. And for myself.'

When she went to give him the ring, he refused to take it. 'I don't want that ring back, Isabel. It's yours. I gave it to you. You keep it, or sell it if you want to.'

Isabel came close to crying again. He really was the nicest man. He'd have made a wonderful father.

She shrugged and slipped the ring onto her right hand. 'If you insist,' she said, using every bit of her will-power to keep it together. 'But I won't sell it. I'll wear it. It's a beautiful ring. Fortunate, though, that I didn't find any wedding rings I liked yesterday, so at least we don't have to return *them*.'

Isabel was still amazed by the fact that less than twenty-four hours ago Luke had been very happy with her. But, as they said in the classics, there was many a slip 'twixt the cup and the lip.

She sighed, then stared regretfully into her now empty glass. 'I'd better go get you your credit card while you're here.' And while she could still stand. That whisky was *really* working now.

'That can wait,' Luke said before she could get up. 'I want to finish discussing the rest of my financial obligations first.'

She frowned. 'What other financial obligations could you possibly have?'

'I owe you, Isabel. More than a ring's worth.'

'No, you don't, Luke. I never lived with you. I have no claim on you other than the expenses for the wedding.'

'That's not the way I see it. You gave up your job to become my wife. You expected to be going on your honeymoon in a fortnight's time and possibly becoming a mother in the near future. Aside from that, married to me, you would never have had to worry about money for the rest of your life. I can't help you with the honeymoon or the becoming a mother bit now, but I can give you the financial security for life that you deserve.'

'Luke, truly, you don't have to do this.'

'Yes. I do. Now listen up.'

Isabel listened up, amazed when Luke insisted she

have his town house in Turramurra, as well as a portfolio of blue-chip stocks and shares which would provide her with an independent income for life. It seemed his father had been a very rich man. And now so was Luke.

She thought about refusing, but then decided that would just be her pride talking. At least now she wouldn't have to worry about having to live here under her parents' roof till she found another job. Her mother was going to be very upset when she found out the wedding was off.

She smiled a wry smile at this wonderful man she had hoped to marry. 'I always knew you were a winner. But I'd have preferred you as my husband rather than my sugar-daddy.'

'You've no idea how sorry I am about all this, Isabel,' Luke apologised again. 'I wouldn't have hurt you for the world. You're a great girl. But the moment I saw Celia, I was a goner.'

Isabel's mind flew straight to the moment she first saw Rafe Saint Vincent today. She hadn't been a goner. But she might have been, if he'd come on to her. Thank heaven he hadn't.

'She must be something, this Celia.'

'She's very special.'

And very beautiful, no doubt, Isabel deduced, with a body made for sin and eyes which drew you and held you and corrupted you. Just as Rafe's eyes had today.

He'd fancied her. Isabel hadn't liked to admit it to herself before this, but she'd sensed his male interest at the time. She'd sensed it from the first second they'd looked at each other. She always sensed things like that.

You could go back for your phone after Luke leaves. You could tell Rafe the wedding's off. You could...

No, no, she screamed at herself. Not again. Never again!

'Okay, so tell me all,' she demanded of Luke, desperately needing distraction from her escalatingly dangerous thoughts. 'And don't leave out anything...'

CHAPTER FOUR

RAFE noticed the phone she'd left behind almost immediately. He snatched it up from the coffee-table and was running out after her when he stopped and waited to see if she remembered and came back for it herself.

But she didn't, and he just stood in the hallway and listened to her drive off.

It was crazy to want to see her again this side of the wedding. Crazy to force her to return.

She wasn't the type to let him have his wicked way with her. She wasn't the type to let *any* man have his wicked way with her without a band of gold on her finger.

Maybe not a virgin, but close. The way she'd frozen when he'd dared touch her hair. The way she'd bolted out of his place, probably in fear that he might do more.

And he'd wanted to. Oh, yes. Being that close to her—actually touching her—had turned him on something rotten. When her bag had hit him as she'd hurried out, he'd just managed not to visibly wince. Luckily, she hadn't stopped and looked down at where her bag had hit him, or she'd have been in for one big fright!

That was another reason why he hadn't run out into the street after her just now. Looking a fool was not his favourite occupation.

Hopefully, by the time Isabel realised she'd left her phone and turned round to come back, he'd have himself under control again.

And then what, Rafe? What is the point of this exercise? Is it some form of sexual masochism?

Even if you were the kind of man who seduced other men's fiancées—which you're not, usually—you haven't one chance in Hades of defrosting *this* one.

So, if and when she does come back, have the damned phone handy near the front door, give it to the lady and send her on her merry way.

His decision made, Rafe dropped the metallic-blue cellphone on the hall table and headed upstairs for some breakfast. After that, he came back downstairs to his darkroom, where he set about developing the rolls of film he'd shot last night at Orsini's summer fashion parade, and at the after-parade party, which had gone well into the wee small hours of the morning. The women's magazines would be ringing first thing Monday morning, wanting to see the best of them.

Two hours later, Rafe was still in his darkroom, going through the motions, but his mind simply wasn't on the job. The object of his distraction hadn't come back, and he simply could not put her out of his head.

The truth was, she intrigued him. Not just sexually, but as a person. He wanted to know more about her.

In the end, Rafe stopped trying to put her out his mind. He abandoned his work, pulled the business card she'd left him out of his pocket, went back upstairs, picked up his phone and punched in the number she'd written down.

The line rang and rang at the other end, with Rafe about to hang up when someone finally picked up.

'Hello there.'

Rafe frowned. It was a woman, but he wasn't sure if it was Isabel. She sounded…odd. 'Isabel?'

'Yep? To whom do I have the pleasure of speaking?'

Rafe couldn't believe his ears. She was drunk!

'It's Rafe. Rafe Saint Vincent. The photographer.'

Dead silence. Though he could hear her breathing.

'You left your mobile phone at my place.'

More silence.

'I thought you might be worried about it.'

She actually laughed.

'Isabel,' he said with concern in his voice. 'Have you been drinking?'

'Mmm. You might say that.'

'I am saying it.'

'So what?'

Rafe was taken aback. This wasn't the woman he'd met today. This was someone else. 'You said you didn't drink,' he reminded her.

She laughed again. 'I lied.'

His eyes widened with shock, then narrowed with worry. 'Isabel, what's wrong? What's happened?'

'I guess there's no point in not telling you. You'll have to know some time, anyway. The wedding's off.'

He couldn't have been more taken aback, both by the news *and* her manner. 'Why?' he asked.

'Luke's left me for someone else.'

Rafe experienced a small secret thrill at this news, but his overriding emotion was sympathy. He knew what it was like to be left for someone else, and he wouldn't wish the experience on a dog.

'I'm so sorry, Isabel,' he said with genuine feeling. 'You must be feeling rotten.'

'I was, till I downed my third whisky. Now, I actually don't feel too bad.'

He had to smile. That was exactly what he'd done the day Liz had left him. Hit the bottle. 'You should never drink alone, you know,' he warned softly.

'Oh, I'm not drunk,' she denied, even though her voice was slurring a little. 'Just tipsy enough so that my pain is pleasantly anaesthetised. Why, you offering to drink with me, lover?'

Rafe's smile widened. It seemed Isabel's ice-princess act melted considerably under the influence of three glasses of Scotch.

'I think you've had enough for one day.'

'That's not for you to say,' she huffed.

'Maybe not, but I'm still saying it.'

'Did anyone ever tell you that you are the bossiest person alive?'

'Yeah. My mother. She threw a party the day I left home.'

'I can well imagine.'

'But she loves me all the same.'

'I doubt other people would be so generous.'

Her alcohol-induced sarcasm amused him. 'Did any-one ever tell you you're a snooty bitch?' he countered.

He liked it when she laughed. Being drunk suited her. No more Miss Prissy. How he wished he was with her now.

There again, perhaps it was wise that he wasn't. When and if he took her to bed, he didn't want her drunk. Or on the rebound. He wanted her wanting him for himself, and no other reason.

'I guess you won't be needing my services now,' he said.

'As a photographer, you mean?'

Rafe sucked in sharply. What a provocative reply! Perhaps she didn't disapprove of him as much as he'd thought she had.

Or perhaps it was just the drink talking.

'Actually, I'd still like to photograph you,' he said, truthfully enough.

'Really? Why?'

'Why? Well, firstly, you are one seriously beautiful woman, and I have a penchant for photographing beau-tiful women. Secondly, I just want to see you again. I want to take you out to dinner somewhere.'

'You mean…like…on a date?'

'Yes. Exactly like that.'

'You don't waste much time, do you? I've only been dumped for two hours. And you've only known about it for two minutes! What if I said I was too broken up over Luke to date anyone for a while?'

'Then I'd respect that. But I'd ask you out again next week. And the week after that.'

'I should have guessed you'd be the determined type,' she muttered.

'Being determined is not a vice, Isabel.'

'That depends. So why is it you don't already have a girlfriend? Or *do* you? Don't lie to me, now. I hate men who lie to me,' she added, slurring her words.

'I'm between girlfriends at the moment.'

'Oh? What happened to the last one?'

'She went overseas to work. I wasn't inclined to follow her.'

'Why?'

'My career is here, in Australia.'

'Ahh. Priority number one.'

'What does that mean?'

'It means no, thank you very much, Rafe. I've been down that road far too many times to travel it again.'

'Now I'm confused. What road are you referring to?'

'Dating men who want only one thing from me. You do only want one thing from me, don't you, Rafe?'

Rafe considered that a loaded question.

'I wouldn't say that, exactly.' He liked talking to her, too. 'But I have to confess that marriage and kiddies are not on my list of must-do things in my life.'

'Well, they're on mine, Rafe. And sooner, rather than later. But I appreciate your telling me the truth. That's a big improvement on some of the other men I've become involved with in the past.'

His eyebrows shot up. It sounded as if there had been

scads. Any idea that she might almost be a virgin went out of the window. It just showed you first impressions weren't always right.

'Did your fiancé lie to you?'

'Luke? Oh, no...no, Luke was no liar.'

'But he was obviously two-timing you,' he pointed out.

'No. He wasn't. Look, it's rather difficult to explain.'

'Try.'

So she did, explaining the circumstances which had led up to Luke's meeting Celia.

'So he hasn't been two-timing me,' she finished up. 'He only met Celia yesterday.'

'Perhaps, but he didn't tell you the truth about why he was going up to his dad's fishing cabin on Lake Macquarie in the first place, did he?'

'No, but I can understand why. He'd been thrown for a loop when the solicitor told him his Dad wanted to leave his weekender to some strange woman.'

'You make a lot of excuses for him, don't you? He was still unfaithful to you. And he hurt you, Isabel.'

'He didn't mean to. Look, I'm sorry I told you about it now. It's really none of your business. Thank you for ringing and for making me feel a little better, but I think we should leave it right there, don't you? As I said, we want different things in life. I wonder...could you possibly post my phone back to me?'

'I'd rather drop it off to you.'

'And I'd rather you didn't.'

'You're afraid of me,' he said, startled by this real-isation.

'Don't be ridiculous!'

Oh-oh. She was definitely sobering up. And returning to her former stroppy self.

'Just tell me one thing.'

'What?'

'Did you love him?'

'I was marrying him,' she snapped. 'What do *you* think?'

'I think that's a very evasive answer. For a person who demands the truth from others, you're not too good at delivering it yourself.'

She sighed. 'Very well. I liked and respected Luke, but, no, I did not love him. Satisfied?'

'Not even remotely,' Rafe said ruefully. 'Did you think *he* loved *you*?'

'No.'

'What on earth kind of marriage was *that* going to be?'

'One that lasted.'

'Oh, yeah, right. It didn't even get through the en-gagement. For pity's sake, Isabel, what did you expect? Men want passion from their wives. And sex. At least in the beginning.'

'You think I didn't give Luke sex?'

'Not the kind which his new dolly-bird obviously does.'

'You don't know what you're talking about. Look, I'm sorry I started this conversation. You simply don't have the capacity to understand what Luke and I had together. How could you? You're one of those men who lives for himself and himself alone. A woman is just a passing pleasure to you, a bit of R&R from your work. You don't want a real relationship with one. As for children, you probably see them as inconveniences, little ankle-biters who'd get in the way of your lifestyle. Luke wasn't like that. He wanted a family. Like me. He wanted for ever. Like me. We might not have been madly in love but we were good friends and extremely compatible, *in* bed as well as out. We could have had a happy marriage. I don't believe he's in love with this new dolly-bird, as you call her. He only met her yesterday. I think it's just sex, the kind that obsesses you so much sometimes that you can't think straight.'

Rafe's eyes widened. It sounded as if she'd been there, done that. She was becoming more interesting by the minute.

'That kind of physical affair never lasts,' she finished bitterly.

Yep. She'd been there, done that, all right. Rafe didn't know if he felt tantalised by this knowledge, or jealous. Either way, the thought of Isabel in the throes of an all-consuming sexual passion was an intriguing one.

'Is that what you're hoping?' he suggested. 'That maybe this thing your Luke is having with this girl won't last? That maybe he'll wake up on Monday morning, realise he's made a big mistake and beg you to take him back?'

'Well, actually, no. I hadn't been hoping that. But now that you've mentioned the possibility…'

Luke could have kicked himself.

'Don't start grasping at straws, Isabel.'

'I'm not. But I'm also not going to repeat the mistakes of my past. So, thank you for thinking of me, Rafe. But find someone else to photograph, and to take to dinner, because it isn't going to be me.'

'Isabel, please…'

'No, Rafe,' she said sternly. 'I realise you have difficulty in accepting that word, but it's definitely no. Now I must go. Goodbye.'

And she hung up on him.

Swearing, Rafe slammed down his end of the phone. He'd handled that all wrong. Totally abysmally wrong!

Still, perhaps it *was* for the best. Isabel wanted marriage. Whereas he most definitely didn't.

But she was wrong about what he wanted from her. It wasn't just sex.

Oh, come now, the voice of brutal honesty piped up. It's always just sex you're looking for these days. All that other stuff you offer a female is nothing but foreplay. The chit-chat. The photographing. The dinner dates. All with one end in view. Getting whatever pretty woman has taken your eye into bed and keeping her there on and off till you grow bored.

Which you always do in the end. Admit it, man, you've become shallow and selfish with women, exactly as Isabel said you were. You haven't been worth two bob since Liz left you. She stuffed you, buddy. Took away your heart. Isabel was right not to get involved with you. You're a dead loss to someone like her. Go back to work. That's the only thing you're good for. Creating images. Anything real is just too much for you.

He stomped downstairs, still muttering. Till he saw Isabel's shiny blue cellphone on the hall table. How odd that just seeing something she owned gave him a thrill.

Did he dare still take it back to her?

No, he decided. She'd said no. He had to respect that. He'd post it to her on Monday, as she'd asked.

Feeling more empty and wretched than he had in years, Rafe returned to his darkroom and tried to bury himself in the one thing which had always sustained him, even in his darkest moments.

But, for the second time that day, his precious craft failed to deliver the distraction he craved.

CHAPTER FIVE

ISABEL groaned. She'd handled that all wrong; talked too much; revealed too much.

Alcohol always made her talkative.

She thanked her stars that she'd pulled herself together towards the end—and that she'd had enough courage to resist temptation.

But oh, she'd wanted to say yes. To everything he'd offered. The photography. The dinner date. Sex afterwards, no doubt.

Isabel closed her eyes at the thought.

They sprang open again at another thought. Her mobile!

Would he still post it to her after all she'd said to him? Her assassination of his character had been a bit brutal, even if correct. He hadn't denied a single word. Okay, so the man did have a sweet side. But how much of that was real? Maybe he'd just learnt that you caught more with honey than with salt.

If he was really sweet, then he'd post her phone back. If not?

Isabel shrugged. She couldn't worry about a phone. If she never got it back, then she'd report it lost and get another one. After all, she didn't have to watch her pennies any more. She was an independently wealthy woman now. Or she would be soon.

Luke would be as good as his word. That, she knew.

Isabel wandered down the hallway to her mother's kitchen, thinking about Luke. Was it possible he might change his mind about this Celia? Or was she simply looking for an excuse not to tell her parents the wedding was off when they came home?

Just the thought of their reaction—especially her mother's—made Isabel shudder. If she hadn't been over the drink-driving limit, she'd pack up her car right now and make a bolt for the town house Luke had given her. She had her own set of keys.

Unfortunately, as it was, there was nothing but to stay here and face the music.

The music, as it turned out, was terrible. Her father recovered somewhat after Isabel explained Luke was going to recompense them for everything they'd spent. But her mother could not be so easily soothed, not even when Isabel told her what Luke was doing for *her* in a financial sense. When Isabel repeated Luke's suggestion that her parents go on their pre-booked holiday to Dream Island, her mother's face carried horror.

'You think I could be happy going on what should have been your honeymoon?' she exclaimed. 'No wonder Luke left you for another woman. You have no sensitivity at all! I dare say he worked out that you were only marrying him for his money. So he gave you what you wanted, then looked elsewhere for some genuine love and warmth.'

Isabel was stunned by her mother's harsh words. 'You think I was only marrying Luke for his money?'

Her mother flushed, but still looked her straight in the eye. 'You weren't in love with the man. *That*, I know. I've seen you in love, girl, and what you felt for Luke wasn't it. You cold-bloodedly set out to get that man. I didn't say a word because I thought Luke would make a fine husband and father, and I hoped that you might eventually fall in love with him. You played false with him, Isabel. And you got what you deserved.'

'Dot, stop it,' Isabel's father intervened sharply. 'What's done is done. And who knows? Maybe it's all for the best. Maybe someone better will come along, someone our girl can like *and* love.'

Isabel gave her father a grateful look. But she was close to tears. And very hurt by her mother's lack of sympathy and understanding. 'I...I have to go and ring Rachel,' she said, desperate to get away from her mother's hostility. Rachel would at least be on her side.

'What about everyone else?' her mother threw after her. 'Who's going to make all the other phone calls necessary to cancel everything?'

'I'll do all that, Mum.'

'On *our* phone?'

Isabel closed her eyes for a second. Phones. They were her nemesis today. 'No,' she said wearily. 'I'll be moving into the town house Luke gave me tomorrow. I'll make all the calls from there.'

'You're moving out?' Suddenly, her mother looked wretchedly unhappy.

Isabel sighed. 'I think I should.'

'You…you don't have to, you know,' her mother said, her voice and chin wobbling. 'I don't really care about the phone bill.'

Isabel understood then that her mother had been lashing out from her own hurt and disappointment. She'd always wanted to see her only daughter married. And now that event seemed highly unlikely.

Because her mother was right, Isabel conceded. She *had* set out to get Luke rather cold-bloodedly, and she simply couldn't do that again. Which left what? Falling in love with another Mr Wrong?

No! Now that was on *her* list of never-do-again.

'It's all right, Mum,' Isabel said, giving her mother a hug. 'Everything will be all right. You'll see.'

Her mother began to cry then, with Isabel struggling not to join in.

She looked beseechingly at her father over her Mum's dropped head and he nodded. 'Go ring Rachel,' he said quietly. 'I'll look after her.'

Rachel, who was Isabel's only real female friend and now the owner of an unused wine-red bridesmaid dress, answered on the first ring.

'Can you talk?' was Isabel's first question. 'Have I rung at a bad time?'

Rachel's life was devoted to minding her foster-mother who had Alzheimer's. She'd been doing it twenty-four hours a day, seven days a week, for over four years now. Despite being a labour of love, it was a grinding existence with little pleasure or leisure.

Rachel's decision to take on this onerous task after her foster-mum's husband had deserted her, had cost her her job as a top secretary at the Australian Broadcasting Corporation, and her own partner at the time. Sacrifice, it seemed, was not a virtue men aspired to.

Nowadays, Rachel made ends meet by doing clothes alterations at home. Her only entertainment was reading and watching television, plus one night out a month which Isabel paid for and organised. Last night had actually been one of those times, Isabel taking her friend to Star City Casino for dinner then a show afterwards. It was a pleasing thought that she'd have the time and the money to take Rachel out more often now.

'It's okay,' Rachel said. 'Lettie's asleep. Thank goodness. It's been a really bad day. She didn't even know me. Or she pretended not to. She's always difficult the day after I've been out with you. I don't think she likes anyone else but me minding her.'

'Poor Rachel. I'm sorry to ring you with more bad news.'

'Oh, no, what's happened?'

'The wedding's off.'

'The miserable bastard,' was Rachel's immediate response, which rather startled Isabel.

'What makes you think it was Luke's doing?'

'I know you, Isabel. No way would you opt out of marrying Luke. So what was it? Another woman?'

'How did you guess?' Isabel said ruefully.

'It wasn't hard. Men are so typical.'

'Mum blames me. She says Luke looked elsewhere because I didn't love him.'

'You *confessed* it wasn't a romantic match?'

'No, she guessed.'

'Oh, well, you have to agree she had a few clues to go on. Luke wasn't your usual type. Too traditionally good-looking and far too straight-down-the-line.'

'Mmm. It turned out he wasn't quite the Mr Goody-Two-Shoes I thought he was. Not once he met the sexy Celia.'

'So who is sexy Celia? Where and when did he meet her?'

'He only met her yesterday, and she's his father's mistress's daughter.'

'*What*?' Rachel choked out. 'Would you like to repeat that?'

She did, along with the rest of Luke's story. Isabel had to admit it made fascinating listening. It wasn't every day that a son found out his high-profile hero-status father had been cheating on his mother for twenty years. Or that the same engaged and rather strait-laced son would jump into bed with the mistress's daughter within an hour or two of meeting her.

Isabel still did not believe that Luke was in love with this Celia, but he obviously thought he was after spending all night with her doing who knew what. Even now he was speeding back up to his dad's secret love-nest on Lake Macquarie for more of the same!

It sounded like an episode from a soap opera.

No, a *week* of episodes!

Rachel's ear was glued to the phone for a good fifteen minutes.

'You didn't tell your mother all that, did you?' she asked at the end of it.

'No. I just said he'd met someone else, fallen in love with her and decided he couldn't go through with the wedding.'

'At least he was decent enough to do that. A lot of guys these days would have tried to have their cake and eat it too, a bit like Luke's father did with this Celia's poor mother for twenty years.'

'Yes. I thought of that. But I also wondered if Luke might eventually realise it wasn't love he felt for Celia, but just good old lust.'

'Could be. So you'd take him back if he changed his mind?'

'In a shot.'

'Maybe I shouldn't alter my bridesmaid dress just yet, then.'

'Maybe not.'

'And maybe you shouldn't cancel the reception place, or the cake, or the photographer. Not for a couple of days, anyway.'

Isabel wished Rachel hadn't mentioned the photographer. She didn't want to think about Rafe.

'Oh, dear, I think Lettie's just called out for me,' Rachel said. 'Amazing how she's remembered my name now that I'm on the phone. I must go, Isabel. And I am sorry. But…'

'Don't you dare tell me it's all for the best,' Isabel warned.

Rachel laughed. 'All right, I won't. Keep in touch.'

'I will.' When Isabel got off the phone, she realised she hadn't told Rachel about her financial windfall. But she would, the next time she rang her.

Meanwhile, she set about packing her clothes. She was emptying the drawers in her old dressing table when her mother came into the bedroom, looking miserable and chastened.

'I feel terrible about what I said to you earlier, Isabel. Your father said I should have my tongue cut out.'

'It's all right, Mum. You were upset.'

'What I said. I…I don't think you were marrying Luke just for his money. I know you liked him a lot, too.'

'Yes, I did.'

'Do…do you think he might not have fallen for this other girl if you'd slept with him before the wedding?'

Isabel turned to stare at her mother. Truly, what world did she live in? 'Mum,' she said with a degree of exasperation, 'I did sleep with him. Quite often.'

'Oh…'

'And he liked it. A lot.'

'Oh!'

'Sex wasn't the problem. It was passion.'

'Passion?'

'Yes, that overwhelming feeling you get when you look at a person and you just have to be with them.'

'Jump into bed, you mean?'

'Yes. Luke and I never really felt like that about each other.'

'I used to feel that way about your dad,' her mother whispered, 'when we were first married. And he felt that way about me, too.'

Isabel smiled at her. 'That's good, Mum. That's how it should be.'

'Maybe your dad's right. Maybe you'll find someone nicer than Luke, someone you'll fall deeply in love with and who'll feel the same way about you.'

'I hope so, Mum. I really do.' It would be cruel to take away her mother's hope. She'd always had this dream of seeing her daughter as a bride. Isabel had had the same dream.

But not any more.

'You're still going to move out?' her mother asked a bit tearily.

Isabel stopped what she was doing to face her mother. 'Mum, I'm thirty years old. I'm a grown woman. I have to make my own life away from home, regardless. I only moved back in for a while because it was sensible and convenient, leading up to the wedding.'

'But I...I've liked having you home. You are very good company.'

Isabel thought the compliment came just a bit late.

'You're a good cook, too. Your dad and I are going to miss the meals you've cooked for us.'

Isabel relented and gave her mother another hug. 'What say I come over and cook you a meal once in a while? Will that do?'

'Just so long as you come over. Don't be a stranger.'

'I won't. I promise.'

'And you've forgiven your old mum?'

Isabel smiled a wry smile. 'Have you forgiven me for not giving you some grandchildren by now?'

'Having children isn't everything, Isabel.'

Isabel gave her a dry look. 'Said by a woman who had five.'

'Then I should know. What you need to do is find the right man. Then the children will follow.'

'Don't you think I've been trying to do that?'

'Don't try so hard. You're a beautiful girl. Just let nature take its course.'

Isabel was tempted to tell her that nature always led her up the garden path into the arms of men who'd never give her children.

But it was too late to confess such matters. She'd never told her mother the bitter truth about her boyfriends. She hadn't wanted to shock her. To reveal all now would only make her look even worse than she already did in her mother's eyes.

'Are you sure you don't want to go on that Dream Island holiday, Mum?' she asked, deciding a change of subject was called for.

'Positive. I'm too old that for that kind of holiday, anyway. Look, why don't you go yourself?'

'It's not a place you go alone.'

'Then ask a friend to go with you.'

Isabel thought immediately of Rafe… He'd jump at the chance of going with her, all expenses paid!

It was a tantalising idea. Did she dare? Could she actually *do* something like that without getting emotionally involved?

Perhaps she could. Her experience with Luke had changed her, made her stronger and much more self-reliant. She'd gone after what she wanted for once, listening to her head and not her heart. She'd actually gone to bed with a man she didn't love, and quite enjoyed it. Her mind no longer irrevocably linked sexual pleasure and being in love.

Just because Rafe was more like the type of man she'd used to fall in love with willy-nilly, that didn't mean she would fall in love this time. She also had the added advantage of knowing in advance that he wasn't interested in marriage or children. There would never be any fooling herself that she had a future with him.

He'd just be a passing pleasure. A salve to her pride and a comfort to her bruised female ego. Not to mention a comfort to her female body!

By the time she got through the next fortnight, cancelling everything and putting up with everyone's condolences, she'd need comforting. And what better way than on a balmy tropical island in the arms of a gorgeous man you fancied like mad, and who seemed to fancy you in return?

'Isabel?'

Isabel shook herself out of her provocative thoughts.

'Yes, Mum?'

'Well, what do you think about finding a friend to go

away on that holiday with you? If you can't get your money back, it does seem a shame to waste it.'

'We'll see, Mum.' She'd better sleep on the idea. She'd been knocked for a couple of sixes today. And she *had* been drinking. The booked holiday on Dream Island didn't start for another fortnight and she doubted Rafe was going anywhere in a hurry. Maybe if she felt the same way in the cold light of Monday morning…

A shiver ran down Isabel's spine at the thought of doing something that bold. It was one thing to deliberately go to bed with a man like Luke, when your intention was marriage. Quite another to contemplate a strictly sexual affair with the likes of Rafe Saint Vincent!

CHAPTER SIX

RAFE didn't sleep well that night, which wasn't like him. Usually, he was out like a light soon after his head hit the pillow.

But not this time. He tossed and turned. Even got up on one occasion and poured himself a stiff drink.

The trouble with that, however, was it reminded him even more forcibly of the reason for his insomnia.

Had she drunk some more after hanging up on him? Was she also up, wandering around the house in her nightie with another glass of whisky clutched in her hands?

He carried that image of her back to bed with him and tossed and turned some more, his hormone-revved head wondering what kind of nightie it might be. Short or long? Provocative or prissy?

Various alternatives came to mind. She'd look delicious in long creamy satin, and wickedly sexy in short black lace. Better still in nothing at all.

His groan was the groan of a man suffering from a case of serious sexual frustration. Which would never do if he wanted to get some sleep. And he did. He hadn't finished his work today and he'd have to beaver away at it all day tomorrow. No Sunday brunch down at

Darling Harbour with his mother. No slouching around watching the cooking shows on satellite.

Dragging himself up again, he made his way into the bathroom, where he had the hottest of hot showers, a technique he'd found worked much better on him than cold. The heat sapped his energy, and relaxed his tense muscles and other aching parts. After a good twenty minutes of sauna-type soaking, he snapped off the water, dried himself with one of his extra-fluffy white bath sheets, then fell, naked and pink-skinned, back into bed.

An hour later he was still wide awake.

Swearing, he rose, pulled on his black silk robe, made himself some very strong coffee and trudged downstairs to his darkroom where he surprised himself by working like a demon for several hours. It was light when he emerged, but by this time he was too exhausted to care. He went upstairs, switched off his mobile, took his other phone off the hook, closed the roller shutter which he'd recently installed on his bedroom window and collapsed into bed.

If his oblivion was ravaged by erotic dreams, he certainly didn't recall them, but he was embarrassingly erect when he was wrenched out of his blissful coma by the sound of his front doorbell ringing. It was just as well, Rafe decided as he struggled out of bed, that the robe he was still wearing provided discreet coverage. Because he had no intention of getting dressed. He was going to get rid of whoever was at the door, then go back to bed for the rest of the day.

It was Isabel, looking as if she was on her way to afternoon tea with the Queen.

Cream linen trouser suit. Blue silk top. Pearls. Pink lipstick. And that lovely blonde hair of hers, slicked back up in that prissy roll thing.

Her perfect grooming highlighted his own dishevelled appearance. Why couldn't he have any luck with this woman?

'I presume you've come for your phone,' he grumped.

She looked him up and down with about the same expression she had when she'd first arrived yesterday. 'Sorry to get you out of bed,' she said drily. 'But it *is* two in the afternoon.'

Rafe decided there was no point in telling her the truth, that he'd worked most of the night because of her.

'Yeah well, we party animals do get tired. And last night *was* Saturday night. I didn't get to bed till dawn.'

'Alone?'

He crossed his arms. 'Such a personal question for a lady who's just come for her phone.'

'*You* said I'd just come for my phone. *I* didn't.'

Rafe stared at her. Was he about to get lucky here?

'Do you think I might come inside?' she went on in that silkily cool voice of hers, the one which rippled down his spine like a mink glove.

'Be my guest,' he said eagerly, stepping back to wave her inside.

'I need to go to the bathroom,' she said straight away. 'I've just driven straight down from Gosford Hospital.'

Rafe frowned as he swung the front door shut behind

him. 'What were you doing up there?' And, even more to the point, what was she doing *here*? The suburb of Paddington was not on the way from the Central Coast to her address at Burwood. So she wouldn't have dropped in just to use his toilet!

His heart was already thudding with carnal hopes.

'Luke was in a car accident on the F3 freeway yesterday,' she said.

'Is he all right?'

'A few bumps and bruises. Nothing too serious. But he knocked his head and was unconscious for a while. The police found my number in his car and contacted me early this morning, so of course I had to go and see how he was.'

'He's having some rotten luck on the road lately, isn't he? First his parents and now him. Does his new girlfriend know about this?'

'Yes, I was there when she arrived. With her mother.'

'The infamous mother. What was she like?'

'The bathroom first, please, Rafe?'

'Oh, yes—yes, of course. This way.' He had the presence of mind to take her upstairs, instead of to the small downstairs toilet. The main bathroom upstairs was quite spacious and luxurious, another recent renovation. He'd been steadily renovating his terraced home since he'd bought it a couple of years back. It had cost him a small fortune, despite being little more than a dump. But, as in all big cities, you paid for position.

After showing her where the bathroom was, he dashed into his bedroom to dress. Hurrying into his walk-in robe, he ran his eye along the hangers, wondering what to wear. The day wasn't hot, but neither was it cold. Lately they'd had typical spring weather in Sydney, fresh in the morning but warming up as the day progressed, provided it wasn't cloudy. And it wasn't today, judging by the sunshine on his doorstep just now.

By the time Isabel emerged from the bathroom Rafe was looking and feeling a bit better in his favourite black jeans and a fresh white T-shirt. But his face still sported a two-day stubble and his feet were bare.

There was only so much a man could achieve in just over three minutes, the time it took for Isabel to emerge. Clearly she wasn't a girl who titivated.

'Nice bathroom,' she said crisply.

He'd known she'd like it. It was all white, with glass and silver fittings. Cool and classy-looking, like she was.

'You might not like this room as much,' he said as he led her into his main living room, which was decorated for comfort rather than style. No traditional lounge suite, just huge squashy armchairs to sit in, functional side tables, far too many bookcases and an old marble fireplace which he never used, although the mantelpiece was good for leaning on and holding glasses during a party. He had a hi-fi set in one corner and a television and video in the other.

'I like the doors,' Isabel said, as she sat in his favourite armchair, a reclining one covered in crushed claret-coloured velvet.

He glanced at the white-painted French doors which led out onto the small terrace. 'They're purely decorative,' he said. 'I never open them because of the traffic noise.'

'What a pity.'

He shrugged. 'You can't have everything.'

'No,' she agreed with a touch of bitterness in her voice. 'You certainly can't.'

Rafe sank down in a cream leather armchair facing her, and tried to guess at why she'd come to see him.

'The mother was stunningly good-looking for a woman of forty plus,' she said abruptly. 'And the daughter was…well, let me just say that I don't think Luke is going to have a change of heart and marry me after all.'

'Were you seriously hoping he would?'

'Stupidly, I think I was beginning to. Which is really pathetic. But on the drive back to Sydney today I decided I had to stop hoping for some man to come along and give me what I want out of life. I have to go out and get it for myself. And if it's not quite what I've dreamt about all these years, if I have to compromise, then that's just the way life is.'

'That sounds sensible,' Rafe said, even though he had no idea exactly what she meant. 'So what is it you're going to do? And where do I come into the equation?'

She smiled. She actually smiled. Only a small, wry little smile, but it was even better than he'd imagined. Or worse. He'd do anything she asked of him, *be* anything she wanted him to be. If only she'd let him make love to her.

'The thing is, Rafe, I've always wanted a baby,' she announced baldly and Rafe nearly died of shock.

Hold it there, buddy, he reassessed. Now that was one thing he *wasn't* going to do, even if it did mean he'd get to do what he wanted to do most at that moment.

'Naturally, I would prefer to have a husband,' she went on, with an elegant shrug of her slender shoulders, 'or at least a live-in partner before having a child.'

'Naturally,' he said with heavy emphasis.

'But that's simply not going to happen in my case in the near future, and time is running out for me. So I've decided to opt for artificial insemination from a clinic which supplies well-documented but anonymous donors.'

Rafe was both relieved and confused. Why was she telling him all this?

'Now that Luke is going to make me an independent woman of means, I don't need a man's financial support to have a child,' she elaborated. 'I can well afford to raise one on my own. I could put the child in daycare and go back to work, if I so desired. Or hire a nanny. Of course, I do realise it's not an ideal situation, but then, it's not an ideal world, is it?'

'No,' Rafe agreed. 'But why are you telling me all this, Isabel?' he finally asked.

'I'm just filling you in on my plans so you can understand the reasons behind the proposition I am going to make you.'

'And what proposition is that?'

'I want you to come to Dream Island with me on the honeymoon Luke and I booked.'

Rafe tried not to gape. 'Er…run that by me again?'

'You heard me,' she said in a straight-down-the-line, no-nonsense fashion.

Rafe stared at her. Wow. Talk about a shock.

He might have been ecstatic if he hadn't been just a tad wary. The thought that she might have some sneaky plan to use his sperm to impregnate herself without his knowing did not escape him. Though, if that was the case, why tell him about her intention to have a baby at all? Better to keep that a secret if that had been her hidden agenda.

'Why?' he demanded to know.

'Well, it isn't because I don't want to waste money,' she threw at him with a measure of exasperation. 'Even though the honeymoon package was all prepaid and it's too late to cancel. I *want* you to come with me because I want you to come with me.'

Rafe had difficulty embracing the possibility that she just wanted him for sex, even though it was the most exciting thought. All his fantasies of the night before coming true!

'As what, exactly?' he persisted. 'If you think I'm going to pretend to be your husband as a salve to your pride, then you can think again.'

'Don't be ridiculous. I wouldn't insult you like that. You'll be with me as my…my lover.'

Mmm, she'd choked a bit over that last word. He stared deep into her eyes and tried to see what was in her mind.

'Yes, but is my role as lover just a pretend one, or do I get to have the real thing with you?'

She blushed, and it enchanted him as much as it had the first time. It also didn't gel with her wanting him as little more than a toy boy. She just didn't seem to be that kind of girl.

'Spell it out for me, Isabel. I might be being dense but I'm still not getting the full picture here.'

She sucked in deeply, then let the air out of her lungs very slowly, as though she was gathering the courage to say what she had to say. He watched her, fascinated and intrigued.

Isabel hadn't thought it would be as difficult as this. When she'd made the decision on the drive down to ask Rafe to come away with her, she'd thought it would be easy. He'd just say yes and that would be that. She hadn't anticipated that he'd question her so closely, or make her confess her desire for him quite so bluntly.

It was embarrassing, and almost…shameful.

Yet why *should* she be ashamed? came the resentful thought. Had Luke been ashamed, taking what he wanted? At least she wasn't guilty of jumping into bed with Rafe the same day she met him, or while she was engaged to someone else. They wouldn't be breaking anyone's heart by going away together.

Not that Luke had broken her heart exactly. But he'd certainly shattered her dreams.

Isabel cleared her throat, determined not to start waffling, and doubly determined not to feel one scrap of shame!

'The bottom line is this, Rafe. Just because I've decided to have a baby alone doesn't mean I always want to be alone. I happen to like sex. Actually, I like it a lot. Perversely, I seem to like it most with men like you.'

Rafe's eyebrows shot upwards, then drew darkly together. 'Hey, hold it there. What do you mean by men like me? That sounded like an insult.'

Isabel winced. She hadn't worded that at all well. 'It wasn't meant to be an insult. It was just a fact. I'm always attracted to men who aren't into commitment. That used to be a big problem, given I wanted marriage and a family. It was the main reason I decided on a marriage of convenience with Luke, because I was sick and tired of falling in love with Mr Wrong. Now that I've made the decision to have a baby on my own, I don't have to worry about the intentions of the men I sleep with, because I won't want to marry them. I just want to have sex with them. Is there some problem with that? I thought that was what you wanted, too.'

Rafe frowned. He'd thought that was what he wanted, too.

'I guess I still like my girlfriends to think I'm an okay guy, not some selfish sleazebag who uses women for one thing and one thing only.'

'Oh, but I don't want to be your girlfriend, Rafe. After the honeymoon holiday is over, I don't want to ever see you again.'

He was truly taken aback. 'But why not?'

Isabel was not about to tell him the truth on this occasion—that she didn't want to push her luck by spending too much time with him. It was one thing to live out a fantasy fortnight with him on Dream Island, quite another to have him popping around all the time after they came back to Sydney. He really was too nice a guy to allow that. She was sure to end up wanting more from him that he could give.

Right at this moment, however, she just wanted him for sex, and nothing more. One look at his gorgeously rakish self on his doorstep this morning had confirmed that. Isabel didn't want to risk changing that status quo.

'I have my reasons, Rafe,' she said firmly. 'This is a take-it-or-leave-it proposition. I'm sure I could find someone else to go with me if you turn me down.'

The thought of her going with someone else made up Rafe's mind in a hurry. 'No need to do that,' he said hurriedly. 'I'd love to go with you.'

'On my terms and no questions asked?' she insisted.

'None except essentials. Firstly, how long will I be away?'

'Two weeks.'

Two weeks. Fourteen days and fourteen nights. Fantastic! 'And it's on Dream Island.'

'Yes, you've been there before?'

'No, but I've heard about it.' It was the newest and most exclusive of the tropical island resorts off the far North Queensland coast, specialising in romantic holidays for couples and honeymooners. He wondered if they would have one of the special bures overlooking their own private beach. That would be really something. To be totally alone with her with nothing to do but eat, sleep, swim and make love. His kind of holiday!

'When, exactly, do we fly out?' he asked eagerly.

'Today fortnight, at ten in the morning. I'll pick you up here at eight. Be ready.' She stood up abruptly.

'Hey.' He jumped up also. 'You're not leaving, are you?'

'I have no reason to stay any longer,' she returned, her manner firm. 'You said yes. We have nothing more to discuss.'

'What about contraception?'

She stared hard at him. 'I presume I can rely on you to see to that.'

'You're not on the pill?'

'No, and even if I was I would still want you to use condoms.'

He supposed that was only sensible, but he still felt mildly insulted. Which was crazy, really.

'Fine,' he said. 'But there's still no reason to rush off, is there? I mean…fair enough if you don't want to see me afterwards, but it might be nice to spend some time together *before* we go off on holiday together. Get to know each other a little better.'

'I'm sorry but I don't want to do that.'

'Why not, for pity's sake?'

'Look, Rafe, may I be blunt?'

Did she know any other way? 'Please do,' he bit out.

'We both know what the term 'getting to know you' means in this day and age. No, please don't deny it. I'm being brutally honest with you and I would appreciate the same in return. Aside from the fact my period is due this week and I'm suffering considerably from PMT right now, I simply don't want us to go to bed together beforehand.'

'Why not?'

She gave him another of those small enigmatic smiles. 'Maybe I don't want to risk you finding me a disappointment in bed and running a mile.'

Never in a million years, he thought. She only had to lie there and he'd be enchanted. Anything more was a bonus. But, since she openly confessed to liking sex, then he figured she was going to do more. How *much* more was the intriguing part.

'Don't *you* want to try before you buy?' he said with a saucy smile, and she laughed.

'I've seen all I need to see. You really shouldn't come to your front door half asleep and half dressed, Rafe darling. Now, show me where you put my phone, please. It's high time I went home.'

CHAPTER SEVEN

RAFE paced the front room, waiting for Isabel to arrive. She'd said she'd pick him up right on eight. But it was eight-ten and she hadn't shown up yet.

Maybe she wasn't going to. Maybe this had all been some kind of sick joke, revenge against the male sex.

This ghastly thought had just occurred to Rafe when he heard a car pulling up outside. Peeping out through the front window, he was relieved to see that it was her. Snatching up his luggage, he was out of the door before she could blow the horn. By the time he'd reached her car she'd alighted and was waiting beside the hatchback for him, looking gorgeous in pink pedal-pushers, a pink and white flowered top, and sexy white slip-on sandals. Her lipstick was bright pink, her hair was bouncing around her shoulders and her perfume smelt of freshly cut flowers.

'Sorry I'm a bit late,' she apologised as she looked him up and down. Without contempt this time. 'I had this sudden worry that you might have forgotten some essential items so I stopped off at a twenty-four hour chemist on the way.'

He grinned at her. 'Not necessary. They were the first thing I packed. But no worry. We won't run out now, will we? Which might have been a possibility if you're going to look as delicious as you look this morning all the time. Love the pink. Love the hair. But I especially love that perfume.'

Isabel tried not to let her head be turned by his compliments. Men like Rafe were always good with the charm.

At the same time, she'd come here today determined to enjoy what he had to offer. Cancelling everything for the wedding had been infinitely depressing, as had Luke's call telling her that he and Celia were now officially engaged. Isabel was in quite desperate need to be admired and desired, both of which she could see reflected in Rafe's gorgeous brown eyes.

'It's new,' she told him brightly. 'So are the clothes. I splashed out.'

That had been the only positive thing to happen during the last fortnight—Luke coming good with his promise to set her up financially. To give him credit, he hadn't let the grass grow under his feet in that regard. Guilt, no doubt.

Still, she was now the proud owner of a brilliant portfolio of blue-chip stock and shares, the deed to the Turramurra town house and a bonus wad of cash, some of which she'd recklessly spent on a wild new resort wardrobe. She'd given the more conservative clothes she'd bought to take on her honeymoon with Luke to Rachel, who was grateful, but wasn't sure where she'd ever get to wear them.

'You should splash out more often,' Rafe told her. 'I like the less formal you.'

'And I've always liked the less formal you,' she quipped back.

He was wearing fawn cargo slacks and a multi-coloured Hawaiian shirt, his bare feet housed in brown sandals. He must have shaved some time since she last saw him, but not that morning. Still, he looked and smelt shower-fresh, his silver phantom earring sparkling in the sunshine.

He smiled and rubbed a hand over his stubbly chin. 'You could have fooled me. So you like it rough, do you?'

'No lady would ever answer such a question,' she chided in mock reproof.

'And no gentleman would ask it,' he said, smiling cheekily. 'Happily for you, I'm no gentleman.'

'I'm sure you have your gentle side. Now, stop with the chit-chat and put your bag in here. If we don't get going we'll miss the plane.'

'Nah. At this hour on a Sunday morning we'll be at the airport in no time flat. The plane doesn't go till ten, does it?' he asked as he swung his one suitcase in beside her two.

'No,' she said, and slammed the hatchback down.

'Then we have time for this.'

When he pulled her abruptly into his arms, Isabel stiffened for a second. But only for a second. What was the point in making some silly show of resisting? This was why she found him so attractive, wasn't it? Because this was the kind of thing he would do.

Not like Luke. Luke always asked. He never took. Luke was a gentleman.

Not such a gentleman with Celia, however. He'd whisked her into bed before you could say Bob's your uncle! A matter of chemistry, Isabel realised.

As Rafe's lips covered hers, Isabel knew the chemistry between *them* was similarly explosive.

Sparks definitely flew and her head spun.

This was what she craved! Forceful lips and an even more forceful tongue. She leant into him, wanting more. She moaned before she could stop herself.

Rafe was startled by her response. The way she melted against him. The way she moaned. Wow, this was no ice princess. This was one hot babe he had in his arms!

When his head lifted, she made a small sound of protest.

He gave her one final peck on her wetly parted lips before putting her away from him. 'I can see this is going to be one fantastic holiday, honey,' he murmured throatily. 'But perhaps you're right. Perhaps we should get going before we really do miss that plane.'

Isabel hoped she wasn't blushing. She'd done enough blushing since meeting this man. Blushing was for female fools. And wishy-washy wimps. Not for a woman who'd decided to fashion her own destiny in every way.

So Rafe turned her on with effortless ease. Good. That was his job for the next fortnight.

But what about after that? she wondered, throwing him a hungry glance as she climbed back in behind the wheel. Mmm, she would see. Maybe she would keep his number in her little black book for the occasional night of carnal pleasure. Depending on how good he was at the real thing. If his kissing technique was anything to go by, she was in for some incredible sex.

Rafe didn't know quite what to make of the smug little smile which crossed that pink mouth.

Frankly, he didn't know what to make of Ms Isabel Hunt at all!

But he wasn't going to worry about it. He'd lost enough sleep over her this last two weeks. The next fortnight was going to be a big improvement, particularly in the insomnia department. He always slept like a log after sex.

'So, who did you tell your mother you were going away with?' he asked as soon as they were on their way.

She slanted him a curious look. 'What makes you sure I told her anything?'

'I have a mother,' he said drily. 'I know what they're like. They want to know the ins and outs of everything. Often, you have to resort to little white lies to keep them happy. I keep telling my mother that the only reason I haven't married is because I haven't met the right girl yet.'

'And that works for you?'

'I have to confess it's losing its credibility. I think by the time I'm forty she'll resort to taking out ads for me in the newspapers. You know the kind. ''Attractive single male seeks companionship view matrimony from attractive single female. Must be able to cook well and like children.'''

'If she does, I might answer. I cook very well and I adore children.'

'Very funny, Isabel. Now answer the question. Who is supposed to be going with you?'

'Rachel.'

'Who's Rachel?'

'My best friend. The one who was going to wear my wine-red bridesmaid gown.'

'And your mother *believed* you were taking a woman to Dream Island with you?'

'Yes.'

'Wow. My mother would never have believed that.'

'That you were taking a woman to Dream Island?'

'My, aren't we witty today?'

She smiled. 'Amongst other things.'

'What other things?'

'Excited. Are you excited, Rafe?'

He stared over at her. What was he getting himself into here? Whatever it was, it was communicating itself to that part of himself which he'd been trying to control for fourteen interminable days and nights.

'That's putting it mildly,' he confessed.

Her head turned and their eyes locked for a moment. He'd never felt a buzz like it. He could hardly wait.

But wait he had to. For two hours at the airport when the plane to Cairns was delayed. Then another short delay at Cairns for the connecting helicopter flight to Dream Island.

It was almost five in the afternoon by the time they landed on the heliport near the main reception area of the resort, then another hour before they were transported by luxury motor boat to—*yes*! Their own private bure on their own private beach!

Rafe was over the moon. Talk about fantasies coming true!

As he helped Isabel from the boat onto the small jetty, he glanced up at where the bure was set, on the lushly covered hillside on a natural terrace overlooking the water. Hexagon-shaped, it looked quite large, with what looked like an outdoor sitting area, a fact confirmed as they came closer. There was even a hammock strung between two nearby palm trees. Rafe eyed it speculatively when they walked past, wondering what it would be like to make love in a hammock.

The young chap named Tom who'd brought them there in the boat took them through the place, explaining all the mod cons which were state of the art, especially in the bathroom. The spa was huge. There was no expense spared with the white cane furniture and linen furnishings either, all in bright citrus colours with leafy tropical patterns.

No air-conditioning, Tom pointed out. Apparently that didn't work well in the humidity. But the bure had a high-domed ceiling and quite a few fans. Rafe wasn't sure how comfortable visitors would be in the height of summer, but at this time of year the climate was very pleasant, especially with the evening sea breeze which was at that moment wafting through the open doors and windows.

The bed, Rafe noted, had a huge mosquito net above

it on a frame which they were warned should be used every night. If they wanted to sit outside in the evenings, they were to spray themselves with the insect repellent provided and light the citronella-scented candle lamps dotted around.

Holidaying in the tropics, it seemed, did have some hazards.

'Because of all your travelling today,' Tom told them, 'the manager thought you'd be too tired to return to the main resort for dinner, so he had the chef pack you that special picnic dinner.' And he nodded towards the large basket he'd placed on the table in the eating nook.

'The refrigerator and cupboards are well stocked with more food and wine. The bar in the corner over there has every drink on its shelves you could possibly imagine. As I'm sure you are aware, all drink and food is included in the tariff here, so please don't stint yourself. Each day, you can either eat in the various restaurants in the hotel on the main beach or have something sent over. You only have to ring for service. Cigarettes are included also, if you smoke.'

'We don't smoke,' Isabel said for both of them, before frowning up at Rafe. 'You don't, do you?' she whispered and he shook his head.

'I'll be going, then,' Tom said crisply. 'There are brochures on the coffee-table explaining all the resort's facilities. You have your own little runabout attached to the jetty which I will show you how to operate before I leave. You must understand, however, that you can't walk to anywhere from here, except up to the top of the hill we're on. The path is quite steep from this point, but the view's pretty spectacular, especially at sunrise. Worth the effort at least once. I think that's all, but if you have any questions you only have to pick up the phone and ring Reception. Now, if you'd like to come with me, sir, I'll show you how to start the runabout's motor and how to steer.'

Isabel watched them leave, then walked over and sat down on the side of the bed, testing it for comfort. It was firm. Luke's bed had been firm, she recalled.

Luke…

He'd rung her yesterday and told her he and Celia were getting married in a couple of months. For a honeymoon, he was going to take her around the world. For a whole year. After that, they were going to start trying for a baby.

Isabel didn't envy Celia the trip. She'd travelled a lot herself. Saved up during her twenties and gone to those places she'd always thought exotic and romantic. Paris. Rome. Hawaii.

But she envied her that baby. And Luke as its father. He was going to make a truly wonderful father.

Suddenly, all her earlier excitement faded and she wanted to cry. Before she knew it she *was* crying, tears flooding her eyes and overflowing down her cheeks.

Isabel dashed them away with the back of her hands, angry with herself. If only she hadn't let Luke go racing off to Lake Macquarie that Friday. If only she hadn't been so darned reasonable she would have been here tonight, with him. They would have been married, and she would have been making a baby in this bed. Or at least trying to.

Instead, she was here with Rafe!

Throwing herself onto the bed, Isabel buried her face in the mountain of pillows and wept.

Rafe was taken aback when he walked back in and found Isabel crying on the bed. He hated hearing women cry. His mother had cried for a long time after his Dad had been killed. It had upset Rafe terribly, listening to her sob into her pillows every night.

'Hey,' he said softly, and touched Isabel's trembling shoulder.

With a sob, she turned her back to him and curled up into a ball on the green-printed quilt. 'Go away,' she cried piteously. 'Just go away.'

Rafe didn't know what to do. He hadn't a clue what was wrong. She'd said she hadn't loved her fiancé. Had she lied? Had she taken one look at this place and this bed and wanted not him, but Luke?

Dismayed, Rafe went to leave, but then decided against it. She shouldn't be left alone like this. She needed him, if only to comfort her for now.

He lay down on the bed and wrapped his arms around her from behind. 'It's all right, sweetheart,' he soothed, holding her tightly against him. 'I understand. Honest, I do. I'll bet you've been holding your hurt in this last fortnight, and now that you're here, where you should have been with Luke, his dumping you for that Celia girl has hit you hard. Look, I know what it's like to be chucked over for someone else. And it's hell. So cry all you want to. I did.'

Talking to her and touching her seemed to do the trick. Her weeping subsided to a sniffle and she turned over in his arms to stare up at him. 'You did?'

'Yep. Maybe it's not the done thing for a bloke to blubber, but I was like Niagara Falls for a day or two. Heck, no, longer than that. I was a mess on and off for a week. I didn't dare go out anywhere. It was most embarrassing. I drank like a fish too, but that didn't help at all. Made me even more maudlin.'

'Why did she dump you?'

'Ambition. And money. And influence. Be assured it wasn't because the other chap was better in bed,' Rafe added with a grin, and she laughed. It was a lovely sound.

He took advantage of the moment and kissed her. Not the way he'd kissed her back in Sydney this morning, but slowly, softly, sipping at her lips, showing her with his mouth that he *did* have a gentle side. He kept on kissing her, nothing more, and gradually he felt her defences lower till finally she began to moan, and move against him. Only then did he start to undress her—and himself—still taking his time, touching and talking to her as he went, reassuring her of how much he admired and desired her.

It wasn't easy, keeping his head, especially when he uncovered her perfect breasts and sucked on their perfect and very pert nipples, but he managed, till they were both totally naked and she was trembling for him.

It almost killed him to leave her and go get a condom. But a man had to do what a man had to do.

He was quick. Real quick. After all, he'd been slipping on condoms for years. Though rarely when he'd been as excited as this. Had he *ever* been as excited as this, even with Liz?

Maybe his memory was defective but he didn't think so. This was a one-off experience, perhaps because Isabel had made him wait two weeks to consummate what she'd evoked in him the first time he'd looked at her. This was lust at its most tortuous. And frustration at its most fierce.

He was thankful she felt the same way.

Or so he'd thought, till he hurried back to the bed and saw her looking at him with something like fear.

But why would she be afraid of him?

'What *is* it?' he asked as he joined her on the bed once more and drew her back into his arms. 'What's worrying you?'

'Nothing,' she said, shaking her head. 'Nothing.'

'Is it still Luke?'

'No. No!'

'Is it me, then? You're worried I might hurt you.'

She blinked her surprise at his intuition.

'Oh, honey, honey,' he murmured. 'I would never hurt you. I just want to make you happy, to see you smile and hear you laugh again. I want to give you pleasure. Like this,' he said as he stroked her legs apart, his fingers knowing exactly where to go and what to do.

She gasped while he groaned. How wet she was. It

was going to feel fantastic, being buried to the hilt in that.

Waiting any longer was simply not on. And possibly counter-productive. He would feel safer inside her. Less tense. He might even relax a bit.

As though reading his mind, she shifted her thighs apart and bent her knees, inviting him in, murmuring yes in his ear over and over. His fingers fumbled a fraction as he sought to push his suddenly desperate flesh into hers.

Rafe sighed with relief, then just wallowed in blissful stillness for a few seconds. But any respite was short-lived.

As soon as he began to move, her legs were around him like a vine. Or was it a vice? She was squeezing him with her heels and with her insides, rocking backward and forward.

Rafe felt a wild rush of blood along his veins, swelling him further, compelling him to pump harder as he sought release from his agony.

And he'd thought he'd be more relaxed inside her.

Foolish Rafe!

'Rafe,' she cried out, her arms tightening around his neck, her lips breathing hot fire against his throat. 'Rafe…'

Her first spasm sent him into orbit, to a place he hadn't known existed. Was it pleasure or pain as his seed was wrenched from his body? Agony or ecstasy as her almost violent contractions kept milking him dry, making him moan as he'd never moaned before.

Rafe didn't know if he was experiencing happiness, or humiliation. All he knew was that no sooner did he feel himself falling away from that place she'd rocketed him to, than he wanted to be there again.

'You're right,' she murmured, kissing his throat and stroking his back, his shoulders, his chest. 'You didn't hurt me.'

His eyes opened to stare down at her.

'You looked so big,' she explained breathily. 'I haven't been with a man that big before.'

Rafe was startled. He'd always thought of himself as pretty average. What she'd been seeing was mostly *her* doing. Still, he was secretly flattered.

'I'd thought you were worried I might hurt you emotionally,' he said.

'Oh, no,' she said, shaking her head. 'No, that won't happen. I won't ever let that happen.'

Now Rafe felt piqued. Which was crazy. She'd spelled out what she wanted when she'd propositioned him and he'd agreed. Sex on tap for a fortnight without any strings and without any follow-up.

He'd thought such a set-up was every man's fantasy come true. Now, for some reason that he hadn't anticipated, Rafe wasn't so sure.

Oh, for pity's sake, stepped in the voice of cold reason. What's got into *you*? This *is* every man's fantasy come true. Stop playing the sensitive New Age guy and start being exactly what she thinks you are. Rafe the rake!

The trouble was Rafe wasn't really a rake. Never had

been. Still, it might be fun. He could do every outrageous thing he'd ever wanted to do and get away with it. Make the most wicked suggestions. Play Casanova to the hilt, with a bit of the Marquis de Sade thrown in.

He had to smile at that. Him, into bondage and stuff? Wasn't his usual cup of tea, but that hammock had possibilities...

'Why are you smiling like that?' she asked.

'Like what?'

'Like the cat who got the cream.'

'Perhaps because I just did. You are the best in bed, sweetheart. Simply the best.'

She looked slightly uncomfortable with his compliment, as though she didn't like her performance being rated. Yet she must know she was good at sex.

She was a complex creature, and a maze of contradictions. Cool and ladylike on the surface whilst all this white-hot heat was simmering away underneath.

Rafe aimed to keep her furnace well stoked for the next fortnight. She wasn't going to be allowed to retreat into that ridiculous touch-me-not façade, not for a moment. She might think she'd hired him as her private toy boy, but in fact *she* was the one going to be the toy, to be played in whatever way he fancied.

Rafe might have been shocked by the wickedness of his thoughts under normal circumstances. But these were hardly normal circumstances, and it was what she wanted, after all.

'Hey, but I'm hungry,' he said. 'Aren't you?'

'A little. But I could do with a shower first. We've been travelling all day.'

'Mmm. Me, too. But why have a shower when there's that lovely big spa? We could pop in together. What say we take that picnic basket with us as well, kill two birds with one stone?'

'But...'

'But, nothing, honey. You just do what good old Rafe tells you and you'll have the time of your life.'

CHAPTER EIGHT

RAFE was right, Isabel thought two days later. She *was* having the time of her life. He was exactly what she needed just now.

Oversexed, of course. He never left her alone.

But she wasn't complaining. If she was brutally honest, she wanted him as much as he wanted her. He was wonderfully flirtatious and fun, with just the right amount of bad boy wickedness to his lovemaking which she'd always found exciting.

'So what do you think?' she said as she modelled her new red bikini for him.

Rafe was still sitting on the terrace in the morning sunshine, partaking in the slowest, longest breakfast. He was naked to the waist, a pair of colourful board shorts slung low around his hips. He was all male.

His eyes lifted and he stared at her. She hadn't worn this particular swimming costume for him as yet and it was scandalously brief. All the swimwear she'd bought with Luke's money was scandalous in some way, selected in a mood of rebellion and defiance.

And with Rafe in mind.

The white one-piece she'd worn yesterday went totally transparent when wet. Swimming had come to a swift end on that occasion, which was perhaps just as well, since her fair skin couldn't take too much sun. As it was, she was slightly pink. All over.

'Turn round,' he ordered.

She did, knowing full well what the sight of her bottom in nothing but a thong would do to him. Still, that was the general idea. She'd been like a cat on a hot tin roof since he'd come up behind her as she'd been setting out breakfast on the terrace an hour ago, and proceeded to have her right then and there, out in the open. No foreplay whatsoever. Just him, whispering hot words in her ear as he lifted the hem of the sarong she was wearing, then commanding her to stand perfectly still whilst he quite selfishly took his pleasure.

She'd nearly spilled the jug of orange juice she'd been holding at the time. She hadn't come, of course. He'd been much too fast and she'd been much too tense. It had left her terribly turned on, though. She was still turned on an hour later. Hence the red bikini.

Isabel hadn't brought Rafe along with her to remain frustrated for long.

When he said nothing, she spun back round and glared at him, her hands finding her hips.

'Well, what do you think?'

'I think you should come over here,' he said, and downed the rest of his orange juice.

A quiver ran all through her as she walked towards him. What was he going to do to her? Or make her do to him?

When he handed her the empty glass, she just stared at him.

'What's this?' she said.

'I've finished. I thought you might like to clear the table.'

'Then you thought wrong,' she snapped.

'In that case, what do you want to do? Or should I say, what is it you want *me* to do to *you*? If you tell me in minute explicit detail, Isabel, I'll do it exactly as you describe. Anything you want, honey. Anything at all.'

Her mouth had gone dry. '*Anything*?'

'Uh-huh.'

'I…I don't know what I want…'

He took the empty glass out of her hands, put it back on the table, then drew her down onto his lap. 'Yes you do,' he murmured as he moved aside the tiny triangles which barely covered her breasts and began playing with her nipples. 'You know exactly what you want.'

'I…' She could hardly think with him doing what he was doing. Her nipples had tightened into twin peaks of heightened sensitivity, and he was rolling them with his fingertips in exquisite circles.

'Tell me,' he said, his breath hot in her ear. 'Tell me…'

She shuddered and squirmed. 'No,' she croaked. 'No, I can't.'

'Why not?'

'It's…it's too embarrassing.'

'Then I'll tell you what you want. You want me to give you a climax first. With my tongue. You want *me* to wait this time, till I'm climbing the walls like I was our first time together. Even then, you want to torment me some more with this sexy mouth of yours.'

His right hand lifted from her aching nipples to touch her lips, making them gasp apart. She automatically sucked in when he slipped a finger inside.

'Yes, just like that,' he said thickly, sliding his finger in and out of her mouth. 'You'd like to do that to me, wouldn't you, Isabel?'

She shuddered all over.

'And then,' he went on in a low seductive whisper, 'you want me to do it to you like there's no tomorrow. You want me to scatter your mind, to make you feel nothing but the wild heat of the moment, and the beautiful blissful oblivion that will follow afterwards.'

When his hot words finally stilled, so did that finger. A charged silence descended, with no sounds but the heaviness of his breathing and the waves on the beach.

Isabel wasn't breathing at all!

Suddenly, his chair scraped back and he was up and carrying her, not over to the bure and the bed, as she was desperately hoping, but down the path which led to the beach. She was startled when he dumped her into the hammock on the way past then continued on himself to run across the sand and plunge into the ocean. Meanwhile, she had to clutch wildly at the sides of the swinging hammock to stop herself from falling out.

When he returned less than a minute later, all wet and smiling, she threw him the blackest look. 'You did that deliberately, didn't you?' she growled, still clutching at the hammock. 'Turned me on, then made me wait some more.'

'Nope. It just happened that way. Perversely, I turned myself on even more than I was trying to do to you. I had no idea just talking about sex like that was so powerful. Had to go cool myself off before things became downright humiliating. But I'm back now, ready and able to put my words into action. So where shall we begin, lover? Right here in the hammock?'

'Don't be silly. The darned thing won't stay still. And you don't have a condom with you.'

'I wasn't going to have actual sex with you here, Isabel,' he said drily. 'If you recall, that doesn't come till much later in the scenario I outlined, by which time I'm to carry you back to the bure.'

Her mouth gaped open. 'You…you mean you're going to do what you…d…d…described?'

'Every single bit of it. And so are you.'

Her face flamed.

'You'll like it, I promise,' he purred as he pulled her round crosswise and began peeling off her bikini bottom.

She did like it. Too much. Way too much.

But he was wrong about afterwards. He might have fallen into blissful oblivion on the bed afterwards, but she lay there wide awake, her thoughts going round and round.

She wasn't going to be able to give him up after a mere fortnight. That was the truth of it. She was going to want him around for much longer than that.

Why? That was the question. Was it the way he *could*

make her forget everything but the moment? Was it for the brilliant and blinding climaxes he could give her? Or was it something more insidious, something she'd vowed never to do, ever again?

Fall in love…

Rolling over onto her side, she looked at him lying there, sprawled naked on the lemon sheets, his arms flung wide, his silky brown hair. Leaning forward, she lifted one heavy lock from across his eyes and dropped it onto the pillow, then removed another which was covering his nostrils and mouth.

As if sensing that he could now breathe more easily, he sighed a deep, contented sigh, his mouth almost smiling in his sleep.

Isabel found herself smiling as well. Maybe she wanted to keep him around because she just liked him. And because he seemed to really like her in return.

Liking was good, she decided. She could live with that.

Finally, Isabel's worries calmed, she curled up to Rafe and went to sleep.

CHAPTER NINE

'NO RINGING for a dinner drop tonight, Isabel,' Rafe told her. 'We need to get up, get dressed and get away from here for a while. Do something else for a few hours. Have a change of scene.'

Isabel's head lifted and she smiled at him. 'Yes, Rafe darling, but surely you don't want me to get up and get dressed right at this precise moment.'

He stared back down into her cool blue eyes and wished he had the strength to tell her, yes, stop. Stop tormenting me. Stop enslaving me. Stop making me addicted to your body. And to you.

It was Wednesday, and they were back in bed, not long awake from an afternoon nap after a rather rigorous morning. They'd gone for a dawn swim after minimal sleep the night before and hadn't bothered with swimwear. There was no one to see them, after all. No one to see what they did in the water. Or on the wet sand. Or in the hammock again.

The hammock…

Rafe swallowed as he thought of what he'd done to her in the hammock last night, how he'd used the silk sarong she'd been wearing to bind her hands to the rope up above her head. He'd never done anything like that before. And neither had she, if he was any guess.

But what a sight she'd been stretched out there, naked, in the moonlight. Rafe had been incredibly turned on. And Isabel...Isabel had been beside herself. She'd come so many times he lost count. In the end, she'd begged him to stop.

But he hadn't been able to stop, not for a long long time.

And now he wasn't able to stop *her* as she drew him deep into her mouth once more.

He moaned at the heat of it. And the wetness. It was like being sheathed in molten steel. He was going to come. He knew he was going to come.

His raw cry of warning stopped her, leaving him dangling right on the edge.

'You have a problem, lover?' she drawled huskily as she reached for one of the condoms they kept beside the bed.

He choked out a rueful laugh. 'You're cruel, do you know that?'

'Now you know how I felt last night,' she said as she protected them both. 'Just as well my perfume acts as an effective insect repellent or I'd have been covered with insect bites.'

'Instead, you have a few bites of another kind.'

'Beast.'

'You loved it.'

'And you're loving this. So why don't you just lie back and enjoy?'

He sucked in sharply when she bent to take him in her mouth once more.

'No, don't,' he groaned, and her head lifted, her eyes surprised.

'No?'

'No.' He shook his head. 'Not like that.'

He reached down and pulled her up and onto him, spreading her legs outside of his, then pushing his tormented flesh inside her once more. With a primal groan he grabbed her buttocks, kneading them as he rocked her quite roughly up and down on him. They came together, backs arching, mouths gaping wide apart, bodies throbbing wildly in unison.

'Oh, Rafe,' she cried, collapsing face down across his chest, her insides still spasming.

He held her to him till she stopped, though a shudder still ran through her every now and then.

Too much, he began thinking. This is all getting too much.

'I have to go to the bathroom,' he told her a bit brusquely.

'No, don't leave me,' she begged, clinging to him.

'Sorry. Nature calls.' He was out of her and off the bed in a flash, lurching across the sea matting floor and into the bathroom. Closing the door, he leaned against it for a few air-sucking seconds before staggering over to the toilet, not really needing it except to do some essential personal housekeeping.

When he went to do just that, he stared down at himself in horror.

'Oh, no…' he muttered.

Not once had Rafe had a condom break before on him. Not once!

Till now...

His heart sinking, Rafe inspected the damage and it was the worst scenario possible. The darned thing had totally failed. Ripped asunder. Right across the tip.

Immediately he thought of Isabel and in his mind's eye he could see millions of eager little tadpoles careering through her cervix and into her womb, swimming around with more energy than the Olympic water-polo team, watching and waiting to score a home goal.

What were the odds of their doing just that? he wondered frantically, his mind scouring his memory to recall what Isabel had said to him that Sunday just over two weeks ago. Something about her period being due that week. Probably early on in the week, he guessed. She'd said something about suffering from PMT that day.

Rafe did some mental arithmetic and worked out that if Isabel was a normal regular female with a normal monthly cycle, then she had to have already entered, or be entering, her 'most likely to conceive phase' right now.

Rafe sank down on the side of the spa bath. He might have just become a father!

His head whirled. So did his stomach. She was going to kill him when he told her.

Then don't tell her, came the voice of male logic. It will only spoil everything. And there's nothing you can do about it now. Besides, it might not happen. It might not be the right time. Even if it was, couples sometimes tried for years—hitting ovulation day right on the dot—and the woman didn't fall pregnant. Let's not be paranoid about this.

But what if Isabel *had* fallen pregnant. What then?

Cross that bridge when you come to it, Rafe.

Right. Good advice.

Rafe stood up, jumped into the shower and turned on the water. Picking up the shower gel, he poured a generous pool into his hands and slapped it onto his chest.

But a *baby*, he began thinking as he washed himself. *His* baby. His and *Isabel's* baby.

Talk about the best plans of mice and men.

Isabel lay there listening to Rafe in the shower and thinking she could do with a shower herself. She felt icky. But no way was she going to join him in there, not after the way she'd just carried on, clinging to him and pleading for him to stay with her like some lovesick cow.

How typical of herself! And how humiliating!

No wonder he'd bolted out of the bed.

Rafe was right. It was high time they did something else instead of have sex. She was beginning to fall into old ways.

Isabel sighed. If only he was less skilful in the lovemaking department. If only he didn't know exactly the sort of thing which excited her unbearably. If only he didn't always turn the tables on her such as just now.

She'd thought she was being the boss in the bedroom, as she'd used to be sometimes with Luke, but in a flash Rafe had whipped control out of her hands and she'd become his willing little love slave again, as she'd been last night.

Isabel's face flamed as she thought how crazy it had been of her to let him tie her up like that. But, ooh, it had been so deliciously thrilling. And really, down deep, she'd never felt worried. There'd been no fear in her, only excitement.

It had been a game, an erotic game. Just as this holiday together was a game. Rafe knew that. And she knew that.

So why did she keep forgetting?

No more, she resolved. From now on she would stick to the rules. And to the agreed agenda. As for any silly idea she'd been harbouring of seeing Rafe occasionally after this fortnight was over… That was not on. Experience warned her if she saw Rafe outside of this fantasy setting she was sure to fall in love with him, or start relying on him for her day-to-day happiness. She'd been there, done that, and she wasn't ever going there again. Heaven help her, if she couldn't learn from her past mistakes!

Isabel was lying there under a sheet, feeling relatively in control once more, when Rafe emerged from the steaming bathroom, rubbing his brown hair dry with a bright orange towel, a lime-green one slung rather hazardously low around his hips.

Wow, she thought as her gaze ran hungrily over him. He really was gorgeous, even more so now that he was sporting an all-over tan. She loved the long lean look on a man, loved broad bronzed shoulders which tapered down to a small waist. *Loved* tight little buns.

Not that she could see his buns at that moment. But she had an imprint in her memory bank.

'It's time you got up, lover,' he said, draping the orange towel over his shoulder and finger-combing his hair back from his face. 'It's just gone five. I want to be gone from here by six.'

'Fine. I was just waiting for you to finish,' she replied, but, when she swung her feet over the side of the bed and sat up, Isabel hesitated. There wasn't anything for her to put on at hand. She hadn't worn any clothes all day and the sarong she'd been wearing last night was still tied to the hammock. The rest of her clothes were in the walk-in wardrobe, and it was actually further to walk over there than it was to the bathroom.

It was silly that walking around naked in front of Rafe should bother her. He'd seen every inch of her up close and personal. Too silly for words!

Gathering her courage, she tossed aside the sheet she'd been clutching and stood up, wincing a little once she started walking. Oh dear, she *was* icky. That was another thing she found a bit embarrassing. How wet she was all the time.

Not that Rafe minded. He said it was a real turn-on.

Still, once Isabel reached the shower she lathered herself up down there with some degree of over-enthusiasm, as if by removing the evidence of her ongoing heat, she could better keep her cool around him. A waste of time, she realised on remembering she had nothing to wear to dinner tonight but the choice of three highly provocative outfits, all bought to tease and tantalise, herself as well as Rafe.

Which one would do the least damage? she wondered. The little black dress?

No. It was way *too* little, halter-necked with no back and a short tight skirt which looked as if it was sewn on, owing to the material being stretchy.

What about the blue silk petticoat-style number with the swishy skirt?

No. Not with her nipples standing out all the time like ready-to-fire cannons. The material was too thin and the bodice too clingy.

It would have to be the emerald and gold trouser suit. Although still provocative, she at least got to wear a bra, of sorts. But the outfit did have other hazards. Such as the fulfilling of an old fantasy of hers to look like a harem girl. The pants were harem-style, and the emerald material semi-transparent, shot with gold thread. The outfit was only saved from indecency by being overlaid with a thigh-length jacket. The bra of sorts was a strapless corselette, heavily beaded in green and gold glass beads and designed to manoeuvre even the smallest of breasts into a cleavage. Isabel's breasts, though not large, were not small either. The result was eye-catching to say the least.

Once dressed and made-up, Isabel stared at herself in the floor-length mirror which hung on the back of the walk-in wardrobe door and thought she'd never looked sexier. Her hair was up, though not in its usual French roll. She'd just bundled it up loosely in a very casual topknot, leaving strands of various lengths to fall around her face. The long green and gold crystal earrings in her ears would swing when she walked. *If* she could walk, she amended as she squeezed her feet into the outrageously high gold sandals she'd bought to go with the outfit.

'Shake a leg in there, lover,' Rafe called out. 'It's gone six.'

With a shudder which could have been excitement or apprehension, she dragged on the gauzy green jacket, sprayed on some perfume, then went to meet her master.

Rafe was out on the terrace, admiring the view in the dusk light and thinking that this place really was a fantasy come true when Isabel emerged from the bure, looking like something out of the Arabian Nights.

'Well,' he said, smiling wryly to her as he scraped back the chair and stood up. 'If ever there was an outfit designed to turn a gay man straight, then you're wearing it tonight.'

She laughed a slightly guilty-sounding laugh. 'I didn't bring any let's-do-something-else clothes with me, I'm afraid.'

'I see,' he said drily. And he did. She was only here with him for the sex. She'd made that quite clear from the start.

And he'd been with her all the way. Till their little mishap this afternoon. Now, suddenly, everything had changed. Now, suddenly, when he looked at her, he didn't see a delicious bedmate but a possible pregnancy.

Not that he didn't still desire her. He'd have to be dead not to. It was just that other thoughts were now overriding his X-rated ones. Such as perhaps he should still tell her what had happened. It wasn't too late for her to get the morning-after pill. They had a doctor on the island, he knew. And a chemist shop. He'd read the list of services available in one of the coffee-table brochures.

But, oddly, he hated the idea of her ridding her body of his baby—if his baby *was* in there. Peculiar, really, when he'd never wanted to be a father before. He still didn't.

But *she* did. Want to be a mother, that is. She wanted one enough to have one on her own. So why not his? Better than having herself artificially inseminated. Bad idea, that.

'Rafe! Why are you just standing there, frowning at me like that? What on earth are you thinking?'

'What am I thinking?' He took her arm and started propelling her down the path towards the jetty. 'I was thinking that your idea of having a baby all by yourself is not a good one. In fact, it's a very bad one. My mother found it extremely difficult raising me by herself, and she had help for the first eight years.'

'Yes, well I can understand how raising *you* would have tried the patience of a saint,' Isabel said. 'But my baby won't be having your impossible genes, Rafe, so hopefully my job won't be quite so difficult.'

'Is that so?' Rafe smiled. He couldn't help it. Irony always amused him.

'Yes, that's so!' she pronounced haughtily.

'But if you go through with this plan of yours to be artificially inseminated with some unknown donor, then you won't have any idea what kind of genes your baby will inherit from its father. Surely even *my* genes would be better than the lucky-dip method.'

'All that will be unknown is his name and address,' she informed him somewhat impatiently. 'I will know a lot of information about the donor. A complete physical description, all aspects of his health, his level of education, plus other personality traits such as his sporting interests and hobbies. That's how I aim to choose him. I will look at the list of available donors and select the one which best fits my prerequisites.'

'Fascinating. Here, I can see you're having trouble walking in those heels. I'll carry you.' She went to object but he just swept her up into his arms and carried her across the sand towards the jetty.

'Mmm. You're as light as a feather. You know, I think you've lost weight since coming to this island. Too much exercise and not enough eating,' he said, at which she pulled a face up at him.

'We have to make sure you're in tippy-top health, you know, if you're planning to have a baby soon. Three good meals a day, and no silly dieting.'

'Yes, Dr Saint Vincent,' she mocked.

'Just talking common sense. Of course perhaps you're not serious about having a baby soon, or on your own at all. Maybe that was just talk.'

'I'm deadly serious. We're on the jetty now,' she said curtly. 'Please put me down.'

Rafe stared down into her eyes, suddenly aware of how stiffly she was holding herself in his arms. It hadn't occurred to him when he picked her up that she might be turned on by it. Whilst her vulnerability to his close-ness was very flattering, taking advantage of it wasn't a priority of his at this precise moment.

He lowered her carefully onto those wicked-looking shoes. 'So tell me, Isabel, what *are* your prerequisites for choosing the father of your child?'

'No.'

'No? What do you mean, no?'

'I mean no, Rafe,' she said firmly as she marched on ahead of him out along the jetty. 'I am not going to have this conversation with you,' she threw over her shoulder. 'I wish I hadn't told you about my plans now. Why you're even interested is beyond me.'

He hurried after her. 'Oh, come on, don't be like that. If we're going to sit across the table and have dinner for a couple of hours we have to talk about something. And I'm curious.'

She spun round to look him straight in the eye. 'Why?'

'Why not?'

For a moment her eyes flashed with frustration, but then she shrugged. 'I might as well give in and tell you whatever you want to know, because you won't give up, will you? You'll get your way, like you did with the black and white photos. You're like that Chinese water torture.'

He grinned. 'I've been told that before.'

'I can imagine. But you can't have it *all* your own way *all* the time. If I'm to answer such highly personal questions then I have a few of my own I want answered.'

'Fair enough.' He had nothing to hide and, frankly, was intrigued over what she might want to know. More than intrigued. Rather pleased. Maybe she didn't want him just for sex. Maybe she wanted more, whether she admitted it to herself or not.

The prospect of having a more permanent relationship with this beautiful and spirited woman brought a rush not dissimilar to sexual arousal. He'd never been entirely happy with the thought of never seeing Isabel again after this fortnight was over, but had brushed aside any qualms over the rather cold-blooded terms she had set down because he wanted her so much.

But things were different now.

If she was carrying his child, then going their separate ways was simply not on.

Rafe couldn't stop his eyes from drifting down her body, first to her breasts—his baby was going to be very happy with *those*!—and then to her stomach—athletically flat at this moment. But he could imagine how it would look in a few months' time, all deliciously soft and rounded.

Isabel's insides contracted when she saw the direction of Rafe's eyes. He was thinking about sex again. She could tell. The way he'd just gobbled up her cleavage, and now he was undressing her further. He was making her all hot and bothered inside again, like he had when he'd been carrying her just now.

'Now you stop that!' she snapped, and his eyes jerked up to her face.

'Stop what?'

'You know what, you disgusting man. Now help me into this darned thing.'

The runabout rocked wildly when Isabel first stepped down into it, with Isabel almost tipping into the sea. 'Maybe we should have called Tom to take us over,' she said in a panicky voice as she clutched at the sides.

'If you'd just sit down in the middle of the seat, Isabel,' Rafe pointed out calmly, 'everything would be fine.'

Isabel did just that, and everything was fine, with Rafe starting up the motor as though he'd been doing it all his life, then steering her safely back to the main beach where he eased the small craft expertly into another jetty. His confidence and competence at things marine and mechanical reminded Isabel that men like Rafe *did* have their uses in life, other than to give women mind-blowing climaxes.

If she kept him coming around occasionally, he could also be called upon to change light-bulbs, put new washers in leaking taps and even mow the lawn. Now that she was a home owner she'd have to do things like that from time to time.

When he climbed up onto the jetty with his back to her she ogled his body quite shamelessly, especially those tight buns, housed as they were tonight in tight black jeans.

'Now you stop that,' he said, turning and grinning down at her.

'Stop what?' she managed to counter, but her cheeks felt hot.

'You know what, you disgusting woman.'

'I have no idea what you're talking about,' she parried. 'Now, help me out of here, and don't let me fall in the water.'

'Might do you good. Cool you down a tad.'

Isabel decided she really couldn't let him get away with mocking her. Her glance was cool as a cucumber. 'I thought you liked me hot and wet, not cold and wet.' And she swept past him.

Rafe watched her stalk off up the jetty and smiled. She was a one all right. More sassy and sexy than any woman he'd ever met.

But he had her measure. She liked him. She didn't want to but she did. That was why she was going to such great pains to put him in his place all the time. What she didn't realise was that fate might have already propelled him out of his role as temporary lover into possibly something far more permanent. Father of her child.

Mmm. That was another thing he had to check up on. What the odds were of that.

'Where are we going for dinner exactly?' she asked him when he caught up and took her arm.

'To the Hibiscus Restaurant. This way.' He guided her

along the planked walkway which connected the jetty to the main resort buildings which sat in several acres of tropical gardens just behind the beach.

Aside from the reception area, which also encompassed the island store, there was a five-star hotel nestled amongst the palms which boasted two à la carte restaurants, a buffet-style bistro, a couple of bars, a casino games room and a pool which, from the brochures, had to be seen to be believed. One of the restaurants was called the Hibiscus, named no doubt after the lovely tropical flower which grew in abundance on the island.

'I booked a table there while you were in the shower,' he told her. 'The woman on the other end of the phone said it was the most romantic of the restaurants here. I gather she thought we were honeymooners.'

'And you didn't tell her we weren't,' Isabel said drily.

'Goodness, no. That way, we were assured of a good table. She said since it was a balmy night she'd give us one of the ones on the terrace overlooking the pool.'

'Con artist,' Isabel scorned.

'Just being my usual clever charming self.'

'Arrogant and egotistical, that's what you are.'

'You like me arrogant and egotistical.'

'Only in bed.'

'People spend a third of their lives in bed. Except when they're on a pretend honeymoon. Then, they spend nearly *all* of it.'

Isabel laughed. And why not? Rafe had to be one of the most entertaining men she'd ever been with. It was impossible not to surrender to his charm, or be amused by his wit, which was wicked and dry, just the way she liked it.

'I love it when you laugh,' he said. 'You look even more beautiful when you laugh.'

'Do stop flattering me, Rafe. I might get used to it.'

'Ooh, and wouldn't that be dreadful?'

'Not so dreadful. Just unwise.'

'Why?'

She sighed as her good humour faded. 'I told you once before, Rafe. I don't want to have another relationship with a man whose idea of a relationship begins and ends in the bedroom.'

'And you think that's all I'd ever want from you?'

'Isn't it?'

'That depends.'

'On what?'

On whether you're carrying my child…

'On how good you can cook,' he quipped.

Her eyebrows shot up. 'You're saying the way to your heart is through your stomach? I don't believe it.'

'I *do* like my food. This way to the Hibiscus,' he directed on seeing an arrowed sign veering off to the right through the gardens. 'Mmm, I wonder what their wine list is like? Since there's no extra charge, I'll order a different bottle with each course.'

'I'm not going back in that tin-can with you if you've been drinking heavily,' she warned.

'Me, neither. If I feel I'm over the limit, we'll get someone else to take us back. Okay?'

'Okay.' She nodded. 'And don't encourage me to

drink too much, either. I still haven't got over the hangover I had from my last binge.'

'Yes, but that was hard liquor. A few glasses of wine won't hurt.'

'Mmm. You'd say that. You're probably trying to get me drunk so that you can have your wicked way with me.'

He laughed. 'Honey, I don't have to get you drunk to do that.'

Isabel winced. 'I asked for that one, didn't I?'

He gave her an affectionate squeeze. 'Don't be silly. I love the way you are.'

Isabel didn't doubt it. Men had always been partial to whores.

Her stomach turned over at this last thought. She wasn't a whore, but maybe, in Rafe's eyes, she was acting like one. There again, maybe not. Rafe was not a narrow-minded man, and he didn't seem to be afflicted with that dreadful set of double standards which some men dragged up to make women feel guilty about their sexuality.

Her mother, however, wouldn't be impressed with the way she'd been behaving.

Isabel suppressed a groan. Why, oh why did she have to think of her mother? The woman was out of the ark when it came to her views on such things. She didn't appreciate that the world was a different world now. Marriage couldn't be relied upon any more to provide a woman with security for life. And men…men couldn't be relied upon at all!

'You've gone all quiet on me,' Rafe said worriedly.

'Just thinking.'

'Thinking can be bad for you.'

'What do you recommend?'

'Talking is good. And so, sometimes, is drinking. You could do with a measure of both.'

'You conniving devil. You just want to find out all my secrets.'

'You mean you have some?'

'Don't we all?'

'My life is an open book.'

'Huh! Any man with designer stubble and a phantom's head in his ear has to have *some* secrets.'

'Not me. What you see is what you get. If you think I'm indulging in some kind of pretentious arty-farty image with the way I look, you couldn't be more wrong. The phantom's head belonged to my father. I wear it all the time because when I look in the mirror I'm reminded of him. I don't shave every day because it gives me a rash if I do. As far as my clothes are concerned, I dress strictly for comfort, and in colours which don't stain easily. I am who I am, Isabel. And I like who I am. Can you say the same? Aah. Here we are. The Hibiscus.'

CHAPTER TEN

THE Hibiscus lived up to its recommendation, with even the indoor tables having a view of the spectacular pool, courtesy of glass walls on three sides of the restaurant.

Still, given the balmy night, it was going to be very pleasant sitting outside under the stars, and the table they were shown to *did* overlook the pool directly.

Round and glass-topped, the table was set with hibiscus-patterned place-mats, superb silverware and crystal glasses to suit every type of wine. The menus were printed with silver lettering on a laminated sheet which matched the place-mats.

After seeing them seated, the good-looking young waiter handed Rafe the wine list, then lit the lantern-style candle resting in the circular slot in the middle of the table, possibly where an umbrella would be inserted during daylight hours. The wine list was small but select, and Rafe ordered an excellent champagne to start with whilst Isabel silently studied the menu.

Even after the waiter departed she didn't glance up or say a word, leaving Rafe to regret the crack he'd made about her perhaps not liking who she was. She'd looked down-in-the-mouth ever since.

But if she was going to keep firing bullets, then she had to expect some back.

Still…he hated seeing her sad.

But what to do?

'Find anything there to tempt your tastebuds?' he asked lightly on picking up his own menu. A quick glance showed there were three choices for each course, rather like a set menu.

'I'm not that hungry, actually,' she murmured, still not looking up.

Rafe put down his menu. 'Look, I'm sorry, all right? I didn't mean to offend you.'

Now she did look up. 'Don't apologise. You're quite right. I don't think I do like who and what I am. I suspect I never have.'

'What rubbish. What's not to like, except the way you used to do your hair? I hated that. And it wasn't the real you at all.'

'The real me? And what's that, pray tell? Slut of the month?'

Rafe was truly taken aback, then annoyed with her. 'Don't you *dare* say that about yourself. So you're a sensual woman and enjoy sex. So what? That's nothing to be ashamed of.'

'If you say so,' she muttered unhappily.

'You should be jolly well proud of yourself. A lot of females would have folded after what you've been through just lately. But not you. You lifted your chin, squared your shoulders and went on. I might not agree with your decision to have a baby all alone, but I do admire the guts it took to make such a decision.'

Isabel was taken aback, both by his compliments and

his apparent sincerity. He liked her, and not just because she was good in bed.

'Good grief, Isabel, don't you ever go putting yourself down like that again. You have to be one of the most incredible women I've ever met, so stop that self-pitying nonsense and choose something to eat, or I'll lose patience with you and not even want to play sheikh to your harem girl at the end of the night.'

She laughed, her eyes sparkling with returned good humour. 'I knew I did right to ask you to come here with me. You are so…so…'

'Sensible?' he suggested when she couldn't find the right word.

She smiled. 'I was thinking more along the lines of refreshing.'

'Now, that's something I haven't been called before. Refreshing.'

'Take it as a compliment.'

'Oh, I will, don't worry.'

Her head tipped to one side as her eyes searched his face. 'You really are a nice man, Rafe Saint Vincent. And a very snazzy dresser. Love that black and white shirt. Can I borrow it some time?'

'You can borrow anything of mine you like. Sorry I can't return the compliment. I have a feeling I wouldn't look too good in any of your clothes.'

They were both smiling at each other when the waiter materialised by their side again with the champagne, which he duly poured, then asked if they'd like to order. Rafe did, with Isabel surrendering the choice to him, saying she liked the look of everything on the menu anyway and had recently used up all her decision-making powers.

He grinned and chose a Thai beef and noodle dish for an entrée and a grilled barramundi for the main, with a salad side plate.

'And mango cheesecake for dessert,' he finished up. 'We'll also be ordering more wine with each course. Do you have any half-bottles?'

'I'm sorry, sir, but we don't. However, you can order any of the wines listed by the glass.'

'Really? What happens to the rest of the bottle if no one else orders it?'

The waiter gave a small smirk as he whisked the menus away. 'It doesn't go to waste, sir. Be assured of that.'

'I'll bet,' Rafe said drily after the waiter departed. 'I'd like to be a fly on the wall of the kitchen every night after closing.'

'There are always perks to any job,' Isabel pointed out.

'Oh? And what were the perks of being a receptionist at a big city architectural firm?'

Isabel frowned. 'How did you know that was my job?'

'I found out when I rang Les and told him your wedding was off. We had quite a chat about you. He thinks you're a dish and wanted to know what I thought of you.'

'And you said?'

'I was suitably complimentary but discreet. Not a

word about this little jaunt, since it was obvious he knew your family fairly well.'

'Fancy that. Rafe Saint Vincent—the soul of discretion.'

'I have many hidden virtues.'

'Some not so hidden,' she said saucily.

'Naughty girl. But back to the original question. What perks were there in your job beside meeting multimillionaire architects?'

'Not too many, actually. Free ball-point pens? And we won't count meeting Luke, since that didn't work out. I don't have to ask you what the perks of *your* job are. I've seen them on the walls of your office.'

Rafe frowned. 'What do you mean?'

'Oh, come now, lover, those photographs speak for themselves. They have foreplay written all over them.'

'You think I slept with all those women?'

'Didn't you?' Isabel picked up her crystal flute of champagne and began to sip.

'Heck, no. There were at least one or two who held out.'

Isabel spluttered into the glass.

'But they were lesbians.'

Isabel had to put down her glass.

'Stop it,' she choked out, and mopped up around her laughing mouth with her serviette.

'Would you like me to photograph you like that?'

Isabel swallowed. 'In the nude, you mean?'

'Good heavens, no. You saw my photographs. I never take full nudes. You can wear earrings, if you like. And those shoes.' One eyebrow arched wickedly as he peered at her sexily shod feet through the glass table. 'Oh yes, *definitely* those shoes.'

'You're teasing me.'

'Yep. I didn't bring my camera with me. Unfortunately.'

Thank Heaven, she thought. Because no doubt she would have let him photograph her *just* like that. Her behaviour with him since arriving on this island had been nothing short of outrageous.

'So!' she said, and swept up her champagne glass again. 'Tell me why you're opposed to my decision to have a baby alone.'

He smiled a wry smile. 'A change of subject, I presume. A wise move.' Just *thinking* about photographing her in nothing but earrings and those shoes was making him decidedly uncomfortable, especially since he was wearing rather tight jeans.

Rafe picked up his champagne, took a couple of sips and put his mind to answering her very pertinent question. If she hadn't brought up the subject of having a baby herself, he would have worked his way round to it. He hesitated to tell her what he *really* thought of her decision to have a baby alone by artificial insemination. She was determined anyway, and they'd just end up arguing. What he needed to know was the likelihood of her having conceived *his* child today.

'I just think it was a hasty decision, and one made on the rebound after Luke. You're still a young woman, Isabel, with well over a decade of baby-making capabilities left. You have more than enough time to find a suitable father for your baby before launching into motherhood alone. I think you should wait and see if he turns up.'

'Look, I told you. I tried finding Mr Right both with my heart and then my head and I bombed out both ways. No. I can't keep on waiting. And you're wrong about my having a lot of time. A woman might be theoretically capable of having a child right up until menopause, but the odds of her conceiving and carrying a healthy baby full term start to go downhill after she reaches thirty. No, Rafe, my biological clock is ticking and, knowing my luck, it's probably about to blow up. The time for action is now.'

Rafe had a bit of difficulty keeping a straight face. Little did Isabel know but the time for action might very well have been this afternoon!

'I see,' he muttered, dropping his eyes towards his champagne for a few seconds before looking up again. 'So if your marriage to Luke had gone ahead, you were planning to get pregnant pretty well straight away, then?'

Isabel sighed. 'Yes.'

'On this honeymoon?'

'Uh-huh. I had it all worked out, right to the very hour and the day.'

'Hard to pinpoint ovulation with that kind of accuracy, isn't it?'

'Not when you're as regular as I am, and when you've taken your temperature every day for three months.'

'And?' Rafe prompted. 'When would the critical time have been?'

'What? Oh, not till tomorrow, I think. Yes, Thursday. I do everything on a Thursday. Ovulate and get my period. Regular as clockwork, I am. Twenty-eight days on the dot. My girlfriends at work always used to envy the fact I was never taken by surprise, which was true. I used to pop into the loo at morning tea on P-day because I knew, come noon, the curse would arrive.'

'The curse?'

'That's what we women call it. You don't think it's a pleasure, do you? Oh, but this is a depressing topic. Would you mind if we changed the subject again? Let's talk about you.'

'Fine,' Rafe said, his head whirling. Thursday. Did sperm live for a full day? He was pretty sure it was possible, but she'd got up and had a shower soon afterwards. The odds weren't on his side.

Weren't on his side! Was he mad? He should have been relieved. He didn't really want to be a father, did he? *Did* he?

He looked at Isabel and realised he did. With her, anyway.

The realisation took his breath away.

He reefed his eyes away and stared down at the pool. Stared and stared and stared. And then his eyes flung wide. Who would have believed it?

'Rafe? Rafe, what's wrong? You look like you've seen a ghost or something.'

His gaze swung back to her and he almost laughed.

'I have. In a way. See that blonde frolicking down in the pool?'

'The one with the really big bazookas?'

'Yes, well she didn't have such big bazookas when I knew her. She must have had a boob job. Anyway, that's Liz—the girl I told you about. The one who dumped me.'

'Really?' Isabel was close enough to see the buxom blonde quite well, even better once she swam over and hauled herself up to sit on the edge of the pool. When she lifted her hands up to wring out her hair, her boobs looked like giant melons pressed together. Truly, they were enormous!

The grey-haired man she'd been canoodling with in the water climbed out via the ladder and walked over to where he'd left his towel. Whilst Liz looked in her late twenties, her companion was sixty if he was a day.

'Let's go, honey,' Isabel heard the man say with a salacious wink as he walked by. 'Time you earned your keep.'

'Coming, darls,' the blonde trilled back, though her face behind his back was less than enthusiastic.

'Is that the man she threw you over for?' Isabel asked, unable to keep the distaste out of her voice.

'No. I have no idea who that is, although I presume he's rich. No, the man Liz left me for was a fellow photographer. A more successful one at the time, though I'd heard rumours he had associations with some less than savoury video productions. I wondered what had become of Liz when I didn't see any more of her in the fashion world. I think the answer lies in those double D cups. A lot of models, especially ones who want fame and money too quickly, get sucked into doing things they shouldn't do. Pity. She could have been really someone. Instead, she's turned into *that*.' And he nodded towards the sight of her hurrying after her sugar-daddy, her gigantic breasts jiggling obscenely.

'You seem slightly sorry for her,' Isabel said, rather surprised.

'Oddly enough, I am.' He sounded surprised, too. 'Seeing her again, in the flesh so to speak, has given me a different perspective. And it's laid quite a few ghosts to rest.'

'You loved her a lot once, didn't you?'

'Yes. Yes, I did. Stupid, really. In hindsight, I can see she wasn't worth it, but love is blind, as they say.'

'I know exactly what you mean. I couldn't count the number of creeps and losers I've fallen for over the years. But, dear heaven, the last fellow I was involved with before Luke made the others look like saints. Still, I didn't know that when I first met him.'

'And where was that?'

'I was working my way around Australia and had taken this job as a salesgirl in a trendy little boutique on the Gold Coast which sold Italian shoes. One day, this sophisticated guy came in and I served him. He bought six pairs of shoes, just so he could spend more time with me, he said. Naturally, I was impressed.'

'Mmm. A bit naïve of you, Isabel, falling for a line like that.'

'That's me when I fall for a man. Naïve.'

'You weren't with me.'

'I was *attracted* to you, Rafe. I didn't fall for you.'

Terrific. Well, he'd asked for that one, hadn't he?

'So what happened next?'

'What do you think? He took me out to dinner that night, then straight home to bed afterwards.'

Rafe decided not to pursue that conversation further. He felt decidedly jealous of this Hal and his instant sexual success. Isabel had given him icicles the first day they'd met. Still, she *had* been a bride-to-be at that stage, and possibly still suffering from the once-bitten twice-shy syndrome after this fellow.

'So how did it end? Did he dump you?'

'No. Actually, he didn't. In a weird way I believe Hal did love me. As much as a man like that is capable of love. No, something happened and I could no longer pretend he was Mr Right.'

'Oh-oh, sounds like you found out he was already married.'

She laughed. 'If only it were as simple as that.'

'Now I'm seriously intrigued. What happened?'

'He was arrested. For drug importation and dealing. He got fifteen years.'

'Wow. And you never suspected?'

'Not for a moment. He didn't use drugs himself, and he never did any dealing in my presence. Even when he made numerous trips to Bangkok I didn't suspect. He said he was an importer. Of jewellery. I should have known by past experience that he was too good to be true, but as you said…love will make a fool of you every time. I thought all my dreams had come true. Hal was handsome, successful, exciting, masterful. Materially, he had it all as well. The mansion on the water. The car. The yacht. He swept me right off my feet, I can tell you. Told me he adored me. It was just a matter of time, I thought, till he proposed. I was on cloud nine till I picked up the paper one day and saw his photograph on the front page.'

'Must have been one bad day.'

'That's an understatement, I can assure you. I was devastated.'

'Did you have to testify at his trial?'

'No. Which was fortunate. Also fortunate that this all happened in another state. I hadn't told my parents about Hal, you see. But I was going to, once we were engaged. I thought he'd be a pleasant surprise after all the going-nowhere men I'd been with in the past. Some surprise he'd have turned out to be!'

'Just as well he was arrested when he was, then.'

'I didn't quite see it that way at the time,' Isabel muttered.

'No. Just as I didn't see I was better off without Liz. But we're both better off without both of them, Isabel. Much better off. And you're better off without Luke, no matter what you think now. He didn't love you.'

'Love I can do without from now on.'

Rafe looked at her. 'Oh, I don't know. Love still has a certain appeal.'

'I can't see what. It makes you do things. Stupid things. Irrational things.'

'Mmm. You could be right there.' Because for the next two days he was going to do the stupidest, most irrational things in his life!

'Where on earth is that food?' Isabel said irritably.

'It'll be here soon. Meanwhile, have some more champagne,' he added, and topped up her glass. 'Good, isn't it?'

'Yes. But if I don't eat soon it'll go straight to my head. I have a very low intoxication level with champagne. It can make me tipsy quicker than anything else.'

'Is that so? Well, there's no worry in being a bit tipsy, is there? It won't make you do anything later that you wouldn't be doing anyway.'

The eyes she set upon him over the rim of her glass were very dry. 'My, aren't we full of the sauce tonight?'

I hope so, Rafe thought ruefully. Because my sauce is going to have to work very hard to do the job from now on. He didn't dare cut the whole top off every condom he used during the next two days. She might notice. He really could only risk a pin-prick or two. Except perhaps tonight…

Isabel's powers of observation could very well be limited if she got well and truly sloshed. If he was clever with what position he used, he might get away with not using anything at all.

The thought excited, then worried him.

It was a stupid thing to do, as she said. Stupid and irrational. She didn't love him. She wouldn't marry him.

At best, he would be a father to their child at a distance, having limited access.

But so what? he thought recklessly. He was still going to do it, wasn't he?

CHAPTER ELEVEN

ISABEL woke with a moan on her lips. The sun was shining in through the open doorway of the bure, indicating Rafe was already up, probably having his early-morning swim.

'That man must have a constitution of iron,' she muttered as she dragged aside the mosquito net and tried to sit up. But the room spun alarmingly and there was a bongo drummer—complete with drums—inside her head.

With a low groan, Isabel sank back carefully onto the pillows then ever so slowly rolled onto her side. The room gradually stopped spinning.

It was then that she saw the tall glass of water sitting next to the bed, alongside a foil sheet of painkillers.

'What a thoughtful thing to do,' she murmured, though not yet daring to move. In a minute she would take a couple of those pills Rafe had left her. Meanwhile, she would close her eyes and just do nothing.

Isabel closed her eyes and tried to do nothing, but her mind was by now wide awake. She began thinking about last night after dinner. In the end, they hadn't got anyone else to run them back to their jetty. Rafe had said he was fine to operate the boat and she'd been far too tipsy to worry.

Tipsy! Hardly an adequate word to describe her state of intoxication. She'd been seriously sloshed. Not Rafe though, yet he'd consumed as many glasses of wine as she had. Or had he? Perhaps not. He'd talked a lot between courses, and she'd just sat there, sipping her wine and listening to him like some fatuous female fool, thinking how gorgeous he was and how stupid Liz was to dump him.

No, Isabel finally conceded. Rafe hadn't consumed nearly as much wine as she had. If he had, he wouldn't have been able to make such beautiful love to her as he had after they'd come home.

Not that she could remember it all. Some bits were pretty hazy. But she could remember the feel of his hands on her as he undressed her and caressed her. So gentle and tender. The same with his kisses. His mouth had flowed all over her and she had dissolved from one orgasm to another.

She'd never known climaxes could be like that. Blissful and relaxing. Her bones had felt like water by the time he'd rolled her onto her side, rather like she was lying now. Only last night Rafe's naked body had been curled around her back.

Isabel's stomach contracted at the thought. That was one thing she hadn't forgotten. How he'd felt when he'd first slipped inside her. She moaned at the memory. It had felt so good. Even better when he'd begun to move.

Never had she been so lost in a man's arms, her mind and body like mush. She hadn't come again. But, Rafe must have. She had a vague recollection of his crying out. But after that, all memory ceased. She must have fallen asleep. And now here she was the next morning with a parched mouth and a vicious headache, whilst Rafe was down at the beach, no doubt bright-eyed and bushy-tailed.

A shadow fell across the corner of her eye and she rolled over just enough to see Rafe walk through the sun-drenched doorway. His dark silhouette eventually lightened to reveal that she'd been right. He had been swimming, thankfully dressed in board shorts. She couldn't cope with him in full-frontal nudity this morning.

'How's the head?' he said as he walked towards the bed.

'Awful. Many thanks for the tablets and the water.'

'My pleasure. And it *was*,' he added with a devilish grin.

'Don't be cocky. I was pretty plastered.'

'So I noticed. You know you're very agreeable when you're plastered.'

'I really couldn't say. Last night is somewhat hazy.'

'You mean you can't remember anything?'

Isabel caught an odd note in Rafe's question. Was he pleased or offended? 'I didn't say that. I said hazy, as in…hazy.'

'Ahh. Hazy. Hazy word, hazy.'

'You were pretty good, if that's what you're waiting for.'

He smiled. 'That's nice to hear.'

'Different, though.'

Rafe's stomach flipped over. 'Different?' he asked, trying not to panic. 'In what way, different?'

She shrugged. 'Gentler. Sweeter. Different.'

Rafe smiled his relief. 'Well, I didn't need to rush it. You weren't making any of your usual control-losing demands.'

Isabel was taken aback. 'What do you mean, control-losing demands?'

'Honey, you have a very impatient nature when it comes to sex. It's always faster, Rafe. Harder. Deeper. Again. More. No more. Stop. Don't stop. The list is endless.'

'That's not true!' she denied hotly.

'Perhaps a slight exaggeration on my part. But it was still a rather nice change to know I could take my time and do exactly what I wanted to do with your total co-operation. I really enjoyed it.'

And how! Rafe thought.

Any apprehension over his bold decision not to use any protection had disappeared once he'd put his plans into action. Knowing that a child could possibly result from his lovemaking had added an emotional dimension Rafe hadn't anticipated. When he'd felt his seed spilling into her he'd thought his heart would burst with elation. And when she'd gone to sleep in his arms afterwards he'd been consumed by feelings so powerful and deep that they'd revolutionised his ideas on what loving a person was all about.

Seeing Liz last night was the best thing that could have happened to him. What a fool he'd been, choosing a solitary life for fear of being hurt again. Fair enough to withdraw into his cave for a while. But it had been years, for pity's sake. Years of keeping women at a distance, except sexually, and telling himself—and everyone else—that he didn't want marriage and a family, when the truth was he'd become too much of a coward to risk his male ego a second time. He'd been afraid of being dumped again, afraid of rejection.

Not any more. He was going to take a leaf out of Isabel's book and go after what he wanted. Which was *her* as his wife as well as the mother of his child. Or children. Heck, he wasn't going to stop at just one. He'd hated being an only child.

But he couldn't tell her all that yet. He couldn't even tell her how much he loved her. She wasn't ready for such an announcement. But she would be, in time. And when Mother Nature eventually took her course.

It was to be hoped that last night had done the trick. But if it hadn't, he'd already doctored a few more condoms for today. If at first you don't succeed, Rafe, then try, try again.

Trying again had never looked so pleasurable. Pity she had a hangover. Still, that would pass.

'God, I can't stand people looking perky when I'm dying,' Isabel grumbled.

'What you need is a refreshing swim,' Rafe suggested.

She groaned. 'My head is already swimming, thank you very much. Do you think I could con you into getting me a cup of coffee?'

He jumped up off the foot of the bed. 'One steaming mug of sweet black coffee coming up!'

Isabel groaned again. Not only perky, but energetic. He even started whistling.

Still, she had to concede Rafe wasn't anything like she'd first thought. Oh, she didn't doubt he was a bit of a ladies' man. And marriage and children were not part of his life plan. But he wasn't at all arrogant, or selfish. He was actually quite considerate, and highly sensitive. That Liz female had really hurt him, stupid greedy amoral woman that she was.

His dad's death had scarred him as well. Isabel had been moved last night when Rafe had told her how his father had been a country rep for a wine company, travelling all over New South Wales, selling his products into hotels and clubs and restaurants. Rafe had been just eight when his dad's car had hit a kangaroo at night and careered off the road into a tree, killing him instantly. Unfortunately, his father hadn't been a great success as a salesman—a bit of a dreamer, though in the nicest possible way—and money had been tight for his widow and son after his demise.

But he'd been a great success as a dad. Clearly, Rafe had adored him. His voice had choked up when he'd told Isabel that the only things his father had left him in a material sense were a camera and a pair of phantom's-head cuff-links. Father and son had had a real thing for the Phantom, his Dad always bringing Rafe home a *Phantom Comic* after he'd been away. They would always read it together that night. Isabel had been moved to hear that, when one of the prized cuff-links had been lost during a house move Rafe had had the other made into an earring and never took it off for fear of losing it as well. How he must have loved that man!

It was a pity he shied away from being a father himself. With his dad's example to go by, he'd probably be a very good one.

She sighed. That was the incorrigible romantic in her talking again. Next thing she'd have him returning with her coffee and saying he'd changed his mind about what he wanted in life, after which he'd declare his undying love and beg her to marry him.

Fat chance!

'Here's your coffee, lover. Now, stop all that sighing and drink up. Oh, for pity's sake, you haven't even taken your headache tablets yet. Or drunk the water. How do you expect to feel better unless you rehydrate yourself? No, no coffee for you till you've done the right thing. And there'll be no more drinking to excess in future. It's no good for you.'

Isabel glared at him. 'And there I was, thinking you weren't the bullying bossy pain in the neck I'd first met. But I was deluding myself. The only reason you want me to feel better is so that you can have more of what you got last night.'

He grinned the cheekiest sexiest grin. 'You could be right there.'

Isabel glowered at him as she popped two tablets into her mouth and swallowed the water.

'A shower or the sea?' he said, eyeing her rather salaciously where the sheet had slipped down to her waist.

Isabel didn't have to look down to know what he was seeing. Maybe *she* wasn't too perky this morning, but her nipples still were.

And she was so wet down there it wasn't funny.

'I think a spa bath is in order,' she said. 'Alone,' she added firmly.

'I could scrub your back,' Rafe offered.

'No.'

'Spoilsport.'

'And then, after breakfast, I'd like to do something unenergetic. I noticed there was a pack of cards in the cupboard over there.'

'Cards,' he repeated drily. He hated playing cards. His mother was a fanatic at euchre and cribbage, and used to rope him in when she couldn't find another partner. She always won so there hadn't been much fun in it for him.

'There's plenty of other games in there as well, if you'd prefer,' she went on, no doubt hearing his reluctance.

Rafe eyed her with determination. The only games he aimed to play today were those of the erotic kind. He couldn't afford to waste the whole of this very critical twenty-four hours. She might be ovulating at this very second.

But then an idea came to him.

'Okay,' he agreed. 'But, to make it interesting, let's bet on the outcome of each game.'

She frowned. 'For money, you mean?'

'Don't be silly. What would be the fun in that?'

'What, then?'

'If I win, you have to do whatever I want. And vice versa.'

Her eyes widened. 'Are we talking sexual requests here?'

'Not necessarily. I might ask you to go for a swim with me. Or cook me a meal. Or give me a massage.'

Yeah, right, she thought ruefully.

'I won't agree to *anything*, Rafe, especially sexually. There has to be limitations.'

'Nothing too kinky, then. Nothing you think the other person wouldn't like.'

That was far too broad a canvas! 'I...I don't want to be tied to that hammock again.' Not in the daylight. That would be just too embarrassing for words.

'Fair enough. What would you rather be tied to?'

'Rafe!'

'Only kidding.' Hell, he didn't want to tie her up. He just wanted to make her a mother.

Isabel could feel the heat spreading all through her body. This was just the kind of thing which turned her on. Oh, he was wicked.

'Let me have that bath and some breakfast first, then,' she said, trying not to sound too eager. 'You find whatever game you think you would prefer.' And hopefully one that he was darned good at playing. Because she didn't want to win, did she? She wanted him to win.

He chose an ingenious little game called Take It Easy,

and by eleven they were sitting on the terrace, playing. The trouble was luck rather than skill played a large part and, even if you didn't try, sometimes you still won. Each game didn't last all that long and the rules suggested you play three games then totalled up the scores to see who won.

Isabel won the first round, by one point, despite not concentrating at all.

'Oh,' she said, trying not to sound disappointed by the result.

Rafe eyed her expectantly across the table. 'Well? What cruel fate awaits me, oh, mistress mine?'

'You said nothing kinky,' she reminded him.

'No, I said nothing *too* kinky.'

'You also said it didn't have to be a sexual request.' Surely she would lose next time and then she would be forced to do what *he* wanted. That would be much more fun. She would wait. 'So I'd like a toasted ham, cheese and tomato sandwich, please. And a tall glass of iced orange juice.'

'What?' he snapped, his face frustrated. 'You just had breakfast half an hour ago.'

'I'm sorry but I'm still hungry,' she said blithely.

When he just sat there, scowling at her, she crossed her arms. 'Are you welching on your bet already?'

'You'll keep, madam,' he muttered, then went to do her bidding.

Five minutes later he returned with the sandwich on a plate and a very tall glass of frosted orange juice. The fridge and freezer really were very well stocked, especially with the ingredients for easy-to-make snacks. Honeymooners and illicit lovers—who were the likely bookers of the private bures—apparently didn't surface back at the main resort for meals all that often.

Isabel accepted the toasted sandwich and ate it very slowly, pretending to savour every bite. In actual fact, she wasn't at all hungry. She just hadn't been able to think of anything else to ask for. The orange juice was nice, though, and she drank it down with deep gulps. Her hangover had long receded but she was still probably a bit dehydrated.

'Ahh,' she said, and placed the empty glass on the empty plate, pushing them both to one side. 'That was lovely, Rafe. Thank you. Shall we get on with the next round?'

'By all means.'

Rafe won. Easily.

'Oh, dear,' Isabel said.

'My turn, it seems,' Rafe said with cool satisfaction in his voice, and a smouldering look in his eyes.

Isabel began to tremble inside.

'Take off your sarong,' he commanded.

When he didn't add anything else, she just looked at him. 'That's it? Just take off my sarong?'

'Yes. Do you have a problem with that?'

She gulped. It was far less than she was expecting. And yet...

It suddenly hit her that he meant for her to sit there, playing the next round of the game, in the nude. The deviousness of his mind excited her, as did the idea.

Isabel felt her blood begin to charge around her veins as she stood up and slowly undid the knot which tied her sarong between her breasts. Their eyes met and she was just about to drop it down onto the terracotta flagstones when the phone rang.

'Leave it,' Rafe commanded thickly. 'It's probably just Reception wanting to know if we want a picnic lunch brought over.'

Isabel tried to do what he said. Tried to ignore it. But she couldn't, especially when it just kept on ringing.

'I can't,' she blurted out and, retying the sarong, she hurried in to answer it.

'Hello,' she said breathlessly.

'Isabel?'

'Rachel!'

'I'm so s...sorry to bother you,' she cried, her voice shaking.

'Rachel, what's wrong?'

'It's Lettie. She...she's gone, Isabel.'

'You mean...passed away?'

'She wandered out of the house a couple of nights back when I was asleep and got a chill. She... she wasn't wearing any clothes, you see. She often took them off. Anyway, by the time I realised she was gone and the police found her, wandering in some park, she was shivering from the cold and it quickly developed into pneumonia. Her doctor put her in hospital and pumped her full of antibiotics, and they said she was going to be all right, but last night she...she had a heart attack and they couldn't save her.'

'Oh, Rachel, I'm so sorry.'

'You know, I thought I'd be relieved if and when she died,' she choked out. 'You've no idea what it's been like. The endless days and nights. The utter misery and futility of it all. Because I knew she'd never get better. She was only going to get worse. And worse. I used to lie in bed some nights and hope she wouldn't wake up in the morning. But now that she has died, I…I'm not relieved at all. I'm devastated. I look at her empty bed and just cry and cry and cry. I…I can't function, Isabel. I needed to talk to you. That's why I had to call. I needed to hear your voice and know that somewhere in this world there was someone who loved me.' At that, she broke down and wept.

'It's all right, Rachel. I'll ring Mum and Dad straight away and get them to go and bring you home to their place. And I'll be back in Sydney as soon as I can.'

'But…but you can't,' she cried, pulling herself together. 'Your mum will know, if you do that.'

'Know what?'

'That you didn't go to Dream Island with me. She'll know you went with…with some man.'

'Oh, never mind that. What does that matter? So she'll think I'm wicked for a while. She'll get over it. Now, you hang in there, Rach, and don't go doing anything silly.'

'Such as what?' Rachel sniffled.

'Such as drinking too much of Lettie's sherry. Or sleeping with the gardener.'

'I don't have a gardener,' she said mournfully. 'But

if I did I would sleep with him, no matter what he looked like. I'm so lonely, Isabel.'

'Not for long, sweetie. Just hang in there. I'll ring Mum straight away and get her to ring you.'

'All right.'

'You are home, aren't you?'

'What? Yes, yes, I'm home.'

Isabel's heart turned over. The poor darling. She sounded shattered. 'Okay, don't go anywhere till Mum rings you.'

'Where would I go?'

'I don't know. Shopping, perhaps. Or back to the hospital.'

'I don't want to ever go near that hospital ever again.' And she started to weep again.

'Oh, Rachel, please don't cry. You'll make me cry.' Isabel's chin was already beginning to quiver.

'S…sorry,' Rachel blubbered. 'Sorry.'

Isabel swallowed. 'Don't be sorry. Don't you ever be sorry. I'll try to get a flight back today. At worst, it will be tomorrow. Meanwhile, you do just what Mum tells you to do. She'll bombard you with cups of sweet tea and plate-loads of home-made lamingtons but don't say no. You could do with fattening up a bit. Do you realise you've lost most of those fantastic boobs of yours? You know, I used to be jealous of those at school. You've no idea. But they'll bounce back. And so will you, love. Trust me on that.'

'I knew I was right to ring you,' Rachel said with a not so distressed-sounding sigh.

'If you hadn't, I'd have been very annoyed. Now, I must go. Loads to do. See you soon, sweetie. Take care.'

Isabel hung up with a weary sigh. Rachel was right about one thing. Her mother was not going to be pleased with her little deception over this holiday.

But that was just too bad. Squaring her shoulders, Isabel swept the receiver up again, and asked Reception for an outside line.

'I gather the honeymoon's over.'

Isabel spun round to find Rafe standing in the doorway.

'How much did you hear?'

'All of it.'

'Then you know I have to go home. You can stay for the rest of the fortnight if you want to.'

He stared at her as though she were mad. 'Now, why would I want to do that? Without you here with me, Isabel, it would just be a waste of time. No, I'll be coming back to Sydney with you. If you find there aren't any available seats going back this afternoon, you could have Reception offer the rest of this pre-paid jaunt to all the couples on the island whose holiday ends today. Someone is sure to take you up on it.'

'That's an excellent idea, Rafe. Thank you.'

'I am good for some things besides sex, you know.'

Isabel frowned at the slightly bitter edge in his voice. What had got into him? Did he think she was happy about having to leave?

'Look, I'm sorry, Rafe. I hardly planned this. I'd rather be staying here with you than going back home to a heartbroken friend. But fate has decided otherwise. Rachel needs me and she needs me *now*. I'm not going to let her down.'

'I appreciate that. Honest I do. I admire people who are there for their friends when they're needed. I guess that's the crux of my discontent. The fact you didn't consider I'd be there for *you* during the next few undeniably difficult days. You just dismissed me like some hired gigolo whose services were no longer required. I thought we'd moved beyond that. I thought you genuinely liked me.'

'I…I do like you. But what we've had together here… We both knew it was just a fantasy trip, Rafe. It's been fantastic but it's not real life. Come on the plane with me by all means, but once we get back to Sydney I think we should go our separate ways.'

'Do you, now?' he bit out. 'Well, I don't.'

'You don't?'

'No. As far as what we've had here… Yes, it has been fantastic, but I think we can have something better once we get back to Sydney. And we can be good friends as well.'

'But…'

'But nothing. You like me. I like you. A lot. On top of that, we are very sexually compatible. Face it, Isabel, you're not the sort of woman who's ever going to live the life of a nun. You like sex far too much. So don't look a gift-horse in the mouth. Where else are you going to find a man who's prepared to be your friend as well as your lover? A man, moreover, who knows how to turn you on just like that.' And he snapped his fingers. 'You'll go a long way before you come across that combination again.'

He was right, of course. He was ideal.

Too ideal. She was sure to fall hopelessly in love with him. Sure to. But she hadn't as yet. She could still walk away.

But then she thought of what Rachel had said about being so lonely that she'd sleep with anyone, and she knew she wouldn't be able to walk away for ever. One night, when she was alone in that town house at Turramurra, she'd pick up the phone and call Rafe and ask him to come over.

Take what he's offering you now, came the voice of temptation. And if you fall in love with him?

She would cross that bridge when she came to it.

'So you want to be my day-time friend and night-time lover, is that it?'

'No. I want to be your friend *and* lover all the time. I see no reason to relegate our sex life just to night.'

An erotic quiver rippled down her spine. She didn't stand a chance of resisting this man. Why damage her pride by trying? But that same pride insisted she keep some control over the relationship. She could do that, surely.

'You're so right, Rafe,' she said, adopting what she hoped was a suitably firm woman-in-control expression. 'Things *have* worked out between us far better than I ever imagined they would. You're exactly what I need in my life. But please don't presume that my agreeing to continue with our relationship gives you any rights to tell me how to run my life. I know you don't agree with my decision to have a baby on my own, but I aim to do just that, and nothing and no one is going to stop me!'

CHAPTER TWELVE

RAFE sat silently beside Isabel on the flight to Sydney late that afternoon, planning and plotting his next move.

He'd been furious with fate at first for interrupting them. But, in the end, things hadn't worked out too badly. Isabel had at least agreed to go on seeing him. As for her declaration that nothing and no one was going to stop her from having a baby…little did she know but he was her best ally in that quest. He hoped to have her pregnant well before she got round to doing that artificial insemination rubbish.

The captain announcing that they'd begun their descent into Sydney had Isabel turning towards him for the first time in ages.

'I'll drop you off on the way home,' she said.

'Fine. What about tomorrow?'

'What about tomorrow?'

'Will you be needing me?'

She stared at him. 'I thought you said you didn't like my treating you like some gigolo,' she said agitatedly. 'That was a rather gigolo-sounding question.'

'I meant as a friend, Isabel,' he reproved, thinking to himself he had a long way to go to get her trust. That bastard Hal had a lot to answer for.

148

'Oh. Sorry. I'm not used to men just wanting to be my friend.'

'I thought you said you were friends with Luke first.'

'Yes, well, Luke was the exception to the rule.'

'St Luke,' he muttered.

'Not quite, as it turned out.'

'No. So what about tomorrow?'

She sighed. 'I think I should spend tomorrow with Rachel.'

Rafe had no option but to accept her decision. Which meant if she hadn't conceived this month he'd have to wait till her next cycle before trying again.

Still, he admired Isabel for the way she'd dropped everything and raced to this Rachel's side. There weren't too many people these days who would have done that. He liked to think he was a good friend, but he suspected he'd become somewhat selfish and self-centred during his post-Liz years, another result of his bruised male ego which he wasn't proud of.

'What about the next day?' he asked.

'The funeral's then.'

'I'll take you.'

'No.'

'*Yes*. I'm not going to let you hide me away like some nasty secret, Isabel. Your mother already knows you went off to Dream Island with a man. I heard you tell her on the phone. I also gather you took quite a bit of flak about it. I didn't like that. In fact, I wanted to snatch that phone right out of your hand and tell your mother the truth.'

'The…the truth?'

'Yes. You are *not* cheap or easy, which I gather was the gist of her insults. You are one classy lady and I'm one lucky guy to be having a relationship with you. You're also a terrific friend and, I'll warrant, a terrific daughter. Someone should tell your mum that some day, and that someone just might be me.'

'That's sweet of you, Rafe, but you'd be wasting your time. Mum suffers from a double generation gap. She's still living back in the fifties and simply can't come to terms with the fact I'd go away with you like that so soon after meeting you. She was not only shocked, but ashamed.'

'Sounds like she suffers from double standards as well,' Rafe pointed out irritably. 'I'll bet she wasn't shocked when she found out your precious ex-fiancé leapt into bed with his new dolly-bird less than an hour after meeting her. And I'll bet she thought that was perfectly all right!'

'No. No, I don't think she thought that at all. It's hard for her to accept modern ways, Rafe. She's seventy years old.'

'That's no excuse.'

'No, but it's a reason. She'll calm down eventually. Meanwhile, I think it's best not to throw you in her face.'

'Isabel,' he said firmly, '*you* are *thirty* years old. Way past the age of adulthood. You say you're going to live your life as you see fit. Well that should include in front of your mother.'

'That's all very well for you to say. You don't practise what you preach. You told me you lie to your mother all the time. You even pretend you're going to get married some day when you know very well that you're not.'

'That's all in the past. I'm going to be honest with her in future.' No trouble, Rafe thought. Because he *was* going to get married now. To Isabel.

'Yeah, right. Pity I won't be there to see the new-leaf Rafe.'

You will be. Don't you worry about that.

'I'm coming with you to that funeral, Isabel. And that's that!'

Isabel glared at him. The man simply couldn't be told!

'Be it on your head then,' she snapped. 'And don't say I didn't warn you.'

By five o-clock on the day of the funeral, Rafe almost wished he'd heeded her warning. The service was over and they were back at Isabel's parents' place for the wake, and he was looking for a place to hide.

Unfortunately, there weren't too many people for Rafe to hide behind. It had been a very small funeral. Isabel and Rachel, whom Rafe had warmed to on first meeting today, had been cornered by some large woman, leaving Rafe to fend for himself.

The chill coming his way from Mrs Hunt was becoming hard to take, so were the disapproving looks at his earring. Goodness knew what would have been the woman's reaction if he hadn't shaved that morning. Or put on his one and only dark and thankfully conservatively styled suit.

Rafe valiantly ignored the dagger-like glances he was getting from his hostess as he filled his plate from the buffet set out in the lounge room. After checking that Isabel and Rachel were still occupied in the corner, he headed out to the front porch, where he'd seen a seat on the way in, and where he hoped to eat his food in peace, without having to tolerate Mrs Hunt's deadly glares.

But fate was not going to be kind. He'd barely sat down when she followed him through the front door and marched over to stand in front of him. Rafe looked up from the plate he'd just balanced on his lap, keeping his face impassive despite his instantly thudding heart.

Formidable was the word which came to mind to describe Isabel's mother. Handsome, though. She would have been a fine-looking woman when she was younger. Though she did look trapped in a time warp, her grey hair permed into very tight waves and curls, and her belted floral dress with its pleated skirt reflecting a bygone era.

'Mr Saint Vincent...' she began, then hesitated, not because she didn't know what she was going to say, Rafe reckoned, but because she wanted to make him feel uncomfortable.

Her strategy worked. But be damned if he was going to let it show.

'Yes, Mrs Hunt?' he returned coolly, picking up a sandwich from the plate and taking a bite.

'Might I have a little word with you in private?'

He shrugged. 'We're perfectly alone here, so feel free to go for it.'

Her top lip curled. 'That's rather the catch cry of your generation, isn't it?' she sneered. 'Feeling free to go for whatever you want.'

'Good, isn't it? Better than being all uptight and hypocritical, like your generation.'

'How dare you?' she exclaimed, her cheeks looking as if they'd been dabbed with rouge.

'How dare *you*, Mrs Hunt? I am a guest in your home. Are you always this rude to your guests?'

'I have every right to be rude to a man who's taking wicked advantage of my daughter.'

'You think that's what I'm doing?'

'I know that's what you're doing. Isabel would never normally go off like that with some man she'd only just met. You knew she was on the rebound. But that didn't stop you, did it?'

Rafe decided to nip this in the bud once and for all. He figured he had nothing to lose, anyway. 'No,' he agreed, putting his plate down on the seat beside him and standing up, brushing his hands of crumbs as he did so. 'No, it didn't stop me, Mrs Hunt. And I'll tell you why. Because I'm in love with your daughter. I have been ever since the first moment we met. I love her and I want to marry her.'

The woman's eyes almost popped out of her head.

'Of course, I haven't told her this yet,' he went on. 'She's not ready for it. She won't be ready for it for a while, because at this moment her trust in the male sex is so low that she simply won't believe me. She, like you, thinks I'm only with her for the sex. Which is not true.'

'You mean you're…you're *not* sleeping with her?'

Rafe had to smile. 'Now, ma'am, let's not get our wires crossed here. I didn't say that. I *am* a man, not a eunuch. And your daughter is *very* beautiful. But Isabel has much more to offer a man than just sex. She's one very special lady with a special brand of pride and courage. It's a shame her own mother doesn't recognise that fact.'

'But I *do*! Why, I think she's just wonderful.'

'Funny. I get the impression you haven't told her that too often. Or at all. I gather she thinks you think she's some kind of slut.'

'I do not think anything of the kind! The very idea!'

'Well, she must have got that idea from somewhere. Get with it, Mrs Hunt, or you just might lose your daughter altogether. She's a woman of independent means now and doesn't need you to put a roof over her head. She doesn't need your constant criticisms and disapproval either.'

'But… But… Oh, dear, me and my big mouth again…'

She looked so stricken that Rafe was moved to some sympathy for her. Perhaps he'd been a bit harsh. But someone had to stand up for Isabel. None of the men in her past had, least of all St bloody Luke!

'She needs you to love her unconditionally,' he went on more gently. 'Not just when she's doing what *you* think is right. Because what you think is right, Mrs Hunt, just might be wrong. And please...don't tell her what I said about being in love with her. If you do, you'll ruin everything.'

'You really love her?'

'More than I would ever have thought possible. I'm going to marry your daughter, Mrs Hunt. It's only a question of time.'

Her joy blinded him. 'Oh. Oh, that's wonderful news. I've been so worried for her. All her life, all she's ever wanted was to get married and...and... Oh, dear...' She broke off and gnawed at her bottom lip for a few seconds, worrying the life out of Rafe. What now?

'You do know Isabel wants a baby very badly, don't you?' she finally went on. 'That won't be a problem, will it? I know a lot of men these days aren't so keen on having children.'

Rafe smiled his relief. 'Not a problem at all, Mrs Hunt. Hopefully, it's the solution.'

'The solution?' She looked mystified for a moment. But then the clouds cleared from her astute grey eyes. 'Oh,' she said, nodding and smiling. 'Oh, I see.'

'I trust Isabel will have your full approval and support if I'm successful in my plan? You won't start judging and throwing verbal stones again.'

'You can depend on me, Rafe.'

'That's great, Mrs Hunt.'

'Dot. Call me Dot.'

'Dot.' He grinned at her. 'Wish me luck, Dot.'

'You won't need too much luck, you sexy devil.'

'Dot! I'm shocked.'

'I'm not too old that I can't see what Isabel sees in you. But I'm not so sure that not telling her you love her is the right tactic.'

'Trust me, Dot. It is.'

'If you say so. Heavens, I have to confess you've surprised me. Look, I'd better go inside or Isabel might come out and catch us together, and she might start asking awkward questions. She thinks I don't like you.'

'Gee. I wonder what gave her that idea?'

Dot's fine grey eyes sparkled with a mixture of guilt and good humour. 'You are a cheeky young man too, aren't you?'

'Go lightly on the young, Dot. I'm over thirty.'

She laughed. 'That's young to me. But I take your point and I'll try to get with it, as you said.'

Dot was not long gone and Rafe had just sat down again to finish his food when Isabel burst out onto the porch. 'I've been looking for you. Mum said you were out here. What on earth did you say to her just now?'

'Nothing much.' Rafe hoped his face was a lot calmer than his insides. The more time he spent with Isabel the more hopelessly in love with her he was. And the more desperate for all his plans to succeed. 'Why?'

'Well, she actually smiled at me and told me how much she liked you. You could have knocked me over with a feather. She's been giving you killer looks all day, then suddenly she *likes* you? You must have said something.'

'I told her she had a wonderful daughter and I was going to marry you.'

Isabel blinked, stared, then burst out laughing. 'You *didn't*!'

'I did, indeed.'

'Oh, Rafe, you're wicked. First you lie to your mother about getting married, and now to mine. Still, it worked.'

Rafe almost told her then. Told her it wasn't a lie, that he was crazy about her and did want to marry her. But it simply was too premature for such declarations.

'How's Rachel coping?' he asked, deftly changing the subject.

'Not too bad, actually. Did you see that woman we were talking to?'

'The one built like a battleship?'

'That's the one. Her name's Alice McCarthy and Rachel does alterations for her. Did I tell you that's how Rachel's been making some money at home?'

'Yes, I think you did mention it.'

'She's a darned good dressmaker, too, but alterations pay better and take less time. Anyway, Alice has this son. His name's Justin.'

'Oh, no, not another match-making mother. Poor Rachel. She's deep in grief and some old battleaxe is already lining her up for her son.'

'Oh, do stop being paranoid. And Alice is not a battle-axe. She's very sweet. Anyway, this Justin doesn't want a wife. He wants a secretary. As for Rachel being in grief, she needs to get out and about as quickly as possible, otherwise she'll get even more lonely and depressed than she already is. A job is ideal. She'll have to interview, of course, but Alice is going to twist her son's arm to at least give her a go for a while.'

'That's nice of her, but can Rachel do the job? Has she ever been a secretary before?'

'Has she ever been a secretary before!' Isabel scoffed. 'I'll have you know that Rachel was a finalist in the Secretary of the Year award one year. Of course, that was a few years ago, and she has lost a bit of confidence since then, but nothing which can't be put to right with some boosting up from her friends.'

'Mmm. Tell me about this Alice's son. What does he do for a crust?'

'He's some high-flying executive in the city. One of those companies with fingers in lots of pies. Insurance. Property development. You know the kind of thing.'

'What happened to his present secretary? He must have one.'

'The story goes that she suddenly resigned last month. Flew over to England a few weeks back for her niece's wedding, realised how homesick she was for her mother country, came back just to get her things, and quit. He's been making do with a temp but he's not thrilled. Says she's far too flashy-looking and far too flirtatious. He can't concentrate on his work.'

'My heart goes out to him,' Rafe said drily. 'Still, I guess his wife might not be pleased.'

'He's divorced.'

'What's his problem, then?'

Isabel sighed. She should have known a man like Rafe

wouldn't see a problem. If he was in the same position, he'd just have the girl on his desk every lunchtime and not think twice about it.

'Office romances are never a good idea, Rafe,' she tried explaining. 'This is something you might not appreciate, since you don't work in a traditional office. *And* since you're not female. If a female employee has an affair with a male colleague, especially her boss, it's always the girl who ends up getting the rough end of the pineapple.'

He laughed. 'What a delicate way of putting it.'

Isabel rolled her eyes with utter exasperation. 'Truly. Must you always put a sexual connotation on everything?'

'Honey, I'm not the one putting a sexual connotation on this. This divorced bloke thinks his sexy temp has the hots for him and he doesn't like it. Rather makes you wonder why. Is he mentally deranged? Otherwise involved? Gay? Or just bitter and twisted?'

'Maybe he's the kind of man who doesn't like mixing business with pleasure. Unlike *some* men we know.'

'Man's a fool. He's got it made by the sound of it. Still, Rachel should suit him. She's hardly what you'd call flashy. *Or* flirtatious.' More like shy and retiring. Sweet, though. Rafe really liked her.

'No, not at the moment. But she used to be very outgoing. And drop-dead gorgeous.'

'Mmm. Hard to visualise.' The Rachel he'd met today had been a long way from drop-dead gorgeous. Okay, so there were some lingering remnants of past beauty in her thin face and gaunt body. Her eyes certainly had something.

But the hardships of minding a loved one with Alzheimer's twenty-four hours a day for over four years had clearly taken its toll. Isabel had told him Rachel was only thirty-one. But she looked forty if she was a day.

'She just needs some tender loving care,' Isabel said.

'And a serious makeover,' Rafe added. 'New hair colour. Clothes. Make-up.'

'Don't be ridiculous, Rafe. Haven't you been listening? This man doesn't want a glamour-puss for a secretary. He wants a woman who looks sensible and who doesn't turn him on.'

'Oh, yeah, I forgot. Better get her a pair of glasses then, because she has got nice eyes.'

'Yes, she does, doesn't she?'

'And get her to put on a few pounds. That anorexic look she's sporting is considered pretty desirable nowadays.'

'Are you being sarcastic?'

'Not at all. Oh, and tell her to wear black for the interview. It looks bloody awful on her. Unlike you, my darling,' he whispered in her ear, 'who looks so sexy in black that it's criminal.'

'Stop that,' Isabel choked out, shivering when he began to blow softly in her ear.

But she didn't really want him to stop. It felt like an eon since they'd been alone together, since he'd held her in his arms. She was going to go mad if she wasn't with him soon.

'Stay with me tonight,' he murmured.

'I…I can't,' she groaned. 'I'm taking Rachel home to Turramurra with me for a few days. I don't want to leave her alone just yet.'

'When, then?'

'I don't know. I'll give you a call.'

Rafe didn't want to press. But he wanted her so much. He *needed* her. And it had nothing to do with getting her pregnant.

Being in love, he decided, was hell, especially if the person you loved didn't love you back.

And she didn't. Not yet. No use pretending she did.

It was a depressing thought. The confidence which Rafe had projected to Isabel's mother suddenly seemed like so much hot air. What if she never fell in love with him? What if she never fell pregnant to him?

Then he would have nothing.

She had to fall pregnant. *Had* to. Which meant that he had to do absolutely nothing to frighten her off. He had to keep her wanting him. Had to keep her sexually intrigued.

'How about a couple of hours, then?' he suggested boldly. 'After Rachel's gone to bed. I'll pick you up and we'll go somewhere local for a nightcap, then I'll find a private place for us to park.'

Isabel was startled. '*Park*?'

'Neck, then.'

'I haven't necked in a car since I was a teenager.'

He grinned. 'Neither have I.'

'Your car has buckets seats.'

'It has a big back seat.'

She stared at him, her heart hammering inside her chest.

'Well, Isabel, what do you say?'

What did she say?

What she would always say to him.

'Make sure you bring protection with you.'

CHAPTER THIRTEEN

As RAFE turned down Isabel's street in Turramurra he glanced at the clock on the dash. Just after seven. It had taken him over an hour to drive through the rush-hour traffic from the airport to Turramurra.

Rush-hour traffic through the city was the pits at the best of times, and he wouldn't normally venture outside his front door, let alone catch a flight which landed at Mascot, anywhere near the evening peak. Unless there was a dire emergency.

In Rafe's eyes, there had been more than a dire emergency. It had been a case of life and death.

Two weeks had passed since the funeral, and almost a week since he'd seen Isabel, work having taken him to Melbourne for some magazine shoots this past week.

He'd rung her, of course. Every evening.

She'd been very chuffed on the night after Rachel got the job with Justin McCarthy. Rafe had been subjected to an hour of girl-talk stuff. Not that he'd minded. He loved hearing Isabel happy.

The next night she'd been even more excited. The two girls had spent the day shopping for a new work wardrobe for Rachel. All non-flashy, non-flirtatious clothes, Rafe had been assured. He'd received a dollar-by-dollar description of everything they'd bought.

The night after that, she'd raved on about how she was now helping Rachel clear out and clean up Lettie's house. Rachel was going to sell it, then buy a unit closer to the city. Isabel was going to look around for one for her, since she wasn't working and wasn't going to get herself another job for a while, if ever.

The following evening, however, she had been very subdued. When Rafe had asked her what was wrong she'd been evasive, saying in the end that she was just tired. But Rafe believed he knew what was bothering her. Her period—that event she could always set her clock by—hadn't arrived as expected that day.

He'd contained his own secret elation at being successful so soon, and had rung her again today from Tullamarine Airport just before he'd caught an earlier plane than he'd been intending. His original booking had been for a later flight, but he was anxious to get back to Isabel.

She'd been even more distracted during this phone-call, and when he'd said he was coming over as soon as he'd landed she'd fobbed him off, saying she was cooking dinner for her parents that night and to give her a call on the weekend.

Rafe suspected she'd come up with another excuse not to see him then as well. Which was why he'd decided to just show up on her doorstep.

The lights on in her town house told him she'd lied about going to her parents, and that really worried him.

What on earth was going through her mind? Had she

realised she didn't want a baby so badly after all? Or was it just *his* baby she didn't want?

Rafe hoped it wasn't anything like that. He hoped she was just a little shocked, and perhaps worried over what to do where he was concerned. Perhaps she'd decided not to tell him. Naturally, she'd think the pregnancy was an accident on his part and not deliberate. Perhaps she was worried he wouldn't want the child. He stupidly hadn't thought of that. Perhaps she was going to break it off with him and have his baby on her own, as she'd always planned to do.

He didn't want to entertain that other awful worry that she might get rid of his baby. Surely Isabel wouldn't do that. Even if she was late, and thought she was pregnant, she couldn't be sure yet. Even the most regular women were sometimes late.

But she wasn't late, Rafe believed as he sat there, mulling everything over. She was pregnant with his child. That was why she was acting out of character.

The time had come for a confession.

A wave of nausea claimed his stomach as he alighted from his car. Rafe hadn't felt this nervous in years, in fact, he'd *never* felt this nervous. This was worse than having his photographs exhibited, or judged. This was *him* about to be judged. Rafe, the man.

What if Isabel found him wanting in the role as father of her child? What if she didn't think him worthy? What then?

Rafe had no idea. He'd just have to take this one step at a time.

*   *   *

Isabel couldn't settle to anything. She wandered out into the kitchen and started making herself a cup of coffee. Not because she really wanted one but just to do something.

She *couldn't* be pregnant, she began thinking for the umpteenth time as she waited for the water to boil. Rafe had religiously used protection.

But condoms *weren't* one hundred per cent safe, came the niggling thought. Nothing was one hundred per cent safe except abstinence. And they certainly hadn't abstained during the few days they'd spent together on Dream Island. It had been full-on sex all the time. Mind-blowing, multi-orgasm sex. The kind of sex which might cause a condom to spring a little leak.

And a little leak was all that it took. Isabel recalled seeing a documentary once where just a drop of sperm had millions of eggs in it. Millions of very active eggs with the capacity to impregnate lots of women, if the timing was right.

And the timing had been pretty right, hadn't it? Perhaps not optimum time, she conceded. That had been from the Thursday till the Saturday. But they'd had sex late on the Wednesday night and that could easily have done the trick. Sperm could live for forty-eight hours, that same documentary had proudly proclaimed. Surviving half a miserable day was a cinch.

Oh, dear…

Her front doorbell ringing had Isabel spilling coffee beans all over the grey granite-topped bench. It wasn't

Rachel calling round. Isabel had not long got off the phone to Rachel, who'd told her not to be silly, she was only a day and a half late, she probably wasn't pregnant at all. Rachel had sensibly suggested buying a home-pregnancy test in the morning and putting her mind at rest.

But Isabel already knew what the result would be. She was pregnant with Rafe's child. She just knew it.

The doorbell rang a second time with Isabel still standing there, her mind still whirling.

It wasn't her parents. Tonight was raffle night down at their club. Nothing short of her giving birth would drag her mother away from that raffle.

Which event was a little way off yet.

Unlikely to be any of her new neighbours—whose names she didn't even know—wanting a cup of sugar. People rarely did that kind of the thing in the city.

No, it was Rafe. She'd heard the puzzled note in his voice when she'd put him off from coming round. But she simply hadn't been in a fit state to face him.

The fear had first begun yesterday, within hours of her not getting her period around noon, as usual. By this afternoon she'd been in a right royal flap.

Already, she could see it all. Rafe not wanting this child. Rafe making her feel terrible about her decision to have it. Rafe perhaps trying to talk her into a termination.

No, no, she could not stand that. He was the one she had to get rid of, not the baby.

The ringing changed to a loud knocking, followed by

Rafe's voice through the door. 'I know you're in there, Isabel, so please open up. I'm not going away till I speak to you.'

Isabel valiantly pulled herself together. Now's your opportunity, she lectured herself as she marched towards the front door. He already knows you lied to him about tonight. He'll be wondering why. The timing is perfect to tell him you don't want to see him any more. That this relationship—despite the great sex—isn't working for you.

Rafe knew, the moment she opened the door, that he was in trouble. She had that look in her eyes, a combination of steel and ice. He'd seen it before, the day they'd first met at his place.

'Come in,' she said curtly. 'Please excuse my appearance. I wasn't expecting any visitors tonight.'

She was wearing a simple black tracksuit and white joggers. Her hair was down and her face was free of make-up. Rafe thought she looked even more lovely than usual.

'I was just making coffee.' She turned her back on him and headed across the cream-tiled foyer towards the archway which led into the living room. 'Would you like a cup?' she threw over her shoulder.

Rafe decided to circumvent any social niceties and go straight to the heart of the matter.

'No,' he said firmly as he shut the door behind him and followed her into the stylishly furnished living room. 'I didn't come here for coffee.'

She watched him walk over to one of the cream

leather armchairs. He had a sexy walk, did Rafe. Actually, he had a sexy way of doing most things. Once settled, he glanced back up at her, his dark eyes raking her up and down, reminding Isabel that she was braless underneath her top.

Feeling her nipples automatically harden annoyed her, self-disgust giving her the courage to do what she had to do. 'If you came for sex, Rafe,' she said as she crossed her arms, 'then you're out of luck. There won't be any more sex. In fact, there won't be any more us. Period.'

'Mmm. Was that a Freudian slip, Isabel?'

Her resolve cracked a little. 'What…what do you mean?'

'I mean that's the problem, isn't it? You haven't got your period.'

She literally gaped at him, her crossed arms unfolding to dangle in limp shock at her sides.

Rafe sucked in sharply. Bingo! He was right. She was pregnant.

Suddenly, he was no longer afraid. He felt nothing but joy and pride, and love. Isabel didn't know it yet but he was going to make a great father. And a great husband, if she'd let him.

'I understand your reaction,' he said carefully. 'But you have no reason to worry. I'm here to tell you that if you are pregnant, then I will support you and the child in every way.'

She still didn't say a word.

'You *are* late, aren't you?' he probed softly.

She blinked, then shook her head as though trying to

clear the wool from her brain. 'I don't understand any of this,' she said, her hands lifting agitatedly, first to touch her hair and then to rest over her heart. 'Why would you even *think* I was pregnant?'

'I have a confession to make. There was this one occasion on Dream Island when the condom failed.'

Isabel gasped. 'Oh, that's what I thought must have happened. But why didn't you tell me?'

'I didn't want to worry you. It was too late to do anything after the event, other than get you to a doctor for the morning-after pill. And I didn't think you'd want to do that. Was I wrong, Isabel? Would you have taken that option?'

He could see by the expression in her eyes that she wouldn't have even considered it.

'I thought as much,' he said.

She almost staggered over to perch on the cream leather sofa adjacent to him. 'When…when did this happen?'

'On the Wednesday.'

She frowned. 'That night after dinner?'

'No, earlier on in the day.'

Her frown deepened. 'So all those questions you asked about my plans to get pregnant on my honeymoon… You were trying to find out what the likelihood was of my getting pregnant that day?'

'Yes,' he admitted.

'You had to have been worried.'

'No. Actually, I wasn't.'

'But that's insane! You yourself told me you never wanted to become a father.'

'Oddly enough, once it became a distinct possibility, I found I was taken with the idea.'

'*Taken* with the idea?' she exclaimed, stunned at first, then angry. 'Oh, isn't that just like a man? *Taken* with the idea. A baby's not just a fad, Rafe. It's a reality. A forever reality. A forever responsibility.'

'You think I don't know that?' he countered, his own temper rising. 'I've had longer than you to get acquainted with the reality and the responsibility entailed in my being the father of your baby, and I still like the idea. If you must know, when it seemed like a pregnancy might only be a fifty-fifty possibility, I made a conscious decision to up the odds in favour of your conceiving.'

The words were not out of his mouth more than a split second before Rafe recognised his mistake. Isabel was having enough trouble coming to terms with her 'accidental' pregnancy without his confessing to such an action. His desire to reassure her that he really did want her child could very well rebound on him. All of a sudden what he'd always considered a rather romantic decision that Wednesday night on Dream Island began developing various shades of grey about it.

'What did you do?' she demanded to know, her eyes widening.

His guilty face must have been very revealing.

'Rafe, you *didn't*!'

'Well, I…I…'

'You *did*! You had sex with me without using anything. And you deliberately got me drunk so that I wouldn't notice.'

'Well, I…I…' He'd turned into a bumbling idiot!

'How dare you do something like that without my permission? How dare you think you had that right? What kind of man are you?' She jumped to her feet, her hands finding her hips as she glared down at him.

Her ongoing outrage finally galvanised his brain, and his tongue. 'A man who's madly in love with you!' he roared back, propelling himself to his feet also. 'And I'd do it all over again. In fact, I *intended* to do it all over again, as often as I could get away with it. I even doctored a whole lot of condoms in readiness!'

Her eyes became great blue pools.

'I couldn't bear the thought of the woman I loved artificially inseminating her body with some stranger's child, when I wanted to give her *my* child. I was prepared to do anything, break every rule and cross every line, to do just that, and I don't mind admitting it. I love you, Isabel,' he claimed, grasping her shoulders, 'and I think you love me, only you're too scared to admit it, and you're too scared to trust me.

'But you shouldn't be,' he pleaded, his hands curling even more firmly over her shoulders. 'I'm nothing like the other losers you've been involved with. A fool, maybe, up till now. But a fool no longer. Seeing Liz again on that island cured me of my foolishness by making me see I was heading for the same kind of future she's ended up with. Empty and shallow, without really loving anyone or being loved in return. I took one look at you that night and thought, *This* is what I want. This woman, as my wife and the mother of my children. I love you, Isabel. Tell me you love me, too.'

Isabel searched his face, her own a tortured maze of mixed emotions. Shock. Confusion. Anguish. Maybe a measure of desperate hope in there somewhere.

'Love is more than sex, Rafe.'

'I know that.'

'Do you? Do I? Sometimes the lines between lust and love can be very blurred. I've thought myself in love so many times before, and all I've ended up with is a broken heart. And broken dreams.'

'I can understand your fear. I used to be afraid of love, too. But life without love is no life at all. Even your stupid bloody Luke found that out. Look, just tell me if you *think* you're in love with me.'

She moaned her distress at having to admit such a thing.

'All right,' Rafe said. 'You don't have to say it. I'll say it for both of us. We love each other. We've loved each other from the start. That's the truth of it and I won't let you deny it. But I also won't ask you to marry me. Not yet, anyway. All I'm asking is that you let me be a part of your life, and our baby's life, on a permanent basis.'

Isabel could hardly think. Everything was going way too fast for her. 'I...we...we don't know if there is a baby yet. Not for sure, anyway.'

'Then let's find out. Go see a doctor. We'll find one

of those twenty-four hour-surgeries. There has to be one open somewhere around here.'

'There's no need to do that. All we need is a chemist. And they're open till nine tonight.'

'Let's go, then.'

Rafe could feel the tension in her growing during the time it took to drive to a local mall, buy a pregnancy testing kit, then return. They read the instructions together, then Isabel retired to the bathroom to do what had to be done. In a couple of minutes she would confirm what he already knew. She was expecting his child.

Rafe waited patiently for the first few minutes, but when she hadn't come back downstairs after ten he marched halfway up the stairs and called out.

'Isabel? What's taking so long?'

She eventually appeared at the top of the stairs, pale-faced.

Rafe melted with love and concern for her obvious distress. 'Oh, darling, there's no need to be upset. A baby is what you wanted most in the world after all.'

'There's no baby,' she choked out. 'The test was negative.' And she burst into tears.

CHAPTER FOURTEEN

'OH, RAFE,' she sobbed, the tears spilling over and streaming down her face.

Rafe brushed aside his own disappointment to leap up the remaining steps which separated them and pull her into his arms.

'It's all right, darling,' he murmured as he pressed her shaking body to his. 'We'll make a baby for you next month. You'll see. There, there, sweetheart, don't cry so. You know what they say. If at first you don't succeed, try, try again.'

But nothing he could say would console her. She wept on and on, as though her very soul was shattered. In the end he didn't believe her pain was just because the test was negative. He believed it was caused by the build-up of all the disappointments in her life so far, culminating in this last most distressing disappointment.

When she virtually collapsed in his arms, he picked her up and carried her to bed. He didn't bother to undress her, just pulled back the covers and tipped her gently onto the mattress. Though he did yank off her joggers before covering her up with the quilt.

'Don't leave me,' she cried as he tucked her in.

'I won't,' he promised. 'I'll just go make you a hot drink.'

'No, no, I don't want a drink. I just want you. Hold me, Rafe. I feel safe when you hold me.'

He sighed at the thought. How could he stop at just holding her? Yet, at the same time, how could he refuse her? She needed him. Not as a lover, but as a friend.

Kicking off his own shoes, he climbed in beside her with the rest of his clothes on, hoping that would help. And it did. For a while. But, in the end, neither of them was content with such a platonic embrace. Yet it was Isabel who started the touching and the undressing, Isabel who decided she needed him as women had been needing the men they loved since the Garden of Eden.

Rafe could not resist her overtures and, strangely, their lovemaking turned out totally different from anything they'd shared before. It was truly *love*making. Soft. Slow. And so sweet.

Nothing but the simplest of foreplay, just face-stroking and the most innocent of kisses. Rafe's hands were gentle on her breasts and hers caressing on his back. And when the yearning to become one over-whelmed them both they merely fused together, Rafe on top, Isabel gazing adoringly up at him. They took a long time in coming, but when they did it was with such feeling, waves of rapturous pleasure rippling through their bodies, bringing with them the most amazing peace and contentment.

'I do love you,' she murmured as she lay in his arms afterwards.

Rafe sighed and stroked her hair. 'Good.'

'And I will marry you,' she added. 'If you still want me to.'

'Even better.'

'But I don't want to wait till we're married before we try again for a baby. Can we try again next month, like you said?'

'I'm putty in your hands, Isabel.'

When she hugged him even more tightly, Rafe was startled to feel tears pricking at his eyes. But that was how much he loved her, and how much her loving him meant to him. At that moment, his cup indeed runneth over.

He lay thinking about their future for a long time after she was fast asleep.

'I want you to come to lunch with my mother tomorrow,' he told her the following morning over breakfast.

Isabel pushed her hair out of her face as she glanced up at him. 'Oh, dear. Do you think she'll like me?'

'She's going to adore you.'

'You really think so? Mothers worry me a bit. She's had you all to herself all these years. I'll bet you're the apple of her eye.'

Rafe had to laugh. His mother had always found him a very difficult child. And an even more difficult teenager. He'd been one-eyed and extremely focused, determined to be a famous photographer, and even more determined never to be poor, as they'd been for many years after his father had died. At sixteen, he'd used money he'd saved from various after-school jobs to convert their single garage into a darkroom, consigning his mother's car to the street.

She'd been thrilled when he'd finally moved out of home. He believed the only reason she was fanatical about his getting married was because she was paranoid that one day fate would step in and he'd have to come home for some reason.

'Trust me, Isabel,' he said. 'My mother is not one of those mothers. She has her own life, with her own friends, pleasures and pastimes. She just wants me settled and safely married because she doesn't want to worry about me any more. Of course, she would love a grandchild or two. I won't deny that. By the way, any sign of that missing period yet?'

'No. I can't imagine where it is. I'm never late.'

'You don't think that test could have been wrong, do you?'

Isabel's stomach fluttered. She hadn't thought of that. 'I...I'm sure I followed the instructions correctly.'

'Yes, but you're not all that late yet. How far along do you have to be for it to be a reliable test?'

'It's supposed to work from two weeks.'

'Yes, but you would have only been two weeks and a day at best yesterday, Isabel. That's borderline. Perhaps we should buy another test and try again in a couple of days' time.'

Isabel recoiled at the idea. She didn't want to build up her hopes only to have them dashed again. Her emotions had been such a mess last night after Rafe arrived and made all his most amazing confessions. She'd swung from distress to delight to despair, all in the space of an hour.

She hadn't cried like that ever in her life, not even when she'd found out Hal had been a drug-dealer. Still, crying her heart out in Rafe's arms had been a deeply cleansing experience, and their lovemaking later had filled her with such hope and joy for the future that she didn't need to be pregnant now to make her happy. She was already happy just being with Rafe and knowing that he really loved her. They'd have a baby eventually. It had been silly of her to be so disappointed. And it would be silly to torture herself with another test. Better to just calmly wait for her period to arrive, then make plans for trying again during her next cycle.

'No,' she said. 'I don't want to do that. I'm sure my period is going to arrive any minute now, provided I don't start stressing about it. I think that's the problem with it. Stress.'

'I think you could be right. From now on, you are going to be relaxed and happy.'

'Sounds wonderful. So what are we going to do to-day?'

'I'm going to take you shopping for an engagement ring. That way, at lunch tomorrow, Mum will know I'm deadly serious about marrying you. Though it's going to cost me a pretty penny to top that rock you're still sporting on your left hand and which I presume Luke gave you.'

Isabel frowned. 'You're not jealous of Luke, are you, Rafe?'

'Well...'

'There's no need to be. I didn't love him.'

'Maybe, but you do have a lot of reminders of him around you. That ring, for starters. And this place. I don't mind the money he gave you but do you have to live in his house?'

'This was never really Luke's house. I mean, nothing in it reflects him on a personal basis. He bought it already furnished. And he wasn't living here all that long. Still, I'm quite happy to move in with *you*, Rafe, if you like. Though a terrace is not really suitable for a family. What say we sell both places and buy another one? Together.'

'Done.' Rafe smiled his satisfaction at that idea. 'Now, let's get dressed and go into the city for some serious ring-shopping.'

'Are you sure you can afford this?' Isabel asked Rafe later that morning, after she'd selected a gorgeous but expensive-looking diamond and emerald ring.

'No trouble. I'll just go ring my bank manager for a second mortgage.'

Isabel looked at him with alarm. 'I don't mind getting something cheaper.'

Rafe smiled and kissed her. 'Don't be silly. I was only joking. I can easily afford this ring, Isabel. I might not be a multi-millionaire but I have more than enough to support a wife and family. I am a very successful photographer and an astute investor, even if I say so myself.

I'll tell your dad that when I officially ask for your hand in marriage tonight.'

'When you *what*?'

'As you once pointed out to me, Isabel, your parents come from a different generation. I want to get off on the right foot with your father as well as your mother.'

'You'll get off on the right foot with my mother by just marrying me,' Isabel said drily.

Rafe smiled. 'That's what I gathered when I told her I was going to do just that at the funeral a couple of weeks back.'

Isabel was astonished, then amused. 'So that's what you did to make her like you! You are a mischievous and manipulative devil, Rafe Saint Vincent. But I love you all the same.'

'You'd want to after costing me this much money.'

'Don't worry,' she murmured, reaching up to kiss his cheek. 'If you ever run out, I have plenty.'

'Huh. Now I'm not so sure I like Luke giving you all that money, either. A man likes to be his family's provider, you know. He likes to be needed for more than just his body.'

Isabel giggled and Rafe bristled. 'What's so funny?'

'You are, going all primal male on me. Who would have believed it from the man who let me buy his body to do with as I willed for a whole fortnight?'

'I did not!'

'Oh, yes, you did. You didn't pay for a single thing on that jaunt to Dream Island.'

'I did so, too.'

'Name one.'

'I paid for the condoms.'

'Only half.'

'The three dozen I bought should have been more than enough. How was I to know I was going way with a raving nymphomaniac?'

They both realised all of a sudden that everyone in the jewellery shop had stopped what they were doing and were listening to their highly provocative bickering.

Isabel blushed fiercely whilst Rafe laughed.

'How embarrassing!' Isabel cried once they'd paid for the ring and fled outside. 'Lord knows what they thought of us.'

'Probably that you're a rich bitch and I'm your gigolo lover.'

Rafe loved it when she looked so mortified. She was such a delightful contradiction when it came to sex. So wildly uninhibited behind closed doors, but so easily embarrassed in public. Being with her was like being with a virgin and a vamp at the same time. It was a tantalising combination and one which he aimed to enjoy for the rest of their lives.

'Let's get right away from here,' Isabel urged, grabbing his arm, 'before someone comes out of that shop.'

Rafe found himself being dragged forcibly down the street. 'That's better,' she said, stopping at last. 'Oh look, Rafe, a chemist. I think I will buy another of those tests.'

'I thought you said you didn't want to.'

'I know but I...I've changed my mind.'

'Oh. Why's that?'

'Well, just now I felt kind of funny in my breasts.'

'What do you mean? Kind of funny?'

'All tingly and tight around the nipples.'

He gave her an amused glance. 'There are other explanations for that besides pregnancy, sweetness. You were just embarrassed by what happened in that shop. You find embarrassment a turn-on.'

'I do not!' She was taken aback by such an idea, and even more embarrassed.

'Yes, you do. But let's not fight about it in public. We'll pop in and buy another test, then go home. My place this time.' Thinking about her being turned on had turned *Rafe* on. He couldn't wait to get her behind closed doors again. He had a mind to photograph her as well. Afterwards. She always looked incredible afterwards. Relaxed and dreamy. He'd been wanting to capture that look with his camera for a long time. Not a nude shot. Just her face.

But she dashed upstairs for the bathroom as soon as they arrived back at his place, taking that damned test with her. A disgruntled Rafe collected his favourite camera from the darkroom, but he already knew he was wasting his time. Her mood would change once the test came back negative again. He'd been foolish to suggest the first one might have been wrong. It had just seemed logical at the time. Now he wished he'd never opened his big mouth.

Once again, she was gone ages. Lord, he hoped she wasn't up there crying again. Eventually he trudged up the stairs, not even bothering with the camera. He knew when he was beaten.

'Isabel,' he said wearily as he knocked on the bathroom door, 'please let's not go through all this again.'

The door opened and there she stood, and, yes, she was crying again, though not noisily. The tears were just running silently down her lovely cheeks.

'I should never have let you buy that bloody thing,' he muttered, hating to see her in such distress. 'Isabel, there's no need to get all upset again.'

Her smile startled him. So did the sudden sparkle in her soggy eyes.

'You don't understand, darling,' she said. 'I'm not upset. I'm crying with happiness. The test was positive, Rafe. We're pregnant!'

Rafe was to wonder later in his life exactly what he felt at that moment. Time and distance did fog the memory. But it had to go down as one of the great moments in his life. He'd put it on a par with their wedding day, just over a month later, even if he had been forced to tolerate Les taking a zillion photographs and both mothers hugging and kissing him all the time.

Nothing, however, would ever eclipse the magic moment when his firstborn entered the world.

Rafe would never forget the look in Isabel's eyes as she cradled her son to her breast, then looked up at him and said, 'I'd like to call him Michael, Rafe. After your father.'

Oh, yes, that was the moment he would remember above all others.

Perhaps because he was weeping at the time.

HER SECRET
PREGNANCY

by

Sharon Kendrick

Sharon Kendrick started story-telling at the age of eleven and has never really stopped. She likes to write fast-paced, feel-good romances with heroes who are so sexy they'll make your toes curl!

Born in west London, she now lives in the beautiful city of Winchester – where she can see the cathedral from her window (but only if she stands on tip-toe). She has two children, Celia and Patrick, and her passions include music, books, cooking and eating – and drifting off into wonderful daydreams while she works out new plots!

Don't miss Sharon Kendrick's exciting novel,
The Greek Tycoon's Baby Bargain, **out in May 2008 from Mills & Boon® Modern™.**

To Judy and Rob Hutson
with thanks for their vision and imagination.

CHAPTER ONE

THE lawyer was slick and smooth and handsome—with the most immaculately manicured hands that Donna had ever seen.

'Okay, Donna, if you'd like to sign just there.' He jabbed a near-perfect fingernail onto the contract. 'See? Right there.'

Donna was tempted to giggle. 'You mean where your secretary has helpfully drawn a little cross?'

'Ah, yes. Sorry,' he amended quickly. 'I didn't mean to patronise you.'

The tension of the last few weeks dissolved. 'Don't worry. You weren't.' She signed her name with a flourish. 'I'm just glad it's all over.'

Tony Paxman did not look as though he echoed her sentiments. 'I shall miss seeing you!' he sighed. 'Still, the premises are yours and you've got your liquour licence. Now it's over to you. Congratulations, Donna!' He held his hand out. 'And I wish you every success for the future!'

'Thank you,' said Donna, hoping she didn't sound smug. Or triumphant. Because she knew she should be neither. She was just lucky—though some people said there was no such thing, that you made your own luck in life.

She picked up her cream silk jacket and gave Tony Paxman a grateful smile. He had guided her through all the paperwork concerning the purchase with the care of a soldier negotiating a treacherous minefield. Most importantly of all, he'd kept the whole deal quiet. She owed him. 'Would you like to have lunch with me, to celebrate?'

Tony blinked with the kind of surprise which suggested that a lunch invitation from Donna King had been the very last thing in the world he had been expecting. 'Lunch?' he said weakly.

Donna raised her eyebrows at him. She wasn't proposing an illicit weekend in Paris! 'Or have I broken some kind of unwritten law by inviting you?'

He shook his head hastily. 'Oh, no, no, no! I often have lunch with my clients—'

'That's what I thought.' She glanced down at her watch. 'Shall we say one o'clock? In The New Hampshire?'

'The New Hampshire?' Tony Paxman gave a regretful smile. 'Marcus Foreman's place? I'd absolutely love to—but we won't get a table today. Not at such short notice, I'm afraid. Not a chance in hell.'

'I know that.' Donna smiled. 'Which is why I took the precaution of making a reservation weeks ago.'

He frowned. 'You were so sure we'd wrap up the deal?'

'Pretty much. I knew that the court hearing to get my licence was today. And I didn't foresee any problems.'

'You know, you're a very confident woman, Donna King,' he told her softly. 'As well as being an extremely beautiful one.'

Time to gently destroy his embryo fantasies. It was just a pity that some men saw a simple gesture of friendship as an invitation to form some deep and meaningful relationship.

'Please don't get the wrong idea, Tony,' she told him softly. 'This is purely a business lunch—a way of me thanking you for all your hard work. That's all. Nothing more.'

'Right.' He began to move papers around on his desk with a sudden urgency. 'Then I'll see you in The New Hampshire at one o'clock, shall I?'

'Yes, indeed,' said Donna. She reached for her bag and rose to her feet, the high heels of her brown suede shoes making her look much taller than usual. 'I shall look forward to it.'

'Me, too,' he said wistfully.

Outside the lawyer's office, Donna sucked in the crisp April air, scarcely able to believe she was back in the city she loved. Her visits over the last few weeks had been secretive, but there was no need for secrecy any longer. She was here—and here to stay.

It was a perfect day. Blue sky. Golden sun. The white waxy petals of a magnolia shining out like stars. A grey stone church whose spire looked like the sharpened tip of a pencil. Perfect. And the cherry on top of the cake was that she had swung the deal.

People had said that she was crazy to open up a tea-room in a city like Winchester, which was already bursting to the seams with places to eat. And they'd had a point. But most of those places were indifferent, and most were owned by large, faceless chains. Only one stood out from the crowd. And it belonged to Marcus Foreman.

Donna swallowed down excitement and nerves and something else, too. Something she hadn't felt in so long she had thought she'd never feel it again. A lost, forgotten feeling. But it was there, potent and tugging and insistent just at the thought that very soon she would see Marcus again. Excitement.

And not the kind of excitement you got the night be-

fore you went on holiday, either. This was the kind that
made the tips of your breasts prickle and your limbs
grow weak.

'Oh, damn!' she said aloud. 'Damn and damn and
damn!' And, turning her collar up against the sudden,
sharp reminder that the breeze which blew in springtime
had an icy bite to it, Donna set off down the street to
window-shop until lunchtime.

She walked slowly around the shops, only half seeing
the clothes in the expensive boutiques which studded the
city like diamonds in an eternity band. Exquisite clothes
in natural fibres of silk and cotton and cashmere. Clothes
which would normally tempt her into looking, even if
she couldn't always afford to buy.

But today was not a normal day. And not just because
it wasn't every day that you ploughed your savings into
buying a business which several people had predicted
would fail from the start.

No, today was different, because as well as going forward—Donna would be going back. Back to the place
where she'd met Marcus and learned about love and
loss—and a whole lot more besides.

It was just past one when she sauntered her way into
the reception area of The New Hampshire, hoping that
she looked more confident than she felt. Behind the
smooth, pale mask of her carefully made-up face, she
could feel the unfamiliar thumping of nerves as she
looked around her.

The place had changed out of all recognition. When
Donna had worked there it had been during the chintz
era, when everything had been tucked and swagged and
covered with tiny sprigs of flowers.

But Marcus had clearly moved with the times. The
carpet had disappeared and so had the chintz. Now there

were bare, beautifully polished wood floorboards and simple curtains at the vast windows. The furniture had been kept to a minimum, and it looked simple and comfortable rather than in-your-face opulent. Definitely no overstuffed sofas!

Donna remembered how overwhelmed she'd felt the very first time she'd walked in through those doors. It had been like entering another world. But she'd been just eighteen then—nine years and a lifetime ago.

She walked up to the reception desk on which sat a giant glass bowl containing scented flowers. The fleshy white lips of the lilies were gaping open, surrounded by spiky green foliage which looked like swords. It was an exquisite and sexy arrangement, but then Marcus had always had exquisite taste.

The receptionist looked up. 'Can I help you, madam?'

'Yes, hello—I have a table booked for lunch,' smiled Donna.

'Your name, please?'

'It's King. Donna King.' Her voice sounded unnaturally loud, and she half expected Marcus to jump out of the shadows to bar her way. 'And I'm meeting a Mr Tony Paxman.'

The receptionist was running her eyes down a list, and ticked off Donna's name before she looked up again.

'Ah, yes. Mr Paxman has already arrived.' She gave Donna a look of polite enquiry. 'Have you ever eaten at The New Hampshire before?'

Donna shook her head. 'No.'

She'd made beds and cleaned out baths and sinks in the rooms upstairs, and had worked her way through some of the more delicious leftovers which had found their way back to the kitchen. And just once she'd eaten with the rest of the staff in the private function room upstairs, when Marcus had been jubilantly celebrating a glowing newspaper review.

Donna swallowed down that particular memory. But she'd certainly never eaten a full meal in the fabulous restaurant.

'No, I haven't.'

'Then I'll get someone to show you to your table.'

Donna followed one of the waiters, determined not to feel intimidated, telling herself that she'd worked and eaten in places just like this all over the world.

Yet her heart was still racing with anticipation that she might see him, and she wondered why.

Because she was over Marcus.

She had been for years.

The restaurant was already almost full and Tony Paxman rose to his feet as she approached. 'I was beginning to think you'd stood me up!'

'Oh, ye of little faith!' she joked, smiling up at the waiter, who was hovering attentively. 'Some house champagne, please. We're celebrating!'

'Certainly, madam.'

Tony Paxman waited until he was on his second glass before remarking obscurely, 'Let's hope you'll still have something to celebrate six months down the line.'

The bubbles inside her mouth burst. 'Meaning?'

He shrugged. 'Just that Marcus Foreman won't exactly be overjoyed when he finds out that you're opening up a new restaurant in the same town.'

'Oh?' Donna slid a green olive into her mouth and chewed on it thoughtfully. 'Everyone knows he has an awesome reputation in the catering industry—surely he's man enough to take a little honest competition?'

'I should imagine he's man enough for most things,'

remarked Tony Paxman drily. 'Just maybe not in the very same street.'

Donna placed the olive stone in a small dish in front of her. 'Anyway, I'm hardly going to be a *serious* rival, am I? Think about it—his hotel only serves afternoon tea to its residents.'

'True. But what if they start coming to you instead?'

Donna shrugged. 'It's a free country, and there is always room for excellence.' She gave a huge smile as she lifted her glass in a toast. 'So may the best man win!'

'Or woman?' Tony murmured.

Donna looked down the menu, spoilt for choice. 'Let's order, shall we? I'm starving!'

'Sounds good. Then you can tell me your life story.' He frowned. 'You know, your hair is the most amazing golden-red colour. I bet you used to dress up as a princess when you were a little girl!'

'No, I was the one with the long face, wearing rags!' Donna joked, though it wasn't really a joke at all.

She'd experienced just about every emotion it was possible to feel about her itinerant childhood with a loving but ultimately foolish mother. At her knee she had learnt the arts of exaggeration and evasion, and had then learnt that they were just different words for lying. And lies could grow bigger and bigger, until they swamped you like a wave and dragged you under with them.

She smiled at Tony Paxman. 'Let's talk about you instead. And then you can tell me all about Winchester.'

He began to talk, and Donna tried very hard to enjoy the meal and his company. To make witty small-talk as adults always did. Pleasant chatter that didn't mean a thing.

But she was too distracted by her surroundings to be able to concentrate very much. Even on the food. Weird.

She hadn't banked on Marcus still being able to affect her desire to eat.

He'd always employed the most talented chefs—even in the early days, when he hadn't been able to afford to pay them very much. And it seemed that his standards hadn't slipped. Not by a fraction. Donna gazed at a perfect pyramid of chocolate mousse which sat in a puddle of banana sauce.

Maybe she *was* completely mad to set herself up in some sort of competition with a man who had always been regarded within the industry as having both flair and foresight.

'Donna,' said Tony suddenly.

She pushed the pudding plate away from her and looked up. 'Mmm?'

'Why did you ask me to have lunch with you today?' He swallowed a mouthful of wine and refilled his glass, then began answering his own question without appearing to notice he was doing it. 'Because it sure as hell wasn't because you wanted to take our relationship any further.'

She stared at him in confusion. 'But I told you that back in the office.'

'I guess you did.' He shrugged. 'Maybe I hoped I could change your mind.'

'Sorry,' she said softly, and sat back in her chair to look at him. 'The lunch is to say thank you.'

'For?'

'For tying up the deal without complications and for keeping it secret.'

'Ah, yes.' He sipped his drink and watched her. 'I meant to ask you about that. Why the big secret? Why wasn't anyone allowed to know?'

'It's no secret any more.' She smiled. 'You can tell who you like.'

He leaned across the table. 'You told me that you'd never eaten here before.'

'Well, I haven't.'

'But this isn't the first time you've been here, is it?'

Donna's eyes narrowed with interest. She hadn't been expecting perception. Not from him. 'What makes you say that?'

'Your body language. I spend my life observing it—goes with the job. I'm an expert!' he boasted.

Not such an expert, Donna thought, that he had been able to recognise that she was sending out don't-come-close messages. Still, there was no point trying to exist with misunderstanding and deceit flying around the place. She knew that more than anyone. 'I used to work here,' she told him. 'Years ago. When I was young.'

'You're hardly ancient now.'

'I'm twenty-seven!'

'Old enough to know better?' he teased.

'Oh, I don't think so,' came a silky drawl from behind Donna's right shoulder. 'Not if past experience is any-thing to go on. Don't you agree, Donna?'

She didn't turn around. She didn't need to. She would have recognised that voice if it had come distorted at her in the dark from a hundred miles away. A split-second of dazed recognition stretched out in front of her like a tightrope. She moved her head back by a frac-tion—and she could almost *feel* his presence, though she still couldn't see him.

'Hello, Marcus,' she said carefully, wondering how her voice sounded to him. Older and wiser? Or still full of youthful awe?

He moved into eyeshot—though heaven only knew

how long he'd been in earshot for. But he didn't look at
Donna straight away. He was staring down at Tony
Paxman, so that Donna was able to observe him without
him noticing.

And, oh. Oh, oh, *oh*! Her heart thumped out of control
before she could stop it.

She had known that she would see him again, and she
had practised in her head for just this moment. Some
devil deep in her heart had wondered if his hair might
be thinning. If he had allowed his wealth and success to
go to his stomach and piled on weight. Or if he might
have developed some kind of stoop. Or started wearing
hideous clothes which didn't suit him.

But he hadn't. Of course he hadn't.

Marcus Foreman was still the kind of man who most
women would leave home for.

'Tony,' said Marcus easily.

The lawyer inclined his head. 'Marcus.'

'Do you two know each other?' Donna asked Tony in
surprise.

'Oh, everybody knows Marcus,' he responded, with a
shrug which didn't quite come off.

But Donna had detected a subtle change in her lunch
companion. Suddenly Tony Paxman did not look or
sound like the smooth, slick lawyer of earlier. He
sounded like a very ordinary man. A man, moreover,
who had just recognised the leader of the pack.

Marcus turned to her at last, and Donna realised that
she now had the opportunity to react to him as she had
always vowed she would react if she ever saw him again.
Coolly and calmly and indifferently.

Her polite smile didn't slip, but she wondered if there
was any way of telling from the outside that her heart-

rate had just doubled. And that the palms of her hands were moist and sticky with sweat.

'So. Donna,' Marcus said slowly, and she met his dark-lashed eyes with reluctant fascination, their ice-blue light washing over her as pure and as clear as an early-morning swimming pool.

'So. Marcus,' she echoed faintly, eyes flickering over *him*. Okay, so he hadn't become bald or fat or ugly, but he'd certainly changed. Changed a lot. But hadn't they all?

'Do you want to say it, or shall I?' His voice was heavy with mockery, and something else. Something she couldn't quite put her finger on, but it told her to beware.

'Say what?'

'Long time no see,' he drawled lazily. 'Isn't that the kind of cliché that people usually come out with after this long?'

'I guess they do,' she said slowly, thinking that nine whole years had passed since she had seen him. How could that be? 'You could have said, ''Hi, Donna—great to see you!'' But that would have been a whacking great lie, wouldn't it, Marcus?'

'You said it.' He smiled. 'And you're the world's expert where lying is concerned, aren't you, Donna?'

Their gazes clashed and she found herself observing every tiny detail of his face; a face she'd once loved—but now she told herself that it was just a face.

She'd known him at the beginning of his rapid rise, before success had become as familiar to him as breathing. Before he'd had a chance to fashion himself in his own image, rather than one which had been passed down to him.

Gone was the buttoned down, clean-cut and preppie look which had been his heritage. The polished brogues and the perfectly knotted tie. The soft Italian leather shoes and the shirts made in Jermyn Street. The suit had gone, too. Now he wore pale trousers and a shirt. But a silk shirt, naturally. With—wonder of wonders—the two top buttons casually left undone. He looked sexy and sensational.

He had let his hair grow, too. A neatly clipped style had once defined the proud tilt of his head. Now strands of it licked at his eyebrows and kissed the high-boned structure of his cheeks. Stroked the back of his neck with loving, dark tendrils. He looked as rugged and as ruffled as if he'd just tumbled out of some beautiful girl's bed after an afternoon of wild sex.

Maybe he had.

Her smile froze as she found she could picture the scene all too clearly. Marcus with one of those long-legged thoroughbred type of girls wrapped around him. The kind who'd used to hang around waiting for him like groupies.

She searched in desperation for something cool and neutral to say, her gaze fixing with a pathetic kind of relief on his shoes. 'You're obviously not working.'

Only his eyes hadn't changed, and now they chased away faint surprise. As if her reaction had not been what he had expected. He glanced down at the navy deck shoes which covered his bare feet. 'What's wrong with them?' he demanded.

'Well, nothing really, I suppose. Just not the most conventional of footwear, is it?' she observed wryly. 'You look like you're about to go sailing, rather than running a business.'

'But I don't run a conventional business,' he growled impatiently. 'And I don't feel the need to hide behind a suit and tie any more.'

'My! What a little rebel you've become, Marcus!' commented Donna mildly, noticing the watchful spark which darkened his eyes from aquamarine to sapphire.

There was a small, apologetic cough from the table, and Donna and Marcus both started as Tony Paxman looked up at them. Donna bit her lip in vexation.

She'd forgotten all about her lunch partner! How rude of her! And how unimaginative, too. Just because Marcus Foreman had walked in, that didn't mean that the rest of the world had stopped turning.

It just seemed that way....

'Er, shall we order coffee, Tony?' she asked him quickly.

But Tony Paxman looked as if he'd taken about as much rejection as he could handle in one day. He shook his head as he rose to his feet—master of his own destiny once more as he made a big pantomime out of gazing at his watch.

'Heck! Is that the time? Time I wasn't here! Client meeting at three.' He held his hand out towards Donna and she took it guiltily. 'Thanks very much for lunch, Donna. I enjoyed it.'

Suddenly Donna felt bad. She hadn't meant for this to happen—for Marcus to disrupt her whole lunch, her whole *day*. Which left her wondering just what she *had* expected. She'd known that there was a strong possibility she would see him today. Had she naively supposed that he would pass by her table without a flicker of recognition? Or that they would exchange, at most, a hurried nod?

'Thanks for everything you've done, Tony! Maybe we'll do this another time.'

'Er, yes. Quite. Goodbye, Marcus.' Tony gave a grimace as Marcus clasped his fingers in what was obviously an enthusiastic handshake. 'Fantastic lunch! Wonderful food! As always.'

'Thanks very much,' murmured Marcus.

The two of them watched in silence while Tony Paxman threaded his way between the tables, and suddenly Donna felt almost light-headed as Marcus turned his head to study her. As though she'd just plunged into the swimming-pool-blue of his eyes without having a clue how to swim.

'Congratulations, Donna,' he offered drily. 'You've latched onto one of the town's wealthiest and brightest young lawyers.'

'His bank balance and his pretty face don't interest me—I chose him because he was the best.'

He raised his eyebrows. 'At what?'

'Not what you're obviously thinking! He was recommended to me,' she answered, with a sigh. But even as she said it she realised that she didn't have to justify herself to Marcus. Not any more. He wasn't her boss. He wasn't anything except the man who'd given her such a disastrous introduction into the world of love-making.

And then dumped her.

'And did the person who recommended him also tell you that he has just come through a mud-slinging divorce which was *very* nasty? That he's ready and available—but only if you don't mind half his salary going out on his ex-wife and two children? I know that financial embarrassment tends to put some women off.'

And then he gave a brief, unexpected smile which half blinded her. 'Heavens,' he murmured. 'I sounded almost *jealous* for a moment back there.'

'Yes, you did,' she agreed sweetly. 'But there's really

no need to be, Marcus—my relationship with Tony Paxman is strictly business.'

'I couldn't care less about your relationship with anyone!' He stared insolently at her fingers, which were bare of rings. 'But I presume that you *are* still in the marriage market?'

Donna stared at him. 'I'm still single, if that's what you mean by your charming question. How about you?'

'Yeah,' he said softly. 'Still single.' His eyes narrowed. 'So what are you doing back here, Donna? Are you planning on staying around?'

Was she willing to be interrogated by him? To lay herself open to his opinion and probably his criticism. 'I'd love to tell you about it, Marcus.' She smiled as she realised that there were a million and one things she could be legitimately occupying herself with. 'Pity I don't have the time right now.'

Something in her manner told him it wasn't true. But no surprises there. Hadn't she lied to him before? Only then he'd been too young and too blind with lust to see it. 'I bet it's nothing urgent,' he commented silkily. 'Nothing that can't wait.'

'But I might be rushing off to an urgent appointment,' she objected.

'Might be. But you're not,' he breathed, his voice thickening as he recalled the wasted opportunity of the one night he'd spent with her. 'You've got the pampered air of a woman who has taken the day off work.'

He pulled out the chair opposite her with a question in his eyes. 'So, why don't I join you for coffee now that your silver-tongued lawyer has flown?' he suggested softly. 'And then you can tell me exactly what you're doing here.'

CHAPTER TWO

DONNA was torn. Wanting to stay—because when Marcus was in a room it was as though someone had just switched on the lights. Even now. Yet also wanting to run out of the restaurant as fast as her feet would carry her.

And wouldn't that just convince him that she was still an emotional teenager where he was concerned?

Smoothing the cream silk dress down over her hips, she sat further back on her seat. 'Okay, then,' she answered coolly. 'I will.'

Marcus expelled a soft breath of triumph. He'd seen her hesitate before sliding that irresistible bottom back. So she had overriden her better judgement and decided to stay, had she? A pulse began to throb with slow excitement at his temple. The die had been cast. A smile curved the corners of his lips almost cruelly as he lowered his powerful frame into the chair facing her.

He gave a barely perceptible nod across the room at a watching waitress, and that was the coffee taken care of, then found himself in the firing line of a pair of eyes which were as green as newly mown grass. Eyes which these days were darkened with mascara which had teased the lashes into sooty spikes. Not the bare, pale lashes he'd always used to tease her about.

'You look completely different, Donna,' he observed slowly.

She gave him a disbelieving stare. 'Well, of course I do! I'm nine years older, for a start. People change.

Especially women.' And yet for a moment back there she had felt just like the unsophisticated teenager he obviously remembered. 'And I can't look *that* different,' she declared, in surprise. 'Seeing as you recognised me straight away.'

'Yeah.' Just from one, swift glance across a busy restaurant. He'd surprised himself. Maybe it had been the unforgettable fire of her hair. Or the curves of her body. Or that rope of amber beads at her throat—golden beads as big as pebbles. He swallowed as he remembered the only other time he had seen her wearing *those*. 'Maybe you're just printed indelibly on my mind,' he drawled.

'I *do* tend to have that effect on people,' she agreed, mock-seriously, and she could tell that her new-found sophistication surprised him.

Marcus might not know it, but he'd been largely responsible for her transformation from chambermaid to business woman. How many times had she planned to knock him dead if ever she saw him again? Well, now he was sitting just a few feet away from her. Was he *really* as indifferent to her as he appeared to be?

'So, how have I changed, Marcus?' she asked him sweetly.

He leaned back in the chair and took the opportunity to study her, which gave him far more pleasure than he felt comfortable with. Donna King had turned into a real little head-turner, he recognised wryly—despite her unconventional looks and her even more unconventional background.

He'd worked long enough in the high-octane world of upmarket restaurants to recognise that the deceptive simplicity of her cream silk dress would cost what most people earned in a month. As would those sexy high-heeled shoes he'd glimpsed as she'd slid her ankles beneath the table. Shoes like that cost money. He'd bet she had a handbag to match. He glanced at the floor to where, like most women, she had placed it, close to her feet. Yes, she did!

She was looking at him expectantly, and he remembered her question.

How had she changed?

'You used to look cheap,' he said honestly, not seeming to notice her frozen expression. 'Now you look expensive. A high-maintenance woman. With expensive tastes,' he added. 'So who pays for it, Donna? Who's the lucky man?'

Donna bristled. 'Heavens—but you're behind the times!' she scoffed. 'Women don't need to rely on men to pay for their finery, not these days. Everything I'm wearing I paid for myself!'

Marcus swallowed. Then it was money well spent.

Someone had threaded a cream satin ribbon though the fiery strands of her hair, sending out a seductive and confusing signal of schoolgirl sophistication. And her breasts were partially concealed behind a cleverly cut jacket. So that one moment he could see their erotic swell, only to have the jacket shield them when she moved her body slightly forward. It was maddening! He felt the intrusive jerk of desire, and willed it to go away.

'And you're wearing make-up,' he observed, almost accusingly. 'Yet you never used to wear a scrap!'

Donna laughed. 'Of course I didn't! When you get up at six in the morning to start stripping the beds, slapping on make-up is the very last thing on your mind. Believe me—a chambermaid's life doesn't lend itself very well to glamour.'

'Not unless you get lucky with the boss.'

She stared at him. 'But I didn't get lucky, did I,

Marcus? In fact the best bit of luck I had was having the courage to walk away from this place without a backward glance.'

'Yet you're here today?' he said bluntly. 'Why?'

'I'm celebrating.'

'How very intriguing,' he murmured. 'Shall I guess why, or are you going to tell me?'

Well, he would find out soon enough, whatever she said—and then he might sit up and wipe that smug smile off his face and take notice of something other than her body—which she noticed he hadn't stopped looking at.

Donna had opened her mouth to reply, when a very beautiful woman wearing a sleek black dress carried a tray of coffee over to their table.

Donna watched the woman's gleaming black head, with its perfectly symmetrical centre parting, as she set down the tiny cups and the cafetière in front of them, and the plate of thin almond biscuits. Then she heard her ask, 'Anything else for you, Marcus?' in a soft French accent, and noticed that she looked at him with politely concealed lust shining from her dark eyes.

'No, thanks!' He shook his head, his attention momentarily distracted as he watched the girl glide away.

'She seems very efficient,' observed Donna.

'Yes, she is.'

'And very good-looking.' Now why had she said *that*?

He raised his eyebrows. 'Very.'

'But not one of the waitresses—judging by her dress,' she probed.

He gave her a perplexed smile. 'Do you want to talk about my staff, Donna?'

'Of course not.'

He poured out the coffee, automatically offering Donna the sugar bowl, and she felt a little tug of nostalgia as she wondered whether he'd actually remembered her excessively sweet tooth.

'No, thanks. I've given up sugar in tea and coffee.'

'What, even when you're mysteriously celebrating?'

'It's no mystery.' She sipped her coffee and smiled. 'That's the reason I was having lunch with Tony Paxman, if you really want to know. I've just tied up a deal.'

'What kind of deal is that?'

She heard the condescension in his voice and her determination not to be smug or triumphant threatened to fly out of the window. But she hauled it back. 'A business deal,' she told him coolly. 'Which I happen to have set up.' She sat back in her chair and waited to hear what he would say.

He frowned at her, looking as puzzled as if she'd just announced she was running for mayor. 'You mean you're going to be working for someone else?'

'What a predictable and irritating conclusion to jump to! Actually, I'm going to be working for myself.' Donna even allowed herself a smile. 'I'm the boss.'

His hand stilled only briefly on its path to the sugar bowl, and he picked a cube up between his fingers, dipped it into his coffee and bit into it. 'Doing what?'

She savoured the moment like a hot bath at the end of a long, hard day. 'Running a restaurant, actually,' she answered serenely.

'Where?'

'Right here in Winchester.'

His interest was stirred, along with his imagination. It was far too close to home to be mere coincidence, surely? The same business, in the same *town*.

So why?

Was she seeking revenge for what had happened all

those years ago? Or was her extraordinary decision to come back based on a far more basic urge? Had that last night left a dark, demon blot on her memory, as it had on his?

Did she want…? Marcus felt the sweet, slow throbbing of sexual excitement begin… Did she want to play out that scene once more—only this time with a far more mutually satisfactory ending?

'Well, you really must have come along by leaps and bounds, Donna,' he mused, 'if you're planning a capital venture on a chambermaid's salary.'

If the remark had been made in order to inflame, then it served its purpose. 'Do I *look* like a chambermaid?' she demanded.

His groin ached. No. Right now she looked as he had never imagined she could look. Beautiful and proud and refined and, well…classy.

'Do I?' she persisted.

'No,' he growled. 'But that's what you were the last time I saw you.' His eyes narrowed. 'It makes me wonder what you've been doing in the intervening years to put you in the position of being able to buy a restaurant.'

'What do you *think* I've been doing? No—don't bother answering that! I'll tell you! I happen to have worked extremely hard since you kicked me out on the street!'

'Spare me the Victorian imagery,' he sighed. 'I gave you a generous pay-off *and* a job in London to go to. You were the one who decided not to accept.'

'I didn't want anything more to do with you!' she said bitterly.

He shrugged. 'That was your prerogative—but I refuse to be cast in the role of unfeeling bastard just because it suits your story!'

Donna glared. 'I managed very well on my own, thank you. I travelled to New Zealand and cooked on a sheep station. I worked in a bar in Manhattan—*and* on a cruise-liner! I know the hotel and restaurant industry inside out. I worked hard and saved hard—'

'And played hard, too, I imagine?' he cut in.

'That's something you'll never know!' She stared at him curiously across the table—expecting him to show *some* kind of reaction. But there was none. Just that barely interested, faintly bored expression.

'Well, I shan't be losing any sleep over it,' he offered drily, as he stirred his coffee. 'It's a precarious profession. I see new restaurants going under all the time.'

'Thanks for the few words of encouragement!'

'That's a fact, not a scare story. You know what they say—if you can't stand the heat then get out of the kitchen!' He gave a slow smile. 'Want to tell me all about it, Donna—or are you worried about industrial espionage?'

'No, my only worry is that I might lose my temper!'

He laughed, enjoying the hidden fires of conflict, and his smile sent her blood pressure soaring. 'Feel free,' he murmured.

Ignoring the sultry innuendo, Donna paused for effect. 'I've bought The Buttress Guest House!' she announced.

Marcus narrowed his eyes. So. Not just in the same town, but on the same street. Neighbours as well as rivals? He hid a smile. Not really. No one in their right mind would dream of comparing a run-down boarding house to a five-star hotel! 'You're opening up a *guest* house?'

'That's not what I said,' she contradicted. 'I've bought it and converted it.'

Of course she had, thought Marcus, as all the facts began to slot into place.

The Buttress Guest House had gone bankrupt a couple of years ago and no one had wanted to touch it. It was small and it was tired—with tiny, impractical rooms and, more importantly, no parking facilities.

But recently the house had seen a plumber's van parked outside it for the best part of a month. Painters and decorators and French-polishers had been employed to work there. Hammers and drills had been heard as you walked past. Interesting pieces of furniture had been seen disappearing into the beautiful old house.

Marcus, along with most other people in the town, had assumed that the house was being converted back to a private residence before being put on the property market again. Now it seemed he'd been wrong.

'You've *converted* it,' he breathed, and stared at her assessingly. 'Into what?'

'A tea-room, actually.'

'A tea-room?'

'That's what I said!'

He very nearly laughed, but something in the proud way she'd said it stopped him. 'How quaint,' he murmured.

'I'll take that as a compliment.'

'It wasn't supposed to be a compliment.' He frowned, and instead of feeling angry he felt a maddening rush of the protectiveness she'd always used to bring out in him. 'Have you taken any business advice, Donna? Seriously?'

'If only you knew just how insulting that question sounded! Or maybe you do! Of course I took advice! *And* I did accounting at night school!' Her eyes narrowed suspiciously. 'Why?'

'Because there's no parking for any cars, that's why!' he exploded. 'Didn't it occur to you to ask why the place had been on the market for so long? Or did you think it was a bargain, just waiting for you to breeze along and buy it?'

'For your information, I don't need any parking!'

'Oh, really?'

'Yes, really! The property happens to be on the route of at least two official Winchester Walks. The tourist office know all about me. They're going to help get me started and I'm hoping that word of mouth will do the rest. People won't need cars—and that's the kind of customer I want! People who are interested in history and sightseeing, and can be bothered to walk down the road for a cup of tea and a piece of cake instead of polluting the atmosphere in some horrible gas-guzzling machine!'

There was silence.

'You're crazy!' he said at last. 'Crazy and impetuous!'

'What's the matter?' She gave him a steady, cool look. 'Do you think that being my own boss is too good for someone of *my* pedigree?'

'What your mother did for a living didn't concern me,' he said coldly. 'But the fact that you deceived me did. But then our whole relationship was built on a tissue of lies, wasn't it?'

'Relationship?' she scorned. 'Oh, come *on*, Marcus! To describe what we shared as a ''relationship'' is not only inaccurate—it's insulting to relationships!'

He sat back in his chair and studied her, the ice-blue eyes as cool as she had ever seen them. 'So tell me—is this whole enterprise of yours some naive plan for revenge?'

Donna blinked at him in genuine astonishment. 'Revenge?'

'It's a natural progression, if you stop to think about it,' he mused. 'You striking out, in a primitive kind of way, to make me pay for what happened between us.'

For a moment she was dumbfounded, and it took a few incredulous seconds before she could speak. 'Marcus—please credit me with a little more intelligence than that. I'm not stupid enough to set myself up to be miserable—and pursuing some sort of vendetta against you would make anyone miserable.'

'Maybe being miserable is a price worth paying.' He shrugged. 'Depends how badly you want to pay me back!'

She gave him a look of undiluted amazement, realising that maybe he didn't know her at all. 'What a disgustingly over-inflated ego you have, Marcus! Do you really think that I would stake everything I own on a venture like this unless I thought I could make some kind of success of it?'

'I have no idea. Maybe I've misjudged you,' he said, sounding as though he didn't think he had at all. 'But in that case—how did you manage to keep it so quiet for so long?' he mused. 'And why?'

'How?' She smiled. 'I hired a good lawyer. You said yourself that Tony Paxman was expensive. Well, he's good—and you always get what you pay for—that's something else I've learnt. As for why...' She met his gaze steadily. 'I suspected that you might try and block the sale if you knew who was behind it.'

And she was right—damn her! Not because he feared competition—he'd always been able to deal with *that*. No, it was more to do with the effect she had on him... Marcus was silent as he dragged oxygen into his body and fought to swamp his instincts. He felt unwelcome heat invade him. She always made him want what he didn't need...

Seconds ticked by as his heart thundered and the tiny hairs on the back of his neck stung like pin-pricks. He didn't speak. Didn't dare to. Not until he was sure that his feelings were under control once more. Only then did he speak, lacing his words with sarcasm. 'So, it's open warfare, is it, Donna?' he drawled.

'Of course not! I'm sure there's room for both of us,' she said mock-generously. 'People will choose where they want to eat.'

'As you did today,' he remarked obscurely. 'But maybe you had your own special reasons for wanting to eat here.'

Donna held her breath. 'Like what?'

'Like me.'

'You?'

'Mmm. Me. There are plenty of other places you could have taken your lawyer to. Maybe you just couldn't wait to see me again.'

It was partly true—but not for the reasons he was implying, that she was still vulnerable where he was concerned. Seeing Marcus again had been intended to be the final proof that not only had she turned her life around, but she had succeeded in forgetting the man who had brought her nothing but heartache.

Donna opened her mouth without thinking, and the words came fizzing out before she could take them back. 'And why would I want to see you again, Marcus? Why would I want to re-acquaint myself with a man who gave me nothing but grief? The man who strode in and took exactly what he wanted and found he couldn't handle it afterwards! Was that the real reason you sacked me, Marcus—not because I'd lied to you, but because I reminded you of what you'd done? Were you feeling guilty that you'd seduced a poor little virgin?'

'You're talking like a victim, Donna—and I can assure you that you were nothing of the kind. For an innocent you certainly knew how to be provocative.' His mouth tightened as he lowered his voice. 'As for seduction—that's too fine a word to describe what was a very regrettable incident all round.'

'A "very regrettable incident"?' she repeated in disbelief. 'My God—I'm going to enjoy becoming the most popular eaterie in town! I hope all your clients come flocking to *me*!'

He gave a sad shake of his head as he rose to his feet. 'Oh, Donna,' he sighed. 'You may be older—but you don't seem to have acquired a lot of wisdom along the way. Your hare-brained scheme won't work. Believe me.'

'Only time will tell!'

His smile was wry. 'I'll try very hard not to gloat when my prediction comes true.'

'And I'll be laughing all the way to the bank when it doesn't!'

'We'll see.' He tore his eyes away from that riveting glimpse of her breasts and walked out of the restaurant, leaving Donna and just about every other female in the room staring wide-eyed after him.

CHAPTER THREE

DONNA paid her bill and then made her way out of the restaurant, trying not to notice that people were staring and wondering if it was because she'd been sitting with Marcus.

It had not been the meeting she'd fantasised about. She *had* been naive. *And* stupid. Imagining that all those sparks of sexual attraction would have been extinguished over the years.

Outside, the afternoon sunshine was beginning to fade, and a tiny breeze had blown up which made her shiver, turning her flesh to goosebumps beneath the cream silk jacket.

She turned and walked up the street towards her newly purchased future, her high-heeled shoes clipping over the familiar pavements until she stopped outside The Buttress and looked up at it. At the worn, wooden door and the ancient brick—all warm and terracotta-coloured in the dying light of the sun. Hers.

The new sign would be erected tomorrow, and the notices would go out in all the trade press. The tea-room had been dominating her thoughts for so long now. She'd been bubbling over with excitement about all her plans and hopes for it—but seeing Marcus today had made her confront the fact that he still had the power to affect her in a way that no other man had ever come close to.

She felt the beat of her heart, heavy and strong, as she remembered the way he looked. Different. Older and rougher round the edges. All tousled and tough—and radiating an earthy sexuality she knew she was incompatible with.

The first time she had met him he'd been kind to her. Kind and caring, yes—but in the way that a Victorian benefactor might throw a bone to a starving dog...

As a teenager, Donna had arrived in Winchester on a rainy December day, dressed in jeans and a jumper and a worn tweed jacket she'd picked up at a car-boot sale and which had been too thin to withstand the constant drizzle. She'd been soaked. Her face had been bare of make-up, her lashes matted with raindrops and her hair a wild ginger mess frizzing all the way down down her back.

There had only been one week to go until Christmas, and there'd been fairy-lights threaded everywhere: outside all the shops and pubs, woven into the bare branches of the trees—their colours blurred like jewels through the grey of the relentless rain.

As she'd turned the corner into Westgate street Donna had seen the welcoming blaze of The New Hampshire hotel and had shivered. It was the sort of place you usually only saw in story books—a beautiful, elegant old building, with two bay trees standing in dark, shiny boxes outside. The windows were sparkly-clean and the paintwork gleamed. It was the kind of place which reeked of money. You could tell just by looking. And places like this were always looking for seasonal workers.

Clutching onto her holdall with frozen fingers, she'd pushed the glass doors open and walked into the foyer, where a man had been standing at the top of a ladder, positioning a huge silver star on top of a Christmas tree whose tip was brushing against the high ceiling.

Donna had quietly slid her holdall onto the thick carpet and watched him. He'd been wearing dark trousers, which had looked new and neatly pressed, and his shirt had been exquisitely made. Quality clothes on a quality body.

She had waited until the star was firmly in place. 'Bravo!' she cheered, and he looked over his shoulder, frowned, then came slowly down the ladder to face her.

His hair was thick and dark and tapered neatly into his neck, and his eyes were the most extraordinary colour she had ever seen. Icy and pale. Clear and blue. As if they had been washed clean. And Donna felt the first tiptoeing of an emotion she simply didn't recognise.

He frowned again as he looked her up and down, and his voice matched his clothes. Rich. 'Can I help you?'

The implication being that he couldn't. That she was in the wrong place. The story of her life, really. She decided to brazen it out.

'Do you have a room?'

The surprise in his eyes was gone almost as quickly as it had appeared, and he shrugged his shoulders apologetically. 'I'm sorry. I'm afraid we're fully booked. It's our busiest time of year and—'

'Actually, I don't want a room,' she interrupted quickly, thinking that it was nice of him to pretend that she could afford a room in a hotel when it was pretty obvious she couldn't. 'I'm looking for work.'

His eyes narrowed. 'What kind of work?'

'Anything. You name it—I can do it! I can wait tables—'

He shook his head. 'I'm sorry. We're a silver-service restaurant,' he said politely.

'Or peel potatoes?'

He smiled. 'We have our full complement of kitchen staff.'

'Oh.' She pursed her lips together to stop them wobbling and went to pick up her holdall. 'Okay. Fair enough. Merry Christmas!'

The man sighed. 'Now you're making me feel like Scrooge.'

'You don't look like Scrooge.' She grinned. Too cute by far.

He thought how thin her cheeks looked. And how pale. 'Ever done any work as a chambermaid?'

'No. But I learn fast.'

'How old are you?'

'Nearly twenty.' The words were out before she could stop them, and she told herself that it wasn't a lie, merely an exaggeration. Because she also told herself that this man was the kind of man who would try to send her home if he knew she was barely eighteen.

And then where would she go?

'Been travelling?' he asked, flicking a pale blue glance over at the holdall, then at the worn elbows of her jacket.

'Kind of.'

She had been moving around for most of her young life. She liked it that way. It meant that she didn't have to give away too much about herself. But she could see him looking at her curiously and knew she ought to say *something*.

'Bit of a nomad, that's me,' she explained with a smile—wondering what had possessed her to add, 'My mother was an actress. We moved around a lot when I was a child.'

'Oh, I see.' He nodded, wondering what he was letting himself in for. But through the glass doors he could see that the rain was now lashing down, to form lake-sized puddles on the pavement outside. It was the kind of night you wouldn't throw a dog out into. 'I'll take you on until the New Year. But no longer—do you understand?'

'Oh, thanks!' Donna breathed, looking for a moment as though she was about to fling her arms around him.

Marcus took a hasty step back.

She wasn't the kind of woman he would normally find attractive in a million years—with her curly ginger hair and pale eyelashes and freckles.

But there was something indomitable about her. Something that made her look small and tough and brave. Something feisty, which was oddly attractive and made him feel strange and warm and prickly inside.

'Don't mention it,' he growled. 'What's your name?'

'It's Donna. Donna King. What's yours?'

'Marcus Foreman.'

She lifted her shoulders in a tiny questioning movement. 'Should I call you Mr Foreman?'

It was such a sweetly old-fashioned proposition that he almost laughed, then checked himself in time. He didn't want her thinking he was making fun of her. 'You're only a year younger than me.' He smiled gently, not noticing her wince. 'Marcus will do just fine.'

'Marcus,' she said shyly. 'Are you the boss?'

It took a moment for him to answer. 'Yes,' he said abruptly. He still couldn't quite get used to the fact that this place was now his. But then his father had only been dead a year. He looked down at her and his features softened.

Her face was so pale that her freckles stood out like tiny brown stars, and her cheekbones looked much too sharp. She could do with a little fleshing out. 'Have you eaten?'

Donna's eyes grew wary. Could he tell? That she hadn't seen a square meal in getting on for a week? And what kind of conclusions would he draw from that?

He watched her reaction and was reminded of a stray cat his mother had once let him keep. The creature had been starving, yet stubborn—mistrusting any attempts at kindness—and Marcus had learnt that the only way to handle that cat was to seem not to care. He shrugged, sounding as if she could take it or leave it. 'There's plenty of food here if you want some.'

'Okay.' She shrugged too. 'Might as well.'

He took her down to the kitchen and introduced her to the staff, and then found things to keep him occupied while she ate and he watched her out of the corner of his eye.

He had never seen anyone eat with so much greed, or so much hunger. Especially a woman. Yet she didn't tear at the food like an animal. Hers was a graceful greed. She savoured every single mouthful with pleasure—and when she'd finally finished she wiped her mouth delicately with a napkin, like some sort of princess, and beamed him a smile.

And that smile pierced Marcus's armour like a ray of sunshine hitting a sheet of ice.

As spring slid into early summer, Marcus showed no sign of asking her to leave. And Donna heaved a huge sigh of relief, because she loved the town and she loved the hotel and she wanted to stay.

She loved the grey flint walls of the ancient buildings and the sound of the choristers' voices spilling their pure, sweet notes into the scented air around the cathedral square. She loved the lush green and crystal streams of the water meadows, where you could walk for miles and feel that you'd stepped back a century. And maybe more than a bit of her loved Marcus, too. Who wouldn't?

It was the first place that had felt like home for a long time. Maybe ever.

She made herself indispensable by working as hard as possible. And Donna could work. If there was one thing her childhood had taught her it was that you didn't get anything for nothing.

Her mother had been a stripper—spending her nights performing in run-down theatres along the coast and her days mostly sleeping. In a way, Donna had brought herself up—making herself as invisible as she knew how. Because a little girl had fitted uneasily into the kind of life her mother had chosen.

She knew that Marcus's father had died the year before, and one day she plucked up enough courage to ask him what had happened to his mother.

Mistake!

The icy-blue eyes narrowed suspiciously. 'Why?'

'I j-just wondered.'

'She's been dead for a long time,' he snapped.

She thought that it was an odd way to put it. As though a chapter of his own life had come to an end with his mother's death. Maybe it had.

'And how old were you?' she asked.

He scowled at the intrusion. 'I was nine, and, yes—before you make the obvious response—it *was* awful. Okay? And I don't want to talk about it. Okay?'

End of subject. But Donna was relieved, in a funny kind of way. The kind of person who didn't like to explain was also the kind of person who didn't ask too many questions. Although it wasn't as if a man like Marcus would be interested in one of his chambermaids, was it?

But sometimes she caught him watching her, when he thought she wasn't looking. And sometimes he even let his guard down enough to laugh at something she said. And sometimes he would tease her about her pale eyelashes, and the way she used to nibble the tip of her thumb when she was nervous.

One day he found her in the staffroom, playing cards with one of the waiters, and he challenged her to play. Only to discover that she could beat him at every card game he'd ever learnt.

Marcus was a man who admired expertise in whatever field it was demonstrated, and he seemed to look at her in a completely different light after that. He told her that watching her shuffle the cards was like poetry in motion, and Donna beamed with pleasure at the praise.

'Where ever did you learn to play like that?' he questioned.

'Oh, here and there,' she told him airily. 'You don't want to know.'

'No, you're right. I don't!' he laughed.

And it was at times like these that Donna had to remind herself that there were some men you should never start getting attracted to, on account of who they were.

And Marcus Foreman was one of them.

He had a younger brother called Lucas, who was nearly as good-looking as his brother, but foxy in a way that Marcus wasn't foxy. And blond, not dark. He was a photographer, of sorts, and he was away travelling, somewhere in Thailand, He hadn't even bothered coming back for Christmas. But Marcus didn't seem to mind.

The first time Donna met Lucas she was on her hands and knees brushing up some crumbs from behind a large pot plant on the first-floor landing, when she heard a low wolf whistle from behind her.

She whirled round, bashing her elbow in the process, and saw a man with blue eyes who looked like a fallen angel. She recognised the likeness immediately. 'You must be Lucas!' she cried.

'And you must be a hallucination,' he murmured, licking his bottom lip like an old-fashioned villian. 'Wow! Stand up. Go on!'

He was the boss's brother. So Donna did as he asked and rose to her feet, not much liking the smile on his face as he looked her up and down as if he'd never seen a woman before.

'Oh, my word!' he breathed softly. 'No wonder big brother wasn't crazy about me coming home—he obviously wanted to keep a living, breathing Barbie doll all to himself!'

'Stay away from her, Lucas—do you hear that?' came a soft command, and Marcus walked up behind his brother as soundlessly as a wraith, silently cursing himself for the attractive enticement having Donna King around the place was proving to be. Those scruffy clothes she'd arrived in had done a remarkable job of concealing a body which regular meals and regular sleep had transformed into something resembling a centrefold.

She was as bright as a button, too. Hard-working. Friendly. And considerate—from what little he knew of her. And he deliberately kept it as little as he could. Knowledge equalled understanding, and understanding could lead on to all kinds of unwanted things.

And whilst Marcus was honest enough to admit that he fancied the pants off Donna King—he was also honest enough to realise that they were worlds apart. Worlds.

Lucas shot Donna a search-*me* kind of look. 'Marcus likes playing the big macho bit!' he grinned.

'Leave that now, will you please, Donna?' snapped Marcus, because she had bent over to flick up the last few crumbs of dust.

'But—'

'Just *leave* it!'

Donna straightened up and smoothed down the pale green uniform which strained so horribly over her bust, slotting the brush onto the dustpan before looking up at Marcus and smiling. 'Are we still on for a game later?'

Lucas's pupils dilated. 'A game of *what*?'

'Not tonight,' said Marcus tightly. 'Just go *away*, Donna, will you? I want to talk to Lucas in private!'

Afterwards, Marcus realised that the worst thing he could possibly have done was to warn Lucas off the luscious chambermaid. His wayward brother loved nothing more than a slice of forbidden fruit.

But what alternative did he have? He didn't think for a moment that she was an unsullied young virgin—but for all Donna's worldliness she had a curious and refreshing innocence about her.

It was a potent combination—and one which caused him to lie awake at night, aching and sweating and pressing his groin hard against the mattress, as if he was trying to punish himself.

Donna saw how different the two brothers were. Marcus was the serious one, with all the responsibilities of the hotel weighing heavily on his shoulders. Lucas was simply devil-may-care. While Marcus seemed reluctant to find out anything about her Lucas wanted to know everything. And a little bit more besides.

But his openness made up for his inquisitiveness. He was so forthcoming—not like his brother at all. Through Lucas she heard about their childhood. About their wild

and beautiful mother—so different from their steady, unimaginative father.

Lucas was candid to the point of indiscretion, Donna
realised. He seemed unfazed by telling her of his
mother's infidelities and the ensuing rows. He explained
that his father had been too much in thrall to his spectacular wife to ever leave her.

He told her things which in her heart she knew should
have remained secret—and maybe that was why she told
Lucas the truth about *her* mother.

He didn't look at all shocked, merely looked her up
and down and said, 'Yes. I can see exactly why she was
a stripper, if her body was anything like yours.'

She could have bitten her tongue out and tossed it
away. 'But you won't tell Marcus?' she begged him.

His eyes were sly. 'Why not?'

'Please!'

'Okay,' he replied easily. 'Don't want to shock my
uptight big brother, do we?' The sly look returned. 'He
likes you, doesn't he?'

Donna shook her head. 'Only as a card partner,' she
said, fervently trying to convince herself.

'I don't think so,' said Lucas. 'He used to play bridge
with the local vicar, and he never used to look at *him*
like that!'

Lucas was pointing out nothing that Donna hadn't noticed for herself. Marcus really *did* seem to like her. That
look in his eyes sometimes…an intense kind of longing
that made her wonder why on earth he didn't just throw
caution to the wind, take her in his arms and…

She knew exactly why. They weren't equals. He was
the boss and she was the chambermaid and she should
never forget that. Because Marcus never did.

Donna saw the hotel grow more and more popular.

Everyone wanted to eat there, and it became the place to see and be seen in. Actors and media-types often drove down from London for dinner and a luxurious bed for the night.

One night a famous restaurant critic from a national newspaper came to review the restaurant. Every member of staff worked their socks off, and they all held their breath until the first edition claimed that it was the 'best-kept secret in the South of England'!

Not for long!

The reservations phone didn't stop ringing, and Marcus announced that he would be providing a meal in the private function room upstairs—to thank all the staff for their hard work.

Donna wore the only thing she had which was suitable—a black velvet dress she'd bought at a thrift shop. It was much too old and too severe for her, but it made her figure look absolutely show-stopping. She wore it with a necklace of huge amber beads which matched the colour of her hair exactly.

She drank champagne and let her hair down—literally and figuratively. In between courses she joined the chefs and waiters and shimmied around the room to the music which played in the background, knowing that Marcus was watching her.

And Donna was her mother's daughter. Whether or not the dancing was learned or inherited—she could dance like a dream.

Marcus couldn't take his eyes off her. He'd never wanted anyone or anything so badly, and once the coffee had been served he gave up trying to resist and slid into the seat next to her.

'Hello, Donna.' He smiled.

'Hello.'

They stared at one another.

'Enjoying yourself?'

'Mmm!' She was now!

He touched one of the pebble-sized amber beads she wore around her neck with the tip of his finger. 'These are beautiful,' he said softly. 'Who gave them to you?'

'My mother.'

'She has excellent taste.'

Donna smiled. 'Actually, she thought they were plastic—that's why she gave them to me. Funny, really— they were the only valuable piece of jewellery she owned, if only she'd known it. She used to walk around quite happily wearing paste.'

'And where's your mother now?' he amazed himself by asking. 'Playing Shakespeare somewhere?'

She wrinkled her nose, not wanting to talk about anything—especially not the stories she'd invented. She just wanted him to kiss her. 'Oh, she's given up acting now! She's running a bed and breakfast on the coast.'

'Whereabouts?'

Donna narrowed her eyes and gave a cynical laugh. 'Oh, nowhere you'll ever go, Marcus.'

The laugh made a hollow sort of sound, and Marcus suddenly caught a glimpse of another world. He saw it all. Seaside rock and greasy eggs on a plate. Ferris wheels and screams and the overpowering smell of chips. And he wanted no part of that world.

If only he didn't want Donna quite so much…

'You look…' His eyes roved over the clinging black velvet and he became temporarily lost for words.

The smile and the way he was watching her made her throw every bit of caution to the wind. She gazed at him provocatively over the top of her champagne glass. 'How do I look, Marcus?' she purred.

'Absolutely bloody gorgeous,' he said honestly.

'Gosh! That good?' Donna wanted him, ached for him, loved him. She knew she would never get another opportunity like this. She leaned forward to softly plant a kiss on his mouth.

He very nearly pulled her into his arms right there and then, until he remembered just in time that almost every member of his staff was watching.

'Let's save that for later,' he whispered.

'Save what?' she teased, automatically slipping into the flirtatious banter she had grown up listening to.

Pulse-points began to throb in places he hadn't even known had a pulse. 'That depends. What say we start with a kiss and see how we get on?'

'Mmm!' She giggled. 'Tell me when you're ready!'

But he noticed that she didn't bite the tip of her thumb the way she normally did when she was nervous. She was twenty years old, for heaven's sake! He wasn't planning on breaking any laws. She liked him and he liked her. He had grown to trust her. Life was too damned short. And you only got one bite of the cherry...

'Oh, I will,' he murmured, and their eyes locked in an unspoken promise. 'You can bet your life on it, sugar!'

When Donna escaped to the loo, she noticed that her face was flushed and that her eyes glittered like a rich woman's diamonds. She patted her wrists with cold water, and smoothed down the wild red tumble of her curls, and was just making her way back along the corridor towards the dining room when a figure slipped out from the shadows.

'Donna!'

Donna started, thinking at first that it was Marcus—until she noticed that the figure was slighter, the shoulders less broad. His voice wasn't so deep, either. 'Lucas!' she breathed, and slapped her palm over her thundering heart. 'You made me jump!'

He looked foxier than ever in the half-light. 'Pretty edgy, aren't you?' he observed. 'My brother has been sniffing round you like a dog all night.'

Donna frowned. 'Lucas, are you drunk?'

'A little. Not drunk enough.' He looked up at the ornate ceiling and scowled. 'Save me from claustrophobia—I need to get out of this place. Lend me some money, Donna.'

'No way! You haven't paid me back the last lot yet!' She made to walk on, but he stopped her.

'Don't you think it might blow things for you if he were to ever find out the truth about you?' he asked her casually.

She stilled. 'Wh-what are you talking about?'

He shrugged. 'The fact that you never knew your father. That your mother stripped for a living. That you spent your life moving around and dodging debts.' He paused for effect. 'Marcus is a very conventional man, Donna. He wouldn't just be shocked, he would be appalled. Do you want me to go on?'

'Are you trying to *blackmail* me, Lucas?'

He laughed. 'Oh, don't be so melodramatic! I'm just asking you a favour, that's all—just as you're expecting me to be discreet!'

She stared at him, her heart sinking as she realised that he could ruin everything. 'How much do you want?'

'Not much. Twenty will do.'

'Wait here.' She sighed, knowing that she probably wouldn't see the money again, but right now it didn't seem important. Nothing did except Marcus. 'I'll go and get my purse.'

When she walked back into the dining room she saw Marcus sitting alone at a table, watching her intently as she crossed the room towards him. And she never gave Lucas another thought.

Marcus was fighting a losing battle with his conscience, and in the end he gave up trying. He went back to her room and the sight of the cramped quarters only intensified his guilt. But the sight of Donna stretched out naked on the beaten gold of the bedspread almost made him lose his mind with desire.

But the act of making love was a disaster—painful and uncomfortable for her, and over far too quickly for him.

He lay awake, staring up through the dark at the ceiling, suspecting that Donna was feigning sleep beside him, but he found he couldn't face talking to her. It was the first time in his life that he had ever failed at anything, but he found that he had no desire to give her the pleasure he knew her beautiful body deserved.

It was supposed to have been a casual fling, nothing more. So why the hell had she kept her virginity a secret? He would have run a mile had he known.

Sliding out of bed, he pulled on his jeans and T-shirt and went down to the kitchen for a glass of milk. And Lucas was there, looking slightly the worse for wear as he flipped the top off a bottle of beer.

Lucas smiled. 'So, did you get your leg over with her?'

Marcus played dumb. 'Who?'

'Donna. Careful there, Marcus—she nearly qualifies as jail-bait!'

Marcus froze. 'She's twenty.'

'She's only eighteen.' Lucas swigged some beer and

his eyes narrowed with mischief. 'Did you know her mother was a stripper?'

It was the final straw, and the excuse that Marcus had been looking for.

Next day, he sacked her.

Donna put the key in the lock and looked down the road. From here she could see the lights of The New Hampshire quite clearly, looking as warm and as welcoming as on that first day, when she had glimpsed it shining like a beacon through the rain.

If Marcus had been standing at the window of *his* office, they could almost have waved at one another.

Not that there was much chance of that happening.

It had made perfect sense to come back here. The ideal spot and the ideal business opportunity—yet now she was wondering how she could have left such a huge factor as Marcus Foreman out of the equation.

She'd somehow thought that his attraction would have dimmed over the years. Well, she'd been wrong. Badly wrong.

The question was what she did about it. Could she ignore him? Act as if he didn't exist?

A cloud crossed over the sun and Donna shivered as she unlocked the front door with a very real sense of something unfinished hanging over her.

CHAPTER FOUR

DURING the next week, Donna was so busy with preparations for the opening of her tea-room that she was able to put Marcus on the back burner of her mind. There were so many different things to organise—flowers to order and staff to settle in and publicity to sort out—and through it all the telephone didn't seem to stop ringing.

She was sitting in her broom cupboard of an office, drawing tiny little teapots on the menus, when there was a rap at the door and a girl with dark curly hair stuck her head round.

'Donna?'

'Yes, Sarah—come in.' Donna smiled at her newest member of staff. 'I can't believe we open tomorrow. Tell me I'm not dreaming!'

'You're not dreaming,' answered Sarah obediently. 'Oh, and Mrs Armstrong—'

Donna blinked. 'Who?'

'The Mayor's wife. She's just phoned to say that they'd both be delighted to come tomorrow. So I've added them to the list.'

'Good. Let's hope we can fit them all in!'

Sarah moved forward and leaned over the desk to lower her voice, like someone about to break bad news. 'Oh, and by the way—there's a man in reception who says he wants to see you!'

'That'll be the photographer from the *Hampshire Times*,' answered Donna absently, thinking how chic the young waitress looked in her pale shell-coloured uniform.

Sarah Flowers had been broke and hungry and eager to learn—just as Donna herself had been all those years ago. In fact she'd deliberately advertised for staff in one of the city's free newspapers, as well as in local shop windows. It meant that she'd ended up with staff who really needed the work—and people who needed to work worked hardest. No one knew that better than Donna.

She glanced down at her watch, and frowned. 'He's a bit early, isn't he? I thought he wasn't supposed to be coming until after lunch.'

'It isn't the photographer,' said Sarah, in an odd, strangled sort of voice.

'Well, who is it, then?'

'Marcus something-or-other.' Sarah screwed up her face with concentration, then dimpled her cheeks as she remembered. 'Marcus Foreman!'

Donna felt her complacency slip. 'Tell him I'm busy. We open tomorrow.'

'I know. I already told him that—but he says he's not leaving until you see him.'

'Oh, does he?' Donna rose to her feet, see-sawing between exasperation and a definite sense of excitement. Because she had been expecting this. Half-dreading it and half-wanting it more than she could remember wanting anything for a long time. Though she hadn't stopped to ask herself why.

She quickly checked her appearance in the mirror which hung on the back of the door, and walked through to the foyer, where Marcus was sprawled on one of the leather sofas. He'd been reading the pink financial pages of one of the broadsheets, but he lowered it onto his chest as she walked in and stood in front of him, her arms crossed protectively over her breasts.

He didn't move an inch, just sat there looking at her with the sort of slow deliberation you might expect from a bloodstock expert seeing a racehorse for the first time.

Marcus had been wondering why he'd been unable to resist the compulsion to come across the road to see this place for himself. Now he knew that the reason was standing directly in front of him. Sweet Lord, but she looked sexy! But schoolmistressy sexy. All buttoned up and covered up in a plain chocolate-brown dress, with just the simple string of amber beads around her neck.

Had her legs always been that long? he wondered distractedly. Or did it have something to do with the three-inch heels which made them seem to reach all the way up to her armpits? And who else could have scraped their hair back as tightly as that and still manage to look good?

But then, Donna King had always managed to break a few rules where looks were concerned, he thought. Hell—he had found her desirable when she had breezed around the place with frizzy hair and no make-up.

'Hello, Marcus,' said Donna calmly, though calm was hardly the way she felt inside. She felt as if there was a nest of vipers wriggling around in the pit of her stomach. She felt squirmy and distracted and odd. 'This is an unexpected pleasure.'

'Say that once more with feeling,' he mocked.

She gave him a prim, I'm-going-to-humour-you smile. 'I'm afraid I haven't got time to see you at the moment. Really.'

He rose silently to his feet and she noticed that even with her highest heels on he still towered over her like a giant. 'Then make time,' he said softly.

She met the challenge in his eyes. 'Or what?'

'Or I'll sit here and distract you all day.'

'I would ignore you.'

'No, you wouldn't. But you could try.'

And she would probably fail. Because a man who looked like Marcus looked would be pretty impossible to ignore.

Today he was wearing some kind of charcoal-coloured silk shirt with a pair of black denims. And while some men never looked good in jeans once they had passed the age of twenty-one Marcus was not among them. She guessed that most twenty-one-year-olds would die to own a body like his!

'Come on, Donna,' he cajoled softly. 'Call it simple professional interest. I only want to see what you've got on offer.'

Now why did everything he said sound like an allusion to sex? Was that his intention? She refused to meet his eyes for longer than a distracting second. Instead, she fixed her gaze on a point midway down his chest. 'We open tomorrow,' she said agitatedly. 'And we're having a party. I even sent you an invitation. Didn't you get it?'

'Yeah. I got it a couple of days ago.' He had ripped open the envelope with its oddly familiar writing which seemed to have become more fluid over the years. And he had felt a mixture of different emotions as he'd pulled out the thick card within. Surprise that Donna had had the audacity to ask him—as well as a burning curiosity to see what she had done to the place. And if the reception area was anything to go by she was onto a winner.

'Were you surprised?' she queried. 'To be invited?'

'A little. I didn't think I'd be number one on your guest list—'

'You weren't,' she agreed calmly. 'More like number one hundred and one.'

'So why bother?'

'Because I suspected you'd probably gatecrash if I didn't! Or go to extraordinary lengths to disguise yourself as an ordinary punter just so you could have a look round. I thought I'd save you the trouble.'

'How very sweet of you.'

'Wasn't it?'

'And maybe because you wanted to show the place off?' he suggested. 'To put my nose out of joint by demonstrating how well you'd done?'

'Maybe there was a bit of that,' she agreed. 'You can't blame me for that, Marcus.'

'No,' he said slowly, looking around. 'I guess I can't.'

'So, are you be coming to the opening, or not?'

That slow, secret smile of hers made him ache in places it was uncomfortable to ache in public. 'I'll think about it.'

'It'll give you the perfect opportunity to see the place properly.'

'No, it won't,' he contradicted flatly. He had been having trouble sleeping over these past few days and he didn't like it. He didn't like it one bit. He glared at the unwitting cause of his sleeplessness.

'You'll have all the great and the good crowded in here, fawning over you like sycophants,' he said. 'You'll speak less than ten words to every person in the room, and you certainly won't be able to give anyone your undivided attention.' He paused. 'And I want your undivided attention, Donna.'

'Do you? And do you always get what you want?'

'Usually.' The light blue eyes hardened. 'Though not always, of course. Honesty is notoriously difficult to come by, isn't it? Especially when you're employing staff.'

'Oh!' she exclaimed sarcastically. 'Was that a pointed remark—directed at me?'

Marcus shrugged. 'Put it this way—I'd certainly have difficulty writing you a good reference.'

'Then it's a good thing I'm not asking you for one!' She realised that his boast of earlier had not been an idle one, and that he had no intention of going anywhere. So why fight it? 'Okay, Marcus,' she sighed. 'You win! Come with me and I'll show you around. What would you like to see first?'

He didn't miss a beat. 'Whatever you'd like to show me. I'm easy.'

'How about the kitchen?' she said brightly.

She could feel her heart bashing against her ribcage as he followed her along to the kitchen and cast a swift, professional eye over the fittings.

'Nice,' he commented, running the flat of his hand over a giant steel oven as if he were smoothing the flank of a horse. 'This is very nearly top of the range. Big investment.'

'It needs to be. I'm going to be doing lots of baking. Scones. Cakes. Meringues.'

He shot her a glance. 'You aren't planning to do all the cooking yourself?'

'Yes, that's right,' she shot back. 'Along with the cleaning, the ordering, the serving and the accounts! Don't be daft, Marcus—I'm going to have people working for me, of course.'

'How many?'

'Well, just a couple, to start with. A waitress—remember Sarah, who showed you in?'

'Vaguely.'

'And a woman called Ally Lawson, who's going to be helping me with the baking.'

Marcus frowned. 'How many covers do you have?'

'We can seat thirty inside, and another thirty in the garden—though obviously we'll only be able to use that when the weather's good enough.'

'Then you simply aren't going to have enough staff,' he told her.

She resented the advice, even though she knew he was right. 'I know that—I'm not completely stupid! I'm going to fill in wherever someone is needed—I can bake and wait tables myself. And I'm going to get some casual staff during the summer, when it gets really busy. There are plenty of students around who want jobs.' She swallowed down her desire to have him praise her, and gestured with her hand instead. 'Come through and see the tea-room.'

'The tea-room,' he echoed faintly, as she pushed the door open into a low room with a beamed ceiling.

Marcus thought that it was like stepping back in time—it had dark wood absolutely everywhere and he could smell furniture polish. Each table had a starched white tablecloth with a lace trim flouncing around the legs, and there were brightly polished copper kettles and old-fashioned jugs filled with bluebells.

Donna was proud of what she had achieved, and Marcus Foreman was respected in the business. His opinion was worth something. 'What do you think?'

He didn't need to. 'It's old-fashioned,' he told her bluntly.

'Well, of course it's old-fashioned—afternoon tea always *is*! People don't come to a city like Winchester and trawl round the ancient streets and gaze up at the cathedral and Jane Austen's house in wonder—and expect something high-tech afterwards! They don't want sushi or a three-bean salad! They want featherlight sponges on bone-china plates! Scones with thick cream and homemade jam—just like Mother used to make!'

His eyes narrowed with cruel perception. 'Why, is that what *your* mother used to make?'

Donna blushed, and hated herself for doing so, and thought that if she was a merciless kind of person she might have brought up the subject of *his* mother. 'You know very well she didn't!'

He shook his head. 'But that's where you're wrong, sugar—I don't. I know nothing at all. I thought that your mother was a noble, committed actress, because that's what you led me to believe.'

'With good reason. Seeing as how you set yourself up to pass judgement on everyone else!'

'I have to admit that it came as something of a shock to me,' he continued, as if she hadn't spoken, 'to discover that she used to strip down to a few strategically placed tassels and then gyrate her pelvis in men's faces!'

'And you w-wonder why I never told you?' she demanded shakily. 'Because you haven't got the imagination to see that it was the only option for her! She was a single mother!'

'Not the only option, Donna,' he grated. 'Thousands of women who are single mothers don't become strippers! There are plenty of other jobs available.'

'I'm not ashamed of my mother, or what she did!' she said proudly. 'And whatever *you* say won't make me! However it may have seemed from the outside—*I* know the truth! She may have been misdirected—but she wasn't promiscuous.' She took a deep, shuddering breath.

'She wasn't really interested in men—she was hurt

too badly when my father left. I certainly didn't grow up knowing a series of ''uncles''. She kept her morals, and she didn't just fritter her money away like so many of her colleagues did. She saved, and set herself up in business on the proceeds—'

'That's the bed and breakfast place you were once so scornful of?'

'Yes!' she snapped. 'And that was because I was of an age where I didn't appreciate all her hard work and sacrifice—so of course I was scornful!' And she'd been desperately trying to hide the truth from him. 'But my mother made a success of her B&B. She worked hard!'

He saw her blinking rather rapidly and felt an intrusive pang of conscience. He found that he wanted to draw her into the circle of his arms and stroke that gleaming, fiery hair. He glanced down at a menu instead. 'And what is she doing now?'

'She's dead. She died two and a half years ago. The money from her business helped me buy this place.'

'Donna, I'm—'

'No, you're not!' she told him fiercely. 'Don't say you're sorry, Marcus—because you're not!'

'Listen to me,' he told her, and his voice was just as insistent. 'Of course I'm sorry that she's dead! I lost my own mother when I was a child. I know how badly it hurts—whatever age you are.'

When he spoke like that—in that soft, urgent way, as if the words came straight from the heart—*that* was when he was at his most dangerous, Donna realised. And the danger lay in thinking that he saw her as his equal. And he didn't. He never had.

But he would.

'Well, thank you for that,' she said stiffly.

'Don't sound so surprised. I'm not a complete bad guy.'

'You just do a very convincing imitation, is that it?'

He laughed, and found that he badly wanted to kiss her. And it was a long time since he had wanted to *kiss* a woman.

Donna looked at him, her courage deserting her as she realised that he still had the power to make her want him. Very badly. Had he taken an exam in how to move, she wondered distractedly, so that a woman would get turned on just by watching him?

He was resting his jeaned bottom against one of the tables, his long legs stretching out in front of him, making the table look like a flimsy little stick of dolls' house furniture. And why was he looking at her like that? As if he'd like to eat her up for breakfast.

He met her eyes. She looked so cool and so untouchable and so damned *superior*. 'I notice that you still haven't asked me anything about my baby brother,' he observed. 'Surprising, really—I thought that you and Lucas were the best of buddies.'

'He always found time to talk to me, if that's what you mean.' She wiped her finger along a gleaming surface, delighted to see it come away dust-free. 'How is he?'

He gave a grim smile. 'Isn't it odd that the two of you didn't stay in touch? After all, what Lucas didn't know about you wasn't really worth knowing, was it, Donna? Such a very *intimate* friendship—'

'I was never intimate with your brother!'

'Of course you were,' he scorned softly. 'You shared thoughts. Secrets. You don't have to rip all your clothes off and have sex with someone in order to be intimate, you know!'

She was unprepared for her own soft venom, but maybe it had been silently building up inside since that long-ago night when his virile body had terrified the life out of her and his face had been that of a wild, dark stranger. 'I'm surprised that intimacy is a topic you want to touch on, Marcus.'

Their eyes met.

'Ouch,' he winced softly. 'Be careful, now. If you're going to accuse a man of being a disaster in bed you're going to hit him where he hurts hardest.'

'What, dent his pride, you mean? Or his ego?'

'I was thinking of somewhere a lot more basic than that, sugar,' he taunted, revelling in the fact that by now her cheeks were as hot and as flushed as if she'd just run up a steep hill. 'Challenge a man like that and he's going to respond in one way only. By demanding a repeat performance. What do you say to that, Donna? Shall we let history repeat itself and hope that the outcome is more mutually satisfactory this time?'

Donna froze. Her mouth felt as dry as unbuttered toast. She ignored the question, and all its implications— though she wondered if she would have been able to if he had put his arms around her, instead of discussing it in that cold, clinical way. 'I thought we were talking about Lucas.'

'Ah, yes. Lucas.'

His mouth relaxed into a smile which surprised her— a proud, elder brother kind of smile.

'Well, Lucas seems to have made good—confounding all predictions to the contrary. He took his camera round the world with him and got as far as South America, where—rather amazingly—he fell in love.'

'What's so amazing about that?'

'Well, he'd never managed to stay faithful to a woman

before.' He searched her expression for disappointment, but if there was any then she was hiding it well. 'He married Rosa and is now the proud father of twin boys. He runs a moderately successful studio in Caracas—taking wedding and christening photos and studio portraits. And he seems very contented.'

'Good heavens!' said Donna faintly.

'Heartbroken?'

'Don't be silly. I just can't imagine Lucas as a husband—let alone as a *father*! He always seemed too restless to ever be described as contented.'

'That's what the love of a good woman does for you.' He paused. 'Pity you didn't qualify.'

'I never wanted your brother—'

'But he wanted you.'

'Maybe he did. But that was nothing to do with me. He knew I wasn't interested in him—not in that way.'

He shook his head. 'You played us off against one another, Donna. You know you did. I was the lucky recipient of all those smouldering looks you used to send out—but it was Lucas who was treated to all the cosy little chats, wasn't it?'

Donna frowned in confusion. He made it sound as if he had been excluded. 'But you didn't want that kind of relationship,' she protested. 'Not with me, anyway. You held me at arm's length, Marcus—you know you did. You used to clam up if anything remotely *personal* ever reared its ugly head. You were so busy being the boss. Keeping your distance.'

'Just not very effectively,' he observed, and his voice sounded bitter. 'Well, not in your case.' He shook his head as the memory buzzed like a persistent fly. 'I thought you were sexually experienced, Donna—I really did. When I discovered you were a virgin I couldn't believe it! I was astonished—'

'But not pleased?'

'No,' he said bluntly.

It still hurt more than it had a right to. 'I thought that it was every man's fantasy. To be the first lover.'

'Not this man.'

She didn't stop to ask him why because she had a good idea what he might say. Virgins were girls who had grown up in dinky houses with fitted carpets. The kind of girl that men ended up marrying. Not the kind of girl they wanted a quick fling with.

She stared at him, dazzled by the beauty of his eyes as their ice-blue light washed over her face. 'So what do you want, Marcus?' she demanded. 'Why have you come here today?'

He narrowed his eyes assessingly. Didn't she know? Couldn't she tell? That he wanted to eradicate all those memories of that night and to replace them with something which would make her ache with longing.

And the way he was behaving towards her—he wouldn't even make it past first base.

'What happened to all your freckles?' he asked suddenly, leaning fractionally forward so that her flesh radiated its warmth towards him.

It was such an abrupt change of mood and subject that Donna screwed her eyes up at him. 'Freckles?' she repeated suspiciously.

'Those tiny brown marks sprinkled all over your face,' he teased. 'You used to have more—your skin was covered in them. Remember?'

'I started staying out of the sun,' she answered.

'And you lost them along the way, with the frizzy hair and the dungarees?'

It should have sounded like a slur, but when he said it in that oddly indulgent way it was very nearly a compliment. Suddenly Donna felt more than nervous. When he was being nice to her, like this, she was just a hair's breadth away from feeling as vulnerable as she'd ever been in his company.

'My hair is still frizzy when it's untied,' she told him repressively. 'And I still wear dungarees when I'm not working.'

'Do you?' He was silent for a moment as he stared down into her smooth, pale face and was filled with a nostalgic desire to see her looking the way she used to. With those big, fat ginger plaits and the freckle-spattered face and her oddly secretive smile.

Unthinkingly, he allowed the tip of his tongue to slick the corners of his mouth, and found her following the movement with eyes which managed to be both fascinated and disapproving.

'Licking your lips?' she observed. 'Don't you get fed properly?'

'Why, are you offering?'

'I've got quite enough catering to be going on with,' she answered coolly. 'Now, I really think it's time you were going, Marcus—you've seen just about everything there is to see.'

'Not the garden,' he objected.

'You'll get your opportunity to see that tomorrow.' She met his eyes. 'If you're planning on coming?'

He fought against his better judgement, and lost. 'I wouldn't miss it for the world,' he murmured.

CHAPTER FIVE

'DONNA—you've worked miracles!'

Donna smiled politely at the Mayor's wife, who had worked something of a miracle herself, she thought. The miracle being how she managed to remain standing after eating three rounds of smoked salmon sandwiches, four scones with cream and jam and an enormous wedge of coffee and walnut cake!

'Why, thank you, Mrs Armstrong! Can I fetch you another cup of tea?'

'Oh, would you, dear? That last piece of cake has made me terribly thirsty.'

'I'll go and get it,' said Donna. She made her way through the tea-room, smiling at people on the way, noting with satisfaction that every single table was full. Just by the kitchen door she passed Ally, who was pushing her way out, bearing a tray loaded with vanilla butterfly cakes and slices of lemon madeira.

'What do you reckon?' whispered Donna. 'Do we have a success on our hands?'

'We most certainly do! I'd even do a thumbs-up if I didn't have my hands full!' laughed Ally. 'You can sit back and rest on your laurels once they've all gone!'

'They don't really show much sign of going, do they?' said Donna.

'Not really. Though I suppose we shouldn't complain. Most restaurateurs complain about the trouble they have getting people *in*—not getting them out! I'd better go and feed the hungry masses. I'll see you later,' said Ally.

In the kitchen, Sarah was busy putting scones onto a beautiful bone-china plate. She saw Donna and turned her eyes up to heaven. 'Just how many did you invite, for heaven's sake? Did no one at all turn you down?'

'Oh, just a couple,' said Donna lightly. 'No one important.' She had tried to tell herself that she wasn't disappointed. So *what* if Marcus hadn't shown?

So why did she keep looking up every time the bell rang on the front door? Only to have to force a smile when she saw that it wasn't who she'd thought it might be.

But the afternoon had been a huge success.

As well as the Mayor, they had managed to get their local Member of Parliament to squeeze a brief cup of Lapsang Suchong into his busy schedule. The press had arrived early, and stayed longer than expected, especially when Donna had produced a wine cask from the fridge because they'd all claimed that they didn't want to drink tea.

A female journalist's eyes had lit up briefly as her antennae tested whether there was a story. 'Are you allowed to serve alcohol here?' she had asked doubtfully.

'Oh, yes—I've got my drinks licence,' Donna had said proudly. 'During the winter I'm going to serve mulled wine and mince pies.'

'Yum!' the journalist had said.

After a good deal of discussion Donna, Ally and Sarah had all worn shiny black short-sleeved dresses which came to the knee, with cute little white muslin aprons over the top. And they had all been convulsed with the giggles while trying them on.

'These are our "special occasion" dresses!' announced Donna. 'For high days and holidays!'

'Donna, I can't wear this!' Sarah had protested. 'I look like every man's fantasy of a French maid!'

'Only if your skirt were half that length—with lacy-topped stockings showing,' Donna had argued. 'Any-way—there's no law written down that says that wait-resses have to wear unflattering clothes. You both look absolutely gorgeous, if you must know!'

'Well, so do you,' Ally had said, with a wink.

When everyone had gone home at last, they cleared the tables, put all the clean glass and china away and swept the kitchen floor. Then the three women flopped down at a table and congratulated themselves on the ef-ficient service they had provided.

'Wasn't that man supposed to be coming?' asked Sarah.

'Man?' Ally did a mock double-take. 'Did I hear you mention a *man*?'

Donna liked Ally, and had been glad to give her the job. She was thirty-three, attractive and blonde. And sep-arated. Her husband had left her—saying that he wanted to spend his life with a woman he had met in a hotel bar. He had told Ally that he was 'sorry' for the disrup-tion he was causing, and what he'd said to Charlotte—their five-year-old daughter—was anyone's guess. So far, according to Ally, she was unable to speak of her father without bursting into noisy tears.

'Which man are we talking about?' persisted Ally, looking round the empty tea-room as if a member of the opposite sex might suddenly materialise.

'Donna's friend,' said Sarah. 'The tall, good-looking one with the dark hair. But he's not here.'

'He's not my friend,' protested Donna. 'I don't even like him.'

'Oh, don't you?' said Sarah, clearly not believing a

word of it. 'So why did you show him round the place yesterday, looking all pink and excited and hot underneath the collar?'

Donna sighed. 'Because I used to work for him. And I *wasn't* pink-faced and excited.'

'Er, *right*,' said Ally, screwing her face up in confusion. 'Has he got a name?'

'Yes, it's Foreman,' said Donna reluctantly, knowing that Ally was a local girl and wondering if she had heard of him.

Ally's eyes widened. She clearly had.

'Not Marcus Foreman?'

'That's the one.'

'Mmm! What's he like?'

Donna hesitated. 'He's—'

'He's standing right over there,' said Sarah, from out of the corner of her mouth.

Donna looked up to see Marcus framed on the threshold of the doorway, a shaft of sunshine gilding the edges of his hair so that he resembled a dark, gleaming angel.

Their eyes connected and then he smiled, and something extraordinary happened to Donna as he began walking towards her. It was like a blurred picture coming into focus. Like coming inside from the bitter cold. The world and her place in it suddenly made sense. Her resistance flew and she stared up at him, feeling as punch-drunk as a boxer.

'Hello, Marcus,' she said weakly.

'Hello, Donna. How did it go?'

'If you'd been here when you should have been you would have found out for yourself.'

He found the rebuke stimulating. But right then he found everything about her stimulating. Especially in that outrageously sexy black dress, with the pure white apron over the top. 'You said you were going to show me the garden, remember?' He gave a crinkly smile at the other two women. 'But maybe you'd better introduce me first.'

Sarah's facial muscles went into a kind of spasm as she gazed up at him.

Donna almost smiled. It would be funny if it wasn't so predictable. 'Sarah Flowers. Ally Lawson. This is Marcus Foreman.'

Sarah and Ally both leapt to their feet as if the movement had been scripted.

'I've been past your hotel millions of times!' babbled Sarah. 'But of course I've never eaten there.'

'Why not?' he asked.

Ally came to Sarah's rescue. 'It's a wee bit too expensive,' she said bluntly.

Marcus smiled. 'People usually find that it's far less expensive than they imagine—in fact it's comparable to plenty of other restaurants with lower ratings. Tell you what,' he added thoughtfully, 'if each of you want to bring a partner—say on a Monday or Tuesday evening, when we're quiet—you can eat there on me!'

'Gosh, thanks!' beamed Sarah.

'Yes, thanks very much!' echoed Ally.

They left soon after, and Donna stood and waved them off down the street, where the cherry blossom was being rained down in a pale pink storm by a suddenly blustery April wind.

She locked the door behind them and went back into the tea-room to find that Marcus hadn't moved, and her heart lurched with a fierce kind of excitement at the way he was staring at her.

'That was very kind of you,' she said unsteadily. 'To offer Ally and Sarah a free meal.'

He raised his eyebrows. 'Don't sound so surprised.'

'I'm not, actually. You like playing the role of bene-factor—you did it to me, remember?'

He bit back his automatic reply to *that* unwittingly provocative remark. 'You have the ability to make an act of kindness sound like a character defect, Donna.'

'Do I? I'm sorry.' She didn't know whether to sit or stand. She felt uncomfortable, too aware of herself. And him.

'You still haven't told me how your opening went.'

'I know I haven't.' She looked him straight in the eye. 'But that's not why you're here, is it? If you were in-terested in the fortunes of my tea-room you would have turned up on time like everyone else and seen for your-self. Wouldn't you?'

His smile was rueful. 'I guess I would.'

'So what, then?'

'You want the truth?'

She nodded.

'You don't need me to tell you, Donna. You know yourself.' His eyes had never been bluer. 'I want to make love to you.'

Her mouth fell open. *'Marcus!'*

He shook his head. 'You should never have come back if you didn't want this to happen,' he told her softly, and his words were like a sweet caress on her skin. 'Nine years ago we blew everything—and I want the chance to put it right.'

'Oh. I see.' Her heart plummeted with disappointment. But then what had she been expecting—a declaration of undying love? 'Was I the one lover who didn't give you full marks for performance? Is that what this is all about?'

'No. It's about getting rid of a desire that isn't going

to go away. Look me in the eye, Donna, and tell me truthfully that you don't want me just as badly. Do that and I'll go away and leave you alone.'

She couldn't.

If only he would play the game. Tell her that he'd never stopped thinking about her, that he couldn't go on living without her. But he was an honest man. She knew that. Everything in his world was black and white. 'Don't do this to me, Marcus,' she whispered. 'Please. I can't fight you.'

'I don't want you to fight me,' he whispered back. 'I want you to give in to what you really want to do.'

His voice moved over her senses and she shook her head distractedly.

The movement made his eyes darken, and unexpectedly he reached up and touched her hair and the gesture took her completely off her guard. 'Amazing,' he murmured. 'I've never met another woman with hair like yours, Donna. Like fire. Rich and raw and hot.' He was conscious of echoing words he had spoken to her once before, as if he wanted to re-run the film and change the ending. 'Why don't you kiss me, huh? Come on, sugar. Kiss me.'

Over the years she had erected a wall around her heart, and Marcus was demolishing it, brick by brick, exposing the emotional wasteland which lay beneath. She jerked her head back with an effort. 'We shouldn't be doing this.'

'I don't agree, and neither do you, not really. I can read it in your eyes. And your body.' His eyes flickered over the black satin dress that made the curves of her body so luscious and irresistible. He could see the swell of her breasts as they strained against the material, their rock-hard tips pushing towards him, and he thought he might pass out with longing. 'See for yourself if you don't believe me.'

Donna glanced down at her swollen breasts, her fingers flying protectively to her throat, and she looked down in horror to discover that her hand was shaking uncontrollably.

And he saw, too. Saw and smiled. 'Yes,' he said slowly. 'Yes, I thought so.' His gaze licked over her like warm syrup as he took her trembling hand in his, locking their fingers together and guiding them to lie over the muffled thundering of his heart. 'Can you feel that?'

Her lips seemed glued together. She wasn't able to answer him. Or look at him. All she could do was feel the pumping of his life-blood beneath her fingertips.

She lifted her gaze to his, her eyes full of question and need, and her breath escaped in a gentle sound as she saw the desire which had darkened his eyes.

'Kiss me, Donna,' he urged again. 'You know you want to.'

She trembled. 'S-sometimes I want to eat more ice-cream than I should—doesn't mean I'm going to do it.'

Without any warning, he brought his mouth crushing down on hers. The last time he had kissed her she had felt like a gawky novice in his arms. She had been too overwhelmed by him not to feel terrible, debilitating nerves. But not this time.

She opened her lips and shuddered, lost in the erotic power of his kiss. 'That…wasn't fair!' she gasped.

'Maybe not, but it was good, wasn't it?' he murmured. 'I know what you want, don't I? Maybe I always did. Just back then I was too selfish. And I'm going to make it up to you.'

He brought the palms of his hands around her back and down her spine until they cupped her satin-covered bottom to bring her into the cradle of his hips, and she whimpered as she felt him rock against her. 'This time I'm going to take it slow.'

'Marcus...' Was that hot, jerky little voice really hers?

He was kissing her neck, the curve of her jaw. 'I'm going to have you calling my name out loud,' he said indistinctly. 'I'm going to give you so much pleasure that you'll be begging me to stop!'

She couldn't believe that he was saying these things to her, and she couldn't believe how much it was turning her on, bringing her to a fever-pitch of excitement that made her gasp something that was muffled and indistinct.

He lifted his head, his eyes glazed. 'What is it?'

'I don't *know,*' she almost wept.

He began to lift up the satin skirt of her dress. The air was like a cool whisper on her thighs and she felt the pooling of unbearable need as she swayed against him.

He looked down at her. 'Want to go somewhere else?'

She wanted... 'I want—'

'Tell me, sugar. Tell me what it is you want.'

'You *know*!' she gasped. Nine years she had waited to have him do this to her again. Only this time she wasn't going to ruin it with her naive hopes and expectations. 'You know damned well!'

He lifted his head from her neck to look at her flushed face and his smile was triumphant and heartbreakingly predatory. Oh, yes, he knew all right.

Hell, much more of feeling her breasts jutting tantalisingly into his chest like that and he... But just imagine if a passing tourist should glance in through the window and see them. Think what *that* would do for his reputation!

Or hers.

He drew a deep breath to clip an urgent sentence out. 'Where's your bedroom?'

Somewhere, even in the hot mists of unstoppable desire, Donna heard warning bells. No, not there. A room where he would be surrounded by all *her* things. Because that was where it had all gone wrong last time, when he had been the big, virile lover and she the foolish, frightened virgin. She didn't want Marcus cramped this time, or daunted by her narrow bed and the starched and frilly white linen she had accumulated over the years. Her room was too feminine for a man like Marcus. He would have no place there.

She shook her head. 'Not my bedroom.'

For one horrific and unimaginable moment he really thought she was going to kick him out, and he could barely get his next words out. 'Where, then?'

'Upstairs.'

'Want to take me there?'

'O-okay.'

'I'm half tempted to carry you,' he growled as he saw her move with the gawky uncertainty of a newborn foal.

'No, don't. You couldn't.'

'Want to bet?' He could hardly believe what he was doing as he took her by the hand and swung her easily over his shoulder in a fireman's lift to carry her up the stairs. What was happening to him? Since when had he decided to play masterful?

He was careful to keep his eyes averted from the obvious distractions of her bottom—otherwise he suspected he might go tumbling back down the way he had come. And in a way he was glad to have the physical diversion of carrying her. It took the edge off his passion, and maybe that was what he needed where she was concerned. For there must be no repeat of last time…

'Just here,' whispered Donna.

He pushed open the door with his knee and set her down, barely noticing the fittings or the decor—just that the bed was huge, thank God. He turned to the woman by his side, her eyes huge and dark and green in a face tight-white with expectation.

He bent his head and negligently brushed his lips against hers. 'Now,' he said indistinctly, 'where were we?'

'I don't remember,' she gasped.

He kissed her until her knees grew weak, and then began to unbutton the tiny satin-covered buttons which ran down the entire length of her dress, but his fingers were trembling and the aching in his groin was unbearable. He couldn't believe that this was happening to him again. He felt powerless—as if some great, ungovernable force was controlling him. He lifted his mouth away from hers. 'Can you do this?' he beseeched.

Her fingers were only marginally less shaky than his, but she guessed it was easier to take off your own clothes than someone else's, and soon the dress had been slung in a far corner of the bedroom.

And Marcus was down to a T-shirt and a pair of black silk boxer shorts.

Donna swallowed and stared at him, unable to tear her eyes away.

He pulled his T-shirt off in a single movement and saw her hand reach round to her back to unclip her bra. He let his eyes drink in the creamy flesh which spilled over the confining black lace.

'No, don't. Leave it on!' he said unsteadily. 'And

come here.' He pulled back the cover and climbed into bed, holding his arms out to her, and she went into them like a child going home, almost falling on top of him in her eagerness to be enfolded in that warm embrace.

'Oh, Donna,' he said softly, and ran his fingertips around the oval curve of her jaw. 'You little beauty.'

She could feel muscle and bone through the warm satin of his skin, and the hot, hard throb of desire nudging against her. 'I can't believe I'm here, like this. Doing this,' she stumbled. 'With you. I told myself I never would, no matter what the provocation.'

He tipped up her chin so that she couldn't escape his penetrating stare. 'For God's sake, Donna—if you don't want to go through with it then tell me—but tell me now!'

She shook her head. 'You know I couldn't let you go, even if I wanted to.' Her lashes fluttered down to partially conceal her eyes. 'And I don't,' she added huskily.

He gave a moan as he pulled her over him, moving her up the bed so that he could unclip her bra, and her breasts came tumbling out, one falling with sweet accuracy into his mouth.

'Mmm. Bullseye!' he murmured, and Donna actually giggled.

'That's better,' he said approvingly.

He suckled her while she moaned and wriggled against him until he thought he would explode with need like a champagne cork.

'Slide my shorts off,' he whispered, and his fingers flicked tantalisingly at her panties as she did so, the tips coming away moist and fragrant with her musky, feminine scent. He placed his middle finger in her mouth, their eyes locking helplessly as she sucked on it.

'Oh, God,' she whimpered.

'Do you like that?'

'*Yes!*' she almost sobbed.

'Want to make love?'

'*Yes!*'

He felt her reaching to find him, exquisitely encircling him as she had once done as an untutored girl. And it was with a feeling of *déjà vu* that something nudged insistently at his memory. 'Are you on the pill these days?'

Her reply was nearly, Of course not—except that there was no 'of course' about it.

And there was no reason in the world for her to be offended by what was, in fact, a very sensible question. Especially under the circumstances. Why wouldn't he think she was on the pill? Most women of her age were. 'No. No, I'm not.'

He swore softly as his hand groped down to find his jeans and fumbled around until he had fished a packet of condoms out of the back pocket.

He slid the protection on with both regret and relief, part of him wanting no barrier between them. But only a foolish, inconsequential part. And that was when he stopped thinking and started feeling as he thrust long and hard and drove deep into her hot, welcoming flesh.

When Donna opened her eyes it had grown dark, and she blinked once or twice, wondering why she was sleeping in the guest bedroom and what exactly had woken her.

Until a slight movement set off the first trigger of recollection and memory washed over her bare skin like a warm bath. She became aware that her breasts were tingling, their tips still prickling with sweet sensation, aware too of an aching deep inside her. As if she had been using muscles she had never used before. Maybe she had. She smiled as she reached out to click the lamp on, and the room was flooded with light.

Stretching lazily, she turned her head to see Marcus pulling on his jeans, the look on his face changing from one of dark and flushed contentment to a closed and wary expression when he saw her watching him.

'Hi,' he said.

She might have hoped for something a little less non-committal, in view of what they had been doing over the last few hours.

Still. Just because they had both enjoyed the best sex ever, that didn't mean he was about to start telling her he loved her! That would just be a bonus, she thought rather wistfully.

'Hi,' she said, and smiled as she sat up, her hair half-in and half-out of the French plait, and strands of it falling over her freckled shoulders.

Marcus averted his eyes from the spectacular movement of her breasts, but it was too late to stop his body responding. He bent down to try and locate his watch and hoped that she hadn't noticed.

He still felt shaken by what had just happened. He had made love to her over and over again—more times than he had ever done to a woman before. But he had been unprepared for the power of their lovemaking. He had experienced blissful abandonment, yes—but it had overwhelmed him in a way that was completely alien to him. And he wasn't sure that he liked it.

'I didn't want to wake you,' he said, as he hunted around for his shoe.

'Was that why you were creeping around like a thief?'

He found the shoe and slipped it on, then buckled up

his wristwatch. 'Actually, you looked so peaceful lying there that I thought I'd leave you.'

Donna sighed. She wasn't going to clutch onto his ankles to prevent him from leaving the room, but neither was she going to act as if they had spent the afternoon talking about the state of the economy! 'And of course the advantage of leaving me to sleep is that you could avoid having to answer any awkward questions.'

He went very still. 'You make it sound like I'm on trial.'

'Not really. I just wondered what the hurry was, that's all. I mean, I presume you haven't got somebody else to rush back to?'

'Shouldn't you have asked that *before* we went to bed?' he drawled.

Like the stereotype of a possessive girlfriend, she heard herself saying, 'Is that a yes or a no?'

His mouth thinned. 'I only ever sleep with one woman at a time.'

That hurt. And so did the dismissive way he spoke, which meant that Donna couldn't pretend any longer even if she'd wanted to. And suddenly she didn't want to. She wasn't a little girl who couldn't face knowing the truth—however much it hurt.

'You know, I'm getting the distinct impression that we have just made our second big mistake, Marcus.'

He tugged the T-shirt down and tucked it into the waistband of his jeans. 'Mistake?' he queried, looking faintly surprised, as if this were perfectly normal behaviour and she was breaking some unspoken code of conduct. 'Oh, Donna, please don't let us go down that route! Nobody had to drag you to bed. Not this time—nor the time before. You were the one who came back to Winchester. You were the one who walked into my restaurant giving me the green light. What did you expect? You must have known that something like this would happen.'

The green light? She kept her voice calm—though heaven only knew how. 'Okay, maybe I'm overreacting. So why the long face and the keep-away body language? And why now—after what just happened. It was good, wasn't it?'

'It was bloody fantastic,' he said softly. 'You know it was.'

'Well, then?'

Marcus screwed his eyes up, as though a light were blinding them. He seemed to choose his words carefully. 'I don't like what you make me become.'

'And what's that?'

His voice deepened. 'You saw for yourself. You don't need me to tell you.'

Donna nodded. She had been stunned by the depth of his passion, at the way he had stripped away layer upon layer of himself—to reveal a tantalising glimpse of what lay at the very core of the man. The free spirit which had been obscured by the burden of responsibility. Surely he had the courage to face up to the truth?

'You mean you're worried that you'll end up like your mother?'

There was a long, fraught silence. 'What do you know about my mother?' he asked icily.

'Lots.'

The blue eyes looked frozen. 'How?'

'Lucas told me.'

'Oh, did he? And what exactly did he say?'

'That she was beautiful. And wild. And that she was unfaithful to your father—time and time again. He said that the rows which resulted were so bad you both had to be sent away to school, but that he couldn't bear to divorce her.'

'And did he say anything else?' he asked, in a deceptively silky voice.

Donna shrugged. 'He said that she was out of control.' She met his furious gaze with a candid stare. 'And that's how you were today, wasn't it, Marcus? Out of control.'

Tense seconds ticked by. 'Your comments aren't just intrusive—they're inaccurate. Passion has nothing to do with fidelity. And fidelity is a matter of personal choice.'

'Marcus—'

'As amateur psychologists I'm afraid you and Lucas leave a lot to be desired,' he continued, and his mouth hardened. 'Don't tell me that you were spinning fantasies, Donna. Expecting to hear me say that you're the one and only just because we had an afternoon of great sex?'

'Of course I wasn't.' Donna pulled the bedspread up to cover her bare breasts.

'The debt I owed you has been cancelled,' he added softly. 'So we're quits now.'

She could scarcely get the words out. 'You mean…you've redeemed yourself—sexually—by giving me the orgasms I missed out on before?'

His look of outrage was worth what it had cost her to reduce their afternoon to simple mechanics.

'I wouldn't have put it quite like that.'

'Oh? How would you have put it, then? Dressed it up with a euphemism? The earth moved! The bell rang!'

'Don't spoil what just happened!' he snapped. 'Just face up to the truth, the same way that I have had to. There's too much history between us, Donna. Too much water has flowed underneath the bridge—not just a gentle stream in our case, more like a bloody great torrent!'

She returned his mocking glance with a face devoid of expression. And why was she cowering beneath the bedclothes as if she was still the humble chambermaid and he was still her lord and master?

She slid her long legs over the side of the bed and heard his gasp as the covers fell away and she stood up like Venus rising out of the waves.

He swallowed. 'What are you doing?'

'I'm going to fetch my clothes from next door. So that I can see you out. There's no crime against that, is there?'

Marcus stood there, open-mouthed. In the heat of passion his vision had been limited to whichever particular area had been given his undivided attention. Seen in isolation, each breast was utterly magnificent, the indentation of her waist just perfect and the swell of her bottom every man's most torrid fantasy.

But put them together and you had sheer perfection.

A comment that Lucas had once made came drifting back over the years. 'You can see why her mother was a stripper!' And the blatantly sexy compliment toughened his resolve.

'I can see myself out.'

Donna's eyes hardened. 'What's the matter? Ashamed to be seen leaving in case anyone knows what you've been up to? Well, don't worry, Marcus—people can't tell you've had sex just by looking at you, you know! Besides, I want to lock up behind you.' And she wiggled out of the room to find some clothes.

He waited, feeling more het-up and confused than he could ever remember. She was nothing but a manipulating little witch! Why had she waited until he was dressed and ready to leave before flaunting her body at him like that?

When Donna reappeared she had redone her French plait and put on a pair of jeans and an old plaid shirt.

Marcus should have felt less agitated, but he didn't. Suddenly she looked so scrubbed and *wholesome*. Funny how that could be just as erotic as satin and lace.

'Let's go,' she said coldly, and she led the way downstairs.

They didn't say a word to one another as he followed her towards the front door, and the loud ringing of the doorbell made them both start.

Now who the hell was *that*? wondered Donna, and she pulled open the door to find Tony Paxman standing on the doorstep, a foolish grin on his face and a bottle of champagne in his hand.

Marcus felt mad jealousy rip through him as the good-looking lawyer handed her the wine and gave a helpless kind of smile.

'Hi, Donna. Sorry I'm late—I had to go to court with a client. This is for you.' He nodded cautiously. 'Hi, Marcus.'

Marcus gave a grim nod.

'Oh, how thoughtful of you, Tony!' enthused Donna, overplaying her gratitude like mad. 'Come in!'

Tony looked at Marcus. 'Oh, but you're—'

'No, I'm not! Marcus is just leaving—aren't you, Marcus? Come and have a drink with me, Tony—I feel like celebrating! Have a wander round while I'm seeing Marcus out.'

The lawyer stepped inside, and Donna almost recoiled from the black, baleful look that Marcus sent searing in her direction.

'Goodbye,' she said quietly.

'Goodbye, Donna.' His glance was unfathomable as he watched Tony Paxman disappearing down the hallway. Then he looked into her eyes. 'A word of advice,' he said softly.

If she had known what was coming she would never have asked him. 'What?'

'Just don't forget to change the sheets first, huh?'

There was a short, breathless pause. She wanted to scream, but she didn't want to make a scene.

Instead, she shut the door firmly in his face.

CHAPTER SIX

TEMPERAMENTAL April drifted into glorious, golden May.

Donna went to an auction and bought a job lot of neglected garden furniture. She spent every evening rubbing it down and painting it all dark green, then she dotted the restored tables and chairs out onto the newly mown lawn.

They looked perfect in her own secret garden, where the spreading branches of the apple trees were bursting into tiny pink and white blossoms. Soon they would be able to start serving tea outside regularly—at the moment it was on sunny days only.

And business was booming. It seemed that Winchester had been crying out for a good, old-fashioned tea-room, because the public had greeted its arrival like an old friend. Every day they were full.

It appealed to people right across the board. The older generation approved because they could remember when afternoon tea had been a regular feature on the culinary calendar. The younger people liked it because they wished it still *was* taken regularly—or so they told Donna. It was popular with courting couples too, because tea was essentially a romantic meal, where people could linger unbothered over the scones. And tourists adored it because it fitted in with their perception of what traditional England was really like.

The days were long and busy, with Donna getting up at the crack of dawn to start making cakes and scones.

She enjoyed the warmth and smell of the baking, and the sound of the radio playing and the birds singing outside. The Buttress had become her haven. After a long time searching, she felt she had at last come home.

In fact, there was only one faint cloud on her horizon, and that was Marcus—or, more accurately, what had happened with Marcus upstairs in the guest bedroom. But as the days blurred by even that became understandable. Acceptable, even. She was determined to be modern and mature about the experience. To remember the good bits and blot out the bad.

As a relationship it was a non-starter, but she could accept that. Of course she could. In fact, she couldn't think of a single other woman of her acquaintance who had not had something similar happen to her.

She had wondered how she would cope if she kept bumping into him, but she did not bump into him. Not once.

She saw him a couple of times from a safe distance, and once when they were both shopping at Winchester's open-air market. She felt an almost savage jolt of recognition as she spotted his tall, dark figure across the square, and she could have *sworn* that he'd seen her. But he didn't come over. Just walked resolutely on.

She realised what insular lives they led. Marcus had his own little world and she had hers. They lived on opposite sides of the same street, but they might have lived on opposite sides of the world for all that their lives collided.

It was towards the end of May that the first niggling little doubt began to bother her in her quieter moments.

She made excuses.

She had been busy/stressed/worried. She had changed jobs/changed area/changed home. But then a couple of days became a couple of weeks, and her anxiety levels shot up—until she convinced herself that there was nothing to worry about.

Lots of women were late—and it wasn't as though she could be pregnant, was it? Donna felt her cheeks burning as she remembered how Marcus had sworn and insisted on wearing a condom. Every time. He had been determined that she shouldn't get pregnant.

No, her lateness was obviously psychological in origin.

She kept telling herself the same thing over and over again, even after May had slipped into June. But when she saw the 'July' written in black and white on the calendar she knew that she had to snap out of her denial mode and see whether her worst fears were about to be realised.

She drove to an out-of-town pharmacy and bought a pregnancy testing kit, and the following morning the blue indicator line in the test-tube told her that, yes, the worst-case scenario had actually happened.

She was pregnant.

Pregnant and alone and frightened. Knowing that she ought to tell someone, and knowing who the someone should be, and unable to face doing it.

She went to see her doctor, who destroyed her last remaining fantasy that maybe the result of the test had been false.

'Yes, you're pregnant.' She smiled. 'And you're a fit and healthy young woman—I can't see there being any problems. Congratulations!' she added, but Donna's lack of response made her frown. 'I *do* take it that congratulations are in order?'

Something primitive and protective stirred deep

within Donna's belly and consigned her doubts to history. 'Yes,' she said. 'They are. Thank you.'

'And the father?' asked Dr Baxter delicately. 'Is he around?'

'Er, not exactly.'

'Well, is he going to be supporting you?'

'I don't know,' said Donna simply. 'I haven't told him yet.'

She was longing to confide in someone. Ally, perhaps—who was a single mother herself. Or Sarah. But the troublesome voice of her conscience knew that she could not talk to them before she had talked to the one person she did not want to talk to.

She put it off and put it off, burying her head in the sand, as if by telling no one it would make it seem as if it wasn't real.

Except that it was real. The tingling weight of her newly aching breasts was real enough. As was the nausea, which seemed to be entirely random in when it hit her. One week she felt sick in the morning, the next her evenings were spent hovering within easy reach of a basin.

She put off telling anyone until one of her regular check-ups, when Dr Baxter beamed at her and said, 'Well, well, Donna. You've started showing at last, haven't you?'

'Sh-showing?'

Dr Baxter sent her a rather odd look and her voice was very gentle. 'That's right.' She smoothed her hand over the barely noticeable curve. 'It *is* usual in these circumstances for a woman to start looking as though she's going to have a baby, you know.'

That was the word which brought Donna swiftly to her senses.

Baby. It was a real word in the way that 'pregnancy' wasn't real. She couldn't put it off any longer. She had to tell him.

As soon as she got back to the tea-room she rang up the hotel before she could change her mind.

The phone was answered by a sexy female voice—all low and husky and French. Donna couldn't imagine the owner of that voice being stupid enough to find herself in the situation that *she* was in.

'Hello, this is The New Hampshire Hotel, Francine speaking. How may I 'elp you?'

'Um, I'd like to speak to Marcus Foreman.'

'And your name, please?'

'It's King. Donna King.' She had a short, humiliating wait before the voice came back.

'I am very sorry, madam, but Mr Foreman is very busy at the moment. Can I take a message?'

Donna was tempted to hang up. Or shout. Or swear. But it wasn't Francine's fault. She drew a deep breath instead. 'Could you tell him to contact me, please? I need to speak to him. Urgently.'

'That's all?'

All? How much more did she want? 'Yes, thank you. That's all.'

'He knows your number?'

'He knows where I live. The number is in the book.' And Donna hung up and went to put the hot water urn on.

He arrived that same day, when she was hanging the 'Closed' sign in the window. He was wearing a grey sweater with his black jeans, and he looked curiously sombre. Donna opened the door to him, thinking that he was going to look even more sombre in a few minutes' time.

'Hello, Marcus.' She managed a smile. 'Come in.'

'Hello, Donna,' he said warily.

He didn't say anything else until they were in her small sitting room upstairs. He looked around him, as if checking that nobody else was in the room.

'I was surprised to get your call.'

'But you didn't,' she said archly. 'Remember? You refused to take it.'

'I was in the middle of a meeting. I'm up to my eyes with plans for opening the new hotel, remember—as well as having a business to run—'

'So do I!'

He gave a short laugh. 'This is chicken-feed in comparison—and I'm not being insulting—'

'Yes, you are!'

He sighed, realising that he'd been right to stay away. 'You see? This is what happens whenever we get together, Donna. We fight—or fall into bed.'

'We never used to fight,' said Donna sadly. 'So what changed?'

Marcus shook his head as though she was being especially gullible. 'I can tell you exactly. It happened once we became involved physically—it's as simple as that. That's what changed our friendship. Sex changes everything, Donna—didn't you know that?'

Donna started feeling nervous. 'Er, yes, it certainly does.'

He looked at her. 'So?' And, on meeting her confused look, elaborated, 'Why did you want to see me?'

'Do you want to sit down? Shall I make us some tea first?' Suddenly any activity seemed preferable to having to tell him her news.

'No. Thank you.' His body had altered, it was full of

tension now, as though his senses had already alerted him of the danger to come.

What way was there to tell him? How on earth could she break it to him softly?

'I'm pregnant,' said Donna bluntly.

He was silent for no more than a split-second. 'Congratulations,' he said evenly. 'Who's the lucky man?'

Donna stared at him. 'Pardon?'

'The father,' he explained. 'Of your child.'

Donna shook her head in disbelief and the French plait felt as heavy as lead as it snaked down her spine. Even in her very worst nightmares she could never have dreamed that he would be so insensitive.

'Why, you are—of course.'

The expression in his eyes was chilling. 'There's no "of course" about it. In fact, as a candidate, I'm least likely to be the father, surely? We used a condom. Remember?'

'Candidate?' She selected the one word which had jarred more than anything else he had said and repeated it incredulously, trying to steady the rapid rise in her breathing. 'Are you…?' She struggled to complete the sentence. 'Are you implying what I think you're implying? That any number of men could be the father?'

He shrugged. 'You tell me.'

Donna resisted the desire to flail her fingernails at his mocking, sarcastic face—something she couldn't even blame on her rocketing hormones. She'd wanted to do something very similar that day when…when he had made that remark about changing the sheets after Tony Paxman had arrived.

Suddenly she got a glimmering of the way his warped mind was working, and she felt quite violently sick.

Her hand flew to her mouth and her words were muffled as a consequence. 'You don't honestly think that I jumped straight from your bed into Tony Paxman's?'

'But you weren't *in* my bed, were you, Donna? You never have been. The action all took place here. Who knows what followed next? I didn't exactly have to mount a long and strategic campaign to seduce you, did I? Why should I flatter myself that Tony Paxman would be any different?'

Donna stared at him, feeling like an animal that had been shot and wounded. Enough to traumatise but not enough to inflict a mortal blow.

Was this what had she agonised over for days and days and weeks and weeks? Was this why she had felt honour-bound to tell him? For *this*?

She felt her knees begin to give way. Saw the bright, blurry stars which danced across her line of vision like a Jackson Pollock painting. Her body was a burning core but her forehead was icy with sweat, and when she spoke her words were almost unintelligible.

'Get out! Go on—out!' she croaked, and sat down abruptly on the sofa and shut her eyes with exhaustion.

When she opened them again Marcus was bending over her, flapping a glossy magazine over her face in an attempt to circulate the air.

His own face, she noted with some satisfaction, was tight with tension.

She tried to sit up, but he shook his head and restrained her, with the flat of his hand pushed gently against one shoulder.

She wriggled like a captive eel. 'Keep your hands off me!'

'It's a little late in the day for that, surely?' was his wry reply. 'Would you like something to drink?'

'I feel like a good, stiff brandy if you must know!'

'Well, you can't have it,' he answered repressively. 'Not in your condition.'

'Condition?' Donna nearly burst into noisy sobs. 'It's such a corny word!'

'It's a pretty corny situation all round,' he said bitterly, and turned towards the door.

'Where are you going?' she choked.

'To make you some tea. *I'll* have the brandy.'

She stretched out on the sofa until the shuddering of her breathing became steady, and she must have drifted off into a light sleep, because when she opened her eyes it was to find Marcus pouring out tea and spooning sugar into it.

'I told you I'd given up sugar,' she said tiredly.

'Shut up,' he answered, but his voice was almost gentle.

She still felt lousy. Physically. And yet some of the burden seemed to have been lifted from her shoulders. He hadn't actually told her not to worry, and she didn't think he would—but at least she didn't feel alone any more.

He waited until she had drunk some tea and a little colour had returned to her face. Then he sat down on a hard chair opposite her.

'So. You say I'm the father?'

She shook her head. 'No. I don't *say*, Marcus—you *are* the father.'

'Are you sure?'

She finished her tea and put the cup down on the carpet. It was no good feeling offended by his assumptions—she hadn't exactly behaved like some sort of saint, had she? But one thing was for sure—if she started behaving hysterically it would not do anyone any good.

Least of all the baby.

She placed a protective palm over her belly, and if Marcus registered the sudden action he didn't comment on it. 'Quite sure,' she said calmly.

He cleared his throat. 'May I ask how?'

'Didn't you do biology at school?' she questioned wildly.

'Don't be flippant at a time like this! I asked you a civil question—I'd appreciate a civil answer!'

'Because…' She floundered for the most delicate way of phrasing it—but what was the point? They'd insulted each other about as much as they could. 'Because you're the only man I've had sex with.' She saw that he still looked unconvinced.

'Since when?'

'A long time,' she said emphatically. 'A very long time.' He still didn't look convinced. 'For…oh, for at least a couple of years.'

He nodded. 'Oh, I see. One of the condoms must have split,' he said to himself. 'How many times did we do it?'

Donna blushed. 'I don't remember.'

'That's probably how it happened,' he sighed. 'Don't they say that human—?'

'Stop it!' She clapped her hands over her ears as she glared at him in outrage. 'I do not need to hear how wonderfully adaptable the human sperm is at a time like this!'

'No,' he agreed slowly, and looked up, the ice-blue eyes looking troubled. 'How far gone are you?'

The words didn't seem to make any sense. She stared at him blankly.

'How many weeks are you?'

'Nearly twenty-two.'

There was a long, loaded silence. His eyes met hers

incredulously. 'You're that advanced?' he asked in a shocked voice.

'Think about it, Marcus. You could have worked it out for yourself!' she retorted.

'You mean it's been that long, since…since we…?'

'Made love?' she questioned. He probably wouldn't have described it that way himself—but now that there was a tiny life growing inside her she needed to feel that the act of creating that life had been more than just sex. 'Yes. It is.'

He was shaking his head as if he had just come out of some long-term trance. Surely it couldn't have been that long ago? Had over twenty-two weeks really passed since he'd told himself that no matter how tempted he was—he wasn't going to go near her again?

'Listen,' he grated. 'Maths is usually my strong point—but not right at this moment. My head is spinning.' The ice-blue eyes burned with a strange kind of intensity. 'Just tell me when the baby is due.'

'Early in the New Year. The first week of January,' she told him at last, and as the words came tumbling out she thought that she had never seen him look quite so shattered by anything.

'You're kidding?'

'I wish I was.'

The blue eyes bored into her. 'And what's that supposed to mean?'

Donna looked at him. What did he expect her to say? That she was overjoyed at the thought of bringing an unplanned child into the world? A child whose father thought so little of her that he had not been near her since that afternoon of passion more than five months ago? 'I don't know what I mean,' she said. 'I'm mixed up, I guess.'

Marcus found his eyes drawn irresistibly to her stomach. He realised that he had only ever looked at a woman's body as an object of desire before now, but suddenly he recognised that Donna's body would nurture his child. He swallowed, the enormity of it all hitting him as he looked closer, but he could detect no tell-tale swell. Not underneath that loose shirt she was wearing. 'God, I could do with a drink.'

'Then have one.'

'No, I'd better not.' He looked at his watch and sighed. 'I have to go out tonight. Very soon, in fact.'

'And that's the difference between us, isn't it?' she questioned, and her voice was filled with a kind of bitterness as she felt her freedom begin to slip away. 'Your life will go on undisturbed, won't it, Marcus?'

'Well, hardly,' he bit out. 'I can't imagine that I'm going to have a rip-roaring time tonight after this bombshell has been dropped in my lap.'

'You're concerned about your social *calendar*?' she demanded incredulously. 'Don't worry about me—I'm just concerned about the rest of my life!'

'For God's sake, will you stop twisting my words, Donna? I was thinking short-term, that's all. You were looking at the wider canvas. Understandably.'

She knew that she had no right to ask where he was going, or with whom, and yet stupidly enough she felt as though she *did* have rights. He was the father of her unborn child, for heaven's sake!

But only through luck. Or bad luck, as he would probably see it. Luck he could have done without.

Donna made her mind up in that moment. This baby had not been conceived out of love. Certainly not on Marcus's part. But one thing was for sure—when their child arrived kicking and shouting into the world in the New Year there would be nothing but love waiting.

She sat up, feeling stronger now, smoothing back a damp tendril of hair. She leaned back against the cushions. 'Maybe it's best if we get a few things straight right from the start, Marcus.'

He became watchful. 'Go on,' he said warily.

'I just want you to know that I'm not asking you for financial support.'

He stilled. 'Oh?'

'And I'm not asking for your emotional support, either.'

'Really?' His eyes burned into her. 'Just what *are* you asking, then, Donna?'

'Nothing.' She bit her lip. 'Nothing at all.'

'No money? No babysitting for the nights you want to go out?'

She couldn't project that far into the future; she simply couldn't imagine it. 'That's right.'

'So why bother telling me at all?'

Surely he understood that? 'Because as the father you have a right to know.'

'Just no right to have any involvement with my son or daughter's life?'

'But you wouldn't want any, surely?' she asked him, her surprise genuine.

'How the hell do you know what I want—when I don't even know myself?' he snarled. 'And how can I possibly make a snap decision about such an earth-shattering piece of information as this?'

'Marcus—'

'I want time to think about it,' he continued remorselessly. 'We've already acted with indecent haste—maybe if we hadn't then we wouldn't have found our-

selves in this situation. We owe it to the baby to work
out our best options. *And we owe it to ourselves,*' he
finished quietly.

Even in the midst of all the emotions which swirled
around her like the thrashing sea above the head of a
non-swimmer, two words pushed themselves to the front
of her mind.

The baby. How cold that sounded.

'It isn't *the* baby—it's *my* baby,' she said aloud, in
case the child growing inside her could hear them, and
might turn distractedly in the womb, feeling unloved and
unwanted.

'My baby, too,' he said quietly. He looked at her
fierce little face and felt a pang of something approaching remorse. If only he hadn't ravished her quite so thoroughly. He swallowed down his self-disgust.

At least they were agreed on something—his behaviour *had* seemed to be way beyond control. Indeed, he
could not remember ever having been so overcome with
desire—but he could hardly blame her for *that*, could
he? And, meanwhile, he should have been somewhere
else ten minutes ago. 'Listen, this is too much to take
on board and try and sort out in one brief meeting.
Besides, I have to go now.'

'Of course you do.'

He stared at her. She looked so damned vulnerable,
lying there. 'Will you be…all right?'

Donna forced herself to get up off the sofa, impatiently shaking off the hand which he immediately
reached out to steady her. 'Of course I'll be all right.
And there's no need to treat me like a fragile old lady!
I'm pregnant, Marcus—not ill!'

'Yeah,' he agreed. The static in the air had made the
loose shirt cling to her, and now he could see the definite

curve of her belly. He felt a lump rise in his throat, and instinctively reached out and put his arms around her in a gesture of comfort.

For a moment Donna let herself be held, sinking into the warm security of his arms where she felt safe. He smelt clean—of lemons and musk—and she found that she wanted to sink into the protection of his body, to rest her head on his shoulder. In that moment she felt really close to him.

How peculiar that a simple hug could be infinitely more intimate than full-scale sex. She pulled away—knowing that it was dangerous to attach more than she should to small acts of support.

'You'd...better go.'

'Yes.' But he seemed strangely reluctant to move. 'Goodnight, Donna,' he said at last.

'When will I see you?' Funny, too, that her new-found 'condition' gave her the right to ask questions like this.

'I don't know,' he told her. 'I honestly don't know.'

CHAPTER SEVEN

JUST as soon as Marcus had left, Donna was asking herself why on earth she'd been so passive. She shouldn't have asked when she was going to see him. She should have demanded to know!

Because things needed to be decided.

Like what official story they were going to give. Winchester might be a city but it was a tiny city—known fondly by its inhabitants as the village with a cathedral! And as the pregnancy became more advanced they were going to have to say *something*. She wouldn't be able to keep it secret from Ally or Sarah for much longer either, that was for sure.

Oddly enough, the subject came up the following morning. Donna had been baking scones in the kitchen since six. Just lately the sickness seemed to come late-morning, and she found that if she could get the bulk of the food preparation over before that then she was usually free of the horrible, dry retching which made her stomach feel like a deflated balloon afterwards.

But this morning the sickness had struck early, and without warning. Donna wondered if it was the psychological impact of having told Marcus and consequently not sleeping a wink all night. By the time Ally came in just after nine—when she'd dropped her daughter Charlotte off at school—Donna was sitting white-faced and trembling at the kitchen table.

Ally took one look at her pinched face and grimaced. 'Tea?'

'Yuck! No!' moaned Donna.

'Sympathy, then?'

'Sympathy is just a word.' Donna shrugged listlessly. 'It doesn't actually do or change anything.'

'No, it doesn't,' agreed Ally calmly. 'But it might just make you feel better.'

Donna shook her head. 'I can't.'

'Can't what? Can't face up to fact that you're going to have a baby?'

Donna stared across the table at her in dry-eyed shock. 'How on earth did you know?' she whispered.

'How?' Ally gave a short laugh. 'I'm a mother myself! I've suspected for weeks, if you must know. It's harder than you think to hide pregnancy, you know, Donna—particularly from another woman.'

'Oh, God,' groaned Donna, and leaned onto the table, resting her head wearily on her arms. 'What am I going to do?'

'You don't really have a lot of choices, do you?' asked Ally crisply. 'How many weeks are you? About twenty?'

'Bit more,' mumbled Donna against her forearms.

'Well, in that case you're obviously going to have to go ahead and have the baby—'

Donna sat up, her expression one of outrage. 'Of course I'm going to go ahead and have the baby!' she stormed. 'Why ever would you think—?'

'Shh!' soothed Ally. 'Keep your hair on! I didn't mean to offend you, or to suggest anything—it's just that a lot of women in your situation would have considered—'

'Don't even say it!' warned Donna, and then her eyes narrowed suspiciously. 'What situation?'

Ally shrugged. 'You're not with the father, I take it?'

'Is it that obvious?'

'Yes.'

'Oh, Ally, I feel so *stupid*! How did I ever get myself into this position?'

'Donna,' Ally sighed. 'You're no more stupid than countless other women have been. These things happen. Have you told him? The father, I mean.'

'Yes.' Donna stared at the table. 'I've told him.'

'And what does he say?'

'That we have to talk about it.'

'That's very good of him,' said Ally drily, and then she creased her nose up. 'I don't suppose there's any chance of the two of you ever—?'

'No,' said Donna firmly. 'None whatsoever. He's made that perfectly clear.' She picked a rosy apple out of the fruit bowl and began to rub it absently against her sleeve, but then another wave of nausea hit her and she quickly put it back. 'You haven't asked me whether he's married.'

'Why should I ask that?'

'Well, it is an obvious assumption to make when a woman has a lover that no one has ever seen. Isn't it?'

'But I know he's not married,' said Ally slowly. 'Marcus Foreman is the father, isn't he?' She saw Donna's dazed expression and gave a short laugh. 'And before you ask, no—I'm not a mind-reader. It was just pretty obvious to me—and to Sarah.'

Donna silently filed away the fact that the two of them must have discussed it. 'How? When I haven't seen him for weeks?'

'You were so distracted after he came to see you the day we opened. You used to jump six feet in the air and snatch the phone up whenever it rang. Then your face would crumple when you discovered it was the wholesalers asking about a jam delivery! But not for long. There was always that gritty smile lying in wait.' Her face softened. 'You were always determined not to look upset when the bastard didn't ring you.'

'He is not a bastard,' defended Donna dully.

'Maybe his mother and father were legally married,' conceded Ally. 'But he's behaved like one towards you, hasn't he?'

'Actually, no.'

'Donna—now you're just being soft!'

But Donna shook her head. 'I'm not. If he really *was* an out-and-out bastard he would have visited me on more than one occasion, instead of just the once. Some men would have done that if there was sex without questions on offer. At least this way he wasn't pretending to feel something he obviously didn't. He made me feel like a mistake, not a prostitute.'

The two of them stiffened as they heard the sound of a key in the lock.

Donna looked at Ally. 'So Sarah knows, too?'

'Yes. She guessed herself. You've been wearing shapeless tops for ages now. And, like I say, it's pretty obvious to another woman.'

'I would have told you weeks ago, except that I was too scared to acknowledge it, even to myself. And I felt I couldn't tell anyone—not until I'd told Marcus.' Donna heard the sound of the telephone ringing, and Sarah's voice calling to say that she would answer it. 'Listen, Ally—please don't say a word to anyone else. Not until I've discussed it again with Marcus.'

'Don't worry, I won't.'

They both looked up as Sarah came to the door, an expectant smile on her face.

'Mmm,' she said pointedly. 'Guess who's on the phone for *you*, Donna?'

'The taxman?'

'Marcus Foreman.'

Donna tried not to look as though she was rushing, but she was puffing slightly as she picked up the receiver. 'Hello?'

'Why are you out of breath?' demanded the voice at the other end.

'Because pregnant women get easily puffed!'

There was a pause while he considered this. 'Will you have dinner with me tonight?'

'Dinner?'

He gave a short laugh. 'Is that such a bizarre request in the circumstances, Donna?'

She heard the sarcasm which coloured his voice and understood it immediately. If there had been a time for sounding shocked it should have been when he had arrived wearing a dark, sultry expression and intent on seduction. Not when he was asking her to share a meal with him as two civilised and consenting adults.

'No, of course it isn't,' she told him quickly. She was about to utter, I'd love to, but that would have been pure convention, not truth. 'Where?'

Another pause. 'I thought at my house.'

She bit her lip. 'The New Hampshire too public for you?'

'Not in the way you're thinking—'

'And how the hell would you know what I was thinking, Marcus?'

He sighed. 'If we go to a restaurant—and that's any restaurant, not just mine—then we're on show, aren't we? People watch us, assess us.'

'Assess *me*, you mean. And how pregnant I am.'

'Donna,' he said patiently. 'Unless you've suddenly been diagnosed as expecting triplets I can't for the life of me see how yesterday your pregnancy was a secret whilst today the whole world would know that secret just by looking at you!'

'Because today I really *feel* pregnant!' she wailed.

'Probably because you told someone,' he mused. 'Anyway, dinner. Come early—is six o'clock okay?'

'I suppose so.'

'Do you want me to come and collect you?'

'No, I think I can probably manage the five-minute walk myself.'

'Well, if you're sure…'

'Marcus, I'm not an *invalid*—I told you that before!'

'No,' he agreed. 'You're just having a baby. My baby, in fact,' he finished, with an unfamiliar note of something she couldn't quite put her finger on. And Donna wondered whether it had been pride or panic she had heard in his voice.

Donna had dressed carefully the day she had got her licence and taken Tony Paxman out for lunch—but that had been nothing compared to the agonised deliberations she indulged in once she'd shut up shop and sent Sarah and Ally home. Dinner with Marcus in the most bizarre circumstances imaginable—so what did she wear?

The sleek cream dress and matching jacket she had worn that day were immediately rejected as much too formal. Donna narrowed her eyes at the dress and guessed that it probably wouldn't do up any more, anyway.

Given her newly expanded waistline, she didn't really have a lot of choice. Pencil skirts were out, for obvious reasons. So were the narrowly cut trousers she sometimes wore. And what self-destructive little imp had prompted her to think that she might be able to get away with jeans and a big cotton T-shirt?

She couldn't even get the jeans past her thighs! This was worse than the days when she was a teenager and used to have to lie on the floor and use a coat-hanger to lever the skin-tight denim flaps together! She was definitely going to have to buy some new clothes to accommodate this baby.

In the end she selected a simple silk trouser suit which she had bought and worn to death when she had lived in New Zealand. The wide, soft trousers had an elasticated waistband and the slip-over top was cool and roomy. She'd washed it more times than she cared to remember, and it had faded from deepest cinnamon to pale topaz. But it still looked good. It hid the swell of her belly and the colour made the most of her pale skin and orange-red hair and green eyes.

She put on a coat of waterproof mascara and a slick of clear lipgloss, then wove a black velvet ribbon into the French plait and she was ready.

Marcus lived in a road just behind the hotel, where the houses were detached and elegant, their gardens shimmering pockets of well-tended lawns with carefully chosen shrubs spilling onto their gravelled paths. It was a balmy evening, the air thick with the scent of roses and the muted sound of a late tennis game somewhere in the distance.

Marcus opened the door before she had a chance to ring the bell, which she guessed meant that he had been watching out for her—and that pleased her. Not because she thought for a moment that he was mooning over her like a lovesick calf—but because it implied that he was nervous, too. Which would even things up a little. And it wasn't like Marcus to be nervous.

He stood in the doorway and looked at her. Despite what he'd said to her on the phone about looking no different he realised that she *did* look different. How you saw someone depended on what you thought about them. And now he knew she was pregnant she suddenly looked like the most pregnant woman in the world. Cool and clean as a glass of water. All glowing and growing and radiant.

'Hi,' he said, and his voice sounded much softer than usual. 'Glad you could make it. Come in.'

'Thanks.' Glad she could *make* it? Heavens, how *formal* they sounded—as though it was a boardroom meeting they were attending. And how surreal—given the circumstances of why she was there!

She stepped into the wide hallway, with its sweeping staircase and softly gleaming wooden banister, and felt herself suddenly cloaked with insecurities.

Marcus noticed her body freeze with tension, and he frowned. 'Is something the matter?'

She shrugged. 'It's a little strange being here, that's all. I mean, I've never even set foot over the threshold of your house before, not in all the time I worked for you. I was never invited, and I suppose I never would have been invited either, if I hadn't got myself into this awkward situation.'

His face darkened. 'I think we have to take joint responsibility for the ''awkward situation'', as you so sweetly put it. As for never coming here.' He gave her a look which was the closest she had ever seen to Marcus looking helpless. 'There was never any reason for you to come here, was there? That wasn't the way things were. How they worked.'

'No, I guess not. You were the boss and I was the chambermaid.' She'd only ever seen him at the hotel. The world had not seemed to exist outside the hotel. It had become their world in microcosm.

Marcus had been working all the hours that God sent. And he'd needed to. His father had been sick and frail for a long time before his death, but he'd been a stubborn man. He hadn't been able to bear to relinquish his control of the family business to his son, even though he hadn't really been fit to run it himself.

And it had only been after his death that Marcus had discovered the disastrous state of the hotel's finances and had set about trying to salvage them.

'And was I a good boss?' he asked suddenly.

He had been a very distracting boss.

'You never seemed to go home,' she said, remembering the time when she had started work one morning and found him fast asleep at his office desk. She'd crept away and made a tray of coffee and put it on his desk before gently shaking his shoulder. He'd woken sleepily, and rubbed his eyes, and an odd, jolting kind of stare had passed between them while a blistering silence had ticked away around them, like a time-bomb.

And that was the precise moment that Donna had decided she was falling in love with him…

'You were the original workaholic.' She smiled wistfully at the memory.

He studied the careful way that she answered him, sensing that he couldn't hold back on this—it just wasn't fair to her. 'I never wanted to go home,' he said simply. 'You made working late the most attractive prospect I could imagine…well, nearly,' he added, then wished he hadn't. If there was one thing he *wasn't* going to do tonight it was to treat her like a sex object.

'Come through,' he said—and gestured towards a door at the end of the corridor. 'To the kitchen.'

It was a huge kitchen, with a big, scrubbed pine table and an enormous old-fashioned range. It looked too tidy to be a room which was used a lot, and Donna wondered how often he ate here. But there were some beautiful pieces of coloured glass dotted here and there, and a terracotta dish containing oranges and lemons. She could imagine a cat sitting contentedly by the range. A ginger cat, licking its glossy coat.

'It's a beautiful room,' she murmured.

The French windows were open, leading out onto a garden which was still a blur of mauves and pinks and blues, although the brilliant greens of high summer were gone. Donna blinked. Were those really children's voices she could hear—or had she imagined those as well?

She turned round to find Marcus studying her intently.

'What would you like to drink?' he asked. 'I've got most fruit juices. Or there's mineral water, if you'd prefer.'

The feeling of losing control over her body was only intensified. Donna frowned at him. 'And what would you say if I asked you for a proper drink? A glass of wine or a beer?'

'I'd probably tell you that although one or two drinks a week are permissible after the first trimester, doctors now recommend—'

'Marcus!' Donna dropped her handbag onto a high-backed chair which stood next to the range and turned indignantly to face him. 'Will you stop it?'

'Stop what?'

'Trying to take control!'

'I wasn't,' he said stubbornly. 'I was just—'

'Yes, I know! Interfering! It's my body,' she declared.

'And you've got my baby growing inside it,' he told her quietly.

Wide-eyed, they stared at one another, his words shocking them both into silence.

Marcus had spent a sleepless night trying to come to terms with her news. Yesterday he had been dazed and confused. And angry. But this morning he'd found himself standing in his garden to see the new dawn break—his feet all bare and soaked with dew. And what had seemed like an out-and-out disaster in the darkest hours had taken on an air of mystery and wonder as the sun had burst upon the sky in a blaze of pink and orange and purple.

A baby...

But that had still been a baby in the abstract sense. Saying those words out loud somehow made it real. And far more real for her than for him. She was the one it was actually happening to. What right did he have to police her every move?

'Have a glass of wine if you'd like some,' he growled.

'I wouldn't, actually,' she answered sweetly. 'But I'd like to be given the choice. You see, over the years I've become rather fond of making my own decisions!'

'Point taken, Donna.' He gave a slightly unsteady smile as he poured out two tall glasses of mineral water, adding ice and lemon before handing her one. 'So. What shall we drink to?' he asked. 'The baby?'

'The baby.' She nodded obediently, wondering if this sensation of unreality would ever disappear. It was as if this was all happening to someone else, not her. She stole a glance at the calm way he was sipping at his drink. 'You seem to have accepted the fact remarkably well.'

'I don't have a choice, do I?' He put his drink down and slid some bread into the oven, then bent to take salad ingredients from out of the fridge and began chopping tomatoes. 'And when you don't have a choice—then you make the best of things. Good lesson for life.'

She thought that, yes, it was. That in a funny kind of way that had been exactly her own philosophy—right from when she had been a little girl. She looked up to tell him that and found his eyes on her, the flash of understanding in them telling her far more clearly than words ever could that he knew.

He put the knife down, and smiled as he said her name, the smile all mixed up with tenderness and regret. 'Oh, Donna,' he sighed.

His eyes were incandescent with a fierce blue light, and for a moment she nearly forgot herself. Nearly reached across and touched her fingertips against the faint shadow on his chin. Wanting to trace the shape of his face, the squared-off curve of his jaw, the sensual pout of his lips. But she had no right to touch him, none at all, and she shrank back.

'What is it?' he demanded urgently. 'Why has your face gone so white? Is it the baby? Are you sick?'

She shook her head. 'No. I just got a short, sharp dose of reality which forced me to accept a few unpalatable facts.'

He severed a piece of cucumber. 'Oh?'

'I remembered that I am only here by accident. That's all. We are not partners, Marcus, not in the true sense of the word. Nor even lovers. And I am not the proud bearer of your child—I am simply a vessel that got filled by—'

'Don't you dare!' He put the knife down and gripped

her upper arms—not hard, but she could feel his fingers burning into her flesh through the thin silk.

'Don't dare tell the truth, you mean?'

He shook his head impatiently. 'That's only your version of the truth. Thinking negatively won't do you any good at all,' he ground out. 'Or the baby. Or the whole damn situation!'

He moved his face closer, and Donna felt helpless beneath a gaze so probing it made her feel that he could look into her mind and read every thought there.

Could he tell that she wanted him with an urgency which had her fingers itching to pull his face down to hers? To meet and meld with those sweet, hard lips which would open under pressure... She swallowed down her desire with difficulty and wriggled out of his grip.

'We have to be positive,' he whispered. 'Both of us.'

She nodded her head. 'I know we do.'

His eyes blazed. 'I don't want you to worry, Donna. Not about anything. Do you understand?'

The attack of lust passed as quickly as it had arrived, in time for her to realise that he was talking to her as if she had just had her brain removed.

'But I'm not worried!' she protested. 'Honestly!'

He shook his head, as if he thought she was just reassuring him for the sake of it, to be polite. 'Well, I am,' he said flatly.

'You're worried?'

'Yes, I am.'

She looked at him expectantly. 'What about?'

'About you living in that flat above the tea-room, for a start.'

Donna fixed him with a furious look. He hadn't

thought the flat so ghastly that it had prevented him making love to her there! 'What's wrong with it?'

'Well, imagine if your kitchen caught fire!' he said heatedly.

Donna frowned. 'Why should it?'

'Because you're living above the kitchen! You cook food in larger than average quantities, don't you? You employ staff, don't you? Therefore the possibilities of some kind of fire breaking out are much greater. Good grief, your oven could explode!'

'And so could yours!' she retorted. 'I've had the premises checked by the environmental and safety officers! I'm not living in a booby-trap, you know!'

'I'm not suggesting you are—'

'And for your information, I check the kitchens myself, every single night before I go around locking up.'

'Exactly!' He beamed with triumph. 'It's too much for you to handle! You're doing that now and you look exhausted, if you want the truth. Imagine when you're dragging yourself around at forty weeks.'

'You're making me sound like an Atlantic whale!' Donna objected mildly. But she was surprised and impressed that he knew how long a pregnancy lasted, and remembered his earlier pat comments about 'the first trimester'. 'And since when did you become such an expert on childbirth?'

He gave an unfamiliar and sheepish grin. 'I went out and bought just about every book there was on the subject.'

'And how many was that?' she asked faintly.

He counted off on his fingers. 'Four books on pregnancy. There's an even bigger section on the first year of life, and then—'

'I've heard everything I need to know.'

'Ah, but that's where you're wrong!' He poured them out some more mineral water, as if playing for time. 'Whatever objections you may put up, you know in your heart that I'm right.'

'If you say so, Marcus,' she said demurely, thinking that if she gave him enough rope he might hang himself!

He breezed on, not seeming to notice her sceptical expression. 'And The Buttress—whilst being an excellent tea-room—' he crinkled an encouraging smile at her '—and I'm impressed with what you've done, believe me.'

'Gee, thanks!'

If he heard the sardonic note in her voice, he didn't react to it. 'But it is *not* the place for a pregnant woman, and neither is it the place for a brand-new baby. And that's why I've decided—' he drew a deep breath, like a man seeking courage to make the ultimate sacrifice '—to let you come and live here.'

CHAPTER EIGHT

DONNA was so thunderstruck by Marcus's suggestion that she just stared at him, her mouth limply falling open. She must have misheard. *Must* have.

'I'm not sure I heard that properly, Marcus.'

He smiled the complacent smile of a man who had never been turned down for anything in his life. 'You can come and live here,' he explained kindly. 'My home will become your home.'

'When you say *live* here…' Donna hesitated as quiet hysteria gave her the terrible temptation to giggle. She tried to find a diplomatic way of wording her question and realised that there wasn't one. 'What do you mean, exactly?'

His eyes were wary. 'It sounds straightforward enough to me.'

'Well, not to me. I'm interested to know just what role I'd be expected to play.'

'What role?' he repeated cautiously.

'Sure. Will I be your partner, in the full sense of the word? Will we be sharing a bed and having sex together? Or am I simply expected to drift around the edges of your life? And, in that case, won't your girlfriends be rather spooked when they see a woman who is heavily pregnant—with your child—walking around the place and treating it like home. What if I unwittingly walked in just as you were about to seduce one of them on the sofa?'

'Donna!'

'It's no good saying "Donna!" like that,' she said serenely, enjoying the look of outrage on his face. 'That doesn't answer any of my questions.'

'Do you really think that I'd be upstairs…?' His voice trailed off in disbelief and it took a moment or two for him to repeat the word. 'Upstairs…'

'Making love?' she put in helpfully, feeling emotionally stronger by the second. 'Well, that would certainly be preferable to you being *downstairs* making love!'

'Just what kind of a man do you think I am?' he demanded.

'Well, since you ask…' Donna met his gaze unflinchingly. 'The kind of man who has sex when he feels like it and doesn't even bother seeing the woman afterwards. Does that sound familiar?'

'Oh. Oh, I see.' His watchfulness transformed itself into a panther-like stealth, and Donna wondered if she had pushed him just a little too far.

'Is that what this is all about?' he queried silkily. 'The fact that it was just a one-off? Is that why you're so angry?'

'I thought I was being more practical than angry,' she reasoned, because anger would imply vulnerability—and she needed to be strong. 'I've learnt to cope with most things in my life, Marcus, and this won't be any different.' She shrugged her shoulders. 'These things happen.'

'Especially to us. One-night stands seem to be our speciality, don't they, sugar?'

He reached his hand up towards her face and Donna tensed, but he was merely brushing a strand of hair from where it had been threatening to glue itself to her lips.

The tiny gesture was oddly touching. It made her feel defenceless when she needed to be tough. Did he recognise that? Was that why he had renewed his campaign?

'And you still haven't answered my question.' He studied her carefully. 'About coming to live here.'

Donna moved away from the work-top, wanting to be out of range of that delectable ice-blue stare, but wanting more than anything to eat. These days she seemed to be controlled by her body.

She smiled at him. 'I can't possibly answer that on an empty stomach. So, can we please have some food now? I'm starving.'

Marcus gave a small, wry smile in response. Had he thought she would agree to come and live here as easily as she had agreed to have such warm and beautiful sex with him? 'Sure we can.' He added some tuna to the salad and took the warmed bread out of the oven. 'Want to eat in here? Or is it warm enough to eat outside?'

'Outside.'

'Then let's go.'

Donna carried out the checkered cloth he gave her and spread it over the grass, while Marcus carried the food and water on a tray.

He spooned her out a generous portion of salade niçoise and watched while she devoured it with an appetite which took him right back to that day when she had arrived—so cold and wet and hungry. And the sense of protectiveness he'd felt towards her then was nothing to what he was experiencing right now.

'Do you always eat that much these days?' he enquired, once she had paused for breath.

She wiped up the last of the dressing with a piece of bread and ate it slowly, waiting until she had finished chewing before she answered his question. 'Not usually. It's this pregnancy business.'

He turned onto his side and stretched out on the grass, tucking the white T-shirt into his jeans as he did so, making Donna horribly aware of how long and how muscular his legs were.

'So, tell me all about it,' he said softly. 'This pregnancy business.'

She pushed her empty plate away and took a sip of water. 'Sometimes you're so sick that you tell yourself you'll never eat another thing—just so you won't be able to be sick.'

'And then?'

She shrugged. 'Then the baby must send some message to your brain, or your stomach—or something. Because suddenly you discover that you could devour just about everything in the fridge—and then some! You feel like one of those locusts you see on nature films— the kind that march around stripping everything bare...' Now why had she said *that*?

His eyes darkened at the way she faltered on those last few words, and his smile grew thoughtful. 'Well, feel free, Donna,' he murmured. 'Strip everything bare, if that's what you really want.'

She glared. 'It isn't really helpful if you're going to make suggestive remarks like that, Marcus.'

'It's the effect you're having on me,' he groaned.

'But I'm not doing anything!' she protested.

'No?' He suspected that if she started reading from the telephone directory he would find it sexy! 'Don't look so shocked! Surely you must realise how damned gorgeous you look sitting there?'

'Gorgeous?' She looked down at herself. All she could see was the swollen breasts and tummy, which, after the gigantic portion of food she had just put away, made it look as though she was due to give birth at any moment.

'Normally I can't stand false modesty—but that

sounds pretty genuine to me.' He shook his head in disbelief. 'Of course you look gorgeous. You're blooming, Donna,' he said softly. 'Blooming like a rose in high summer. Your skin is clear and your eyes are bright as stars. Hell, your figure has always been the best I've ever seen on any woman, but pregnancy has only enhanced it.'

He shut up then. Her mutinous expression told him that now might not be a good time to tell her how magnificent her breasts looked. He rolled over onto his stomach. At least that way there was a chance she wouldn't notice just how she was affecting him. Or where.

Donna saw him wince and thought she knew why. She'd seen the flush which had heightened his colour, emphasising those amazing cheekbones. The hectic glitter in his eyes hadn't gone unnoticed, either. She found herself wanting to touch him. To run her fingertips over the satin of his skin, seeking out all the dark and secret hollows.

She thought how easy it would be to lie back beside him. To pretend that she needed to digest her meal. Or to look at the clouds as they chased one another across the sky. Then it would be only a matter of time before he leaned over to press his mouth against hers.

And she wanted that. Wanted him. He was the only man she had *ever* wanted, in truth.

'So, are you going to come and move in with me, Donna?'

His voice sounded as disconnected as the distant droning of a lawnmower in one of the neighbouring gardens.

The eighteen-year-old Donna would have leapt at the chance, but she was no longer eighteen. Nine years on she had got herself into a crazy situation—but she didn't have to make it even crazier.

She shook her head. 'No, I'm not. I can't think of a worse idea, to be honest. I'm still trying to get used to the fact that in under four months' time I'm going to have a tiny baby to look after. Now is certainly not the right time to start experimenting by living with someone.'

He turned onto his back again, the urgency to possess her disappearing with the moment. 'I might not ask you again.'

Donna laughed. 'Oh, dear!' she teased. 'Then I've missed my chance for ever. Well, there you go!'

Marcus looked up at the darkening sky which domed above them. He couldn't figure her out. He had thought… He frowned.

Donna looked down at him. 'What's the matter, Marcus?' she taunted softly. 'Can't believe a woman has said no to you?'

He was gentle with her because she was pregnant, but there was no hesitation in his movement as he pulled her down on top of him, feeling the lush resistance of her ripening flesh against the sudden hard throbbing of his. 'Maybe I think I can change your mind,' came his soft groan as he tangled his fingers in her French plait and brought her mouth down to his.

He kissed her, and that was all he did. He didn't grapple with her clothing or try to explore the contours of her body. Just lay there with his fingers nonchalantly threaded into her hair, his lips alternatively sweet and soft and hard and hungry.

It was both passive and seeking. Innocent and immensely experienced. It was a slow, drugging seduction and it was entirely new to her.

And Donna was completely unprepared for its impact. With Marcus everything had always been so hot and immediate. As if the world would end if they didn't join their bodies together as quickly as possible. No one had ever told her it could be like *this*.

She lay dazed and unfurling on top of him, feeling the honeyed pulsing of desire as it stealthily invaded her body.

Marcus knew that he had to stop. This was unlike anything in his experience. More beautiful than anything he'd ever felt. And in a minute he'd.... ·

Donna blinked as he tore his mouth away to somehow gather her up into his arms and gracefully manoeuvre them both to a standing position, and only when she felt the ground beneath her feet did he let her go.

'Donna—'

'You're out of breath,' she gasped.

'So are you.' He paused, still disorientated by that kiss. 'And your hair is all over the place.'

She brushed a damp curl off her cheek, feeling the sweat as it pricked her forehead. She brushed a few strands of dry grass from her sleeve and began to walk towards the house.

He walked by her side across the springy turf. 'Can I come to the clinic with you? And see the scan? I want to see the baby's heart beating.'

Suddenly she felt guilty. 'I've already had a scan.'·

He tensed, knowing that he had no right to feel excluded. 'And?'

'And it all looks fine. Absolutely fine.' A smile broke out on her lips and suddenly he was smiling too, and if this had been a normal relationship she would have flung her arms around him and he would have picked her up and twirled her round like a carousel.

But it wasn't a normal relationship. And Donna realised that they had avoided discussing some very practical issues.

'People are going to start noticing soon,' she said.

'Hasn't anyone noticed already?'

'Ally has. And Sarah. But neither of them has said anything. What do you want me to say, if anyone asks?'

Marcus studied her. She was asking his opinion and yet he didn't count, not really. She'd made love to him and was carrying his child as a consequence. Then she had lain kissing on the grass with him—but now he offered to do the decent thing and *live* with her she didn't want to know.

'Marcus?' She butted into his thoughts. 'What do you want me to tell people?'

He felt the anger rising up inside him, and he turned his face away, so that all she could see was a shadowed profile etched softly against the dusky evening light. 'That's entirely up to you.'

She wished he would help her out. Did he enjoy seeing her have to ask these humiliating questions? 'So if I tell people that you're the…father—you won't mind?'

'Why should I? They're going to find out soon enough,' he said flatly. 'Because as soon as the baby is born I shall be applying for custody.'

CHAPTER NINE

'HE SAID *what*?'

Donna willed herself to stop shaking for long enough to repeat what she had just told an incredulous Ally.

'Marcus said…' She took a great gulping breath of air which steadied her voice. 'That he was going to fight me for custody of the baby once he or she is born.'

'But he can't do that,' said Ally.

'Who says he can't? He can do any damn thing he pleases. He's rich. He's powerful. He's influential. What judge isn't going to look at him and compare him favourably to me—a girl from the wrong side of the tracks. Struggling to start her own business and to bring a baby up at the same time.' Donna groaned. 'What about the current backlash against working mothers? The belief that women who put their careers before their babies are uncaring?'

'But you aren't *planning* to put the tea-room before the baby, are you?' questioned Ally patiently.

Donna carried on as if she hadn't heard her. 'There's a big swing in favour of fathers at the moment—you know there is. Fathers are clamouring to be heard—saying that they are just as capable of bringing up a child as the mother. Oh, Ally,' she wailed. 'What am I going to do?'

Ally glowered. 'You can stop acting like you've already lost—that's for sure! Then you take yourself off to a lawyer and you find out exactly where you stand!

121

You know a lawyer, don't you? The guy who brought the champagne round the day we opened?'

'Tony Paxman,' said Donna dully.

'Well, then. He's a friend, isn't he?'

'Not really.'

Donna didn't feel like explaining to Ally that Tony Paxman hadn't really been offering the only kind of friendship she would accept. And somehow she didn't imagine he would look very favourably on the fact that she was expecting Marcus's baby. 'Oh, I just don't know what to do,' she sighed. 'I really don't.'

'Well, I *do*!' said Ally firmly. 'You have all the power in this, Donna—just think about it. You're pregnant, aren't you? *You're* the one carrying the baby. And you're looking after yourself—anyone can see that. Okay,' she amended, as she noticed the huge, dark shadows beneath Donna's eyes, 'you don't look so great today—but that's hardly surprising, is it?'

'Gee, thanks,' replied Donna drily.

Ally gave her an apologetic look. 'Look, what I'm trying to say is that it's *your* baby, Donna—growing inside *you*—'

'And he's the father.'

'He *impregnated* you,' said Ally, in a clipped voice. 'That's all.'

But something deep within Donna fluttered—maybe it was the baby itself, letting its own objections be known—and she shook her head. 'It isn't just a biological function,' she said quietly. 'Certainly not with Marcus. He *is* the father of this baby. In every way which counts.' She didn't know why that should be. She just knew. In the part of her that was beyond logic or reason. The part of her to which Marcus seemed to have unique access.

Ally looked torn between admiration and impatience. 'That may be,' she allowed. 'But even so, he can't just come and take it away from you—that's total male oppression!'

'Or equality,' shrugged Donna. 'Maybe men feel they've been excluded from bringing up children for long enough. That they can offer exactly the same emotional and physical sustenance as women. It all depends which way you look at it.'

'He can't just take the baby away from you,' repeated Ally grimly. 'Can he?'

Donna shook her head. 'That's the trouble. I don't know. That's something I'm going to have to find out.'

'Who from?'

'A lawyer, I guess.'

'Well, that's easy.' Ally smiled. 'Tony Paxman may not be your best friend, but he's a damned good lawyer. You told me that yourself!'

But Donna knew she couldn't go and see Tony. In fact, she couldn't face going to see anyone in Winchester. If Marcus turned this into some sort of battle it was going to be ugly. And she needed some facts at her fingertips before she cast herself in the role of local victim.

'I'm going to make a couple of phone calls,' she said to Ally. 'Can I leave the fruitcake to you?'

'Consider it done!' said Ally, with a quick glance at her watch. 'Listen, Sarah will be in soon. Why don't you take the rest of the day off?'

'Thanks, Boss!' said Donna, laughing in spite of everything.

She phoned Carly Morrison—a woman she had met years ago at an evening class, when she'd first moved to London. They had both been trying to master the art of cake decoration, and Carly had gone on to become a cookery presenter on a cable TV channel. Over the years the two of them had stayed in regular contact, and Carly had promised to come to The Buttress just as soon as her busy schedule allowed. She was unshockable, very likable—and she had lots of contacts.

Donna tracked her down to the television studios, and after Carly had demanded to know 'everything' there was to know about life running a tea-room, Donna plucked up the courage to ask her question.

'Carly, I need a favour.'

A loud, throaty laugh came ringing down the line. 'If it's a loan you're after then I'm afraid you've come to the wrong person, honey!'

'No. It's not that sort of favour. I need the name of a lawyer.'

There was a pause. 'You in some sort of trouble, Donna?'

Donna made a snap decision. If she started on her story she would never get finished, and Carly would see the pregnancy for herself soon enough. And besides, she was not going to think of this baby as anything but a joy. Certainly not trouble. 'Not at all. I just need a little advice, that's all.'

'Okay, hon—here's the number. Got a pen?'

Donna rang the number and the lawyer—who was quite clearly smitten with Carly—told her everything she needed to know.

She put the phone down slowly and went to the kitchen, to find Ally and Sarah buttering scones with the speed of women working on a production line. They both looked up as she walked in.

'Everything okay?' asked Sarah.

'I think so. I'm going to go out for a walk. I need some fresh air.'

'Donna,' said Ally warningly. 'What did the lawyer say?'

She felt light-headed. Weird. 'I'll tell you later. I must get out of here. I feel all trapped and claustrophobic.'

She saw the brief look which passed between the two of them, as if to say, I'm not surprised. They obviously thought that she was starting to feel hemmed in by the pregnancy and Marcus's threat to sue her for custody.

Outside the air was thick, the September sun beating down on her bare head like someone trying to get inside. She felt like a stranger in the place she knew better than any other. Maybe she would walk down to the market and buy herself some flowers.

She took the scenic route to the market, down through the water meadows and past the cathedral. Sweat trickled in undulating streams down her spine, and she began to wish she had worn one of the many hats she owned.

She bought two big bunches of scarlet daisies, and as she fumbled around in her purse for money she felt a slight aching at the base of her belly. Sweat broke out on her face and she saw the market trader frown.

'You all right, love?' he asked, and his voice seemed to come from a long way down a tunnel.

Donna nodded, and cradled the flowers in her arm like a baby. She would go back the shorter way. It wasn't as pretty, true, and it took her directly past Marcus's hotel, but her energy seemed to have been sapped. It was all very well telling herself that pregnancy wouldn't change anything—but for the baby's sake she was going to have to start taking things a little easier. And marching down to the market was simply asking for trouble.

*　　*　　*

Marcus was sitting in his office, drumming his fingers angrily against his desk. He had spent the last hour attempting to dictate letters to his secretary, but his words had made no sense and in the end he had grown tired of her look of surprise.

'Lets go over this again in the morning, can we?' he had growled.

'Certainly.' His secretary had given him a polite, quizzical smile. 'Er, can I fetch you some aspirin, or something, Marcus? You seem a little under the weather.'

'Nothing!' he had roared, and word had soon spread around among all the staff that Marcus was in a *filthy* temper and that no one should talk to him unless absolutely necessary.

He stared out of the window, wondering why the landscape suddenly seemed to have altered beyond his comprehension. The street was the same. The cars still moved past. So why did it all look so fundamentally different?

Because a woman was out there somewhere? he wondered. A woman who carried his child? A vulnerable woman he had threatened with litigation. He felt guilt and anger kick in, spilling around his veins in equal measures. He rested his head against the cool pane of glass and let out a sigh.

How could he have done? How *could* he? Told her that he would fight her in the courts, his very stature and determination implying that if there was a battle ahead he would be the only victor. What kind of man, he wondered, did that?

He was going to have to go and tell her that the words had been fuelled by his frustration. Not a sexual frustration—but the frustration of having set something in motion without thinking where it might lead. But maybe that was just life. People acted on impulse all the time. You could say that he and Donna had just been unlucky. He thought of her swollen belly and his heart raced. Or lucky.

He stared sightlessly at the people who ambled slowly along the pavements. Students walking in large groups, their individual uniform of jeans and T-shirts making them all look the same. Older tourists with a fortune's worth of photographic equipment dangling from around their necks. Girls in light dresses, looking no older than Donna had been that first time she had come to him looking for work.

He screwed his eyes up as one of them crossed the road. The memory could play tricks with the eyes. For a moment there that flash of bright, titian hair had jangled a distant bell of recognition, as had something in the way she walked.

But, no, that could not be Donna. It was too stooped for Donna. Donna didn't have a rounded body like the woman he was looking at.

Marcus froze.

No, of course she didn't. The Donna of his memory was young and carefree—the woman who was crossing the road was nearly a decade older and stooping beneath the burden of his child, her arms full of flowers the colour of blood.

Without thinking he reached his fist up and began to hammer on the window, and she looked up then, and saw him.

Marcus watched the emotions which flitted across her face. Surprise. Anger. And what was that…? He watched her cross back to his side of the road, her face set into a mask of grim determination.

By the time he went to meet her she was already

standing in Reception, her face as pale and as transparent as rice-paper, the blood-red flowers reflecting a sinister glow up into her colourless cheeks.

'I need to see you,' she croaked.

He took her arm, ignoring her weak attempt to shake him off. 'You need to sit down,' he corrected, and spotted his *sous chef* peering from behind a pillar. 'Graham!' he called. 'Bring tea into my office! Quickly!'

'Yes, Marcus!' said the startled chef.

Marcus guided her into his office, thinking how light she felt, boneless almost. He pulled out a chair for her, alarmed by her pallor but even more alarmed by the way she sank down into it without protest.

Donna was glad to get the weight off her feet. She released the flowers onto her lap, her palms all clammy and sticky and cold with sweat.

Marcus bent over her, his face tense. 'Donna—listen—'

'No!' She thought of the baby and that gave her strength. '*You* listen! I've spoken to a lawyer—'

'Donna—'

'Shut *up*!' she told him tiredly. 'And listen. He told me that you do not have any rights to this baby at all—not unless we are married. And as we are not married and are never likely to be—then that's the end of that!' She stared at him defiantly. 'Okay?'

He sat on the edge of his desk and watched her, recognising that she was dangerously close to tears. 'Okay,' he agreed softly.

Donna had wanted a fight. She'd wanted to storm and rage at him and… She sucked in some of the air, which seemed so still and so heavy. 'He also told me that you are able to acquire parental rights by mutual agreement.

So you need my co-operation if you want to see this baby, Marcus.'

'And if you decide not to co-operate?'

'Then you'll have to take me to court!' She paused for effect. 'And I can easily deny everything. I can tell them that someone else is the father.'

'You would do that?' he breathed.

The weight of her head seemed unbearable. 'I would do anything—*anything*—to stop you taking my child away from me, Marcus. You'd better believe that!'

He was the kind of man who needed to have every available fact at his fingertips. And he needed to know how thoroughly she had investigated the whole subject.

'What if I prove that the baby is mine?'

'And how would you do that?' she challenged. 'Certainly not by circumstantial evidence! We only had sex once, and no one has ever seen us together. It would be your word against mine!' She allowed an ironic smile to curve her lips. 'I shouldn't imagine that it would be difficult for the daughter of a stripper to convince the court that you were just one in a long line of lovers!'

His mouth tightened as he found that he couldn't bear to think of her in bed with another man. Then told himself how stupid that was.

'Of course you could always do a DNA test,' she continued. 'But the baby will have to be born first—'

'Donna, stop this right now,' he pleaded, thinking that her skin looked ashen.

'Why should I? You started it.' She locked her fingers together, as if she were about to start uttering some kind of fervent prayer. 'And when the baby is born no one will ever want to take it away—because they'll be able to see how much...' she gulped. 'How much we love one another!'

'Donna—I don't want to take your baby away from you.'

'Yes, you do!' Had he slipped a tight, iron band around her belly and tightened it without her seeing? Donna stared at him in horror, their argument completely wiped away by this new and terrifying intervention. 'Marcus?'

He saw her wince and recognised the pain and fear, sensing that something was happening now beyond both their control. 'Donna.' His voice sounded leaden. He seemed to move in slow motion towards her. He saw her stiffen, and then slump, falling forwards and knocking the daisies to the floor, their wilted scarlet petals scattering like bullets.

He heard a cry, and realised that it was his cry, not hers, because the scarlet petals had not been spilt from the broken flowers, but from the crumpled body of the woman who slid helplessly into his arms.

CHAPTER TEN

EVERYTHING was white. Clean and pure and white.

Even the light that dazzled and hurt her eyes so much that she shut them quickly, only seconds after opening them.

'Donna,' came a low, anguished voice that she knew she ought to recognise. But recognition was difficult because it didn't sound like the voice she knew at all.

'Shh. She's sleeping,' said a voice she definitely didn't recognise. 'Let her rest. She needs to rest.'

Donna heard something else. The familiar/unfamiliar voice murmuring something with an odd, broken kind of urgency. And then peace once more.

Next time she opened her eyes the light had changed. This time it was softer, more golden. Part of her wondered whether she had died and gone to heaven.

'Hello, Donna.'

This time she recognised it properly. Her lips were bone-dry, so she licked them. She blinked as she was caught in the ice-blue spotlight of his eyes, and then recoiled at what she read in them.

Pain. Harsh and unremitting pain which threw the world into sharp focus.

She remembered now. Her own pain. And blood. And Marcus looking drained, speaking urgently down the telephone. An ambulance, its siren screaming like a demented woman. The unresisting cold steel of a hospital trolley. A man in a mask. A light shining in her eyes. Pain and wetness.

'Oh, my God!' She sat bolt upright and then slumped back against the pillows. *'No!'*

He caught her and cradled her against him awkwardly, as if he was frightened to touch her. 'Wait a minute,' he whispered against her hair. 'I'll fetch the midwife.'

Midwife?

Through a sickening daze a bell sounded. Donna became aware of a dark-haired woman with dimpled cheeks who came to the other side of the bed and tried to shoo Marcus away, but he wasn't going anywhere.

The nurse wore a badge which said, 'Midwifery Sister Hindmarsh.' She looked at Donna, her dimples disappearing as she waggled her finger like a teacher. 'You're a very lucky young woman, you know, Donna.'

Donna turned her head to one side and felt a tear slide slowly down her cheek. *Lucky?* Like hell! What was lucky about being alive if you'd lost the only thing which mattered? She shook her head.

'Oh, yes, you are.' The nurse shook her head in an exaggerated manner—as if reflecting on the foolishness of pregnant young women in general and Donna in particular. 'Running around the place like that,' she tutted. 'Working yourself up into a state. Is it any wonder you had a bleed?'

Through her befuddled state something clicked in Donna's mind. The nurse was being bossy. And the nurse wouldn't dare to be bossy if…

'The baby?' she croaked.

The nurse gave a grudging nod. 'Is fine. Absolutely fine. As I said, you're a very lucky young woman.'

Not quite believing her ears, Donna turned to Marcus, a question in her eyes.

He seemed to be having some difficulty speaking, but finally he nodded. 'It's okay, Donna. It's okay.' And then he smiled—weak and watery, but definitely a smile. 'You haven't lost the baby.'

Donna tried to sit up again, but Marcus's hand seemed to be very firmly restraining her whilst at the same time managing to give her shoulderblade the most wonderful massage. If she hadn't felt so drowsy she might have swatted his hand away, but as it was she was enjoying it far too much to want him to stop.

'How long have I been here?' she whispered.

'Only a few hours. The doctor examined you and they scanned you. After that you just wanted to go to sleep—don't you remember?'

She shook her head. 'I don't really remember anything. Maybe the sleep blocked it all out.' Perhaps that was nature's way of protecting you.

'I was there when you had your scan.' His voice held an unmistakable note of pride. 'The heart was beating like crazy and the baby looks *fantastic*!' He laughed. 'Though I guess you could say I'm a little biased!'

She put her hand tentatively over her belly. It still felt big. And full. Another tear slid down her cheek.

'Don't cry, sugar,' he said softly. 'The baby's safe and you're safe. Everything's going to be all right.'

The doctor was even more forthright than the nurse had been.

'You do understand everything I've explained to you, don't you, Donna?'

Donna nodded and looked to Marcus for support, but he looked just as grim as the doctor. Actually, he looked even grimmer.

'You have a condition known as placenta praevia,' the doctor continued. 'Which means that the placenta is lying very low down in your uterus. The risk is that it will rupture and tear.' His face grew serious. 'And if that were the case, then obviously both you and the baby would be put in danger.' He gave a gentle smile. 'But as it is what we call a Grade 1 placenta praevia it is only a *small* risk, as I have already explained to your partner.'

Donna opened her mouth to explain, but when she saw the look on Marcus's face decided that it wasn't worth it. Too complicated, she thought tiredly.

'There is no need for any treatment other than rest. But you *must* rest. Do you understand that, Donna?' He turned to Marcus. 'And you must keep an eye on her. There mustn't be a repeat of what happened today. She can potter around the place, but there must be no exertion. No lifting. No riding of bicycles. And no sex!' he finished severely.

Donna had never blushed so deeply in her life. She willed Marcus to rescue her, and he did—but in a way which made her embarrassment ten times worse.

'You're talking about penetrative sex, I presume, Doctor?'

Now it was the doctor's turn to look embarrassed. 'Er, yes. Obviously—'

'And what about my business?' Donna put in hastily, because she knew that she would curl up and *die* if they said anything else on the subject.

The doctor glowered. 'Just how important *is* your baby to you, Donna?'

'More important than anything in the world,' she told him truthfully.

The doctor hid a smile. 'Good. That's all I needed to know.'

Marcus waited until she was safely strapped into his car before he reinforced what they had both heard. 'You heard what the doctor said, Donna. I hope you're going to take notice.'

Stay calm, she told herself, stay calm. She cleared her throat. 'No matter what the doctor said—I still have a business to run. I can't just pretend it doesn't exist.'

He didn't answer immediately as he manouevered the car out of the hospital gates and drove as carefully as if he had a consignment of raw eggs on the seat beside him. 'You're not to worry about the business. That's all going to be taken care of.'

Not to worry, indeed! 'But *how*, Marcus?' she wailed. 'We can't cope with just two staff and I haven't got enough money to pay someone else if I can't work my-self.'

He stole a glance at her. 'Let me concentrate on the road,' he said abruptly. 'I don't want to have a row in the car.'

'Who said anything about a row?'

'That mutinous look on your face did. We'll talk about it when we get home!'

She sat back in her seat and sighed, knowing that it was pointless to argue.

But she protested when he drew up outside *his* house. 'Would you mind telling me why you've brought me here? I want to go home!'

'I know you do, but your tea-room isn't private enough,' he argued. 'And neither is the hotel. We need to talk without interruption.'

It seemed easier to agree than to protest—and besides, the sensible side of her knew he was right. So she let him lead her into the house. In fact, he actually tried to scoop her up into his arms to carry her, but she drew the line at having *that* happen. Last time he had picked her up it had been to take her up to bed, and look where that had led. 'Don't carry me, Marcus.'

'Why not?'

'Because I want to walk. I need to feel I can.'

'Don't you want to be cosseted?' he questioned softly.

'No, I prefer to be independent.' She smiled serenely. 'It gives a woman security—surely you know that?'

'I think I'm just beginning to find out,' he answered wryly.

But she allowed him to settle her on a beautiful chaise longue which stood in the bay window of the sitting room, overlooking the garden. And she lay watching the trees blowing gently in the breeze while Marcus went away to make tea and sandwiches.

He sat down on a chair opposite her and waited until she had worked her way through two rounds of egg and cress, pleased to see her devouring the sandwiches with that desperate kind of hunger—and the colour slowly returning to her cheeks. His own appetite seemed to have disappeared, along with his unshakeable belief that whatever he wanted in life he would somehow be able to achieve.

Because he had never felt quite so powerless as he had done while he'd endured the long wait through the doctor's examination. He had imagined losing the baby. Losing Donna. The world had tipped and shifted on its axis. It had been a sobering experience.

'Now,' he said. 'I have a proposition to put to you.'

'Go on.'

'Will you promise to hear me through without interruption?'

Donna pulled a face. 'That's a very mean request!'

'A very necessary one in your case. Will you?'

'How can I possibly answer that until I know what you're going to ask me?'

'*Please*, Donna.'

She smiled. 'I guess if you're pleading with me it must be important.'

'I'll take that as a yes.' He smiled back at her, unable to resist her at that moment and thinking what a mass of contradictions she could be. 'I know you said you didn't want to come and live here—' He held his hand up because he could see that she was itching to butt in with an objection. 'Remember what you promised!' he warned.

'But nothing has changed. I still don't want to live here.'

'Of course things have changed! You're not in a position to allow yourself the luxury of pleasing yourself. Not any more. You need to rest, Donna—you heard what the doctor said. You can't possibly go back to work. What if you wake in the night with a pain, or—God forbid—another bleed?'

'Don't!' She shuddered.

'Well, the doctor said it was unlikely—as long as you look after yourself—but it's still a possibility. You need another person around—night *and* day. If you're here I can look after you—and I should be looking after you. Hell, I *want* to look after you!'

Donna looked at him steadily. 'Finished?'

'Yes.'

'Can I speak now?'

He gave a longing kind of sigh. How could she be expecting his baby—slumped and recovering on the sofa—and yet still have the sexy air of the minx about her? 'Yes, Donna,' he said gravely. 'You can speak now.'

'Who's going to run your business for you while you're looking after me?'

'My general manager, of course.'

'*Exactly!*' She leapt on his answer with triumph. 'So who's going to run mine?'

Fortunately, he had anticipated just this question and prepared for it. 'Like I said—there's absolutely no cause for concern. I'm going to send over one of my cooks, who can help Ally with the baking. She's also prepared to wait tables if she needs to, but there are other staff I can supply, too.' He tried to tempt her a little bit more. 'To be honest, Donna, I employ a lot of people, and they are at your disposal for as long as you need them. You'll probably find that you'll be better staffed than you ever were before!'

Her face was stony. 'But you still haven't answered my question, Marcus. Who is actually going to *run* the business?'

He frowned as he tried to remember the name of the blonde who had scowled at him as if he were the devil incarnate. Was it Alison, or something? 'Ally!' he remembered. 'Or Sarah.'

'Wrong,' she corrected. 'Ally is a busy single mum with no desire to put in any more hours than she already does. And Sarah is a twenty-two-year-old with a social life which interests her more than a tea-room, not surprisingly.'

He looked at her. 'So?'

'So I'd like to know who's going to do all the ordering? Sort out rows with the laundry service? Be there to greet the tourists and generally act as host? All the unseen things which make the difference between a business running competently and running *brilliantly*. Who's going to do all that?'

Marcus could see where this was leading, and he could also see that there was only one person who could possibly do what she asked.

He sighed. 'I am, I guess.'

'Exactly! So it obviously makes far more sense for you to come and live with *me*!'

He looked at her with interest. 'How?'

'How, indeed!' she scoffed. 'You bring a suitcase and move in!'

The interest intensified. 'Maybe I should have said where?'

She looked at him steadily. 'Don't get any mistaken ideas. I may not have five bedrooms, like you—but I do have two. That's one for me and one for you. I've converted the whole upstairs into self-contained flat. You'll find all your home comforts there, Marcus. Simple.'

'Simple,' he echoed, realising this meant he would be put in the room where he had made love to her. He was about to be reminded of that afternoon every night and every morning. He sighed, and couldn't help thinking that his new accommodation was going to seem like a sophisticated form of prison.

Ally and Sarah giggled like schoolgirls when Donna broke the news to them.

'Marcus Foreman—Marcus *Foreman*—is going to be working here?' spluttered Sarah.

'Will he wear a pinny?' snorted Ally.

'Well, he could, as long as he wore it with nothing underneath,' said Sarah innocently. 'He's got the kind of body that women fantasise about!'

'Sarah!' cried Donna and Ally, in unison.

'Well, he has,' said Sarah stubbornly.

'Oh, go and make us all a cup of tea!' laughed Donna. 'And take a cold shower while you're at it!'

'So, let me get this straight,' said Ally, once Sarah had disappeared in the direction of the kitchen. 'Marcus will do everything that you usually do, and he will also provide any extra staff we need?'

'That's right. He wants to keep a close watch on me.'

'How close?'

'Ever heard of clams?'

Ally laughed. 'Oh, I see. So that means he's going to be sleeping here as well, does it?'

Donna blushed. 'There's no way round that. He thinks I shouldn't be left on my own, and even the doctor agrees about *that*. So you can stop looking at me like that, because it's not how you think!'

'Really?'

'Really! I shall have my room, and Marcus will be staying in the spare room.'

'Won't that fuel his fantasies—having you so close?'

Donna shot her an incredulous look. 'You're kidding! I don't think Marcus will be having any sexual fantasies about a woman who is beginning to resemble a mountain of lard!'

'What was that?' came an interested male voice as Marcus himself walked into the room.

Donna blushed again. 'Oh, nothing.'

'Just discussing my sexual fantasies, were you?' he enquired idly.

'If you knew, then why did you ask?'

'I just enjoy seeing you blush, Donna.'

'Well, make the most of it! Hopefully I'll become immune to your off-beat sense of humour,' she said sweetly.

'You never did before,' he smiled.

'Ah, but I was younger then!'

Ally stood up. 'Suddenly I feel a little superfluous. I think I'll go and see what's happened to that tea.'

'You don't have to,' protested Donna.

Ally smiled. 'Oh, yes, I do. You know what they say. Two's company and three in this case is most definitely a crowd!'

Ally closed the door behind her and they looked at one another across the room.

'We're going to have to avoid doing that,' said Donna.

'What? Talking about my sexual fantasies? I agree. Because life at the hotel will seem very tame by comparison if that's what counts as normal conversation over here!'

She looked into his eyes and the mischief and humour in them made a pretty potent combination.

She quickly began to straighten a stack of linen napkins. 'You know very well I didn't mean that. I was talking about excluding Ally and Sarah. And we mustn't.'

She wriggled her shoulders, as if trying to ease the tension out of them, and the fire of her hair shimmered like a beacon. Worse than that—it drew his attention to the heavy fullness of her breasts.

He felt the hot flame of desire, and dampened it down to a dull smoulder. 'You started it by talking about me while I was out of the room!'

'Eavesdroppers never hear any good about themselves,' she said serenely. 'Anyway, we were just discussing where you're going to sleep.' She smiled, and looked at the appropriately modest suitcase he had carried in with him. 'Like me to show you your room?'

'Okay.' Feeling a little like a man going off to his own execution, he followed her upstairs—noticing now how the pregnancy had added a little extra flesh to her bottom. But the added curves suited her, he decided. Maybe too much. He hadn't been upstairs since the day they'd made love, and he felt the blood heating his face as they reached the top of the stairs.

The image of that afternoon was burned indelibly into his memory, and it came on him when he least expected it or wanted it. Like when he was sitting round a table in the middle of some stuffy meeting and he would get a flashback of those pale, beautiful limbs entwined around him, or her glossy red hair spread all over the pillow.

He had convinced himself that not only was she bad for him—they were bad for each other. He had regretted that afternoon just as much as he'd revelled in its sweet, erotic memory. He had thought that not seeing her would make that memory recede and that distance would enable him to put her out of his mind—the way he had managed to do all those years before. But nothing seemed that simple any more. Nothing.

Donna saw him tense and guessed what he might be thinking—maybe because she was thinking pretty much the same thing herself. 'This is where it all started,' she observed softly as they drew up outside the spare room.

But he shook his head. 'Oh, it started long before this, Donna. It started when you walked into my hotel, dripping wet. Looking so lost and so small.'

She forced herself not to be seduced by the memory. Or his words. She led him quickly past the room which was to be his, and threw open the door of her own bedroom, and Marcus opened his eyes in surprise—as much at the room itself as the fact that she had allowed him access to it.

It was painted a soft buttermilk, with white muslin curtains billowing like clouds at the window and a snowy drift of a duvet lying like a great heap of snow on the brass bed. On the wall she had pinned different straw hats—some with flowers, some with ribbons, some battered, one scarcely worn.

'I buy a new hat every summer,' she explained, when she saw him looking at them.

'Which one did you buy this year?'

She pointed to the newest-looking one, which was decked with shiny red cherries and a scarlet ribbon. 'That one.'

'Put it on now,' he coaxed softly.

'No.'

'As the acting manager of this establishment, I command you to put it on!' he said sternly.

Funny how he could make putting a hat on seem like a highly erotic invitation. 'No, I won't! Finish looking at the rest of my room instead!'

Aching, he complied. Apart from the bed, the only piece of furniture was a dressing table—with a small stool which stood in front of it. Overall the effect was simple, clean and stylish.

She looked at him, searching his face for a reaction. 'So what do you think?'

'I like it. It's a very attractive room. Feminine without being in the least bit frilly.'

'Is it what you were expecting?'

'I don't know what I was expecting. I wasn't expecting you to come back to Winchester and start your own business.' He smiled. 'I've learnt to expect the unexpected from you, Donna—you're not an easy woman to stereotype.'

'Then let's destroy another stereotype while we're at it, shall we?' She walked over to the dressing table and picked up a photograph in a silver frame which stood among several others.

'Here.' She handed it to him.

Marcus studied it. It was of a woman aged about twenty-five. She was wearing a tiny bikini, made entirely out of silver sequins, and she stared at the camera with a smile which managed to be both saucy and innocent. Her hair was very dark, but apart from that it was easy to see the likeness—the big green eyes and the secret smile which reminded him so much of Donna's.

'It's your mother?' he guessed.

'That's right.' She pointed to the brief bikini. 'See what she's wearing?'

He nodded.

'She used to keep the bottoms on, you know. During her act. And parts of her breasts were covered by tassels. She was never completely naked.'

'You don't have to explain anything to me,' he said uncomfortably.

'Yes, Marcus, I do,' she said firmly. 'I need you to know. The word ''stripper'' is so emotive—but we forget how society has moved on. My mother used to wear nothing that wouldn't be worn on a beach now—or probably to a film première!' She took the photo away and put it back down. 'I'm not saying that I think it was a good job—because it wasn't. It was a lousy, stinking job. She just made it as acceptable as she could. Now look at this one—'

The next photo showed the same woman, aged about fifty. Her hair had touches of silver and she wore a simple woollen dress, a single strand of pearls at her neck. She looked, thought Marcus, like someone you would automatically give the best table in the restaurant to.

'This is some years after she bought her boarding house,' said Donna.

He couldn't keep the astonishment out of his voice. 'What happened?'

'She got herself an education. Oh, I don't mean that she started going to evening classes, or anything—just that she read books. Lots of different books. She learned how to think and she learned how to dress. She stopped believing that paste jewellery was beautiful and pearls and amber were dull. She learned the value of things.'

'But she never married again?'

'She wasn't ever married in the first place. Not to my father, anyway. I'm illegitimate,' said Donna, and gave him a wistful smile as she replaced the photo. 'You see, even that doesn't shock people any more.'

'Did it shock people when you were growing up?'

'Sometimes. But not enough to ruin my life.' She shrugged as she moved towards him. 'I'm not showing you this to get the sympathy vote, you know. My childhood made me what I am today, and I like the person I am today, so I can't regret it. Any of it.'

He reached out and captured her face, cupping it gently in the palm of his hand. 'I like the person you are today, too.'

'Well, that's a good start.'

He rubbed his thumb thoughtfully over the base of her chin. 'There are a couple of things that *you* need to know as well, Donna—and the first concerns your mother.'

She took a step back, away from the distracting feel of his thumb. 'Go on.'

'I never judged either her or you by what she did for a living—I wasn't given the opportunity. *You* were the one who assumed I was prejudiced. I objected to being lied to while you apparently trusted my brother enough to tell him everything.'

'You were always too busy. Too distracted. You put up a barrier which Lucas never did.'

'Maybe.'

'No maybe about it. It's true.' She looked at him, and realised that perhaps she hadn't been as honest as she could have been. 'I wanted you to *like* me, Marcus—not look down your nose at me. That's why I told you my mother was an actress.'

'I realise that now. Besides, I *did* like you—and the way I felt wasn't something I could control. I think I would have felt the same way if you'd told me that you'd just landed in a spacecraft from Mars!'

She looked at him. 'That was the first thing you wanted to say to me. What was the second?'

'Something I tried to tell you when you came to my office yesterday. That I never intended to fight you for custody of the baby.'

'That's what you told me.'

'I know. But I was angry. And frustrated.'

She raised her eyebrows and looked at him.

'Not in the sense that you're thinking. I meant frustrated by the whole situation, and my role as a bit-player. You were going to have my baby and I felt like I was just looking on from the sidelines.'

'I'm sorry,' she said simply, 'that one afternoon of lust—or passion, or whatever you want to call it—should have trapped you with this huge and irrevocable consequence.'

'And I'm sorry, too,' he said quietly. 'You're even more trapped by the situation than I am. It isn't your fault that the contraception failed. Anyway, there's no point in regrets. That's history—not reality. Our reality is here, and now.'

'Yes, I know.' Her words filled a silence made more intense by the realisation that he was still within touching distance.

The desire to kiss her was stronger than anything he had ever felt in his life, but now was not the right time to give in to temptation. Kisses led to inevitable conclusions. She was still pale, and fragile—no matter how much she protested to the contrary.

And the doctor had said no sex, in any case.

'Why don't you lie down and rest,' he suggested easily, 'while I go and see what needs doing downstairs?'

CHAPTER ELEVEN

FOR the first week after Marcus moved in, he and Donna walked on eggshells—behaving as politely as two people who had just met instead of two people who were soon to become parents. Somehow their lives managed to be both intimate and separate at the same time.

Marcus even went over to the hotel every morning to shower and shave, once Ally and Sarah had arrived for work. He told Donna that bathrooms were especially private places and that he wouldn't invade her space.

Donna thought he meant that her bathroom was too small—which it was—and tried not to feel offended—but she did. The same way she felt when they were sitting watching TV in the evenings, and Marcus would leap to his feet and say that he was going to do some work in the office downstairs. But he'd say it in such a growling kind of way that she found herself wondering if she had offended him.

Still, she wasn't going to find out by attempting to read his mind, and after a week she decided that they needed to talk.

She waited until Ally and Sarah had gone home after one particularly busy afternoon, and found Marcus sitting in the office, doing some paperwork of his own. His eyes looked sleep-depleted and he badly needed a shave—so how come he still looked like the most desirable man she had ever seen in her life?

He looked up as she walked in, and frowned. 'Everything okay?'

'Not really.'

He was on his feet in an instant, his face a fretwork of frowns. 'Is it the baby?'

'No, it is not the baby!' said Donna crossly. 'Every time I feel tired or have a negative thought it doesn't mean that I'm going to lose the baby!'

'Don't be so bloody flippant, Donna.'

'I'll be flippant if I like!' she retorted, knowing her voice sounded wild, but blaming it on the hormones which were raging remorselessly around her bloodstream. 'I'm the one who is actually *carrying* this child. Remember? I'm the one stuck with this bizarre situation of having you living here with me like some...some...'

'Mmm?' He raised his eyebrows, instantly on the alert. 'Some what?'

'Some...*stranger*!' she blustered.

He smiled. 'Very mild, Donna. I was expecting much worse than that!'

'*Now* who's being flippant?'

The ice-blue stare had thawed a little. 'Sit down,' he suggested softly.

Now why did Marcus suddenly sound like the host? Donna pulled out the chair opposite him and sat down.

'Tell me what you want, sugar,' he said gently.

She wondered how much she dared say, and then realised that she had nothing to lose by being honest.

'I can't see that you living here is going to work if you're just going to cook for me and bring me cups of tea all day and then hide away in another room. Like some old-fashioned retainer! Or a paying guest who isn't paying!'

'You mean you want rent from me?' he asked, deadpan.

'*No!*'

Marcus laughed. 'Okay. That's what you don't want. Now tell me what would please you.'

Donna swallowed as she studied her hands, which were neatly folded on her lap—it seemed easier that way than having to meet his eyes. He could please her just by existing. But there was being honest and being foolish, and you didn't tell a man a thing like that—especially when he hadn't shown the slightest tendency to come *near* her—let alone make love to her—in months.

She sighed. 'If you're here in body, but not in spirit, then I'm getting all the disadvantages of having someone share my house—with none of the advantages.'

'Such as?'

Donna shrugged. 'Oh, I don't know! The late-night chats over a cup of cocoa—'

'But you're not allowed late nights—remember what the doctor said?'

She pulled a face at him. 'Okay. The soul-searching, then.'

This drew a smile. 'You want to search my soul, do you, Donna?' he mocked.

'Yes, I do,' she murmured. 'If you've got one! You're the father of my baby, Marcus—and I don't want you to be a stranger to me! Or to the baby. I want to be able to answer questions about you, when he or she is older.'

The smile disappeared. 'Questions in my absence, you mean? Isn't that rather assuming that I'm not going to be around to answer them myself?'

'But that's the whole point! *I don't know!* We haven't discussed it, have we? We haven't discussed anything. How much of a hands-on father are you intending to be?' She stared at him intently. 'You can't just move in and pretend that nothing is happening. Something very big *is* happening, and we need to talk about how we're going to deal with it.'

He was silent for a moment. 'Don't you think we should take things slowly?'

'That's rich—in view of how we got ourselves into this situation in the first place! We didn't think about taking things slowly *then*! And there's a difference between taking things slowly and never getting off the starting block!'

Marcus sat back in the chair, his eyes looking very blue against the pale denim shirt he wore. 'But we can't possibly predict how we're going to react to this baby when it feels like we're making everything up as we go along. Doesn't it?' he probed.

'I guess it does.' She gave him a look which she knew was helpless, but she was past caring whether or not she appeared vulnerable. Right then she *felt* vulnerable. But she was pregnant—so she was allowed to! 'Maybe it feels like this for all parents-to-be.'

'Maybe.' He stared down at the yellow roses which stood in a crystal vase on the desk. Donna must have put them there this morning. 'What we *can* do is to make the most of the present and see where we go from there. The relationship we forge together during these next few months is going to be the foundation for the future.'

'Some foundation,' she murmured, 'when you've been actively avoiding me.'

He shook his head. 'I haven't been avoiding you, sugar. I told you. I was giving you space. Trying not to upset your life still further—'

'Marcus!' She leaned across the desk. 'About the only thing which could upset my life further at the moment would be to discover that I'm to give birth on national television!'

'Ah, yes,' he said gravely. 'I've been meaning to speak to you about that!'

Their eyes met across the desk and the sparks of humour which flew between them were unbearably erotic, Donna thought, smoothing her cotton dress down over her bump, as if to remind herself of the consequences of erotic thought.

'Tell me what you want to know,' he said.

'About you, mainly,' she said simply.

Marcus nodded, almost to himself. He'd wondered when this might be coming. He met her gaze with a mocking smile. 'I gather you don't want to hear about the highs and lows of my life as a hotelier?'

'Not really.'

'You want to hear about the other women?'

Donna drew in a sharp breath. That was what she had been hinting at, yes. She hadn't expected him to be quite so blunt about it.

He didn't wait for an answer. 'There's no need to start looking coy all of a sudden. That, presumably, is what you're angling to hear about? My past relationships?'

'I'd be lying if I told you I wasn't interested,' she told him quietly. 'Yet I'm not really certain that I want to hear about them.'

'Maybe you should start the ball rolling by telling me about yours,' he challenged softly.

'Oh, just…the usual.'

'That's a pretty sweeping definition.' He narrowed his eyes. 'Ever come close to marrying?'

'Nope. Have you?'

He shook his head. 'Never. Ever been in love?'

Well, she certainly wasn't going to admit to loving…she deliberately changed the tense…to *having* loved *him*. Honesty should not equal humiliation! 'What's love?' she asked, properly flippant this time.

'Cynic!' he laughed, but oddly he found that her answer disappointed him. Surely he wasn't so arrogant as to suppose that she had once loved him?

'Have you?' she asked him tentatively.

'Oh, there have been times in my life when I sensed that I was on the brink of something that other people might describe as love,' he said slowly. 'It's just that I always pulled back!'

'In the nick of time?' she suggested.

'Yeah. Maybe.' His eyes grew thoughtful. There *had* been women. After he'd sent Donna away, there had been quite a lot of women. As if he'd wanted to prove to himself that he was the world's greatest lover. For a time.

And in the years which had followed there had been some who'd been textbook-perfect wife material in just about every way which mattered. Yet something had always held him back from making a commitment, and he'd never come close to finding out what it was. 'Maybe,' he repeated.

The sun had moved across the sky and shadows fell onto his face, defining the dip of his cheekbones and the darkened curve of his chin. 'Now you tell me something, Donna.' He paused, searching her face for the first flicker of reaction before she had a chance to modify it. 'When you wake up each morning, there's a dreamy little interlude before reality slots into place. Right?'

'Mmm.' She narrowed her eyes, not sure what line he was going to take. 'So?'

'So when that happens, and you remember that you're going to have a baby—my baby—do you groan and turn over and feel trapped? Maybe wish it had never happened?'

Donna smiled. 'I groan, yes—always—and so would you if you woke up to raging heartburn or a feeling of nausea!'

He smiled too.

'As to whether I feel trapped.' She wriggled a bit in her seat as she gave the question some thought. 'Sometimes, obviously I do—especially when I think of the sheer commitment of having a baby. And the birth itself, of course. But I asked some of the other mothers in my antenatal group, and they said they felt exactly the same.' Her eyes softened in response to the question in his. 'As to wishing it had never happened; well, it has. Like you once said, you can't rewrite the past, but…' Her expression grew thoughtful.

'But?' He put in softly, fascinated by the dreamy look on her face.

Donna shrugged. 'It's funny, really—I mean the logical side of you thinks, Help! But then there's this soppy side of you that seems to cut right through all the practical objections. So that even though this is never how you would have planned to have a baby, you're just thinking, Oh, yes, please! I mean, it seems absolutely crazy to me—but I can't *wait*!'

'Can't you?'

'No.' She shook her head as she heard the indulgent note in his voice. 'Sad, isn't it? A psychologist would have a field-day—telling me that I was trying to create the family unit I never had myself and that's the subconscious reason why I became pregnant. Only it won't be a proper family unit at all. I'm doing exactly what my mother did, and raising a child on my own.'

He shook his head. 'Wrong, Donna. Your father deserted you, and your mother. I'm not going anywhere.'

She bit her lip, forcing herself to accept the truth, however unpalatable. 'But one day you might. One day you might not pull back from the brink. You might fall in love with a woman who will resent me—and who could blame her? If I were in her shoes I might feel the same about a casual fling who had got herself pregnant!'

'Donna,' he said patiently. 'You're accepting blame where none is due. The reason you became pregant is because the condom failed—'

'Don't!' she wailed. 'That makes it even worse. Implying that I had an ''accident''—with all the negative baggage that word brings!'

'And the reason the condom failed,' he continued inexorably, ignoring her shocked gasp and her rapidly rising colour, 'was presumably because we had some of the most—' He drew a breath, not sure where this admission was going to take him. 'The *most*,' he emphasised, 'passionate sex I can ever remember.'

There was a short silence.

'Honestly?' asked Donna, her heart pumping like mad, hardly able to meet his eyes.

He noted her use of the word—a word she had used on more than one occasion today. And if he owed her anything it was that. 'Honestly,' he nodded, but then he shut up. Talking about it only made him think about it, and thinking about it didn't really help him sleep at night.

Donna tried not to read too much into his words. Just because the sex had been passionate, it didn't mean any more than that. Nor did she want it to. It was only her wildly fluctuating hormones demanding what nature had determined she should demand. A mate who would love her and provide for their child.

Well Marcus would certainly provide for their child—but that was *all* she could count on. She felt the familiar and gentle fluttering of the baby inside her, and blinked rapidly.

'Are you okay?' he demanded.

She felt oddly shy, praying that he wouldn't ask to feel—and praying that he would. 'It's the baby—it's moving!'

He was longing to touch her belly, but they had already raked up a lot of emotion today—surely any more would crowd her?

He registered all the conflicting emotions he could see on her face. There was fear and uncertainty, joy and disbelief. Heaven knew, he'd experienced them all himself, and a few more besides. 'Donna,' he said softly.

'Mmm?'

'You look tired.'

'I am a bit.'

'Right, then,' he said briskly. 'Go and lie down before dinner.' He saw her expression and knew what it meant. 'And stop worrying. I won't be the unpaying guest any more. Everything will be exactly as you want it to be—you only have to say. In the evening we will talk to your heart's content.' He smiled. 'Do you still play cards?'

'I'm a little rusty.'

'I could give myself a handicap.'

'That would be very sweet of you,' said Donna innocently. 'I'm sure I'd never manage to beat you these days.'

CHAPTER TWELVE

'SO WHAT do you want to do tonight, sugar?'

Donna looked up from her tapestry as Marcus breezed into the sitting room. She was embroidering a snow-white goose with a big blue ribbon around its neck. For the baby.

She'd never thought she would be the kind of person to enjoy precision sewing, but to her suprise she not only loved it, but was good at it, too. It was the perfect occupation for someone who wanted to be doing something but wasn't allowed to move much! And at this late stage in her pregnancy she physically *couldn't* have moved much—even if the doctors had told her she could!

She gave a dreamy sort of smile as she gazed up at him. 'Shall we play cards?'

Marcus pulled a face, and moved around the room restlessly. 'I'm bored with cards.'

'You're just fed up with losing!'

'I only let you win because of your delicate condition!'

'Of course you do!' Donna bit back a smile. 'Anyway, I don't feel in the least bit delicate at the moment.'

'No.' He ran his eyes over her. 'You don't look it, either. You look as healthy as an—'

'Ox?' she supplied drily.

'That wouldn't have been my first word of choice, no.'

'How about—like a barrage balloon?'

He considered this, relishing the invitation for him to look at her properly. Normally he had to do it when she wasn't aware he was watching her. Like when she was asleep. And at thirty-seven weeks into her pregnancy she was sleeping a lot. Then he would feast his eyes on her burgeoning figure with a mixture of pride and lust.

Especially lust.

He'd always found Donna sexually attractive, but it had come as a revelation for him to discover that he found her just as desirable when she was almost full-term with the baby.

Almost as big a revelation as discovering that he *could* reign in his sexual desire for her when he needed to. It hadn't been easy, but over the past few months—somehow—he'd kept the pleasurable, persistent ache of longing well hidden from her.

'Er, no.' He swallowed. 'You don't look like a barrage balloon, either.'

'What then?'

It was that slumberous little side glance that played such havoc with his composure! 'Just stop playing the tease, will you, Donna?' he growled. 'Or you might find you get more than you bargained for!'

Donna looked up at him thoughtfully as she leaned back against the bank of cushions, thinking how disgustingly healthy and vibrant and sexy he looked in a charcoal sweater and dark cords. But he looked distinctly grumpy, too—and just when she had thought that things between them were ticking along so beautifully.

In one corner of the room over by the window stood the Christmas tree which Marcus had dressed the day before—although she had masterminded all decorations from her almost permanent position on the sofa!

It was hard to believe that he had been sharing her

flat for over three months—yet he had slotted into her life as though he had been born for just that purpose. What was even harder to believe was that their baby would be born soon after the month was out. But Donna wasn't scared; she just wanted the waiting to be over.

'You're very jittery tonight,' she observed, in that calm, almost sleepy manner which seemed to be part and parcel of being pregnant.

'Yeah, well.' He scowled.

'Well, what?'

He shook his head. 'Nothing.'

'Marcus,' she said patiently. 'You can't come out with elusive little snippets like that and then not explain yourself. What's troubling you?'

He studied her carefully. 'You are—or rather, your attitude is.'

'Oh? You don't like the way I overrode your opinion on the tinsel?' she suggested lightly, looking in the direction of the Christmas tree, because anything was better than meeting that sizzling blue stare which was making her feel all mushy inside. 'Or do you think we've gone over the top with the angel hair?'

'Hell, Donna!' he exploded. 'That illustrates my point exactly!'

'What does?'

'You take things so lightly.'

She *did* meet his gaze then, and her expression was fierce. 'Are you suggesting that I'm not taking this pregnancy seriously?'

'Yes! *No!* Oh, I don't know!'

'Tell me,' she coaxed.

He ran his hand distractedly through the ruffled dark hair and flopped down onto a chair. 'Physically, you're doing everything the doctors and the midwife tell you—'

'Sounds like there's a "but" coming,' observed Donna drily.

'But I don't know anything about your mental state!'

Donna blinked. 'You think I'm crazy—is that it?'

'Donna!'

'Well, that's what it sounded like!'

'You never tell me about your worries!' he said stubbornly. 'Your doubts, your fears, your uncertainties!'

'You're assuming I've got some?'

'I know you have.'

Donna looked at him steadily. 'Oh? How?'

'Remember September?' he asked.

'That was months ago!'

'I don't need a speaking calendar! I know when it was,' he told her waspishly. 'Remember we were walking back from the cathedral and you saw that whole bunch of schoolchildren?'

The children had been noisy and laughing and wearing uniforms which had looked much too big for them. 'Yes. I remember. What about it?'

'And you went all quiet, didn't you? I saw you looking at one child in particular.'

A child with eyes that had reminded her so much of *his* eyes. 'Yes.'

'And I knew you were trying to imagine *our* child going to school like that—'

'Only I couldn't,' she put in quietly. 'It seemed too far in the future. Too impossible to imagine. Anyway…' She smoothed her hand down over her swollen belly. 'While I'm flattered that you noticed my reaction, that *was* three months ago. Why did it take you so long to get around to asking me, Marcus?'

He gave a sigh. 'Because when the doctor told you to take it easy, I sort of assumed that meant pushing the more awkward issues to one side. I didn't want it to come over as a criticism of *you*.'

'And wasn't it?'

He shook his head. 'Not at all. Surely it's only healthy to be aware of the difficulties which lie ahead of us? If you thought that everything was going to be one hundred per cent perfect for one hundred per cent of the time, then I *would* be worried. Because that would be unrealistic.' There was a brief pause, and his eyes took on an almost luminous intensity. 'Any regrets, Donna?'

She went very still. 'Have you?'

He gave a faint smile. 'That isn't fair.'

'Tell me what *is* fair.' She smiled, but the question in her eyes did not go away.

Marcus hesitated. Analysing how he felt still seemed pretty alien to him—but he owed Donna the truth. Hell, he owed her a lot more than that, but truth came pretty high up the list.

'I did have a few regrets,' he admitted. 'Right at the beginning.'

Donna nodded, respecting the honesty which lay behind his answer and realising how much simpler it would have been for him to have lied to her. 'But not any more?'

He shook his head. 'Now I just want it to happen. Sometimes it seems as though it never will. And sometimes I try to imagine what things will be like when the baby arrives, but I just can't. It's too big.' He stretched his legs out and gave her a lazy smile. 'But then I could never have imagined living with you, like this—'

'And finding it tolerable?' she questioned casually.

'Finding it more than tolerable!' he teased. 'Finding that I like it very much.' Apart from the fact that sexually she was off-limits, of course. And he wouldn't dream of telling her *that*. His face grew serious. 'I just want more than anything for the two of you to be safe and healthy.'

Donna nodded. 'I know you do.' With her finger she traced a line around the circumferance of her bump. 'It's funny—we've been to all the classes and read all the books; I've eaten the right things and done everything I've been told to—but there's still this great sense of uncertainty—of leaping into the unknown. That *is* scary—but then, life *is* scary sometimes.'

He nodded, finding the sight of her swollen body unbearably moving. He thought how brave she had been. She'd never complained of tiredness, or of losing her figure as he knew so many women did. 'Whatever happens between us, Donna,' he said suddenly, 'we have to make things work for the baby's sake.'

It sounded awfully as if he was preparing her for the inevitable—and in Donna's eyes the inevitable was that Marcus would move out as soon as the baby was born. And that she would only see him when he came round to collect the child. She pushed the image away. 'Yes,' she agreed. 'I know we do.'

'Both of us had crazy childhoods, sugar—let's make sure we don't pass the same legacy onto our baby.'

Her smile wasn't as steady as she would have liked, but that wasn't really surprising when he said our baby like that. It was such an emotional phrase to use.

He saw her look of uncertainty and wanted to take her in his arms there and then, but he was terrified that she would misinterpret the gesture. And besides, he wasn't sure that he trusted himself to. Self-control was one thing, but the strain of living so closely with her and not being permitted to lay a finger on her was beginning to tell. He didn't know how she did it, but her inbuilt sensuality seemed to have grown along with the baby—and he would defy any normal, red-blooded male not to have felt the same as he did.

Not that they had been doing anything likely to fan the flames of passion—quite the opposite, in fact. They spent long lazy evenings and weekends together. Marcus cooked and Donna continued to eat enough for two—sometimes three. They played cards and watched television—though the channel was swiftly changed if there was anything on it which was even *remotely* connected to sex.

They read books—sometimes they even read the same books and then they discussed them afterwards. Sometimes the discussions were amicable, when they agreed on something. More often than not they could only have been descibed as 'heated'.

And heated was also the only way he could describe the way she left him feeling most evenings when she demurely went to bed—at some unholy hour. Sometimes as early as nine o'clock! He would try to concentrate on something other than how soft and pale and beautiful and *lonely* she must be feeling, upstairs underneath that snowy-white duvet. While he sat alone, mocked by memories.

'Are you hungry?' he asked her, with a gentle smile.

'Not really.' She lay back against the cushions and clasped her hands over her belly. 'It doesn't feel as if there's very much room in there tonight. Certainly not for food. Ouch!'

Marcus brightened. 'Baby moving?'

'Baby making attempt on prenatal kick-boxing championship, more like!'

'Can I feel?'

There was barely a flicker of hesitation before she

said, 'Of course.' She had never said no to him before, but then he hardly ever asked, even though she sensed he was dying to feel his child moving. She suspected that he found it just as difficult and distracting as she did.

She sat up a little straighter and shifted up the sofa to make way for him, dreading the feel of his warm hand on her belly. Well, not dreading it so much as wondering whether she would manage to sit through it without wriggling—but then it was such an intimate thing to do, when you thought about it.

He nestled up close and gently put the flat of his hand down on her belly, and almost immediately the baby aimed a healthy kick at it.

'Ouch!' He retracted the hand in mock-pain. 'I can see what you mean! Donna, it must hurt like hell.'

She shook her head. 'No, it doesn't. It's a funny, fantastic feeling. I can't really describe it.'

'Look!' he exclaimed, and bent his dark head to study the bump intently. 'You can see the shape of the heel quite clearly. Look—it's like a fish moving around underneath the surface!'

He sounded as excited as a little boy whose favourite team had just won the league! Donna smiled. 'A fish? More like a dolphin!'

He put his hand back over her umbilicus and just let it rest there, then turned his head to look at her. 'Do you think it's a boy?'

'Yes,' she nodded. 'Or a girl!'

'Donna!'

'Marcus!' she teased.

'Do you wish we'd found out?'

During one of her routine scans they had been asked whether they wished to know the sex of their child, and they had looked at one another and shaken their heads at exactly the same time and said, 'No thanks.'

'No, I don't,' said Donna. 'I want there to be a nice surprise at the end of all that labour!'

His heart leapt with anxiety. 'I wish I could do it all for you, sugar.'

'Well, you can't. You're not biologically programmed to!' She snuggled back comfortably against the cushions. 'But it's sweet of you to say so.'

He wondered if she was as aware as he was that his fingers were within touching distance of her breasts, which had been growing bigger by the day. He ached to touch them.

She was wearing a maternity dress that he had bought for her in London. He had travelled up for a meeting— very reluctantly—and only after making water-tight arrangements ensuring that Donna would be well looked after. He had been heading for the Tube, walking down one of those fancy streets in the centre of the city, when he had seen the maternity shop.

He had wandered in without really knowing what he wanted. If anything. But there had been several very helpful sales assistants who had fussed around him as if he were the first father since the world began. They'd asked what colour hair Donna had. And what colour eyes. And they'd complimented him on his descriptive powers, claiming that most men didn't have a clue what colour their wives' eyes were! And he hadn't corrected them.

He had ended up buying a knee-length velvet dress— the pale green colour of a new leaf, expensive and highly impractical. It was fitted on the bust, from where it fell in softly draped folds to just above the knee, showing off her magnificent legs. He thought it made her look like some contemporary Grecian goddess.

'That dress looks wonderful,' he said in a throaty voice.

'Does it?'

'Mmm. You look like a green bud, about to burst into leaf.'

'It's far too good to be wearing round the house like this, but I keep thinking that there are only three weeks to go—so I'd better get as much wear as I can from it.'

'Mmm,' he said again, hardly hearing a word she said, aware only of his child growing deep inside her.

Donna realised that his hand was still lying over her stomach, and she would have moved except that he seemed so contented like that, and to be truthful—she *liked* it. She felt safe. Protected.

Marcus held his breath. He had been expecting her to shift uncomfortably away from him, but he felt no resistance—not even passive resistance. Through the soft green material of her dress he could feel the baby—not belting its limbs around any more, but obviously just squirming around happily.

Donna relaxed. Why not just lie back and enjoy what was a perfectly relaxed and conventional pose between two parents-to-be? Okay—they might be not be the most conventional *couple* in the world, but so what?

She liked the gentle pressure of his hand. In fact she felt so comfortable that she might even think about resting her head on his shoulder. And why not? They had already agreed that he would be present at the birth—and you couldn't get more intimate than *that*.

Marcus's pulse rocketed as he felt her relax against him. It was pitiful! Laughable, really—that such a small crumb of affection should bring him such pleasure. And even more laughable that he should suddenly feel like a complete novice. Except that he *was* a complete novice in this situation. He had never made love to a pregnant woman before...

And you're not going to make love to one now, he told himself firmly. All she's doing is resting her head on your shoulder!

Donna closed her eyes and felt herself drifting into a place somewhere between wakefulness and sleep. Where sight and sound retreated to a distant place, and where sensation overwhelmed everything else. She could feel the weight of the baby, and its occasional bubbling little movements. She snuggled into the hard contour of Marcus's shoulder, and felt the firm flesh and the whispering of silk as his shirt brushed against her cheek. She sighed.

Unable to resist any longer, Marcus let his thumb brush lightly against the base of her swollen breast, and held his breath while he waited for her reaction. But she just sighed again.

This time the touch of his thumb was more deliberate, and this time the breath which escaped her sounded deliciously dreamy. He grew bolder. Drew slow, light circles round and round the nipple until he felt her moving impatiently beneath him, making a protesting little cry.

'Donna?' he said softly.

She opened her eyes to find him watching her. 'Mmm?'

'Did I wake you?'

'I wasn't asleep.'

'Were you pretending to be?' he asked suddenly.

She felt lazy and comfortable, the blood pulsing through her veins like honey. 'Yes. Naughty of me, wasn't it?'

'Why bother pretending?'

The baby was impeding her ability to shrug. 'I suppose I thought that if I pretended, then I could just lie back and enjoy what you were doing. Without having to question whether I should be letting you.'

'Don't feel guilty,' he urged.

'It's easy for you to say that. Men don't seem to have the same hang-ups about sex...as women.' She had very nearly said sex without love.

'Don't have hang-ups. Just enjoy it.'

'Mmm.' She was keeping her eyes open only with the greatest of concentration. 'What's the matter, Marcus? I've never seen you looking so edgy before.'

Because he had spent every day and every night under her roof in a state of near-permanant excitement, while he behaved in the most decent way he knew how. Knowing that he couldn't—no, *mustn't* go near her. If it had been anyone else he might have tried, but not Donna. Not after the urgent way they had fallen into bed last time. And she was pregnant—so he had all the protective baggage which went with that.

It was just that the thought that maybe she'd wanted him to do this to her all along was nearly driving him out of his head with excitement. 'I thought you were about to leap up and slap me around the face.'

'I don't think I could leap anywhere at the moment,' she said drily.

'Oh.' He recognised the husky note in her voice. She wanted him to carry on—he would have staked everything he owned on that. 'Well, maybe I should just continue with what I was doing,' he said thickly. 'Who knows? It might even send you to sleep.'

'I suppose it might,' she agreed unconvincingly, and she lay back and closed her eyes again.

He was almost frightened to begin, for fear that he would never be able to stop. And he must be able to stop. The slightest hint of resistance or second thoughts on Donna's part and he would put an end to it without her having to utter a word.

His whole hand cupped her breast while the thumb began to tease the swollen, tightened centre. He watched the unconscious way her body communicated its pleasure to him. Her lips were parted and her breath beginning to quicken. He watched the way her head tipped back, as if its weight was too great a burden for the pale column of her neck and that great heavy rope of hair hanging down her back. He noticed the slow unfurling of her fingers, like petals warming to the sun. And he knew that if her eyes were open the pupils would be huge and black and dilated.

He idly changed the direction of his thumb and heard her purr with pleasure in response, and it was only then that he bent his head and began to kiss her.

'Oh,' she sighed with longing against his mouth. She just couldn't stop herself. Only a self-deluding fool would claim that she hadn't wanted him to do this for days. Weeks. Months, even.

He smiled into her lips. 'I could kiss you all night.'

Her eyes flickered open. 'I might even let you.'

'Really?' he murmured.

'Mmm. Really.' Donna had thought that he would immediately start removing her clothes, but he didn't. Instead, his hand went to the band which was tied tightly around her plaited hair, and he pulled it free. Unravelled the emerald velvet ribbon woven into the strands until her hair hung in crude ringlets around her face.

'Shake your head,' he whispered.

She did as he asked and her hair erupted and casaded like amber around her shoulders.

'You're my fantasy come to life, Donna. Do you know that?'

No, *you're* the fantasy, she thought. You're *my* fantasy come to life. And I love you.

His hand began to sculpt her body from breast to thigh, over and over again, until she felt weak with wanting. And then he carefully rucked the velvet dress up to her waist, exposing her vast belly in the tent-sized knickers. She drew her knees up immediately.

'Don't,' she objected.

'Don't what?'

'Don't even look at me.'

'But you're beautiful.'

'No, I'm—'

'*Yes,*' he contradicted, and traced a lazy line across the drum-tight bump, and it seemed like the most arousing gesture he had ever made. 'Big and proud and beautifully ripened.'

She gave up fighting and let him slide his hands round to cup the firm jut of her buttocks. Let him kiss her eyelids, the tip of her nose and the corners of her mouth. She felt the light touch as his fingers feathered her where she was warm and moist and aching—until she was lost in a dark, erotic world of his creation. She said his name, just once, and then began to move distractedly beneath his touch.

Marcus looked down at her while he continued to caress her, revelling in the frantic little movements of her limbs. He knew it would be more practical to take her upstairs, but he could also see that she was close to the edge. Too close. And too precious and unwieldy to just fling over his shoulder and mount the stairs and take her upstairs to bed.

Which meant staying right here…

He slid his hand inside her panties and she made an agitated little sound that was somewhere between a gasp and a cry as he moved his hand against her heated flesh with a slow, sure rhythm.

This was all going to be over far too quickly, was his one regretful thought as he watched the frantic circling of her hips.

Donna felt the first spasm of pleasure ripple with increasing strength through her body, on and on and on, until she thought she would die with pleasure or astonishment. Or both. She called his name out loud. And then she cried.

He took her upstairs and undressed her like a child, finding a nightdress tucked underneath her pillow and pulling it over her head. It was made of fine white lawn—all tucked and embroidered—and with the thick red hair falling in a bright mane over her breasts she looked impossibly flushed and sexy and beautiful.

She was all sleepy as he pulled the duvet over her, and his body felt dry and aching, and he knew that if he didn't get out of here soon…

He was just tiptoeing out when her voice halted him.

'Marcus?'

He turned around.

Her eyes were wide open. 'Come to bed.'

He shook his head. 'You're tired now and you need to sleep. It doesn't matter,' he lied.

'Yes, it does. I want to hold you. I want you to hold me.'

'What if I said no?'

'You want to make me clamber out and chase you? In my condition?' she mocked.

He smiled. 'Well, I've tried to do the gentlemanly thing.'

'And I'm not going to let you.'

'Oh, well, in that case…' His eyes narrowed like a cat's as he shut the door softly behind him and began to unbutton his shirt.

He was tempted to tear the garment from his body in his eagerness to fall into bed with her, but he didn't want to frighten her. So he made his undressing as unhurried as he could and saw that she was watching the slow striptease through lazy, slitted eyes, clearly enjoying it. And by the time he slipped underneath the sheets to join her, he discovered that she was trembling nearly as much as he was.

She wrapped her arms almost shyly around his neck. 'I'm going to make love to you now.'

He shook his head. 'No, sugar. The baby. Remember what the doctor said. No sex.'

'But there are other ways. Aren't there?'

'There sure are.'

'I want to pleasure you the way you did to me,' she whispered. 'Will you show me how?'

Her innocent question caught him by surprise. So did the trusting way she asked it. Did that mean what he thought it might mean? But then the throb of anticipation blotted out the question. 'You bet your life I will,' he murmured. Marcus took her hand and softly kissed each finger in turn, then the palm. Only then did he let his body relax with anticipation against the mattress as he held her by the waist. 'Lesson number one…' his voice was soft '…you bend your head and you kiss me.'

CHAPTER THIRTEEN

DONNA woke him some time in the night.

'Marcus!' she hissed urgently, shaking his shoulder. 'I think I felt something!'

Lost in the memory of one of the most beautiful orgasms of his life, Marcus felt himself stir. 'Mmm. So did I!'

'I'm serious!'

Moving swiftly out of the memory, he sat up in bed his eyes snapping open. 'You mean it's the baby?'

'I'm not sure.'

He frowned. 'It can't be! There's still another three weeks to go.'

'It could be. Babies come early.'

'Keep still, then.' He slid his arms around her shoulders and cuddled her against him, loving the feel of her bulky stomach pressed up this close to him. 'And we'll wait and see.' He gave the top of her head a perfunctory kiss. 'Okay?'

'Okay.'

They both held their breath almost without realising they were doing so, then let it out in unison as nothing happened.

He stroked her hair and slid a hair-roughened thigh over hers. 'I guess we just wait. I can't think of a nicer way to do it.'

'Me, neither.' She nestled against his bare chest, so comfortable in his arms.

Marcus lay in silence for a moment, just listening to

the sounds of the evening—the ticking of a clock in the room and the distant hum of a car outside. There were things he wanted to ask her, but he wondered if now was the right time. Maybe there never would be a right time.

'What is it?' she murmured sleepily against his chest.

'How do you know it's anything?' He smiled in the darkness.

'You tensed up your shoulders—the way you always do when you want to ask a difficult question.'

He thought about this. 'You know me pretty well now, don't you, Donna?'

Donna felt protected by the cloak of darkness, and secure enough to say what was on her mind. 'I think I always have done. Only I never felt your equal before.'

'But you do now?'

'Oh, yes.'

He took a deep breath, but before he could speak she said it for him.

'You want to know if you're the only lover I've ever had, don't you, Marcus?'

He was stunned by her perception, even if he had already worked out the answer for himself. 'I have no right to ask.'

'Yes, you do. There shouldn't be any no-go areas of knowledge. Only you have to be prepared to hear things you might prefer not to.'

He sighed. 'It was a naive and unrealistic expectation.'

Donna smiled. 'Yes, it was, but so what? We all have them—or did you think that as a man you were immune? I wish you'd never had any other woman than me, but you have.'

'Yes, I have.' He paused. 'But what if I told you that no woman has ever come anywhere close to affecting me the way you do? On any level.'

'And what if I told you that there has only ever been one other man—'

'And did he love you?'

'Yes. Very much.'

'But you didn't feel the same way?'

'No,' she answered quietly, thinking, How could she have done—when she had only ever loved Marcus? She forced her thoughts away from the wishful to the practical. 'You know, we still haven't talked about what's going to happen after the birth.'

'Because we agreed we wouldn't try to predict the future. Especially not about the important things.'

'And what are the important things? The baby is going to be born soon—maybe sooner than either of us think. Surely we're close enough to the future now for me to ask you a question like that.'

He scowled, knowing now another reason why they had always avoided the subject. Too painful. 'Well, most important to me is how often I get to see the baby, I guess.'

'You mean access arrangements?'

Marcus nodded, wincing in the darkness at the coldness of the phrase. 'We can have a lawyer draw up some kind of formal agreement, if you'd prefer.'

Donna took her head from his chest and leaned over him, even though she could only see the smoky gleam of his eyes in the dim light. 'Is that what you want?'

He laughed, only it didn't sound bubbling, or humorous. 'I don't think what I want is relevant.'

'Of course it is!' she said fiercely. 'You're the father!'

'But only the biological father!' he snarled.

'What other kind is there?'

'The real kind! The kind that wipes his nose when he gets a cold. Or kicks a ball around in the park with him.

The kind that shows him how to ride a bike without falling off and how to deal with bullies when they pick on you!'

'And what if we have a girl?' asked Donna primly.

'Exactly the same!' He scowled. 'And don't try to be clever *or* change the subject, Donna King! You blithely talk about what it would be like if I met another woman—don't you ever give a thought to what it would be like for me if *you* met another man? Will I have to stand and watch from the sidelines while he or *she*,' he corrected hurriedly, 'calls another man Daddy? I don't think I could stand it,' he finished ferociously.

'Why are we arguing about a mythical man I might never meet at a time like this?' she asked him. 'I thought we had had just enjoyed a mutually satisfactory experience—'

He sighed. 'That's just the problem. We have.'

'And? How is that a problem?'

'It makes me realise how much I...want you.' It didn't seem quite the right word, but it would do for now. 'I want you even more now than ever before, Donna. If anything, the sex has only made things worse—it's made me realise what I've been missing!'

He was right—the sex had changed everything. Donna had a sneaking suspicion that sometimes men's minds and women's minds were heading in the same direction—only taking two entirely different routes to get there. She loved him. She knew that. She thought that deep down he felt the same way about her. But she wasn't going to put words in his mouth, however much she wanted to hear them.

'You mean you want to start having sex regularly?' she asked casually.

Marcus snapped the light on, and through the blinking

of her eyes in reaction Donna saw him glaring at her as though she had just uttered the most awful blasphemy. *'No!'* he roared.

Donna pretended surprise. 'You don't want sex?'

'Yes!'

'Marcus, if you're going to yell like a hooligan then I suggest you go back to your own room!'

'If you weren't pregnant I'd put you over my knee!' he retorted.

'If I weren't pregnant, then you wouldn't *be* here, buddy!'

'Says who?'

'Says me!'

'Oh, yes, I would!' he said fervently.

There was a pause. 'You would?' Donna gulped.

'Of course I would! Because sooner or later I would have come to my senses and realised just how much I love you. And I do, Donna. I love you very much.'

She gazed back at him, too scared to hope for what had always seemed like an unobtainable dream. He'd said the words, and she believed that he meant them—but was there substance behind them? Enough to withstand all the tests that life threw in the path of love?

She thought how easy they were in each other's company—just as they had been all those years ago. They laughed at the same jokes, they disagreed on all the things that men and women had been disagreeing on for years. Like whether women could read maps or men could do more than one task at a time.

She didn't have much experience of the opposite sex, but she knew that whatever chemistry they had in bed was pure magic.

So did that add up to love?

'I love you, Donna,' he repeated softly, and cradled

her tenderly against him. 'If I hadn't been so damned dense I might have admitted it to myself a whole lot sooner.'

Her heart filled with a feeling of contentment so pure that it made her feel quite dizzy. 'I love you, too.' She turned to rest her head against his chest, and sighed. 'Oh, Marcus!'

He stroked her arm. 'Mmm?'

'This is what it could have been like—if only we'd stayed together.'

He shook his head, secure now, letting go of the last of his regrets. 'No, sugar,' he said softly. 'We were both too young—the gulf was too wide. I was too arrogant and you were too…'

'Too what?'

'Too good for me!' he said fiercely.

Donna smiled and didn't correct him. After all, it didn't do a man any harm to have respect for the woman in his life!

'We needed to part in order to grow, and—'

'*Marcus!*' she interrupted frantically.

'What?'

Donna gasped, and this time she looked scared. 'It's the baby,' she told him, wide-eyed. 'It's coming!'

'How do you know?'

'I just know,' she said firmly, as women had been saying to their men since time began.

The journey to the hospital seemed to take for ever.

Marcus had never felt so helpless in his life as he'd located his car keys with shaking fingers. He had briefly considered calling an ambulance, but decided that the journey would be faster and more reliable if he was in the driving seat.

Which meant that now all his attention was taken up with trying to steer the car as smoothly as possible, with his precious cargo sitting in the passenger seat beside him. It meant that he wasn't able to touch Donna, or to comfort her. He was forced to concentrate on the road—and he didn't need to keep looking at her to know that she was suffering. Her eyes were huge and dark in a snowy-white face as the contractions started coming more frequently and more powerfully.

He saw her stiffen as another spasm passed, and he glanced over at the illuminated clock on the dashboard.

'How often are they coming now?' she croaked.

'About every five minutes.'

'That's quick. I think. *Oh!*' She clung onto her belly.

'Donna, I can't bear to see you this way,' he moaned, as she gave a sudden whimper of distress. 'What can I *do* for you, sugar?'

'Just keep driving.'

'Do you think—'

'No, I don't! I'm not thinking about anything—and neither should you if you're going to fret! If you want something to take your mind off things, Marcus, then try deciding what baby names you could live with, as that's something else we didn't get around to deciding!'

Things got a little better when they arrived at the hospital. At least there were people in uniform who seemed to know what they were doing. For once in his life Marcus was happy to stand on the sidelines and let them take over, while Donna was bundled onto a trolley and rushed up to the labour ward.

'Just grip my hand,' Marcus urged her as they waited for the lift, not seeming to notice that her nails were making tiny red, crescent-shaped lacerations on his palms.

Donna had shut her eyes now, as if to blot out the pain, and he saw her face contort against the force of the new life trying to push its way out of her body. He found himself wishing that he'd told her he loved her sooner. Or maybe wishing that he hadn't been so damned arrogant in the first place, and then they would never have been in this situation.

But he wouldn't have unwished that. Not for the world. Because hand in hand with his natural fears for Donna and their baby came the most breathless excitement he had ever felt. As if a miracle was happening right now and right here. And he was part of it.

The midwife who admitted her onto the labour ward was Sister Hindmarsh—the same rather bossy nurse who had given Donna such a stern lecture when she had been taken there with the bleed, all those months ago. But now her face was wreathed in smiles as Donna was wheeled into the delivery room.

'Hello again, my dear!' she beamed. 'I was rather hoping I might be on duty when you came back!'

'Nurse, I need to push!' moaned Donna.

'Well, you *think* you do, dear,' said the midwife kindly, clearly not believing a word of it. 'That's what all you first-time mothers say—but because it's a first baby, I think you'll find you've got a lot longer to wait than that! Now, let's have a quick look at you...' She lifted up Donna's gown and her face underwent a startling transformation. 'Oh, good heavens!' she exclaimed. 'You're fully dilated!'

'Is that bad?' demanded Marcus.

'No, it's wonderful,' answered the midwife. 'It means we're going to have a baby! And sooner, rather than later!'

'Marcus!' Donna's voice cracked as she gripped onto

his hand, her body tensing up to face the next contraction. 'Please don't leave me.'

'I'm not going anywhere, sugar!'

Marcus had never known an experience as powerful as seeing his child being born—but along with the pride came panic. He tried telling himself that women had been giving birth for centuries, in conditions far more threatening than the clean and antiseptic surroundings of this hospital delivery room.

But nothing seemed to take the edge off his fears for Donna and their baby.

Nothing, that was, until Donna gave one last shuddering groan—and a long, skinny object with a shock of dark hair emerged, shouting, into the world.

'It's a boy!' beamed the midwife, over the baby's first lusty scream. 'A beautiful baby boy.' She creased her brows as she deftly delivered the child onto Donna's stomach. 'And just about the longest-looking baby *I've* ever seen. He'll be tall—'

'Just like his father,' said Donna breathlessly, and smiled up into Marcus's eyes.

'And would you like to cut the cord, Mr King?' asked the midwife.

Marcus would have said that he was one of life's more confident men, but he knew he would rather risk bungee-jumping from the top of the tallest skyscraper than risk harming his baby son. 'I'd rather leave it to the experts,' he answered with a tight smile. 'And the name is Foreman.'

'Oh. Is it?' said the midwife, with studied casualness, and something in her tone made Marcus look up at her with a puzzled frown.

The cord dealt with, the midwife latched the baby onto Donna's breast. 'I normally go and make you both a cup of tea now,' she explained. 'Gives you a couple of quiet minutes alone with your baby.'

Once she had gone, the delivery room was filled with the sound of contented glugging, and their eyes met with delight and disbelief over the small dark head.

'He's here,' said Donna. 'And somehow it feels as though he was always meant to be.'

Marcus swallowed as he bent to wipe a damp strand of hair away from her forehead, and he was overwhelmed with a love so pure that he vowed never to forget the way he felt right at that moment. 'Thank you, Donna,' he said simply.

'You're welcome!' She looked up and her eyes were shining. 'Isn't he beautiful?'

'He sure is. As beautiful as his mother.'

'No. Much *more* beautiful!' she insisted, confidently moving the baby onto the other breast while Marcus watched with wondering eyes.

'Where ever did you learn to do that?'

'I didn't,' said Donna, with a slow smile. 'I just knew he was finished on that side. And we're going to have to choose a name for him soon—I can't keep saying "he" and "him" the whole time! Did you have any ideas in the car?'

Marcus shrugged. 'Sort of. You say first.'

'Well, I quite like Nick.' Donna stroked the downy head. 'Your father was Nick, and my mother's middle name was Nicola, and I thought…'

Her train of thought was interrupted by the return of Sister Hindmarsh, who was looking at Marcus with a definite question in her eyes. 'So. Have you come to any decisions yet?'

Marcus smiled. 'Not quite. Though we both like the name Nick.'

The midwife threw him one of her despairing looks. 'Mr Foreman!' she exclaimed. 'Have you not asked this poor girl to marry you yet?'

The pale blue eyes lit up with amusement as he met Donna's eyes. 'Well, she might not agree to have me.'

The midwife gave a loud sigh which was obviously meant to signify her disapproval of false modesty.

'Will you marry me, sugar?' he asked softly.

Donna was tempted to giggle with sheer happiness as Nick's mouth slid sleepily from the nipple. 'Marcus, you don't have to marry me just for the baby's sake—'

'But I'm not!' he put in quickly. 'I want to marry you because I love you. More than words could ever say. I was intending to ask you earlier, but we...I...' He grinned and shrugged helplessly. 'Fell asleep.'

'Marcus!' she murmured, on a half-hearted note of protest.

He crouched down beside the bed, so that their faces were very close. 'Please say yes, Donna. Say you'll marry me.'

'Yes,' she said, and her smile grew huge. 'Yes, I'll marry you.'

'Congratulations! And about time, too!' The midwife bent and plucked the sleeping infant from Donna's arms and put him gently over her shoulder. 'You and I are going down the corridor while I clean you up, young man,' she crooned softly. 'Because your father has just asked your mother to marry him, and now they want a few moments' peace and quiet to kiss each other. And they'd better make the most of it!' she finished darkly.

Donna sent a half longing glance in the direction of the door as it closed quietly behind Sister Hindmarsh and little Nick. Acknowledging already the first pangs of separation from her child. But he would be back soon.

Then she reached up her arms for Marcus, who was in the process of breaking goodness only knew how many hospital rules—since he had slipped off his canvas deck-shoes and was now sliding a delicious denim thigh forward as he joined her on the bed. He put his arms around her and looked deep into her eyes.

'When shall we get married?' he asked.

'Who cares right now?' she responded softly.

They kissed until Marcus wryly warned her that they had better stop—unless she wanted to get pregnant again! So they wrapped their arms tightly around one another instead.

And that was where Sister Hindmarsh found them when she carried their son back in—the two of them fast asleep, blissfully curled up on the hosptal bed!

The baby gave a cry, and two sets of startled eyes snapped open.

'Your turn,' mumbled Donna sleepily.

'My pleasure,' murmured Marcus. He got off the bed carefully, so as not to disturb Donna, and then tenderly took his son from the midwife's arms and began to rock him.

RICCARDO'S
SECRET CHILD

by

Cathy Williams

Cathy Williams is originally from Trinidad but has lived in England for a number of years. She currently has a house in Warwickshire which she shares with her husband Richard, her three daughters Charlotte, Olivia and Emma and their pet cat, Salem. She adores writing romantic fiction and would love one of her girls to become a writer although at the moment she is happy enough if they do their homework and agree not to bicker with one another.

Don't miss Cathy Williams exciting new novel, *Bedded at the Billionaire's Convenience*, out in June 2008 from Mills & Boon® Modern™.

CHAPTER ONE

RICCARDO FABBRINI stood towards the back of the dim, overcrowded bar, his black eyes narrowed as they moved methodically through the room. He felt another swell of intense irritation hit him as he realised the disadvantage of his situation.

The call had come this morning and the voice at the other end of the phone had been persuasive enough to bypass the rigid series of obstacles that siphoned off all but the most important callers. He hissed an oath under his breath as he continued to scour the room, seeking out the lone female, the woman who had left the message to meet him at an appointed time in this smoky wine bar. If he had personally handled the call he would have made sure to have found out what the hell this meeting was all about. In fact, if he had handled the call there would have *been* no meeting, but Mrs Pierce, competent to the point of meticulousness, had obviously been conned by a soft voice and a fairy story.

Whatever she had to say, it must be good, he thought grimly. It had *better* be good. He was not a man who found it amusing to have his time wasted.

'May I help you, sir?'

Riccardo's dark, impatient gaze focused on a small woman dressed in a waitress's uniform standing next to him, peering up at him, her oval face tinged with pleasure.

He was used to this kind of reaction from the opposite sex and normally he would have automatically fallen back on his charm and flirted with the pretty little thing hovering with her tray tucked neatly under one arm, but this was not a normal situation. He had been manoeuvred into coming here by some woman who had only conveyed to Mrs Pierce that her message was of the utmost importance, relying, no doubt, on his curiosity to grab at the mysterious carrot that had been dangled provocatively in front of his eyes.

Just the thought of it made him catch his breath in another surge of frustrated anger.

'I'm meeting someone,' he answered in a clipped voice.

'What's the name?' The petite blonde moved three steps to a desk at the side and picked up a sheet of paper on which were listed a series of names, most with ticks alongside them, customers who had arrived to take up their reservations.

'That's the one.' He pointed at a name on the sheet, Julia N., with the tick alongside it. 'She's here, is she?' he said grimly, casting his eyes around the room again and failing to find anyone matching up to the woman he had mentally conjured up.

Because conjured her up he had. He would have gone out with her at some point, of that he was sure, which hardly narrowed his options, but he knew his preferences. She would be tall, leggy, blonde and, he had to admit, fairly lightweight in the brains department. That was the way he liked them. Their vanity was his protection from emotional involvement. They enjoyed being seen on his arm, relished the privileges he could offer them but understood their place. Emotional baggage, he had discovered to his cost, did not sit easily on his shoulders.

He also had a good idea of what the woman in question would be after. Money. Weren't they always? However simpering and ingenuous they appeared, his vast bank balance never failed to impress. And he also knew how he intended to deal with any gold-diggers, whatever their trumped-up sob stories. Ruthlessly.

He bit back his anger at finding himself engineered into a meeting he had not initiated and decided, grimly, that now that he had found himself here he would enjoy the situation for what it was worth.

'Just follow me, sir.' The little blonde with the curly hair and the very cute behind walked in front of him and he followed, curious, now that he had come this far, to see where she was leading him. Riccardo anticipated, with a certain amount of relish, a short, sharp and illuminating conversation. Illuminating for the woman in question. Illuminating enough for her to realise that no one, but no one, got the better of Riccardo Fabbrini.

His sensuous lips curved coldly into a smile of antici-pated victory.

He was still feverishly scanning the crowd for the single, blonde female, when he realised that his brief tour of the wine bar, which had taken them from the bustling front to a slightly quieter section at the back, had come to an end. He found himself in front of a table at which was seated a slender, mousy-haired woman who had half risen to her feet and appeared to be holding out her hand in greeting.

'May I get you a drink, sir?' enquired the waitress.

Riccardo ignored the polite question and stared in dis-belief at the figure in front of him, who had now subsided back into her chair, though she continued to watch him. Very cautiously indeed. As though he might very well bite.

Who the hell was she?

'Mr Fabbrini?' Julia stared up at the towering, olive-skinned stranger and nervously tried to gather herself, al-ready regretting her decision to meet him, even while she knew that the meeting was as inevitable as the sun rising and setting. Inevitable and every bit as difficult as she had imagined it would be, judging from the expression on his face.

'Would you care to sit down?' Julia persisted politely, her anxious eyes briefly meeting those of the waitress, whose expression was sympathetic.

'No, I would not like to sit down. What I *would* like is for you to tell me who you are and why you have wasted my time dragging me here.'

Julia felt clammy perspiration break out over her body like a rash. She took a deep, steadying breath and reminded herself that the man in front of her, menacing though he seemed, could do absolutely nothing to her.

The waitress, having hovered indecisively for a few minutes, had retreated to safer waters, clearly intimidated by him.

'I did think about coming to see you at your office,' Julia said weakly, 'but I decided that a neutral zone might be better. I really wish you'd sit down, Mr Fabbrini. It will be impossible holding a conversation with you if you continue to glare down at me like that.'

'Is this better?' Instead of sitting down, Riccardo leant forward, hands firmly planted on the table so that his eyes were on her level and provided Julia, up close, with a vision of such disconcerting masculinity that she flinched back, an automatic response to his aggressive invasion of her space.

Of course, she knew what he looked like. She had seen pictures of him, and she had heard all about his terrifying personality, but nothing had prepared her for the impact of it full-on. Nothing had prepared her for his height, his over-powering maleness that had her breath catching uncomfortably in her throat, the constricting force of his swarthy good looks.

'No,' Julia said as calmly as she could. 'No, it's not, Mr Fabbrini. You're doing your best to threaten me and it won't work. I won't be threatened by you.' Thank goodness she had made sure that their table was situated at the back of the wine bar, where they were at least out of the range of curious ears and eyes. Thank goodness she had chosen somewhere large and very lively, where this little scene was lost amid the babble of voices and the roars of laughter from the groups of after-work men lounging on stools by the bar.

Riccardo continued to look at her without saying a word. Her smoky voice, so at odds with her average appearance, was controlled and self-contained but her hands were trembling. There was nothing her body could do about containing the effect he was having on her, he thought with a hot stab of satisfaction, even though she was doing her best to quell it.

He pulled out his chair and sat. 'My personal assistant said you refused to supply a surname. I don't like mysteries and I don't like women who mistakenly think that I am gullible enough to be taken in by sob stories or fairy tales. You got me here, and now that I'm here you will give me a few answers. Starting with your name. Your full name.'

'Julia Nash.' She waited to see whether he would react, but he didn't. She hadn't been certain whether he would have recognised the name, but Caroline must have kept it to herself after she had made her grand confession all those years ago. Even in the throes of her emotional distress, she had been quick-witted enough to foresee possible consequences.

'The name means nothing to me,' he said dismissively. He inclined his body slightly to catch their waitress's eye, which seemed remarkably easy. She had removed herself physically from the scene of the action, but had remained at a close distance, fascinated by the strikingly commanding man in his impeccably tailored grey suit. As if an outward show of civilised dress could disguise the primitive male beneath. What a joke, Julia thought.

'Nor,' he continued, after he had ordered a whisky on the rocks, 'have I ever met you before in my life.' He had leaned back into his chair but his presence was still as unsettling as when he had been looming over her.

Riccardo had delved into his memory banks and could state that without fear of contradiction. The name meant nothing to him, even though his antennae had sensed her fear that it might have, and he certainly would have recognised her, if only because she would have stuck out like a sore thumb amidst the parade of beautiful blondes who littered his life.

He took his drink from the waitress without even bothering to glance in her direction, instead choosing to focus his unremitting attention on the woman sitting across the table from him.

'Can I get either of you something to eat?'

'I doubt I will be here long enough,' Riccardo said, briefly looking at the waitress, who nodded in utter confusion at her abrupt dismissal.

'How do you know you haven't met me before?' Julia asked, clutching cravenly at any postponement to what she had to impart, and his lips curled into a coldly speculative smile.

'I have never been attracted to little sparrows,' he drawled, knowing that his uncalled-for and cunningly placed attack had a lot to do with the residue of anger lingering inside him.

That stung, but Julia refused to allow her hurt to show. She would also refuse to allow her loathing for the man sitting in front of her to show either. Loathing that had been already formed by the opinions she had made about him from what she had heard.

'You can be reassured that little sparrows find vainglorious hawks equally unappealing,' Julia said with a tight smile.

'So, now that we have done away with the pleasantries, why don't we just get down to business, Miss Nash? Because business is what you have in mind, is it not?' He rested his elbows on the table and swallowed back the remainder of his drink. 'Perhaps you mistakenly thought that an unusual approach might reward you with a job in one of my companies? If so, then I regret to inform you that I am not a man who favours the unusual approach, especially when it encroaches on my limited and hence very valuable personal time.'

'I'm not after a job, Mr Fabbrini.'

The hesitation was back in her eyes. Through thick black lashes he continued to observe her barely concealed nervousness, the way her slim fingers tried to find refuge in clasping her glass, cradling it, using it as something to steady her apprehension.

Very few things in life evoked Riccardo Fabbrini's curiosity. His meteoric rise through his father's ailing firm had been achieved through cold, calculated hard-headedness and a logical ability to scythe through problems. Curiosity was an emotion that deflected from his sense of purpose and nothing in his adult life had had much power to arouse it.

Even women were as predictable as the ocean tides, despite their reputation to the contrary.

Now, though…

The little sparrow in front of him was stirring something in him. Certainly nothing of a sexual nature, although, behind those prim little spectacles, her eyes were an unusual shade of grey and her body wasn't bad, for someone who could do with putting on a bit of weight. Especially around the bust. And her voice. No wonder Mrs Pierce had been taken in. He was almost looking forward to whatever outrageous lie was hovering behind those delicate lips.

'Money, then,' he said carelessly. 'Are you some kind of charity worker? Mission: hunt down prospective bank balances and tout for donations? If that's the case then make an appointment with my secretary. I'm sure something could be arranged.'

'It's not as easy as that.'

Riccardo was almost disappointed that he had guessed correctly and that money was at the root of this ridiculous charade that had forced him to cancel a date with his latest blonde bombshell. Although, to be perfectly honest, the blonde bombshell was due to be cancelled anyway. Regrettably. She had overstepped boundaries which he himself was only vaguely aware of imposing.

'I beg to differ, Miss Nash. It seems a simple equation and not one that called for this level of subterfuge. You want money, I have money. Just tell me the cause and you'll find that I can be generous with my donations.' He pushed back his chair at an angle so that he could cross his legs and draped his arm over the back of the chair, glancing around him.

'There's no equation to be worked out.'

Riccardo glanced at her. 'No equation? Then tell me what you want and let's get this over with. As I said to you, I am not a man who appreciates mysteries and this one is outstaying its limited welcome.'

Julia paled, realising that retreat was no longer an option. Had never really been an option, although there had always been the illusion of one. But how was she going to phrase what she had to say? She was a teacher. She should have had a thousand words at her disposal, but none that catered for this particular reality. Unfortunately.

She lifted her eyes bravely to look at him and was over-whelmed by the dark, brooding intensity of his gaze.

'It's about your wife. Your ex-wife. Caroline.' She watched as the darkly handsome contours of his face stilled. When he made no response, Julia took a deep breath. 'I thought you might have recognised my name,' she said quietly. 'Well, *Nash*. I thought you might have recognised my surname. But Caroline must not have ever told you…'

Surprises are always unpleasant. Riccardo could remember his father telling him that, many years ago, when the biggest surprise of his life had heralded the receivers coming into his company.

This surprise, though, left him winded. Caroline was the memory he had put behind him, buried beneath other willing women and only seeping out in the angry thrashing of his nightmares. And even those had disappeared.

'Aren't you going to say anything?' Julia's anxious eyes met his and he summoned up all the will-power at his disposal, which was considerable, to maintain his cold, un-shaken exterior.

'What is there to say?' he rasped tautly. 'I have no intention of having a cosy chat to you about my ex-wife. May she rest in peace.' He began to stand up and one slender hand reached out, touching him lightly on his fore-arm.

'Please.' Julia's voice was gentle. 'I'm not finished.'

Riccardo looked at the offending hand with distaste, but remained where he was, locked into place by the vile-tasting surge of memories that had risen unbidden from deep inside, like ghouls breaking through the barriers of the earth to roam freely.

Julia had half risen from her chair. Now she sat back down and was relieved when he did as well, though not before he had ordered another drink and wine for her, even though she had not asked for any.

'Why should I have recognised your name?' His voice was flat and hard, like the expression in his eyes.

'Because,' she faltered, 'because my brother was Martin Nash. The man who…who…'

'Why don't you say the words, Miss Nash? The man *who replaced me*.' His mouth twisted into lines of bitter cynicism. 'And to what do I owe the pleasure of this trip down memory lane? From what I recall, she was a very wealthy divorcee when we finally parted company. She and her lover. So, did they thoughtlessly not see fit to leave you in their will when they died?' His voice was an insulting mimicry of sympathy and Julia's back stiffened in a flare of rage.

This man was every bit as bad as Caroline had described. Worse. Julia felt a trace of sympathy for the decision her sister-in-law had made. To break off all contact. To say nothing. At the time she had done her best to persuade her otherwise. Through all those shared confidences she had had to steel herself against the unquiet feelings in her heart that a momentous decision was just morally wrong.

Had she known the true nature of the beast, perhaps she wouldn't have made quite such an effort.

'I loved my brother, Mr Fabbrini. And I loved Caroline as well.' Her voice sounded unnaturally still.

Riccardo felt such rage at that admission that he had to clench his hands into tight balls to stop them doing what they wanted to do. His eyes were blazing coals, however, and Julia could feel them burning her skin, searing through her head like knives of scorching steel.

'In which case, please accept my condolences,' he sneered coldly.

'You don't mean that.'

'No. I don't, and I am quite sure you can understand why. You might have loved my ex-wife. You might have seen her as the paragon of beauty and gentleness that she convincingly portrayed, but she was neither so gentle nor was she so compassionate that she couldn't conduct a rampant affair with another man behind my back!' His voice cracked like a whip around her, causing a group of people at the nearby table to glance around in sudden interest at the explosive scenario unfolding in front of them.

'It wasn't like that,' Julia protested with dismay.

'It hardly matters now, does it,' he said in a dangerously soft voice. 'It was five years ago and life has moved on for me. So why don't you just get to the point of all of this and then leave? Go and find a life to live. If you imagine that you are going to find a sympathetic listener in me then you are very much mistaken, Miss Nash. Any feeling I had for my dearly departed ex-wife dried up the day she told me that she had been seeing another man and was in love with him.'

'I haven't come here searching for your sympathy!' Julia retorted.

'Then why *did* you come here?'

'To tell you that...' The sheer magnitude of what she was about to say made the words dry up in her throat. She removed her spectacles and went through the pretence of cleaning the lenses, her hands unsteady on the wire rims.

Without her glasses, she looked wide-eyed and vulnerable. But Riccardo wasn't about to let himself feel sympathy for this girl. The mere thought that she was his replacement's sister was enough to fill his throat with bile. He could imagine her sitting down in a cosy threesome, nodding and listening to their vilification of him, ripping him apart when he hadn't been there to defend himself.

He finished his second drink and was contemplating a

third, which might at least blunt the edge of his mood, when she replaced her spectacles and looked at him. He decided that he wasn't going to help her. Let her stutter out the reason for this bizarre meeting.

'Caroline and my brother had, well…had been seeing each other for the last four months of your relationship before it all came to a head.' The wine had arrived and Julia gulped down a mouthful to give herself some much-needed Dutch courage. 'But they hadn't been sleeping to-gether.'

Riccardo gave a derisive snort of laughter. 'And you be-lieved them, did you?'

'Yes, I did!' Julia's head snapped up in angry rebuttal of his jeering disbelief.

'Well, I may be a little more cynical than you, Miss Nash, but I could not imagine a man and a woman, both in their prime, spending four months holding hands and whispering sweet nothings into each other's ears without the whispering turning to lovemaking. My ex-wife was re-markably beautiful and highly desirable. I doubt if your brother could have kept his hands to himself even if he had wanted to!'

'They never slept together,' Julia repeated stubbornly. That was what Caroline had told her and Julia had believed every word. It had had nothing to do with sexual attraction and everything to do with the man studying her blackly from under his brows. Caroline had been afraid of him. She had confided that to her over and over in the beginning, and the truth of what she had confided had been plain enough to read on her beautiful, pained face.

Riccardo Fabbrini had terrified her. During their brief courtship, she had seen his dark, brooding personality as exciting, but the reality of it had only sunk home once they had married and she had become suffocated by the sheer

explosive force of it. Nothing in her sweet-tempered re-
serves had equipped her to deal with someone so blatantly
and aggressively male. The more dominant he became, the
less she responded, wilting inside herself like a flower deprived of essential nutrients, and the more she wilted, the
more dominant he had become, like a raging bull, she had
whispered, baffled by her tongue-tied retreat.

Martin, with his conventional, unthreatening good looks
and his easy smile and shy, compassionate nature, had been
like balm to her wounded soul.

But they had not slept together. The thought of physical
betrayal had been abhorrent to her. They had talked, communicated through those long, empty evenings when
Riccardo had taken himself off to his penthouse suite in
central London, nursing his frustration in ways, Caroline
had once confessed, she could only shudder to imagine.

'Perhaps not,' he now conceded with a curl of his beautiful mouth. 'She did have a bit of a problem when it came
to passion. So is this what you came here for? To make
your peace with the devil and clear your brother's name
now that he can answer only to God?' He laughed coldly.
'Consider it an effort well-done.'

Julia drew in her breath and shivered. 'I came to tell you,
Mr Fabbrini, that you have a child. A daughter. Her name
is Nicola.'

The silence stretched between them as agonisingly taut
as a piece of elastic; then he laughed. He laughed and shook
his head in incredulous disbelief. He laughed with such
unrestrained humour that the group of eavesdroppers decided that whatever had been brewing had obviously been
nothing or else jokes wouldn't have been cracked.
Eventually his laughter died, but he continued to grin and
this time there was a trace of admiration in his expression.

'So, Miss Nash, I'm a *papa*. I thought you had come for

money, but I confess I was having a little difficulty knowing what platform you would stand on to get it. Now I know and I take my hat off to you. It is the most ingenious platform imaginable. Except for one small detail. You obviously have not catered for my personality. You must have harboured the strange notion that I was some kind of gullible fool, that you could produce your brother's offspring from behind your back and I would fall for it.' He laughed again, but this time there was no humour in his laughter and his black eyes, when they raked over her, contained no admiration. Only distaste.

'Caroline fell pregnant two weeks before you split up,' Julia informed him in a stony voice. 'You can choose to believe it or not, but it's the truth, and that's what I came here to say. I don't want any money from you, but I felt you ought to know the existence of your daughter. It looks as though I made a mistake.'

She stood up, her head held high, and reached for her bag next to the chair.

'Where do you think you are going?' Having coerced him here against his will, the blasted woman was now about to sally forth with her nose in the air, leaving him sitting at a table, nursing a thousand questions which refused to surface. He did not for one minute believe that he had fathered any child, but now that the seed had been planted he intended to get to the bottom of it and force her to confess that she had made the whole thing up.

'I should never have come here, but I felt I had to. I said what I had to say. I tried.' She proudly made her way through the crowd and was on the verge of acknowledging that she was about to make her escape, when his voice roared through the room, stopping conversation, killing laughter and compelling every head to turn in his direction.

'Get back here!'

Julia didn't look back. She did begin to walk more quickly, though, breaking into a slight run as the exit came into sight, then, once outside, she was running, with the wind bitingly cold against her face and rain slashing down on her head. The pavements were slick and empty and she only slowed her pace because there was the very real possibility that she would fall ingloriously on her face in her heels. They were sensible-enough shoes but by no means the sturdy wellingtons she would have needed for the sudden torrential downpour.

She was concentrating so closely on her feet, her head bowed against the driving rain as she scuttled towards the underground, that she was not aware of the sound of footsteps behind her, increasing in speed until she did finally pause, only to find herself whipped around by Riccardo's hand on her arm.

'You walked out on me!' he threw at her furiously.

'I realise that!' Julia shouted back.

'You think you can just show up from nowhere, start talking about my ex-wife and throw some wild story in my face before walking away!'

'I said what I had to say, now let me go! You're hurting me!'

'Good,' he said. 'Some small satisfaction for me for the stunt you pulled back there.'

'Let me go or else I shall yell my head off! You don't want to end up in a police station for assault, do you?'

'You are absolutely right. That is the last thing I want.' He began pulling her behind him while she swatted her hand at his fingers gripping her trench coat.

'Where are you dragging me? You might be able to get away with this caveman behaviour in Italy, but there are laws over here about men who manhandle women!'

'There are also laws against women who think they can blackmail men out of money using a phoney story!'

He was still pulling her and eventually Julia gave up the unequal fight. If he thought he could spirit her away somewhere to prolong their nightmare conversation then he had another think coming. He would no doubt be heading for a cab, and the minute her feet hit the floor of the taxi she would insist on being driven to the nearest underground. She had said what she had come to say, what she had felt morally compelled to say, and if he chose to disbelieve her story then that was his prerogative.

He wasn't pulling her so that he could hail a taxi.

He was pulling her towards his car, a sleek black Jaguar parked discreetly down a side-road.

Julia shied away but he was much bigger and stronger than her and suffused with angry determination.

There was no way that Riccardo was going to let this little madam escape until she confessed that the whole ridiculous thing had been a web of lies.

He realised that he was furiously trying to remember when he and Caroline had made love for the last time. He knew that it was certainly towards the end of their doomed marriage. He had returned home very late and a little the worse for wear with drink, but clutching a bunch of flowers, his attempt to woo the wife who had already mentally left him. The wife, he only acknowledged later, he had already also left behind.

It hadn't worked. She had patiently allowed herself to be awakened, to be presented with the sad bunch of flowers. She had been polite enough to stick them in a vase of water, even though she would surely have been tired at nearly one in the morning. And she had been polite enough to make love, or rather to allow him to make love to her. If nothing else, he had finally realised that it was over between them. But when had it happened…?

'You're lying,' he said harshly. 'And I want you to admit it.'

'I will not get into that car with you.'

'You will do as I say.'

The sheer arrogance of the man left Julia speechless. 'How dare you speak to me like that?'

'Get in the car! We haven't finished talking!'

'I refuse…'

'Why?' he mocked. 'Do you imagine that your womanly assets aren't safe with me? I told you, I don't favour the sparrows.' With which he yanked open the car door and waited for Julia to finally edge into the seat.

She hoped she left a huge, soaking, permanent stain on the cream leather.

'Now,' he said, turning to her once he was inside the car, 'where do you live? I'm going to drop you back to your house and you're going to explain yourself to me on the way. Then, and only then, do we part company, Miss Nash.'

In the ensuing silence Julia seemed to hear the flutter of her own heartbeat.

This was different from when they were in the wine bar, surrounded by people and noise. Locked in this car with him, she became frighteningly aware of his power and of something else: his potent sex appeal, something she had hidden from in the restaurant, choosing to concentrate her mind on the task at hand. The sparrow, she thought in panic, surely couldn't be drawn to the eagle!

'Well?' he prompted with silky determination, and Julia stuttered out her address.

'Not nervous, are you?' He turned on the engine and smoothly began driving towards Hampstead. 'I told you, your maidenly honour is safe with me. Unless...' he appeared to give this some deep thought '...your fear has suddenly kick-started an attack of nerves. Is that it, Miss Nash? Are you afraid of being found out for the liar that you are?'

'I'm not nervous, Mr Fabbrini,' Julia lied. 'I'm just amazed at your arrogance and your high-handedness. I've never encountered anyone like you in my life before!'

'I'm flattered.'

'Don't be!' she snapped back, her body pressed as far against the door as it was physically possible to be. She looked at his averted profile and shivered. Not a man to cross. Those had been Caroline's words and Julia now had no problem in believing them.

'So when did you decide to concoct your little scheme?' he enquired with supreme politeness.

'I haven't concocted anything!'

Riccardo ignored the interruption. The girl was lying, of that he was convinced, and he would break her before the drive was over. Break her and return to his vastly energetic but essentially uncluttered life.

'So...this so-called child of mine is...what did you say? Four? Five?'

'Five,' Julia said tightly, 'and her name is Nicola.'

'And not once did my beloved ex-wife choose to mention this little fact to me. Surprising, really, wouldn't you say? Considering she always prided herself on her high morality?'

'She thought it was for the best.'

Riccardo felt a pulse begin to beat steadily in his temple. Merely contemplating deception of that magnitude was enough to stir him. Just as well none of it was true. He slid a sideways glance at the slight creature sitting in the car, her body pushed against the car door in apprehension. So convincing, but so misguided. The most successful gold-diggers were the ones who hid their intent well.

The girl might not be a stunner, but she could act. She could act because she had brains, he considered. Which would make it doubly satisfying when she finally confessed all…

CHAPTER TWO

THE remainder of the drive was completed in uncomfortable silence. Rain slashed down against the window-panes, a harsh, clattering noise for which Julia was immensely grateful, because without that background din the silence between them would have been unbearable.

Towards the end she gave him terse directions to her house, which he followed without speaking.

By the time the sleek Jaguar pulled up in front of the three-storeyed red-brick Victorian house, her nerves were close to snapping. She pushed open the car door, almost before the car had drawn to a complete stop, and muttered a rapid thank-you for the lift. There was not much else she could thank him for. He had been insensitive, hostile and frankly insulting throughout those tortuous couple of hours in the wine bar. He had refused point blank to believe a word she had told him and had accused her of being a gold-digger.

Julia hurried up to her front door, the rain washing down on her as she fumbled in her bag for the wretched front-door key. She was only aware of his presence when he removed the key from her hands and shoved it into the lock smoothly.

'I want you to tell me what you hoped to gain by spinning me that ridiculous, far-fetched story,' he rasped, following her into the hall and slamming the door behind him.

Julia looked anxiously over her shoulder towards the staircase, which was shrouded in darkness.

And Riccardo, following her gaze, ground his teeth in

24

intense irritation. She had clung to her fabrication like a drowning man clinging to a lifebelt and he was determined to hear her admit the truth. In fact, hearing her admit the truth had become a compulsion during the forty-minute drive to the house. If not, it would remain unfinished business, even if he never saw or heard from her again, and he was not a man interested in unfinished business.

'I told you…' Her voice was half-plea, half-resigned weariness. Both heated his simmering blood just a little bit more.

'A lie! Caroline would never have kept such a thing from me, whatever her feelings.'

'OK. If you want me to admit that I made up the whole thing then I admit it. All right? Happy?'

Wrong response. She could see that from the darkening of his eyes and the sudden tightening of his mouth. When she had set out on her mission to be honest she had had no idea about the man she would be meeting. She should have. She had heard enough about him over the years, and particularly in that first year, when Caroline had been pregnant and her hormones had unleashed all the pent-up emotion she had managed to keep to herself during her marriage. But time had dulled the impact of her descriptions, and certainly for the past six months Julia had begun to wonder whether her sister-in-law's opinions might not have been exaggerated. Moreover, people changed. He would have mellowed over time.

Looking at his dark, hard face and the ruthless set of his features, she wondered whether anything or anyone was capable of mellowing Riccardo Fabbrini.

'No. No, I am not happy, Miss Nash.' He gripped her arm and leant down towards her so that his face was only inches away from hers. Julia felt herself swamped by him, struggling just to breathe, never mind control the situation.

But her eyes never left his. She was angry and, yes, intimidated, but he could see that inside she was as steady as a rock and he wanted to shake her until the steadiness turned to water.

No woman had ever roused him as much. This was a contest and he sensed that he was losing.

'Come into the kitchen,' she finally said wearily, shaking her arm, which he released. 'I'll explain it all to you, but you'll damned well stop calling me a liar and listen to what I have to say!'

'No one speaks to me like that,' he rasped.

'Sorry, but I do.' Julia didn't give him time to contemplate that assertion. Instead, she turned on her heels and began walking through the dark flagstoned hallway into the kitchen, her backbone straight, refusing to be totally squashed by the powerful man following in her wake.

She could feel him and the sensation sent little shivers racing along her spine. It was a bit like being stalked by a panther, a sleek, dangerous animal that was waiting to pounce.

'Sit down,' she commanded as soon as they were in the kitchen and she had closed the door gently behind them.

This had been Martin and Caroline's house and she wondered whether he would recognise any of the artefacts in the room. Doubtful. Caroline had sold their marital home almost as soon as the divorce had come through and had disposed of the majority of the contents, sending the valuable paintings back to him and selling the rest of their possessions, none of which, she had later told Julia, he wanted. She, along with her lover and every single thing in the house, could go to hell and stay there, for all he cared. The few things she had kept had been little mementoes she had personally collected herself, ornaments and one or two small paintings that had been passed on to her by her own parents when they had been alive.

'Would you like a cup of coffee?'

'This is not your house, is it? Was it theirs?'

Julia looked at him, watched as his shuttered gaze drifted through the room, picking out the homely array of plates displayed on the old pine dresser, the well-worn, much-loved kitchen table with all its scratches and peculiar markings, the faded, comfortable curtains, now blocking out the dark, rain-drenched night.

'Yes, it was. It belongs to me now.'

He began prowling through the room, divesting himself of his jacket in the process and slinging it on the kitchen table. The notice-board, pinned to the wall, was littered with Nicola's drawings. He stared at them for such a long time that Julia could feel the tension searing through her body mount to breaking point. Abruptly she took her eyes off him and began making some coffee.

'Your daughter's works of art,' she said with her back to him.

When she finally turned around it was to find him looking at her, his coal-black eyes narrowed. She took a deep breath and exhaled slowly.

'She started school in September and...'

'Why do you insist on sticking to your ridiculous story?'

Julia didn't reply. Instead, she moved to one of the kitchen drawers and with trembling fingers extracted a photo of her brother, which she handed to him. Martin had been the fair one of them. Even in his thirties, his hair had remained blond, never turning to the mousy brown that hers had. His eyes were blue and laughing.

'That's my brother.'

Riccardo glanced at the picture and very deliberately crumpled it and threw it on the table. 'Do you imagine that

I am in the least interested in seeing what your brother looked like?' he asked in a frighteningly controlled voice. 'I was not curious then and I am not curious now.'

'I didn't show you that picture because I thought you might be interested or curious,' Julia told him. She walked towards the kitchen table and rested his cup of coffee on the surface. She had no idea how he took his coffee but somehow she assumed that it would be black, sugarless and very strong. And she was right. He took the cup, sipped and placed it back on the table, his eyes never leaving her face.

'I showed you the picture so that you could see for your-self how fair Martin was. Almost as fair as Caroline. Of course, he was not nearly as striking as she was, but from a distance they could almost have passed for brother and sister, their colouring was so similar.'

'Where is all this going?'

'I want you to follow me. Very quietly.' She didn't give him time to question her. The more she tried to explain, the more obstinately dismissive he became, the more con-vinced that she wanted something from him. Money. She would reveal her trump card now and hope that proof of her words would make him see reason.

She put her cup on the counter and began walking back through the house but this time up the dark staircase, paus-ing only to turn on the light so that she could see where she was putting her feet. For a large man he moved with surprising stealth. She could barely hear his footsteps be-hind her and, once at the top of the stairs, she turned round just to check and make sure that he was still there. He was. His face grim and set. Julia placed one finger over her lips in a sign for silence and began walking towards Nicola's bedroom.

Her mother, who was already asleep in the guest room,

would have switched on the small bedside light on Nicola's dressing table. Nicola had always been afraid of complete dark. Monsters in cupboards and bogey men lurking under the beds. The stuff of childhood nightmares which no amount of calm reasoning could assuage.

Julia pushed open the door to the room very quietly and went across to the bed and stared down at the child.

Nicola was a living, breathing replica of her father. Her hair, which had never been cut, was thick and long and very black and her skin was satiny olive, the colour of someone accustomed to the hot Italian sun, even though it was a place she had never visited. Her eyes were closed now, but they, too, were dark, dark like her father's, who had joined Julia in contemplation of the sleeping figure.

'You could take a paternity test, but look at her. She's the spitting image of you.'

There was complete, deathly silence at her side, then Riccardo abruptly turned around and began walking out of the room. The sleeping child had aroused sudden, overwhelming confusion in him such as he had never felt before. It had instantly been replaced by rage.

Was it possible to feel such rage? He would have thought not, but he felt it now. Five years! Five years of being kept in ignorance of his own child's existence! His own flesh and blood. Because the minute he had laid eyes on her he had known that the child was his. There could be no doubt.

He thought of his ex-wife and her husband, bringing up *his* child, laughing with *his* daughter, relishing the precious moments of watching those milestones, and his fingers itched with the desire to avenge himself for what he had missed. What had been *his* by right.

He heard Julia running down the stairs behind him and, in the absence of Caroline and her cursed lover, he could feel his body pulsating to unleash his terrible wrath on the slightly built woman following him.

She would have been party to the decision to keep him in the dark about the birth of his child. Whatever her motives for contacting him now, and those motives would surely have something to do with money, she had agreed with the plan to say nothing to him.

He reached the bottom of the staircase and strode into the kitchen. He had to stop himself from smashing things on the way, destroying the contented little nest around him, a contented little nest in which his daughter had been raised. By another man.

Once in the kitchen, he paused and tried to control himself, to regain some of his natural self-composure, which had been blown to smithereens in the space of three short hours.

Somehow he would deal with this. And somehow Julia Nash would be made to pay for the torture she had subjected him to. It mattered not that Caroline and her lover were now no longer around to be held accountable for their vile actions.

Julia Nash was here, accessory to the crime as far as he was concerned, and she would pay the price.

She ran into the kitchen, her face distressed, and he looked at her in stony silence.

'Don't even dare think that you can make excuses for Caroline and what she did! Don't even imagine for one minute that you can justify the immorality of her decision!'

Their eyes locked, Julia helpless to break free from the ice-cold blackness of his stare.

'How dared she think that she could play God and make decisions that would affect my life and the life of my own flesh and blood? And you...' he added in a voice thick with contempt, 'how did you feel watching your brother do the job that should rightfully have been mine?'

'That's not fair!' Julia protested, even though she knew that she was doing little more than shouting in a wind because he was not going to listen to a word she said. But still, she had to defend them both. She might not have agreed with what they had decided to do, but she had been able to see their point. Caroline was terrified that Riccardo, had he known of the existence of his daughter, would do his best to gain custody. The thought of having the fruit of his loins raised by another man would have been anathema to him. So she had silenced Julia's objections. She had reasoned that, however much the courts decided in favour of the mother, Riccardo Fabbrini had the power and the wealth to get exactly what he wanted.

'*How dare you talk to me about fair?*' he gritted. He slammed his fist on the counter, tipping the edge of the saucer resting beneath her cup, and sent both shattering to the ground. She doubted that he was even aware of it.

'You wouldn't have been married to her!' she persisted, mutinously defying the warning in his eyes. 'You're not comparing like with like. You might have seen Nicola on weekends, but you still wouldn't have shared the completeness of a family home. The marriage was over well before she was born. Before she was conceived, even!'

Riccardo refused to hear the sense behind what she was saying. He felt like a man who had suddenly and inexplicably had the rug pulled from under his feet and in the process found himself freefalling through thin air off the edge of a precipice. No, reason was the last thing that appealed.

The small brown sparrow in front of him might be pleading for his understanding, but understanding was the least emotion accessible to him right now.

'Now that you know, we need to talk about Nicola, decide how often you want to see her.' Julia spoke even though her mouth felt dry, and she had to move to the kitchen table and sit down, because her legs were beginning to feel very uncooperative.

She sat down and ran her fingers through her thick shoulder-length hair, tucking it nervously behind her ears. This meeting had all gone so very wrong that she had no idea where anything was heading any more. She had expected a more civilised reaction, a more accommodating approach. She knew that he was a force to be reckoned with in the world of business. She had reasonably deduced that, that being the case, he would respond with the efficient detachment which would have been part and parcel of his working persona. She had not banked on his natural passion, which now flowed around him in invisible waves, putting paid to any thoughts of a reasonable approach.

'A calm, phlegmatic British approach to a problem, is that it? I am supposed to quietly accept years of premeditated deceit with a smile on my face and then get down to visiting rights. Is that it?'

'Something like that,' Julia admitted hopefully.

'I might have been educated in your fine British system, but I am not a phlegmatic British man,' Riccardo informed her icily. 'When it comes to business I may don the clothes of the businessman and speak with the civilised tongue of your country and deal with the savagery of the concrete jungle with cold-headed judgement, but when it comes to my personal life I am a man of passion.'

Julia felt an involuntary shiver of awareness run through her body like an electric shock.

A man of passion. She had seen that for herself and how! *When it comes to my personal life…* The blood rushed to her head as she imagined the personal life he had in mind.

His passion had overwhelmed Caroline. His powerful drive, instead of sweeping her along, had left her flailing. Had it been that way in bed too? Had his passion driven her into a state of numbed frigidity? She imagined that wild, untamed side of him making love, bringing all his suffocating masculinity to bear upon the object of his desire. The picture shocked her with its vividness and for a few seconds reduced her to a state of confusion.

She shook her head, feeling winded. 'Passion won't help us deal with this situation,' Julia said carefully, treading on thin ice. 'Nicola has never met you. She has no idea who you are and she'll be terrified if you suddenly appear on the scene and try to take her over. She's finding it hard enough to come to terms with losing her...' she nearly fell into the trap of saying *her parents* and reined in the instinct at the last moment '...Martin and Caroline. She will need to be approached with gentleness.'

It took supreme will-power not to give vent to the violent host of objections Julia's little speech produced inside him. He could understand her reason, but, like a wounded and raging bull, he simply wanted to strike out.

Had this calmly spoken girl ever felt anything like the hurt searing through his every muscle now? Had she ever felt what it was like to have your world upended through no fault of your own? Because that was how he felt.

This morning he had been in control of his vastly successful life. He had held his dynasty in the palm of his hand and was gratifyingly aware of the sensual magnetism with which he was blessed, and which could draw any woman he wanted to him.

Now he was being lectured to by this seemingly demure but frustratingly obstinate, mousy-haired woman on how to handle a situation the likes of which he had never expected to encounter. Now he was father to a child and a stranger to her as well.

'I need something stiffer than a cup of coffee,' he said abruptly. Julia thought that perhaps she did as well, especially considering that her own cup of coffee lay in splinters on the ground, something she had temporarily forgotten about. She wearily bent down and began gathering the shards of blue porcelain, tipping them into the bin, while he watched her, his face showing his own intense preoccupation with his thoughts.

She was so busy watching him from under her lashes, wondering whether she could second-guess what he would say next, that when the stray splinter of china rammed into her finger it took her a few seconds to register the pain, and only then because of the sight of the blood.

She stood up quickly, holding the injured finger and biting down on her lower lip to stifle the edge of pain. Pain was not a problem, but the blood threatened to bring on a fainting fit.

She hardly expected him to play the knight in shining armour to her damsel in distress, but perhaps it was just part of his nature to take over.

'What have you done?'

'What does it look like? I've cut my finger!'

He took hold of her hand, inspecting the gash left by the shard, and, with a gentleness that took her by surprise, slowly and efficiently pulled out the offending splinter. His hands were steady and assured. Julia felt the warmth of his hand around hers, the slight abrasiveness of his skin, and she stifled a tremor.

'First-aid kit?'

'It's in the… I'll just go and fetch it…'

Instead of releasing her hand, he walked with her to the small utility room, and when she indicated a cupboard to the left he reached up and extracted a cardboard box that was crammed to overflowing with medication of every variety, most of them suitable for young children. He still had her hand in his. Considering what they had just been through and the currents of hostility that had flowed between them, their physical closeness now was like a parody of intimacy.

'*This* is your first-aid kit?' he demanded, and Julia's grey eyes clashed stormily with his.

'Yes, it is. And before you start telling me that it's not up to your high regulation standards, I'd just like to remind you that I didn't ask for your help! I'm quite capable of seeing to a cut finger!'

'You are as white as a sheet. Where are the plasters? All I can see are cough medicines.'

'They're in there somewhere.' She rummaged through the box and extracted a sad looking packet wherein lay a stack of plasters adorned with brightly coloured cartoon characters. 'Nicola likes *Winnie the Pooh*,' she told him tersely, extracting one of the plasters. 'I'll wash my finger before I put this on.'

There was no need. Before she could pluck it from his grasp, he took her finger to his mouth and sucked. The action was so shockingly intimate that Julia stared at him open-mouthed. His dark head was bent, but he raised his eyes to meet hers. Was he caressing her finger with his tongue? she thought dazedly. No, of course not. Her body appeared to be on fire. Another illusion, she thought, distracted.

'Saliva is the best antiseptic,' he said, finally removing her finger and holding it up to inspect it. 'There, that looks a lot cleaner now. Give me the plaster.'

She handed him the plaster and, still ridiculously shaken, watched while he gently wrapped it around the slither of open skin. The sight of the blood must have destabilised her more than she had thought at first, Julia decided. She had always had a peculiarly strong aversion to blood. That was probably why her breathing was as laboured as if she had just completed a ten-mile marathon.

That was probably why she wasn't even aware of her mother's presence until she said, mildly but inquisitively, 'Julia! What's going on here? Have I interrupted something?'

'No, of course not, Mum.'

Riccardo watched the play of emotion shadowing the fine-boned, pale face through narrowed eyes. Her mother had startled her, that was for sure, but more than that. She had sprung back guiltily. Afraid of what…?

'You've been on a date? I thought you said you were going to the pub with some friends! You never told me you had a young man.' Her voice was full of misdirected pleasure and Julia felt herself reddening.

She should have told her mother what she was going to do, that she was going to contact Nicola's father, but she had kept it to herself, reasoning that she would confess when everything had been settled. If he had not turned up or else had walked away from the problem then there would have been no need for painful explanations to her mother afterwards.

'Mum…' Her eyes flickered resentfully towards Riccardo. 'This is…'

'Riccardo Fabbrini. Nicola's father.' The biting sting of anger resurfaced as he extended his hand towards the small, grey-haired woman standing in the doorway.

'Nicola's father.' Jeannette Nash tentatively took his hand while her eyes flicked past him to search out her daughter. 'I do apologise. I thought…'

'Yes, Mum.' Julia briskly stepped away from Riccardo

and edged past her mother back into the sanctuary of the brightly lit kitchen. 'I know what you thought. I didn't want to tell you that I was contacting Mr Fabbrini, just in case...' Her voice faltered and when she turned around it was to meet his steely gaze.

'Just in case the meeting was unsuccessful,' he expanded coldly on her behalf. 'Just in case I was the sort of man who would walk out on his responsibilities. As your daughter has discovered, I am very far from being that sort of man.'

'I wish you'd told me, Julia,' her mother accused and Julia sighed. 'What were the two of you doing in the utility?'

Julia had always known how deeply her mother had felt about Caroline's deception and, in the absence of all those telling confidences about Riccardo's personality, Jeannette had stifled her instinct to intervene with great difficulty. All she had seen was a brief, loveless marriage born in haste and rued at leisure. Something to be mourned but for which he should never have been punished by the absence of his own flesh and blood.

'Cleaning up a cut finger,' Riccardo answered. He shoved his hands inside his pockets and perched against the kitchen counter, his long legs casually crossed at the ankles.

'Nicola isn't awake, is she?' Julia asked suddenly and her mother shook her head with a smile.

'Sleeping like a log. I only woke up to use the bathroom and then I thought I'd come down here and fetch myself a glass of water. You know how difficult it is for me to sleep these days, my love.' She turned to Riccardo and said, with forthright honesty, 'This must be a very difficult situation for you. I'm so very sorry but, well, I'm glad that you're here now.'

Riccardo found that he couldn't resist the genuine sincerity in the faded blue eyes and he offered a half-smile, the first Julia had witnessed since she had first clapped eyes on him.

'I'll leave you two alone. I'm sure there's a lot that you need to sort out between yourselves.' She bustled over to a cupboard and poured herself a glass of water. 'I shall see you again very soon, Mr Fabbrini.'

'Riccardo. You can call me Riccardo.' His mouth twisted. 'After all, I am a member of the family now.

'Several years too late,' he said softly as her mother left the kitchen. 'But here now, Miss Nash. Are you not thrilled to have accomplished what you set out to do?' He flashed her a bitterly mirthless smile and pushed himself away from the counter.

How many more members of this cosy little unit from which he had been ruthlessly excluded? he wondered. Aunts and uncles in the background? Cousins maybe? A full life just lacking the ingredient of father?

Except, he thought with hard-edged cynicism, Nicola *had* had a father. This woman's brother. The only father she had ever known. She'd called him *Daddy* and sat on his shoulders when they went to the park.

Riccardo's shuttered gaze concealed his white-hot fury. For a few seconds back there, as he had dealt with her finger, he had felt a certain uninvited empathy with her. It hadn't lasted. Nor would it return.

'You said you wanted something stronger than coffee,' Julia said, avoiding his rhetorical question. 'I have some wine in the fridge, but that's about it.'

'As frugal in matters of alcohol as your sister-in-law was?'

'I prefer to keep my head.' Especially now, she thought as she opened the fridge and extracted a bottle of Sauvignon. She could feel his heavy-lidded dark eyes rak-

ing over her as she poured them both a glass of
a large glass, which might do something to take t
off that ferocious fury which she could feel him r
keeping in check, hers a smaller glass, just enough to cope.

So in control, Riccardo thought, or at least determined
to be. Which made her little slip-ups all the more intriguing.
She hadn't been in control when he had taken her finger
into his mouth. Her body had become rigidly still and he
had breathed in her unwilling response to him, to the
warmth of his tongue rubbing against the soft flesh of her
finger. And then when her mother had surprised them she
had been startled. The obvious answer was that she felt
guilty to have gone behind her mother's back and contacted
him, but there was something else.

He imagined what it would be like for her to see her
carefully planned life brought to a standstill, just as his had
been.

'Why did you decide to contact me?' he asked, sitting
down at the table and pushing back the chair so that he
could extend his long legs in front of him. His fingers caressed the rounded contours of the wine glass before he
brought it to his lips, sipping some of the wine while he
continued to direct his unsettling gaze on Julia's face.
'Would it not have been easier to have maintained the secret rather than risk kick-starting a situation you might end
up having no control over?' Here's where the money angle
comes in, he thought cynically.

Julia, sitting opposite him, elbows on the table like a
child being interviewed, lowered her eyes. 'I did what I
thought I had to do,' she said. 'When Caroline was alive I
respected her wishes…'

'Because you agreed with her, because you saw nothing
wrong in writing off my existence…'

'Because it was what she wanted. Because I loved my

brother and wanted what I thought was best for them both.' Her jaw hardened and she challenged him to try and pro-long the probing. 'What we have to deal with is reality. What's happening now.'

Riccardo forced himself to let it go. He was so unused to having to let anything go when his instinct told him to pursue that the withdrawal felt like bile in his mouth. 'For which you no doubt have a plan.'

'I don't think you should tell Nicola who you are to start with…' When his mouth opened in outrage she firmly stood her ground, refusing to back away. 'I know this is hard for you to accept, but I don't think she can cope with too much now. Get to know her and when she trusts you then perhaps you can tell her who you are, tell her that you are her blood father.'

'As opposed to what your brother was, you mean?' His lips curled and she met his eyes evenly.

'That's right. She's always known that Martin wasn't her real father. Neither he nor Caroline pretended to her oth-erwise.'

'I will come and see her tomorrow. When she finishes school. What time does she get home? Do you bring her home with you? Does she attend the same school where you teach?'

More at home with being the one who answered the questions as opposed to posing them, Riccardo grudgingly acknowledged the shift in emphasis.

'Yes, I teach at her school, but not in the junior section. I teach the older pupils, and I've been leaving school early so that she can come home with me. I do a lot of my work from home now, after school hours.'

Riccardo had a glimpse of her view of things and it irked him to realise that she was due some sympathy as well. Her life had been changed too, though, he reminded himself grimly, not quite to the same extent as his. He finished his wine and refused the offer of a refill. She, he noted, had toyed with hers, barely drinking any.

'We're normally back home by around four-thirty. If you like, you can drop by around five. She should have had her bath by then.'

Riccardo stood up. It had, he conceded, been the longest day of his life. He slung on his jacket while Julia hovered by the table, keeping herself at a distance, he noticed. He wanted to have another look at his daughter, drink in her sleeping face before he left, but no, there would be time enough tomorrow.

'Does your mother live here with you both?' he asked, as they walked towards the front door, Julia virtually sprinting to keep pace with his long strides.

'She has her own place. She was here to babysit.'

'And you? Where did you live?' He paused by the door, frowning at her as he tried to complete the pieces to this jigsaw that had now become a part of his well-ordered life.

'I rented a flat,' Julia told him vaguely.

'This arrangement must have dented your freedom,' he said without the slightest indication of sympathy in his voice, and when she returned his look with a puzzled one of her own he shrugged. 'Men. A five-year-old chaperon can't have been welcome.'

'It hasn't been a problem,' Julia told him stiffly. She yanked open the front door to find that the rain had softened to a steady, bone-chilling drizzle.

'Because there's no man.' Riccardo watched as her face reddened and the defiant shake of her head couldn't quite hide the fact that his offhand assumption had struck home. 'Is that why your *mama* sounded so pleased when she thought you had brought home a date?' He felt a curl of satisfaction as he watched her flounder. He had spent the past few hours floundering. Now it felt good to have the shoe on the other foot, even though the situations could not be compared.

'You're here because of your daughter,' Julia informed him coldly. 'My personal life has nothing to do with you.' The jeering mockery in his eyes sent her reeling back to that secret place where all her insecurities lay hidden, but never in a million years would she let him see that.

'Which suits me,' he countered smoothly, the hard lines of his face accentuated by the play of shadows from the dim front porch light overhead. 'Till tomorrow. And I am warning you, from now, I will not be open to debate on when I see my daughter. You may hold the upper hand at the moment, Miss Nash, but time has a nasty habit of changing things…'

CHAPTER THREE

'HE SEEMS like a nice man, considering.'

'Considering?' Julia finished plaiting Nicola's hair and tugged both ends so that the child swung around to look at her. Her eyes were almond-shaped and probably not quite as onyx-black as her father's, but the thick lashes were the same. *Nice man?*

'Who seems like a nice man?'

Julia and her mother exchanged a look. 'Just someone who's going to be coming around in a little while, honey.'

'Oh. Can I watch cartoons on TV before tea?'

'Not at the moment. In a while, maybe.'

'Considering...' her mother hissed, doing something comical with her eyebrows that would have made Julia burst out laughing if the subject matter at hand had not been quite so grim.

'What's for tea, Aunty Jules?'

'Chicken.'

'I hate chicken. Do I have to eat it?' Nicola stuck her hands in the pockets of her dungarees and made a face.

'Chicken nuggets.'

'I do wish...' her mother began and Julia flashed her a warning glare. 'Well...and he's very handsome.'

Julia, who had spent the day in a state of muted dread, almost found herself wishing that the doorbell would ring. She had been down this conversational route with her mother countless times before, daily, it seemed to her, since Caroline and Martin were no longer around to provide a buffer, and she wasn't about to go down it again.

'Not interested,' Julia hissed, edging her mother away from curious infantile ears. Amazing, she had discovered, what they managed to pick up when you could swear that their concentration was focused firmly on something else. 'I'm fine, Mum. I have my job. I'm perfectly happy. I certainly don't need a man.' And I most certainly don't need a man like Riccardo Fabbrini, she added silently to herself.

'But it would be nice to see you sorted out, Jules. It won't be easy, you know…' her mother's eyes flitted tellingly to Nicola, who was absorbed in drawing a picture, her face a study in concentration '…*bringing up Nicola all on your own.*'

'Mum. Please. Not now. Please? He's going to be here any minute now.'

'And look at you. Old jeans, checked shirt, flat shoes…'

Julia grinned. 'You know me. Twenty-seven going on twelve. It's a reaction to having to deal with nine- and ten-year-olds all day long.'

'Well, darling, that's as maybe, but…'

Fortunately, Julia was not required to hear the end of her mother's predictable sermon on the joys of marital bliss and the sadness of an old woman's heart when her only daughter appeared to be doing nothing about acquiring any of the said marital bliss.

She wiped her clammy hands on her jeans and slowly pulled open the front door.

Riccardo Fabbrini was every bit as daunting as she remembered. One night's restless sleep had not managed to steel her against the reaction she instinctively felt as their eyes met and the force of his aggressive personality settled around her like a miasma.

This time he was not in a suit. Perhaps he had thought that a suit might have been a little offputting for a casual meeting with his five-year-old daughter.

His informal attire did nothing to deaden his impact, however. The cream jumper and dark green trousers only served to emphasise the striking olive tones of his colouring.

'Is she here?' he asked tersely and Julia nodded, standing well back as he walked into the hall, carrying in his hands two large boxes.

'In the kitchen, with Mum.' No preliminaries. He had come, she thought without much surprise, with his hostility firmly in place. It was stamped in the harsh coldness of his face as his black eyes had swept over her. A night's sleep certainly had done nothing for his temper.

'Your mother is here as well? To give you a bit of moral support, Miss Nash? What do you imagine I am going to do? Kidnap my daughter and spirit her away to foreign shores?'

'For her sake, perhaps, you might want to maintain a semblance of courtesy.'

Riccardo nodded curtly. He had taken the day off work, had gone to Hamley's and spent more hours than he would ever have imagined possible to spend in a toy store, looking for the perfect toy. A difficult task, considering he had not the slightest idea what five-year-old girls liked, and now here he was, already being outmanoeuvred by this chit of a woman with her bookish spectacles and neat outfit.

Overnight, his rage had quietened. But only marginally. He had, however, managed to recognise that he would have to play along with her rules for the moment. Whatever his paternal status, Julia Nash knew his child and he didn't. It was as simple as that. The recognition, far from slaying his thirst for revenge, a revenge thwarted as his ex-wife was no longer around, only muted it slightly. The blood that ran through his veins was too grounded in passion to lightly release the past and calmly accept the future without demur.

The kitchen was warm and cosy. That was his first impression as he walked through the door behind Julia. A scene of perfect domesticity. At the kitchen table, Nicola sat with her head bowed over a piece of paper, and Jeannette Nash bustled by the kitchen counter, stirring custard in a saucepan. He felt like an intruder with his packages clutched in his hands.

Jeannette was the first to break the ice, much to Julia's relief. She turned around and smiled, wooden spoon still in her hand.

'Riccardo, how lovely to see you again. Nicola, darling, we have a visitor.'

Nicola looked up from what she was doing and Riccardo felt a wave of unsteadiness wash over him as he looked at the little girl at the table, her dark hair braided away from her face, her dark brown eyes staring back at him with mild curiosity.

'Hello...' This was such new terrain for him, a man normally in command of any situation life had ever been able to throw at him, that he instinctively looked towards Julia, who read the awkwardness in his eyes and felt her heart soften towards the powerful, aggressive man now hovering uncertainly in front of his daughter.

'Nicola,' she said quietly, 'why don't you show Riccardo what you're drawing? He loves art and he's never seen what a talented five-year-old girl can do.' Loves art indeed, she thought wryly. Although, he did, didn't he? The memory struggled out from the dim recesses of her brain, the memory of Caroline telling her that that was one of the first things that attracted her to him. They had met at an art show and he had been deeply and genuinely interested in the pieces, had been able to talk at length and knowledgeably about paintings. She had misread his interest for an insight into a sensitive nature. Time, she had said more than once, had put paid to that illusion.

But he was certainly doing his level best to maintain it as he walked hesitantly towards Nicola and looked at what she was drawing.

'It's an elephant,' she said. 'There's the trunk.'

'Ah, yes. I see.' He moved a bit closer and bent down, nodding. 'Yes. But it is a very fine elephant. Will it have any legs, do you think?'

'Oh, yes.' She drew four sticks. 'There. Legs.'

'Excellent legs.'

Nicola looked pleased with the flattery and smiled, her curiosity a bit more alive now that the man had passed the crucial test of admiring her work.

'Want to keep it?' she asked and he nodded again.

'Perhaps you could write your name under it.' He could feel his skin prickling with nerves and felt another rush of dislike towards the people who had put him in this situation. Behind him, he knew that Julia was looking at him. Mentally ticking off various boxes in her head, he wondered acidly, labelled *Pass* and *Fail*?

'I…I've brought you something. Well, two things actually. Presents.'

Nicola paused with her pencil raised in mid-air and her eyes slid away from Riccardo towards Julia, who smiled weakly. Riccardo gruffly shoved the wrapped parcels towards his daughter and then stood back with his hands stuffed into his pockets.

'You can open them,' Julia said lightly, and Riccardo gritted his teeth together in frustration. To be viewed with suspicion by his own flesh and blood! To have to seek approval from a woman whose brother had crept into his marital bed and seduced his wife!

The woman in question had approached them, moving

to stand next to her niece so that the three of them formed an uneven triangle around the table. Riccardo refused to look at her, refused to give her the satisfaction of seeing his own uncertainty.

Nicola, oblivious to the tension crackling around her and blithely unaware that she was the focus of his intense concentration, began opening the parcels, her face softening into pleasure as she held up the stuffed Winnie the Pooh bear for them all to see, then the little stack of books, which she looked at one by one, turning each over in her hand until Riccardo muttered uncomfortably, 'I wasn't too sure what you liked and what you did not.'

'Thank you very much.' The almond-shaped eyes were now very curious indeed. 'I love them. Aunty Jules can read one to me tonight,' she added politely, her eyes flicking for support from Julia as she became attuned to the undercurrents zinging through the room.

When Jeannette spoke the strange scenario was broken, thankfully, and then, with tea and pudding and the necessary bustling around the kitchen, something approaching normality was achieved.

Jeannette chatted happily to Riccardo, leaving Julia free to say as little as possible by way of direct address, although her eyes drifted back to him with unnerving regularity. She watched the way he sat in the chair, his long fingers curled around the cup of tea her mother had made for him, his lithe body inclined towards his daughter. The kitchen was warm and he had removed his jumper so that now he simply wore a green and white checked short-sleeved shirt that exposed powerful, swarthy forearms liberally sprinkled with dark hair. Everything about him redefined the word *male*. How gorgeous he and Caroline must have looked together, she thought. He was so tall and dark and forceful and she had been just the opposite, small and blonde and exquisitely pretty. Just the sort of woman a man like Riccardo Fabbrini would be attracted to, Julia thought. Not a timid brown sparrow like herself.

She dragged her attention back to what was happening around her and only realised the time when her mother rose to leave.

'Will I see you again?' Nicola asked shortly after Jeannette had left, pausing by the kitchen door with her small hand in Julia's, ready for her routine of bath and bed. 'Are you and Aunty Jules going out together?'

The innocent question hung thickly in the air. Of course Nicola must have wondered what this strange man, whose resemblance to her she had either not noticed or else only subconsciously acknowledged, was doing in the house. And she had overheard her mother insinuating more than once how nice it would be if Julia could find herself a nice boyfriend and think about settling down before all the nice men were snapped up. Nicola had put two and two together and was now asking whether they came to four.

Julia quickly tried to work out how she could disabuse her niece of this notion without her denial leading to other questions, such as why a perfect stranger who was not going out with her had arrived armed with presents for a child he had never seen.

'Yes, we are, as a matter of fact, little one,' Riccardo said smoothly, before Julia could intervene. He countered her shocked look at him with a bland smile that challenged her to refute him. 'We are most certainly going out.' This time the smile sent a chill of apprehension racing down her spine. It was a smile loaded with intent.

'It's time for your bath,' Julia told Nicola in a breathless voice.

'And you'll read me a story?'

'I will,' Riccardo intervened, 'if you would like.'

'I would rather Aunty Jules. She always reads to me now.'

Only Julia caught the grimness of his expression as their eyes tangled, and she shivered. She would let none of her own apprehension show for Nicola to see, and she didn't, but by the time she returned to the kitchen her seething temper at his casual exploitation of the situation was on the verge of reaching boiling point.

She steamed into the kitchen to find him lounging on one of the kitchen chairs, flicking through Nicola's drawing book, with a glass of wine in his hand. He looked up as soon as she stormed in, in no way apparently intimidated by the light of fire in her eyes.

'Would you care to tell me what the hell you were playing at? Telling Nicola that you and I were going out? How dare you?'

'Why don't you go and pour yourself something to drink and calm your frayed nerves?'

His dark eyes were unreadable. Gone was that glimpse of a man no longer in control of his situation. All that hesitation he had displayed in the company of his daughter had vanished. Every inch of him now breathed self-assurance.

Julia wondered how she could have softened towards him, even momentarily. The only drink she wanted to pour was not down her throat but over his arrogant head!

'If my nerves are frayed then you're the reason!' Julia sat down opposite him and his utter composure only served to fire her up more. 'What did you think you were doing, telling Nicola that you and I…that you and I *were going out together*!'

He took his time answering. He inspected the pale gold liquid in his glass, then tilted it to his lips so that he could swallow another mouthful.

'Did you think that you were going to have things all your own way?' he asked softly. 'You suggested that I don't tell my own daughter who I am because it might destabilise her and she is already coping with the loss of her mother and your brother.' He found that he could not bring himself to refer to Martin in any other way. 'I respected that decision, but tell me this…how am I supposed to put in an appearance without her wondering who the hell I am? And why am I showing such a disproportionate interest in her when I am nothing to you?'

'She's five years old! She's hardly going to sit down and analyse the situation!'

'She might be five years old but she is not a fool!' He leaned forward, his mouth a thin line of ruthless determination. 'She was clever enough to ask me exactly who I was! What do you suggest I tell her? The plumber? And I will be back to pay another visit to take care of the leak? Oh, and by the way, I shall return with more presents? Do you imagine that she would have fallen for something like that?'

'I would have thought of something!' Julia snapped back. 'Eventually. When I thought the time was right.'

'Well, perhaps I am not prepared to play your waiting game, Miss Nash. No, *Julia*. Now that you and I are going out together.'

'We are not going out together!' The way he had said her name. Like a caress. It had stolen over her heated skin and something else had thudded through her. It was something Julia had no intention of focusing on. Instead, she rose to her feet, muttering under her breath, and poured herself a glass of wine.

'And by the way,' she ranted, one hand on her hip, the other holding her full glass, 'make yourself at home, why don't you? Just waltz along and help yourself to the drinks!'

Riccardo looked at her and felt his lips begin to twitch into a smile. The picture she presented! All ruffled outrage, cheeks flushed, her rimless spectacles glinting furiously in the light, five foot three of womanly fury. He had seen many women and in many different lights, but this sort of outspoken fury, unrelated to anything sexual, was a first.

'Are you going to sit down and listen to what I have to say or are you going to stand there exploding?'

'Has anyone told you that you, Mr Fabbrini, are an arrogant swine?'

Riccardo carefully considered the question. 'No, but then you might want to remember that perhaps my arrogance has to do with the situation you have thrust upon me.'

Julia muttered again, but sat down and drank a long, soothing mouthful of her wine.

'I have to get to know my daughter. Gradually. For that, I have to have a reason to visit her, if you don't want her to know who I am. What better way to visit on a regular basis than in the guise of your lover?'

Julia felt a steady heat begin to pulse in her veins. His eyes roved lazily over her flushed face.

'That way, I can get to know her. I can be allowed the chance to know my own daughter. To bring her the presents I have been denied the pleasure of doing for five years, to hold her hand in mine, to receive her trust. Because she loves and trusts you and it might make it easier for her to accept me through you.'

His deep, slightly accented voice washed over Julia, filling the corners of her body like incense. She was dimly aware that he was being reasonable.

'And it is not as though I am competing with anyone

else,' he finished smoothly, dipping his eyes so that his long lashes drooped against his cheek. 'Is it?'

'That's not the point,' Julia said stubbornly.

'No, but it makes things a lot easier. It's a nice house,' he said, looking around the kitchen. 'Nothing at all like the house we shared.'

Julia followed his eyes but said nothing. The house he had shared with Caroline had been, according to her descriptions of it, a show home. A place designed for the sumptuous entertaining of important people.

'It's very comfortable and homely,' he mused. 'A family home.'

'Are you surprised?'

'Surprised because Caroline never seemed interested in homeliness. She always preferred the trappings of wealth.'

Julia laughed and he looked at her narrowly.

'Care to share the joke?'

'The joke is,' Julia said sardonically, 'that Caroline hated the trappings of wealth.'

A dull flush crept into his face. He felt like someone on the edge of some impossibly big secret, a secret that everyone knew about but had managed to keep from him. 'According to you,' he said coolly, and Julia raised her eyebrows.

'According to Caroline, actually. She loathed the army of interior designers who spent weeks swarming through your mansion. When she and Martin bought this house she chose everything herself. From the colours of the paint on the walls to the shade of every tie-back in every room. How on earth could you have lived with someone, been married to them, and not have realised that what they truly wanted was a cottage in the country, and if not the cottage in the country then at least an unpretentious family house in the city?'

'I don't appreciate being patronised, *Julia*. You'll have to be aware of that if this relationship of ours is to stay the course.'

'We don't *have* a relationship, as I've already told you. And I'll be as patronising as I like. You might be able to give orders to all your minions, but I'm afraid I'm not open to being ordered about.'

Riccardo carefully placed his empty wine glass in front of him and proceeded to relax in the chair, hands behind his head. He looked at Julia with interest. Funny, but when she was still she gave the appearance of someone serene, something in the calm set of her features and the way she seemed to observe without comment would lead anyone to assume that she was as placid as a lake. But there were times when she spoke and her face was alive with anima-tion. Like now. Like earlier on, when she had stormed into the kitchen, all fire and brimstone.

His eyes dropped from their interested inspection of her face to the swell of her breasts, just visible under the sexless shirt. His interest became somewhat less dispassionate and he straightened up to conceal an inappropriate stirring in his loins.

'Is it any wonder your mother is tearing her hair out at the prospect of you finding a man?' Riccardo drawled, pull-ing the tiger's tail. He felt a sudden thrill of excitement when she stood up and came across to where he was sitting. She leaned towards him, quivering with aggression, her face pink with anger, hands firmly placed on her boyish hips.

'My mother is not *tearing her hair out at the prospect of me finding a man*,' Julia hissed. 'And I utterly resent you voicing opinions on *my private life*, about which you know *absolutely nothing*! You met me for the first time *yesterday* and *don't you dare* think that you are somehow entitled to *shoot your mouth off* as though you know me. *You don't know me* and you never will!'

'Never say never,' Riccardo informed her silkily. He knew that he was pushing her to the limits of her patience. After what he had been through, that in itself should have been a source of immense satisfaction, but there was something else. He was enjoying her open display of temper. He wondered what she would do if he really gave her something to get worked up about. If he pulled her towards him and kissed her. Covered that angry mouth with his own. He imagined that she would fight him, but then what? Melt? And if she did melt, how would that feel?

'I think it's time you left, Mr Fabbrini.'

'The name is Riccardo. Use it.'

'Or else what?'

'You don't want to lay down any gauntlets for me,' he said softly and watched her grey eyes hesitate as she wondered whether to continue the argument. She backed away, leaning against the kitchen counter, waiting for him to stand up and leave.

'To all intents and purposes, you and I are now an item. Are we not, *Julia*?'

There he went again. Saying her name in that velvety, caressing voice. He was doing it deliberately. Laughing at her. And he talked about *her* patronising *him*!

'If you think it would help you in getting to know your daughter then I shall oblige, but...'

'But...?'

'But don't think that that gives you any rights over me...'

'Rights? What kind of rights?'

Julia didn't know what kind of rights. She knew what she wanted to say but she just couldn't find the words, so she glared impotently at him.

'It's time you left. I have to work tomorrow and I don't want to be late.'

'It's…' Riccardo calmly consulted his watch '…eight-forty-five. Surely not even a primary-school teacher with an over-developed sense of duty could call that late. And what about dinner?'

'What *about* dinner!'

'Perhaps we should have some.' Perversely, now that the object of his visit had retired to bed, instead of rushing to leave, to clear out of the company of this woman whom he had seen from the outset as a conspirator in his ex-wife's plot to deceive him, he wanted to prolong his stay.

Aside from anything else, he had no intention of being seen to be malleable. She might be able to call the shots, *for the time being*, as far as his daughter was concerned, but there her temporary power ended.

'I want to find out about Nicola,' he inserted when she made no move to abandon her mutinous stance by the kitchen counter. 'I know nothing about her and I have a lot of catching up to do.'

'What sort of things do you want to know about?' Julia asked distantly, and he stood up and moved across to her with such speed that she was barely aware of his intent until he was standing directly in front of her, caging her in with his hands, his face dark with sudden anger.

'What do you think? Why don't you use your imagination and figure it out? Pretend for a moment that you're in my shoes. Wouldn't you have just a little shadow of curiosity about your child?'

Julia was finding it difficult to breathe, never mind pretend anything. His face was so close to hers that a sudden movement would involve physical contact of the most disastrous kind.

'All right,' she said weakly. 'I'll…do something for us

to eat and you can ask me any questions you like…' He didn't move and she was formulating a polite way of telling him that cooking was an impossibility while she was being held hostage against a kitchen counter, when he suddenly reached out with one hand and removed her spectacles.

Without them, Julia felt hideously vulnerable. She blinked rapidly. 'What are you d-doing?' she stammered.

Riccardo didn't know what he was doing. He had wanted to see her eyes without the barrier of her glasses. They were a pure shade of grey and without her spectacles concealing them were fringed with thick, long lashes. He stared at them and then abruptly pushed himself away, while she turned and immediately re-armed herself with her glasses.

'When did she start school?' he asked gruffly, sitting back down, shaken by the realisation that he had wanted to kiss that quivering mouth of hers again. He reminded himself that, aside from being on the opposite side of the fence, she was not the sort of woman he was attracted to. 'Does she enjoy it? Does she have friends?'

Julia breathed deeply and began answering his questions while she rummaged in the cupboard for a saucepan and busied herself with chopping mushrooms and onions, efficiently preparing a light pasta dinner for them. Something that could be cooked and eaten within the hour, after which he would have no excuse to stay. His presence in the kitchen was wreaking havoc with her normally very unruffled nervous system and the sooner he cleared out the better.

'And was she happy?' he asked when his plate had been deposited in front of him and he had poured them both another glass of wine. 'Here? With Caroline and your brother? Did she ever ask about me?'

Julia glanced across the table to him. 'I don't know. I

wasn't living under the same roof, so I don't know what questions she asked or didn't ask about you.'

'And you didn't have any thoughts on the matter?' he pressed on mercilessly. 'The three of you were perfectly content to erase my existence? What about your brother? Did he share the same cavalier attitude?'

'We've been through all this,' Julia said tightly.

'And we'll go through it again. Tell me.'

'Caroline felt as if she was caught between the devil and the deep blue sea,' Julia sighed, closing her knife and fork and propping her chin on the palm of her hand. 'You want to make her out to have been without any morals, but she was afraid that if you knew about the pregnancy, about the baby, you would take Nicola away from her. She said that you were fiercely family-oriented, that you came from a big, close family and that the thought of sharing the up-bringing of your child with another man would have been unacceptable to you. And Martin loved her. He agreed because he only ever wanted what made her happy. I know you don't want to hear any of this, but you did ask.'

'Was she *that* scared of me?' he asked and Julia hesitated, not knowing whether he really wanted an answer or whether he had just been thinking aloud, turning over the thought in his mind.

'Answer me!' he commanded, which was Julia's cue to spring to her feet and begin clearing away the dishes.

'You frightened her,' she said eventually, her eyes flicking to his own shuttered, brooding gaze. 'Or maybe I should say that you overwhelmed her.'

'And I suppose she lost no time in confiding all these girlish secrets to you?' he asked acidly. 'Instead of confiding in me and trying to make a success of our marriage, she sought comfort in the arms of a stranger and found release in pouring out her problems on any receptive ear she could find, just so long as it wasn't mine!'

'Stop making yourself out to be the angel, Riccardo!' Julia snapped, only realising afterwards that she had called him by his name, conferring an intimacy on the situation between them that she strenuously resisted.

'Oh, but I was the angel,' he said smoothly. 'There were times when I could easily have taken a lover, when the thought of returning to the house and to a wife who made love as though under sufferance would have been incentive enough, but I didn't.'

'What a saint,' Julia muttered under her breath.

'Sorry? I didn't quite catch that.'

'I *said* that I'm feeling rather tired. Do you want to arrange another day for you to come over and see Nicola? I know that she's going to one of her little friends' for tea tomorrow, but perhaps the day after? Or maybe some time on the weekend?'

Riccardo felt a surge of irritation at her diversion tactic, but he swallowed it back and he hid his natural anger at finding his movements dictated by someone else.

'Perhaps Saturday,' he said, 'I can take you both out to lunch somewhere. Where would she like to go?'

'Oh, any place where the meal comes in a box with a toy,' Julia told him with a smile and he grimaced.

'In other words, French food is out of the question.'

'Out of the question,' Julia agreed. She looked at him curiously. 'This must be, yes, I know, very hard for you, but also…very different. Do you have nephews? Nieces?' She stood by the kitchen sink, arms folded.

'Four nephews, all much older. They live in Italy with my two sisters and their husbands. As for nieces, no. But she has a ready-made family, complete with grandmother.' He grimaced wryly and caught Julia's eye. 'My mother is a very assertive woman,' he said, almost adding *a bit like you*. 'But very fair. She has been longing for a *bambina* in the family. Nicola will find herself swamped by her affection.'

'And you've told them about…the situation?'

'Not yet, no. You have your own timescale as to when you think Nicola should be made aware of who I am, and I have mine when it comes to my family.' He stood up and raked his long fingers through his impossibly dark hair while Julia watched him cautiously from a safe distance.

'And what are your…intentions once Nicola knows that you're her father?' Julia asked, taking the bull by the horns. 'The reason I ask is that if you intend to return to Italy to live and take her with you then I shall do my utmost to prevent it.'

'Is that a threat?' he asked mildly, shrugging on his jacket and preceding her to the front door.

'Of course it's not.' Julia wrapped her arms around her body, hugging herself. 'But this is the only life that Nicola knows. To be removed from it…'

'Would require a little adjustment but would not by any means be an impossibility.' He paused by the door and stared down at her. 'However, for the time being at least, that is not on the agenda. My work takes me all over the world but I am primarily based in London.'

Julia breathed a sigh of relief. For all the changes that Nicola's presence in her life entailed, she would be lost without her. They had always been close, more so now. She uneasily wondered whether Nicola didn't serve the even greater purpose of filling the void in her life, the same void she denied having to her mother whenever the question was raised.

'So I shall see you on Saturday?' she said shakily and he nodded.

'About ten-thirty?' He pulled open the door but instead of walking to his car leaned indolently against the door frame and stared down at her. 'And don't forget.'

'Forget what?'

'Why, Julia, that we're lovers, of course.' His dark eyes roamed over her flustered face, a sensation he enjoyed thoroughly, then he succumbed to the wicked urge that had been plaguing him all night and he lowered his head, covering her startled mouth with his. It was a fleeting kiss, a shadow of a caress, and it tasted as sweet as honey.

And as paralysing as an electric shock, Julia thought numbly as he straightened and turned away as though nothing had happened.

And she had worried about the dangers of him trying to remove Nicola, to take her to Italy to live!

What about the danger lying far closer on her doorstep? She brushed her mouth with the back of her hand but she was still trembling by the time she made it to bed.

CHAPTER FOUR

'I AM beginning to have a whole new outlook on the word *exhaustion*,' Riccardo said to her on the Saturday afternoon as the three of them made their way back to the house.

Julia looked over Nicola's head in the taxi and caught his eye. 'Perhaps it was a mistake to promise that she could choose whatever toy she wanted.' But she couldn't make a big deal of it. It had not been a case of buying his daughter's affections, more trying to win them using the only currency with which he was familiar, namely money. Moreover, she was grateful that in his daughter's presence, he had been the epitome of charm and politeness, with none of those searing looks that were aimed to remind her of her criminal status in his eyes.

She was also grateful that there had been no mention of that farewell kiss of a couple of evenings before, and in fact, she had reached the point of wondering whether she might have dreamt the whole thing.

'I didn't realise that women began procrastinating from as young an age as five,' he responded drily, raising his eyebrows in bemusement.

'Are you talking about me?' Nicola asked, perking up at the mention of her age, and he smiled down at her, tempted to cradle the back of her dark head with his hand. He was aware of Julia looking at him and had to force himself not to look up suddenly and catch the expression on her face.

'We're wondering how come it took you three hours to finally choose your marker set and a handbag,' Julia said, smiling. 'They were the first things you saw!'

'I know, but I wasn't sure… I'm going to draw a picture of Mum and Martin,' Nicola said earnestly, then she turned to Riccardo. 'Would you like me to give it to you?'

Dark eyes clashed with grey ones.

'Of course. That would be very nice,' he said, only the tiny muscle beating in his jaw a sign of his thoughts. Strange, he had been gradually lulled into a sense of family, of belonging, and had almost forgotten that he was still on the outside looking for a way in. He averted his face and stared out of the window, watching the crowded streets race by.

'And maybe you could also draw a picture of a house,' Julia intervened hastily; 'you know how brilliant you are at drawing houses. A lovely tall house like the one you live in, with a red roof and a blue door.'

'Our door isn't blue.'

'Well, cream, then.'

'Will Gran be there when we get back? I want to show her what I got.'

'No, no, I don't think she will be. We can go visit tomorrow.'

'Will you be coming over tomorrow?' Nicola addressed her father and he turned round to look at her. The long, dark hair fell in a tumble along the little shoulders, rippling down her dark green anorak with the patches on the elbows. Her legs stuck out along the seat of the chair, not long enough to dangle over the edge, and her feet were encased in sturdy trainers that, she had proudly pointed out to Riccardo, lit up every time she walked.

He didn't even know whether he could answer that question without first getting permission from her aunt. He knew that it was irrational to continue feeling angry when anger did nothing to alter reality, but he could still feel it take him over.

What did Julia know of loss? he wondered. Loss like he felt whenever, it seemed, he rested his eyes on his daughter. Nothing.

Why shouldn't he make her find out? He had felt the way her mouth had trembled under his and he knew that under the self-control lay passion. He could stoke that passion and then when he walked away from her she too could feel some of the pain he was enduring now. Never as much, but enough.

He raised his eyes slowly to Julia's and held her stare.

'Why don't we play it by ear, Nicky, OK?' Julia said eventually.

'Does that mean yes or no?'

'It means we're not too sure yet,' Riccardo said gently, 'although I would love to come visit tomorrow. Maybe take you to the zoo, check and see how those animals are doing in this cold weather.'

This time when Julia looked at him it was with a frown of disapproval and Riccardo met her eyes with an edge of steel, while between them Nicola began bristling with excitement at yet another weekend treat in store. Not even Julia's dampening suggestion that they might be busy in the morning was enough to deter her enthusiasm.

'You shouldn't have made a promise like that,' was the very first thing Julia said once the taxi had dropped them off at the house, but she had to keep her voice low so that their conversation was not overheard.

'But I have nothing planned for tomorrow.' Riccardo feigned innocence. 'So why not? Did you not think that today was a roaring success?'

Julia didn't answer. She turned the key to the door and was instantly greeted by her mother, face aglow with excitement to find out how their day had gone.

Julia groaned inwardly.

'You didn't tell me you were coming over, Mum,' she said as brightly as she could, harking back with a sense of foreboding to their most recent conversation, during which her mother's seemingly incessant preoccupation with her daughter's man-less state had taken an alarming twist.

'I mean, Jules,' her mother had said coyly, 'he is very good looking, isn't he? And I must say, I've warmed to him since I've seen how he is with Nicola. Not a man to shirk his responsibilities like so many young people today.'

'Where are you going with this, Mum?' Julia had asked, as though she couldn't see very well for herself exactly where it was leading.

'It's not going anywhere.' But there had been no time to release any sighs of heartfelt relief. 'I'm just saying that you don't seem to have met any nice young men yet and why not seize the opportunity to get to know him? You're bound to naturally find yourselves getting close because of Nicola.'

Julia had wanted to point out that Riccardo Fabbrini was about as nice as a roving python on the lookout for its next meal, but she had resisted. Her mother was gradually succumbing to Riccardo's well-directed charm and Julia felt powerless against it.

'Oh, I decided I'd drop by on the spur of the moment, darling. Hope you don't mind that I let myself in.' Her mother's voice brought Julia back from her thoughts and she glanced a little anxiously around at Riccardo, who was listening to their conversation with his head tilted to one side, for all the world as though he could hear every thought running through her head.

'Perhaps you could take Nicky into the kitchen and get her something to drink, Mum,' Julia said with another bright smile. 'I just want to have a quick word with... Mr...um...'

She waited, tense as a coiled spring, until her mother and Nicola had vanished safely out of sight, then spun around to face him, her cheeks ablaze with colour.

'Look…um…'

Riccardo watched her in unhelpful silence. Not so much as a word of encouragement passed his lips as she wiped her hand feverishly across her brow.

'I had to tell Mum about…um…this idea of yours that you and I should appear to be…'

'Lovers?' he supplied, plucking the least helpful expression he could think of and folding his arms.

'Going out!' Julia corrected through gritted teeth. 'I had to just in case Nicky mentioned anything.' She paused and waited for him to fill the ensuing silence, which he didn't. 'It's just a bit of an awkward situation at the moment…um…because Mum's got it into her head that it's a splendid idea. In fact, if she seems to behave as though we really *are* going out instead of just pretending because of the situation, I want you to just ignore her.'

'I'm afraid you've lost me.'

I wish I could, Julia thought desperately. By connecting Riccardo with his daughter she had never envisaged that her own life would be so heavily involved. She was aware of him whenever he was around and had found herself thinking of him whenever he wasn't. When he came too close to her she had the urge to run.

'In words of one syllable, Mr Fabbrini…'

'Riccardo. Try not to forget.'

Julia ignored him. 'Mum might just lay on the encouragement a bit thick, but don't take any notice of her. She's just a little worried about me and she's got it into her head…'

'Worried about you?'

'Worried about me being single and having Nicola under

my care,' Julia snapped. 'She's decided that my life would be a lot better if I had a man around to help and for some strange reason she thinks that you…that you…'

'Might fit the bill?' He raised his dark eyebrows expressively and watched her squirm in embarrassment. It seemed, he thought, that fate was smiling on him.

'Course, she couldn't be more misguided if she tried,' Julia was telling him firmly. 'You're the last person in the world I would look at twice and I know you feel the same about me.'

'How do you know that?'

'The little brown sparrow?' She reminded him of his throwaway remark.

'Were you insulted by that?' he murmured softly and his eyes flicked over her so that she could have kicked herself for mentioning it in the first place. With men like Riccardo Fabbrini, arrogant to the point of distraction, it did not pay to look as though you gave the slightest bit of attention to anything they said.

'I was indifferent to it,' she lied bravely. 'I was merely using your expression as an example of how you felt about me and how I feel about you. Anyway, that's the situation as it stands. And by the way, please don't go arranging anything with Nicola that includes me without consulting me first.' She had added that last bit as a means of regaining some kind of control and she saw his mouth tighten, although he gave her a curt nod by way of concession.

His resolve hardened as he followed her into the kitchen. *Ask permission to arrange anything with his own daughter!* He felt a kick at the thought of wrapping her around his little finger. In fact, he doubted that he had felt such a kick before in his life. Women had come to him. The idea of active pursuit was intoxicating.

Nicola and Jeannette were in the kitchen, chatting animatedly about what they had done. Julia realised that she had not seen her niece so excited for a while. Her markers were already out of their pack and the handbag, a silver sparkly thing with a picture of Tigger embroidered on the front, was open, ready to be filled.

Julia's breath caught in her throat. When was she going to tell her about Riccardo? When would the time be right? She herself might find him arrogant and egotistic but Nicola didn't. Nicola enjoyed the attention he lavished on her. She enjoyed the way he listened to what she said without interrupting, as though every childish word that crossed her lips was of immense importance. It wouldn't be long before he would ask to take his daughter out without the irritating presence of a chaperon, and then he would take her completely. Take her to meet his family in Italy for a holiday, then he would move in for full custody.

'And we might be going to the zoo tomorrow!' Nicola was announcing, her eyes sliding across to Julia to see whether this comment could be slipped past without contradiction.

'Actually,' Jeannette said casually, fussing with the markers, 'I thought you two might like a bit of time of your own. In fact, that was one reason that I thought to come over. I could stay here and babysit Nicola so that you could both go out somewhere, for a meal perhaps.' She looked at Riccardo. 'Julia hasn't had much of an opportunity to go out recently...'

Julia felt a rush of humiliation and anger. She could feel the colour invade her face but she pinned the brightest smile to her lips because Nicola was looking at her.

'It's been a long day, Mum. We're all tired.'

'Nonsense.' Riccardo's voice cut short her litany of excuses and Julia looked at him in veiled surprise. He stepped forward, dominating the kitchen with his sheer size and overwhelming presence. He wasn't looking at her, though. He was looking at her mother and his mouth was curved into a smile of satisfaction. 'What a good idea! I know an excellent nightclub. Very good food and a very good band. After a long day shopping I think we could both do with a bit of relaxation, don't you, *Julia*?' He faced her with a smile and Julia wondered whether it was only she who could read the threat behind it. But why on earth would he *want* to go out with her, when there was no need?

'I—I...' she stammered desperately.

'It's not as though you need to get up early in the morning,' Riccardo continued, pinning her into a corner from which retreat was virtually impossible. 'Unless, of course, you intend to work on a Sunday...'

Jeannette watched these proceedings with delight. If she had harboured any doubts about him it was plain to see that she now genuinely liked him. How had he managed to do that?

'Gran and I will have fun here, Aunty Jules,' Nicola said.

'I'll go home and change quickly,' Riccardo said, moving towards her, 'and I'll be back to pick you up at seven-thirty.' He added in a low voice, 'I hope you'll be ready when I come.' He turned to face her, his broad back towards Jeannette and Nicola, blocking them out. 'And if you're not I shall come to your bedroom and fetch you, whatever your state of dress, so don't think about getting a sudden headache.'

'I refuse to be manipulated!' Julia said feebly, which only served to feed his anger at his own impotent frustration at *her* hands. Every minute spent in the company of his daughter was making him realise just how much he had missed and the slight brunette in front of him was part of the reason he had missed out. No good her denying it. If she had wanted she could have persuaded her brother to take a stand for what was right, persuaded Caroline to let him know about the pregnancy. Caroline had never been able to sustain an argument. She would have listened to reason, would have listened to someone as outspoken and forceful as Julia. For him to hear her talk about being manipulated almost made him laugh.

She would soon discover the nature of manipulation.

'I'll see you at seven-thirty.' With that, he turned to say goodbye to Jeannette, resisting the urge to kiss Nicola, and then stalked out of the kitchen.

He could feel excitement pulsing through his veins as he fired the engine of his car and drove back to his apartment. It took him a mere thirty-five minutes to make it there, using the back-roads of London which were fairly free of traffic. As he showered and changed he looked around his penthouse flat and pictured her there. He imagined her timidly entering, timid because she was not the sort of girl who slept around, who allowed herself to be taken to a man's apartment unless she had spent months building up a friendship first.

But however timid she might be, however cautious, she wouldn't be able to help herself. She would be in the grip of the same urgent need to make love as he would be. She would be excited, apprehensive, shaking with the anticipation of being taken by him.

He towelled himself dry and shaved quickly, with the towel wrapped around his waist. As he shaved he allowed his imagination to roam. To picture how her pale skin would look against the black leather of the sofa in his living room. He slowly stripped her of her sensible clothing, her weekend uniform of jeans and baggy jumpers, he removed her spectacles so that he could see the dark flecks in her grey eyes. He imagined her in tousled, panting disarray on his bed, tangled amid his bedclothes, tangled with *him*, limbs entwining with limbs, hands roving to touch and feel and explore.

She would beg him to bring her to a shuddering orgasm and would blush furiously as she pleaded for satisfaction.

He found that he had to drive at a more leisurely rate back to her house, in order to let his own excitement subside.

Her face was stiff with apprehension and exasperation at being wheedled into a date when she pulled open the front door to him.

'I don't see the point,' she grumbled as she slid into the passenger seat and primly gathered her pale grey flared skirt around her.

'The point of going to a nightclub?' Riccardo enquired, shooting out of the drive and expertly manoeuvring the car along the dark lanes away from her house. 'Or the point of going to a nightclub with *me*?'

'There was absolutely no need to jump at Mum's suggestion.'

'But you hardly ever get out,' he drawled lazily. 'I thought I would be doing you a favour. You know what they say about all work and no play...'

Julia glared ineffectively at his averted profile. She had no idea where they were going, but she suspected that she would not be dressed correctly for the venue. Her grey skirt was smart but hardly the height of fashion, and her strappy silk vest was covered by a dark grey jacket which she had no intention of removing. It left too much of her thin body exposed for her own comfort.

Riccardo, on the other hand, looked as magnificent as she suspected he would. His crisp white shirt emphasised the burnished gold of his skin and his suit, charcoal-grey, was impeccably and she suspected, lovingly hand-tailored.

From where she was sitting, she could smell the clean masculine scent of his aftershave.

'Relax,' he said into the silence. 'You're here now, why not enjoy it?'

'Where are we going?'

'Oh, just a little club I know. Very small. Not very fancy at all, so there's no need for you to feel self-conscious.'

'I don't feel self-conscious,' Julia threw at him, huddling in her unfamiliar outfit and feeling like a badly dressed teenager on her way to a prom night.

'Yes, you do. I can feel it.' He reached out with one hand and curled his long fingers along the back of her neck, gently massaging. Julia gave a squeak of alarm and drew away as much as she could. 'The tension is in your shoulders.' His fingers slipped a little lower, dipping under the collar of her jacket to knead her collar-bone, and just when she was about to tell him to *stop touching her immediately*, he took his hand away and replaced it on the steering wheel.

Julia could feel her heart hammering like a steam engine inside her. His cool fingers against her skin had sent a rush of fire through her, igniting her sensitive breasts and making her body ache.

'So tell me, why is your mother so desperate to have you married off?' Riccardo asked, his voice steady, composed and mildly interested.

'Aren't all mothers desperate to see their children married off?' Julia had to work very hard at keeping her voice as steady as his, but she was uncomfortably aware that her body was still in a state of heady response to his passing touch.

'That may very well be so,' Riccardo agreed. 'I know my *mama* was overjoyed when Caroline and I married. True, she wasn't Italian, but she could overlook that because I had spent so much of my time in England that it was almost natural for me to marry an English girl, and what an English rose Caroline was.'

'She must have been very disappointed when things… didn't work out,' Julia said as she found herself drawn into the conversation against her will.

'Disappointed but not, she afterwards informed me, hugely surprised.'

'Why not?'

'She told me that she worried that Caroline was not fiery enough for me but she had said nothing at the time because she had the notion that opposites might attract and that Caroline's lack of spirit might be just what I needed.'

Riccardo had never confided these personal details to anyone before. He was not a man who shared confidences or even allowed people to know how he felt about matters he deemed private. It felt right, however, to be talking to Julia about it and he decided, with the cool-headed logic which had been his byword for as long as he could remember, that he was simply getting her to relax by throwing her titbits of his personal life. Stirring her interest so that she would no longer see him as a threat. As long as she saw him as her enemy, someone to be distrusted, she would not respond to him and he was aggressively and thrillingly determined to win her response.

'Opposites do often attract,' Julia agreed slowly.

'Or else they repel. In our case, the latter.' He swung his car into a small forecourt jammed with expensive-looking cars, and when Julia looked at the clock on the dashboard she realised with a start that they had been driving for longer than she expected. Driving right out of London from the looks of it, because the street was broader and far less congested with houses and buildings than the streets in central London.

The nightclub itself was brightly illuminated on the outside and resembled someone's house, albeit a commanding, ivy-clad red-bricked house with a doorman incongruously standing to attention outside.

It took several minutes to locate a parking space, and Julia felt another rush of nerves as they walked towards the club, clutching her jacket around her with her little bag hanging from one hand.

The sudden pressure of his hand on the crook of her elbow was surprisingly comforting. As was the ease and assurance with which he led them inside, his hand still cupping her elbow. The room, staggered on two levels with a galleried landing forming a semicircle around the ground floor, was crowded, with people on the dance floor swaying about to the strains of slow jazz music. Waitresses buzzed between tables, carrying enormous trays above their shoulders on the flat of their hands and paying not the slightest bit of attention to the band performing on the podium.

They worked here and were familiar with the atmosphere. Julia, though, was not. As a teenager she had been to one or two nightclubs, noisy, dark places with too many people, no seating to speak of and beer being spilled over shoes and clothes. But this was a new experience for her.

She looked bewildered, Riccardo thought, his dark eyes taking in her open mouth. He felt an irrational swell of pleasure at being the one to introduce her to an experience she had obviously never had before. And she lived in London! What had she done with herself for all her adult life? She was no longer even aware of his hand on her and he took the opportunity to circle her waist with his arm, guiding her towards the table to which the waitress was leading them.

'I take it you have not been to this nightclub before,' he said, swinging his chair closer to hers so that they could speak comfortably above the music. His arm brushed against hers.

'I haven't been to any nightclub for years,' Julia confessed, turning to look at him, taken aback because he was so close to her.

'Not something that responsible teachers do?'

'Are you saying that one has to be irresponsible to come to a place like this?' She hadn't noticed that he had given the waitress an order for drinks but he must have because the young, leggy girl in her small black dress approached them now with a silver bucket in which rested a bottle of chilled white wine, and she expertly placed two wine goblets in front of them and, on a nod from Riccardo, poured them each a glass. Julia dived on hers with the abandon of someone suffering from fluid deprivation.

He laughed and his eyes dipped to the peach-smooth skin visible beneath her cropped jacket. He would be eating that peach later, he resolved, and conquest would taste as sweet as nectar.

'I would not dream of bringing a responsible woman like yourself to a den of iniquity. As a matter of fact, this is a very popular haunt with businessmen entertaining clients. It is more exciting than a restaurant and there is more scope for deals to be discussed than in the bowels of a theatre or an opera house.' Her eyes behind the spectacles were tentative and interested. She was putting aside her natural wariness of him and that in itself gave him a spurt of pleasure. Her face was soft, her mouth parted on a question.

'You come here often, I take it.'

'I have been here several times.' He removed his jacket, transferring his small black leather wallet to his trouser pocket. 'It's a good place to de-stress.'

Julia took another sip of her wine, her eyes drifting to his fingers loosely entwined on the table top. Riccardo, from above the rim of his wine glass tilted to his lips, saw everything, even noticed her slight tremor as she gathered herself and began to stare at the jazz band instead of his hands. Hands that were itching to touch her, and he wryly admitted to himself that evening the score was only part of the deal.

'Where do you go when you want to wind down?' he prompted, placing his glass on the table and circling the rim with one long finger. 'Has Nicola severely curtailed your social life?'

Julia shrugged.

'What does that gesture mean?' He mimicked her shrug. 'That she has or that she hasn't?'

'It's a little harder going out now in the evenings than it used to be. It means I have to make arrangements with Mum in advance. But don't think for a minute that I find it a hardship. I've always adored my niece and she's a joy to have around, even though it's a joy gained through circumstances I would never have wished and could never have foreseen.' Her eyes slipped to his finger trailing the glass and she hurriedly looked away, drowning her confusion by gulping down the remainder of her wine, only to find her glass refilled instantly.

'And where do you go when you make these arrangements?' he asked softly.

'Cinema. Wine bar. Sometimes to the theatre with friends, although on a teacher's salary I've always had to watch where my money went.'

'And now?'

Julia frowned. 'And now what?'

'Do you still have to watch your money? Or did my ex-wife and her husband make sure that you were provided for?' When she had first come to him he had instantly assumed that money must be at the root of her searching him out. Now he realised that she belonged to one of those rare species of women who were not impressed by how much money he had. He sat back in his chair and proceeded to look at her with a closed expression, trying to work her out.

'All of the money from the sale of your house went immediately into a trust fund for Nicola,' she replied coolly, 'and I was left enough to make sure that she doesn't seriously want for anything. So you can rest assured that I won't be knocking on your door, asking for handouts.'

'But it wouldn't be considered a handout, would it?' he told her in a hard voice. 'I've been willing to go along with your game plan, putting my feelings on hold *for the moment*, but I intend to assume full financial responsibility for my child.'

Julia had known that this would arise. In fact, she was surprised that it hadn't arisen sooner. She had a glimpse of a man biding his time and she shivered at the thought of it.

'I understand,' she began quietly, 'but I think you ought to concentrate on the most important thing, which is building a strong relationship with her so that it will be almost natural for her to accept you as her father when the time comes...'

'Don't preach to me on what I should and shouldn't do.' He leaned forward and placed his hands squarely on the table. 'For the moment, I am content to bring presents and then fade obligingly into the background, but rest assured that within the next few weeks I shall want you to produce a complete breakdown of Nicola's expenses, including a financial statement of the money that has been put in trust for her.'

'Because money is so important, isn't it?' Julia said tightly, gripping the stem of her wine glass.

Riccardo sighed heavily. 'It is simply a factor that I intend to take into consideration. Now, instead of sitting here and pointlessly sniping at one another, why don't we go and dance? Enjoy the evening.' He read the hesitation on her face and wanted to yank her out of her indecision by pulling her to the dance floor, but he waited in silence for her answer.

What was it about this woman? he wondered. One minute he was intrigued by her, intrigued enough to almost forget the part she had played in the situation that now existed. The next minute she was firing him up in a way he could recall no one doing in his life before, not even during his long climb to towering success, during which he had had to wage war with his adversaries and establish boundaries beyond which no one would be permitted to cross.

Even in his personal life, the women he had gone out with had respected his boundaries, had known their limits and had never crossed them. This woman boldly ignored every boundary he had laid down without raising her voice and then sat back and watched him rage in stubborn silence.

Dammit, did he want to seduce her to even a score or did he want to seduce her to prove to himself that he was still a man who could control his life, private and public?

'I'm not a brilliant dancer,' Julia was forced to admit awkwardly. And she would probably be even less adequate with this man's arms around her. Just the thought of it was enough to make her feel sick.

'Nor am I.'

'I don't believe you.'

'Then why don't I prove it to you? We can step on one another's feet and decide who is the worse.' He held out his hand and Julia reluctantly slipped her hand into his, feeling his fingers link through hers with a sudden, blinding panic.

'And you have to take your jacket off,' he murmured.

Julia blushed furiously, but obeyed, slipping the short jacket off her shoulders and then instantly feeling exposed in her small, silky top with the spaghetti straps.

She had hardly been listening to the band and was now aware that they were playing a slow number. It seemed that the atmosphere in the club aimed to be mellow, and as such the musicians complied, playing a selection of sexy, downbeat tunes, most of which were vaguely recognisable.

He led her onto the dance floor, which was darkly intimate and pulled her into his arms. His head lowered so that she could feel his mouth brushing her hair and her breasts pushed against his broad, hard chest.

He had been lying, as she had known he was, about his dancing. He was a superb dancer, his movements easy and fluid, and her body gradually picked up the sway of his, moving in time to his rhythm. As they danced he gently ran his finger along her exposed back and it was all Julia could do to keep her feet steady.

'See. I told you I was an abysmal dancer,' he laughed softly into her ear and for one terrifying moment she wished that she could feel his tongue flick there, then move to her lips, explore the soft insides of her mouth, which were trembling in a combination of horror and, she had to admit the truth, sheer, overwhelming craving.

CHAPTER FIVE

RICCARDO, feeling that small shiver of awareness, pressed home his advantage. He coiled his fingers through her hair, enjoying the sensation of it falling silkily over his hand. Most if not all of the women he had dated in the past had been staggeringly beautiful, sophisticated creatures with perfectly styled hair, hair that was secured in place with expensive lotions and hairsprays and was not destined to be threaded through a man's fingers.

Everything about this woman, however, was completely natural. Her thick shoulder-length hair felt smooth and clean. Her perfectly oval face was virtually free of make-up, aside from a pale shade of lipstick and a hint of blusher.

He pulled her fractionally closer to him so that she could feel his body against hers. He wanted her to read the signals he was giving her. He wished, in fact, that he could crawl inside her head and have a bull's-eye view of what was going on in her mind. But he would move slowly. Any direct moves would send her running in the opposite direction.

'Whoever told you that you weren't a good dancer was lying,' he murmured and, just for the sheer hell of it and because he wanted to see how she would react, he nibbled the tender flesh of her ear lobe. 'Now, how hungry are you? The fish here is excellent and not too heavy. We can keep dancing or we can have something to eat and then carry on.'

Had he just done what she thought he had? Had he actually caressed her ear? Julia realised that her feverish

80

imagination was now making her actively hallucinate and she gratefully clutched the lifebelt he had thrown her, nodding vigorously in favour of the food option. In fact, she *was* hungry. Or, at least, she had been when she left the house.

They retired to their table and whilst they waited for their food to arrive Riccardo chatted pleasantly enough about anything and everything under the sun. Anything and everything that had nothing to do with Nicola. Talking about Nicola revived all his old anger at how he had been treated, kept in ignorance of her existence, and with the anger came the inevitable tension. Riccardo didn't want tension. Not right now. He had other plans in mind.

So he laughed and chatted and asked her questions about herself, whilst plying her with drink.

For the first time, the issue that lay between them like a yawning chasm faded into the background as Julia relaxed and told him about her childhood, omitting all mention of Martin. Slightly tipsy she might be, but she was aware of the temporary truce he had declared and she was willing to go along with it because he had been right. She had not gone out and enjoyed herself for quite a while, and it had been over a year since she had gone out on a date with a man. Kind, thoughtful Tim, who had turned from lover to friend to acquaintance all in the space of a short six months. It seemed to be her track record. No wonder her poor mother thought she would never settle down. No wonder, in her most private moments, she herself had her doubts.

'You're not drinking,' she accused when their main course had been cleared away and she had ordered a cappuccino in the hopes that it might sober her up a bit.

'I'm driving, remember? The two don't mix.'

'And I'm talking all about myself. You haven't told me anything about you.' *Talking about herself?* She had been positively garrulous, she thought wryly. What was it they said about alcohol loosening tongues? And with Riccardo, of all people! She had probably been boring him stiff, with her anecdotes about family life and school, but he had been too polite to divert the flow of conversation.

She waited until her coffee arrived and then drank it very quickly.

'What would you like to know?' he asked, watching her flushed face and the way she had the quirky habit of shoving her hair behind her ears when she felt nervous.

'What have you been doing since…is there anyone in your life? I never even thought to ask when I came to see you.'

'Is there anyone in my life…?' Riccardo drawled, sitting back and loosely linking his fingers on his lap. 'Right now I can say with my hand on my heart, that the only female in my life is Nicola. And yourself, of course.'

Yes, and for all the wrong reasons, Julia thought. She felt a puzzling sting of pain.

'You never thought about…getting married again?'

'You have obviously never been through a divorce. Believe me when I tell you that it is one of the most powerful reasons for doubting the institution of marriage. I learned to my cost that the state of wedded bliss can turn two people into strangers and from strangers into hostile opponents.' He laughed mirthlessly. 'Not that I would want to put you off.'

'It *can* be bliss for some,' Julia pointed out. 'My parents were very happily married.'

'As were mine. I guess you just have to say that it's a game of hit or miss, wouldn't you agree? But then again, what relationship isn't hit or miss?' He toyed with his coffee-cup and then took a sip. She had talked to him about her childhood, about what it was like being a teacher, about some of the plays she had seen, the restaurants she had been to, but she had said nothing about the men in her life, and Riccardo suddenly had a burning curiosity to find out about that private side of her. She was as contained as all his previous lovers had been obligingly informative. She retreated with the same speed as they had advanced.

'Shall we dance?' he asked lazily, upturning his hand and waiting for her to accept the invitation.

The dance floor was slightly less crowded than it had been, although the level of noise was higher, a muted but background surge of voices and laughter as the alcohol consumption increased and inhibitions diminished.

The tune carried a more upbeat tempo, and Riccardo swung her towards him, his long legs carrying the tune, his hips grinding gently against her body, his arms circling her back giving her no room to establish any space between them.

Julia felt heady and recklessly alive. It was warm in the room and a fine film of perspiration made her skin tingle.

'So tell me about your love life,' he whispered. 'Do teachers have love lives? I never used to think so at school until I was fourteen and had the pleasure of being in a class with a very voluptuous science teacher. I never realised how fascinating physics could be.' He laughed softly at the memory and Julia's lips curved into a smile.

'I can't imagine you taking apples in for your teacher,' she said.

'Perhaps not the apples but some highly charged fantasies. Until I discovered that she had a husband and a child, at which point I was cured of my adolescent infatuation and started concentrating my charged fantasies on slightly more attainable goals.' His mouth brushed the vulnerable curve of her neck. Any ideas about seduction to even a score had disappeared. He had wanted to taste that soft skin, had just not been able to resist.

Julia's breath caught in her throat. No, she most certainly had not imagined that. But she didn't want to stop him. He was turning her on and she wanted him to carry on turning her on. Three glasses of wine had put paid to her reservations.

'So does *this* teacher arouse fantasies in schoolboys?' he asked, his breath warm in her ear, tickling.

'Eight- and nine-year-old boys don't have fantasies,' she murmured, her face tilted so that her cheek pressed against the smooth cotton of his shirt. 'Or, at least, not of the nature you describe. I think their fantasies run more along the lines of joining the football team or acquiring a new computer game.'

'Shame. And what about your male teachers? Do they look slyly at you when you walk into the staff room? Do they entertain thoughts of stripping you naked and watching you come to them?' He was treading a very fine line here, he knew. He had never dreamed of asking any of his past conquests whether men had fantasised about them. Their responses would have been tediously predictable. A coy laugh and the knowing look in their eyes that told him just how fanciable they knew themselves to be, just what they could do for *him*.

He enjoyed knowing that his risqué questions were probably throwing her into a tizzy of embarrassment and confusion. The lighting was too subdued for him to see whether she was blushing or not, but he would put money on it. He discovered, with a pleasant little jolt of surprise, that the thought was electrifying.

'I don't think so,' Julia laughed nervously, feeling out of her depth now with this turn in the conversation. 'We only have three male teachers. Two are over fifty and the third, from what I gather, enjoys going on wildlife tours more than he enjoys going out with women. We think he might well be gay.'

'Hmm. That's not very stimulating, is it?' He dipped his hand just slightly under her blouse so that his fingers brushed her spine. 'So where do you go to find men who don't enjoy wildlife tours and might not possibly be gay? Mm?'

'I don't have much time to go scouring the city of London for men,' Julia replied vaguely. Teachers were, at least at her school, a fairly sociable lot and her last boyfriend she had met through a friend. It was a subject she did not want to talk about because she knew that he would begin questioning her, and in so doing would discover her appalling lack of an exciting sex life. She had never felt the sizzle of instant attraction, preferring to cultivate a friendship before launching into the dubious waters of romance.

'It's very warm here, isn't it?' she said, desperately trying to find a way of diverting the course of the conversation, and she was relieved when he agreed with her instantly.

'So shall we go back to the table?'

'I have a better idea. Why don't we wander outside for a while? The gardens at the back are quite extensive, believe it or not. One of the advantages of not having a nightclub in the heart of the city. And I could use a bit of cool air.'

Julia hesitated, but in the end she followed him out of the club and round the side, where the thought of cooling off had occurred to a number of people. On the way, they had collected her jacket from where it had been discarded by the table and their waitress had obligingly placed a reserve sign on the table.

The cold air hit her face like a balm and she stood still for a minute, breathing it in with her eyes closed, unaware that he was watching her and the way her slightly old-fashioned outfit emphasised the slenderness of her body. She had a naturally boyish build but seemed refreshingly unaware of how many women would have given their right arm for it. Almost no curves, he thought. Or none that was immediately apparent, although the feel of her breasts on the dance floor, pushing against him, was evidence enough that she was all woman.

He led her past the small groups of people cooling down after the heat inside, and towards the back garden, which was landscaped cleverly to convert a modest-sized plot into the illusion of a small copse. The ground was laced with trees, some evergreen, some bare of leaves, with intriguing, winding paths running between them.

'Perhaps we should head back in,' Julia said nervously as the solitude of their situation hit her. In summer she had no doubt that this garden would be teeming with people relaxing outside with their drinks before returning to the music and food, but in early March most people did not fancy the prospect of dawdling outside.

The cold was already beginning to bite through her thin jacket, and she pulled it tighter around her.

'Cold?' he enquired. In the absence of light, he was just a big, shadowy figure.

'A little.'

'There is that age-old technique for warming up,' Riccardo murmured, stepping closer to her, and Julia blinked furiously behind her spectacles. He ran his hands up and down her arms and felt a rough, primitive urge sweep over him. In every way she had played with his life, turned it on its head, and in more ways than one she had played with his mind, turning his hard-edged dislike into unwilling curiosity, taking the revenge he had coolly plotted and changing it into a genuine quest to control a woman who remained infuriatingly out of reach.

She looked at him. 'I don't think Management would like it if we lit a fire out here.'

Riccardo grinned, his teeth a sudden flash of white in the shadows. 'You're right. They might complain. Besides, I have no matches, have you?' He could feel her shivering beneath his hands. 'Nor do we have sun and a magnifying glass.'

'You were a boy scout?'

'Hardly.' He laughed softly. 'I just read a lot of useful books when I was a kid. I fancied myself marooned on an island, having to survive.'

There was a brief silence, during which they looked at one another, a brief, charged silence, pregnant with the possibilities of the moment.

Then he lowered his head and his mouth met hers. He had not realised the depth of his hunger to taste her lips until he felt hers cool and yielding. Her hands remained clasped protectively around her body as she inclined upwards to him.

'I can't do this with…these on…' He removed her spectacles and Julia whimpered at the brief interlude. She no longer cared about keeping her distance. She was waiting, no, yearning for him to kiss her again, and this time, as his mouth sought and found hers, she returned the kiss, her tongue sliding against his, her lips parted to receive his searing, hungry caress.

He pulled her arms away from her body and, with his hands behind her buttocks, pushed her towards him, grinding her so closely against his body that she could feel his hard erection pressing against her.

A wild abandon coursed through her veins and she moaned as his teeth nipped the arched column of her neck.

Her breasts were aching with the need to be touched, and as if sensing this, Riccardo shoved his hands up the silky top until he felt their soft swell under the strapless lace bra. He felt like a man making love for the first time. Every movement was fuelled with desperate urgency. He didn't want to gently make love to her, he wanted to take her right here and right now and satiate the primal urge tearing him apart.

With one swift movement he dragged the strapless bra down so that he could massage the twin peaks of her breasts with their tight, protruding nipples. As he massaged them she groaned with pleasure and every groan urged him on.

'Touch me,' he commanded, circling her wrist with his hand and guiding it to where his throbbing manhood needed the cool touch of her fingers. He unzipped his trousers and as she gripped his stiffness through his silk boxer shorts she gave a little cry of desire.

'Feeling a little warmer now?' he asked, punctuating the warmth of his breath in her ear with the damp coolness of his tongue.

Julia was beyond answering. The gardens could have been designed, she thought wildly, for this type of activity. The trees were a natural barrier against prying eyes and the scattering of benches a welcome respite for unsteady legs. Riccardo led her to one of these benches, and when she had sat down he splayed apart her legs and positioned himself between them, then he lifted her vest. Her bra was still pulled down and her breasts spilled over the top of it, forming erotic points that reminded him of nothing more than ripe fruits. Ripe fruits ready for eating, which was what he intended to do.

With a stifled groan he buried his face against her breasts

and began sucking, and her hands, hesitant at first, curled into his dark hair while her body slid down the bench until she was arching back to enjoy the erotic sensuous pleasure he was giving her.

She had no idea how this had happened and she didn't care. She had no experience of this sort of raw, carnal lust and she was a willing student. In fact, more than willing—eager. With her head thrust back, she blindly cupped her other breast, offering it to his greedy mouth and she kept her hand there as he suckled, the tip of his tongue flicking erotically over her engorged nipple.

When he removed his feasting mouth she felt the cool air against her bare skin and she twisted in protest, but he was already rucking up her skirt, and Julia's eyes flew open in shock.

He raised his head and smiled wolfishly at her. 'When you say no, do you mean no? Or do you mean yes, please?'

Julia pulled up her bra and shoved down her top but her frantic efforts at rearranging herself stopped there. She looked at him, ready to explore the most intimate region of her body in a way no other man had, and was rocked by excitement.

'I don't think…' she panted breathlessly. 'We can't… I've never…'

'Never felt a man's mouth down here?' To demonstrate the place he meant, he pulled aside her briefs and cupped her with his hands, pressing down until she squirmed. 'And do you want to?'

'We should go back in…side…'

He didn't answer. Instead he bent his head closer to her, his nostrils flaring as he breathed in the musky, womanly scent of her, fragrantly enticing. A thought flickered through his head and was gone before it had time to register. The thought that what he was doing was somehow dangerous, except how could it be? He was in the driving seat and fired with the need to possess. For the first time with this woman, he was on ground with which he was familiar. He would have preferred to have been making love in his king-sized bed in his apartment, but this had a thrilling feel of the stolen moment. He felt like an adolescent and that in itself was so novel a feeling that he thought he should not wish it away.

'If you really want to go inside,' he said unsteadily, 'then, of course, we will.'

Julia twisted like someone in the grip of a fever, a movement he took as surrender, and he lightly skimmed his tongue along the crease of her womanhood, her gasping shudder making him give a grunt of exquisite satisfaction.

He intensified the pressure of his tongue, pushing it deeper within her and holding her firm as she bucked against his hands. It was every bit as erotic as he had imagined it would be. More. He could feel every thread of shock in her at what he was doing and, even more powerful, the need for him to continue. He moved his tongue up and down, sliding into her moistness and licking the tiny bud that had her convulsing with lust.

She curled her fingers into his hair and tugged, her hands pleading with him to stop because he was driving her crazy, but he didn't want to stop. He wanted to take her to the brink and then complete their lovemaking by thrusting into her, like a stallion, so that he could see her face when she reached the dizzy heights of her orgasm.

It took a while for the sound of voices to penetrate Julia's numb, giddy world. It was only when the woman giggled, a high-pitched sound that drifted through the trees and insinuated that another couple had obviously come out for precisely the same as she had been doing, that Julia jerked up and back into the world of the living.

She stared down in horror at Riccardo, barely able to vocalise, but he was already standing up, cursing under his breath.

Julia sprang to her feet and tidied herself with trembling hands.

She had no idea what to say. What was there that she could possibly say? She must have gone completely crazy. She couldn't bring herself to look at him and had turned to head back hurriedly into the club, when he stopped her.

'Don't think you can run inside and pretend that none of this happened,' he grated harshly, furious at their interruption. He had been as fired up as she had been and could already see that she was retreating. Dammit, he was not going to let her retreat on him!

The amorous couple had obviously heard their voices and vanished into another part of the garden, as eager as they had been for privacy. Julia felt sick. Sick with shame and mortification and utterly bewildered by her behaviour.

Riccardo held onto her arms, forcing her to look at him, to acknowledge what had just taken place. He had invaded every pore of her body and now he wanted her to admit it. 'You opened a door and you can't tell me that you can shut it now!'

'*I* opened a door!' Julia spluttered.

'OK, we *both* did.'

'Things got a little out of control. I...I must have had too much to drink...'

'And don't blame the drink! You were as aware of what was going on as I was! And you were enjoying every minute of it!'

Julia stared at him in helpless, frustrated silence. She could feel the cold air wrapping itself around her.

'I'm cold and it's time to leave,' she said unsteadily and after a few seconds he released her.

'Not before we sort this thing out.'

'There's nothing to sort out. I...I don't know how...how we happened to...'

'Stop shying away from the bald truth. How we happened to make love.' With every passing minute she was withdrawing from him, shutting him out, and he was not going to allow her to do that. He had come too far to admit defeat now and walk away. Riccardo Fabbrini never walked away from unfinished business, and this was unfinished business as far as he was concerned.

'We happened to do it because we wanted each other. Still do.'

'It was a moment of madness!' she denied heatedly.

'When is lust ever not a moment of madness?' He sighed and raked his fingers through his hair. The truth was that he was still on fire and the even more gut-wrenching truth of the matter was that he would continue to be on fire until he completed the task he had set for himself, killed off the curiosity to possess her that was driving him crazy. No woman had ever sent his senses rocketing into orbit as this complex creature trembling in front of him had. 'Have you never experienced a moment of madness?' he asked wryly.

'Never.'

'Then you haven't lived.' Their eyes met for the briefest of seconds.

'Maybe not in your eyes.' Her voice sounded high-pitched and defensive. If he couldn't hear the fear in it then she certainly could. Fear of the sweeping tide of physical attraction that had bowled her over the minute he had laid his hands on her. And the attraction hadn't begun tonight. It had been simmering under the surface from the very first moment she had seen him. She had just flatly refused to acknowledge it.

He was so wrong in every respect. He was everything

Caroline had bitterly described him to be. Cold, ruthless, arrogant, a man who got what he wanted whatever the costs and at whatever price. She should have recoiled in disgust at the feel of his hands on her back and the warm breath against her cheek as they had danced, but the opposite had happened and she could not make sense of it. And she should have fled from the touch of a man who had been her sister-in-law's ex-husband, but Caroline had never loved him. Her brief infatuation had been a bright flicker before fading away. There was no betrayal there, but still…

Her heart was still hammering in confusion as they re-entered the club and she preceded him to their table, not bothering to sit down.

'We're not leaving yet,' he informed her, pulling his chair out and sprawling on it, magnificently and gut-wrenchingly masculine, his body lazily indolent as he summoned across their waitress and ordered a refill of coffee for them both. 'So you might as well stop hovering like a startled rabbit and sit down.'

A little brown sparrow? A startled rabbit? Apt that he described her as prey, when she saw him as a predator.

Julia reluctantly perched on her chair and looked at him. 'I don't see the point of conducting a post-mortem on what happened,' she said quietly. 'It did, for reasons I can't fathom…'

'For reasons it *suits you not to fathom*,' Riccardo corrected harshly.

'You're not attracted to me, Riccardo; you made that perfectly clear the very first time I met you. Remember?' Julia sat back to allow her cup of coffee to be placed in front of her, along with the individual plunger, a jug of cream and a bowl of rough sugar cubes.

'And the feeling was mutual, if I recall,' he drawled mockingly. 'Let's just say that time alters everything.' He leaned across the table, invading her space, and she felt her pulses quicken in automatic response. 'If we hadn't been so rudely interrupted we both know where it would have ended.' He smiled wolfishly at her, cutting through her defences and silencing the denial rising to her lips. His eyes locked with hers, making her feel giddy. 'You wanted me in you as much as I wanted to be in you. You were desperate for our foreplay to go further, darling, and I was as desperate as you were. Let's just face the truth and deal with it.'

'But why?' Julia cried. Why what? It was inconceivable that Riccardo Fabbrini was attracted to her. Something else was going on here, under the surface. It was easy for her to see why she had succumbed to him in a moment of passion and, whether he liked to admit it or not, under the influence of alcohol which had lowered her natural reserve. He was devilishly good-looking. There could be very few women who would not respond to his suffocating sexual magnetism. She might hate herself for her temporary weakness, might argue that it defied all logic, but she could still understand her response.

But she possessed no such irresistible qualities of attraction. So why had he seduced her? Because it had all the hallmarks of a seduction.

She was staring at him, trying to find the right words to express what was going on in her head, when a voice cut through the thick silence. Julia sat back and found that her body was rigid with tension and she was breathing rapidly, like someone slowly being deprived of oxygen.

'Riccardo! I've been trying to call you for three weeks! Where have you been?'

Riccardo cursed silently to himself and looked at the platinum-blonde staring down at him with angry, hurt green eyes. There could not have been a worse moment for Helen

Scott to make her appearance. She was dressed, as always, in an outfit that revealed the maximum amount of body without being indecent. Tonight, the colour was red, a bright, eye-grabbing red in the shape of a dress of minuscule proportions, and black shoes that added a further four inches to her already considerable height.

She drew up one of the two free chairs, completely ignoring Julia's presence and fixed him with doleful, accusing eyes.

'I've been busy,' Riccardo told her coolly. 'Have I introduced my date for the evening? Julia, this is Helen. Helen's a model, if you hadn't already guessed.'

'A model and your girlfriend.'

'Ex-girlfriend.' He sighed impatiently, acutely aware that Julia was looking between the two of them and forming opinions. Opinions, for some reason, he did not want her to form. He had never been ashamed of the series of fabulously built, good-looking blonde women who had adorned his arm since his divorce. In fact, he knew that he was the envy of most red-blooded males whenever he went out with one of these women. But he was ashamed now. He could imagine her judgemental, clever brain ticking away, forming conclusions about the kind of relationships he conducted with women, meaningless relationships with women who had never challenged so much as a pore of him. The fact that such relationships had suited him as much as the women in question now sickened him.

Julia, sitting back and watching, felt her heart turn to lead. If she had needed reminding of why exactly a man like him could never be attracted to a woman like her then she had received a very timely reminder. She didn't think that she had ever seen a woman as exquisite as the one sitting next to her, or rather draping her body across the table next to her. Where Caroline had been stunningly pretty, this woman was strikingly beautiful. Every feature was chiselled to perfection, from the arched slant of her eyebrows to the small, perfectly shaped nose and the wide curve of her mouth.

'I've been trying to get in touch with you,' Helen said huskily, the threat of tears in her voice. 'I love you, Riccardo, and I thought you loved me.'

'This is neither the time nor the place...'

'Then where is?' The full mouth trembled. 'I just want to talk with you. In private. I know we can work things out, I know it. I can't sleep, Riccardo, I can't eat. All I can do is think of you, of *us*.'

'There *is* no us, Helen.' His voice was gentle but Julia detected the thread of irritation in it and shuddered inwardly.

'But there could be! If you'll just give us another chance.'

'It didn't work out,' he told her flatly, 'and, if you recall, I never made you any promises. In fact, I was at pains to warn you that I was not on the lookout for commitment.'

'But—'

'There are no *buts*, Helen. You need to move on. I've moved on.' His eyes involuntarily flickered across to Julia and Helen followed his gaze, registering the woman next to her for the first time since she had sat at their table.

'Her? You're going out with *her*?' Her voice wasn't hard with criticism or resentment. It was bewildered, and that struck Julia more forcibly than if she had been punched in the chest by someone in a jealous rage. 'But you can't be. Look at *me*. How could you choose *her* over *me*?'

'Leave this table immediately.' He did not raise his voice by so much as a decibel. He didn't have to. Its very softness was the equivalent of a whiplash, and Helen blanched visibly. When she stood up she turned fully to Julia and spoke in a wavering voice.

'I don't believe Riccardo is going out with you,' she said with tears in her eyes. 'He's always dated good-looking blondes. We used to joke about it, about the way he was always attracted to the same type.' She gave a stifled sob and raised her hand to her mouth, as if pressing down the emotion. 'I don't understand.' She turned away and blindly made her way, head bent, weaving through the tables until she had disappeared towards the other side of the room.

'I apologise for that,' he said roughly. 'Helen and I broke up before I met you. She obviously thought I was joking when I told her it was over.'

Julia didn't say anything. She understood everything and it made her blood run cold.

'I just didn't understand how you could actually be attracted to a *little brown sparrow* like me.' Her voice was mocking. It was easy to use derision to conceal her hurt, her hurt and her anger at herself, because she knew that somewhere deep inside she had half hoped that he really had been attracted to her. 'Now I understand that you weren't.'

'You understand nothing!' he bit out savagely and she smiled, distancing herself from the powerful, potently masculine man leaning towards her, his black eyes burning with intent.

'Oh, no, that's where you're wrong, Riccardo. They say that men go for certain models and very rarely deviate from form. You go for good-looking blondes. Helen said as much herself.' An icy calm had replaced the rampant chaos in her mind. 'You would never in a month of Sundays be seriously attracted to a brown-haired, bespectacled teacher like me. But you were willing to seduce me, weren't you, Riccardo? Because what you wanted wasn't *me*. You wanted to pay me back for what I did, for disrupting your life, for exploding a bomb in your highly organised, perfectly fine-tuned existence. I was the messenger who brought the bad news, and they say we always want to shoot the messenger. That's it, isn't it, Riccardo Fabbrini? You were prepared to set aside your high standards in the opposite sex because it suited you to use your charm on me, to what…make me fall in love with you? So that you could then walk away and teach me a lesson? Was that it?'

She waited for him to at least deny it, hoped desperately that he would, but the hesitation that greeted her accusation was answer in itself, and Julia stood up abruptly, sick to the stomach.

She should have listened to the warning bells in her head, should have kept her distance. She knew better now.

CHAPTER SIX

JULIA could feel the sting of tears at the backs of her eyes as she sat, stony-faced, in the car, her jaw clenched, staring straight ahead. Tears of mortification and hurt.

Riccardo slammed the driver's door behind him but instead of starting the engine he turned to her, leaning against the door.

'Look at me.'

'Take me home, please. Or I shall have to get out of the car and order a taxi.'

'Don't be ridiculous. You would have to wait hours if you ordered a taxi. They're not exactly lining the streets outside.'

'I am *not* being ridiculous! I just want to go home.' Ridiculous, though, was how she felt. Ridiculous in her prim grey outfit, dusted down especially for the occasion, sad and ridiculous.

Riccardo's jaw clenched and he took a few deep breaths. 'I'm sorry about what happened in there. I had no idea Helen would be there or else, naturally, we would have gone somewhere else.'

'Oh, yes, I'm sure you're sorry,' Julia's head snapped round and she glared angrily at him. They had parked at a fair distance from the front of the nightclub, but there was still enough light to throw his handsome face into angled relief. How she could ever have believed, even in the remotest corner of her heart, that this dark, breathtakingly sexy man could ever have touched her body with desire made her shudder with humiliation. 'Sorry because I exposed you for what you are! A man who feels that he can dominate everything and everyone in his life, do exactly what he pleases without thought for anyone else. No wonder Caroline cringed from you!'

'Don't you dare bring my ex-wife into this equation! You've jumped to conclusions and arrived at your own twisted explanations because of your own insecurities.' He was guiltily aware that there was an element of truth in her accusations, but instead of calming him down that only served to stoke his anger further. The minute he had touched her he had been consumed by a need far greater than anything he had experienced before and now…now he realised that his need had been controlling him all along. He had tagged on a few handy reasons to justify his burning desire to touch her, but the brutal truth was that he was attracted to this woman, deeply attracted to the woman who had purposefully wrought havoc with his life. The fact that it made no sense had pushed him into dealing with the unfamiliar sensation of being out of control in the only way he knew how. By trying to take over the reins, by trying to control his inexplicable feelings.

'Don't you dare talk to me about my insecurities,' Julia bit out harshly. 'You don't know a damn thing about me or my insecurities! You pigeonholed me into the enemy from day one and you never bothered to try and understand me or what motivates me! You think you know me because you think you know everything!'

The car was alive with tension; it crackled around them and crawled along her skin and into her bones.

'And you haven't pigeonholed *me*?' He laughed, a dry, unpleasant sound. 'I am Caroline's nasty ex-husband—have you forgotten? I'm the bastard who drove her into the arms of another man. Did *you* ever stop to think that the beast my ex-wife described to you could have felt pain? I might have stopped loving her...maybe I never really did love her. The illusion of love can be powerful but betrayal hurts. Did you ever consider that? Oh, no, you just assumed that I was a bastard and so it was all right to deny me my own daughter because I couldn't possibly have any redeeming features.'

Julia went white as he plucked the unarticulated thoughts from her head and laid them out in front of her in merciless detail.

'You took one look at Helen and decided that she represented the only type of woman I could possibly look at twice. But, as I said, you're looking in the wrong direction for your conclusions. Instead of throwing it at me, try throwing it at yourself. The fact is, you measured yourself against her and found yourself wanting.'

'That's not true! Now drive me home immediately.'

'And cut short this revealing conversation? I think not.' It shocked him to realise that the only thing he wanted to do, really wanted to do, was to finish what had been started in the gardens of the nightclub an hour ago. She sat there, spitting rage at him, as if he had struck a match and tossed it at her, and he wanted to touch her. It made such little sense that he almost shook his head in bewilderment. But he wasn't going to let her squirm away from this. He wasn't going to allow her to throw her frank observations in his face and then turn her back on him before he had a chance to throw a few of his own back at her.

'You have hang-ups about how you look, and your mother probably doesn't help matters by rattling on about marriage and settling down. Underneath that controlled exterior you're burning up with your own insecurities, which is why you think that a man who could bed a woman like Helen would never choose to bed you.'

'Do you have to use such coarse language?'

'Sometimes I'm a coarse man. I don't go around ducking behind civilised phrases when a few blunt words would do much better instead. But do you know what I think?' He leaned forward, crowding her, and Julia felt her heart begin to accelerate. Even though her mind was shrieking disdain, her whole body was reacting to his proximity. Her breasts were hardening and her eyes were compulsively drifting to the narrow line of his sensuous mouth. God, she wanted to touch it, wanted it to devour her, every part of her. It made her sick to think about it.

'I don't care what you think.'

'But you'll listen anyway,' he ground out. 'I think coarse men like me turn you on. I'll bet my house that you've spent your life going out with namby-pamby sissies in touch with their feminine sides.' He made a derogatory sound under his breath and Julia inclined her body towards him, so that their faces were almost touching.

She was so mad that she had to keep her hands clenched on her lap or risk slapping that knowing smirk off his face.

'It may not occur to you that some women happen to like men who are sensitive and kind and considerate and thoughtful! Men who don't act as though the entire universe is their own private playground to do with as they want!'

'Some women, but not you.' He knew that she was itching to hit him. Quite honestly, he could understand why, but God, he wanted her to admit that she had been powerless against him when he had touched her. 'You don't want a man you can order about like one of your schoolchildren. You want a man who will take you, and when he's finished you'll want to beg for him to take you again. Me.'

Julia laughed but to her own ears it sounded brittle and unconvincing. 'You! You flatter yourself!'

'Do I?' he murmured, his eyes flicking to her full mouth.

Abruptly, the atmosphere in the car changed. Julia drew her breath in sharply, wanting to look away but unable to tear her eyes from his lazy inspection of her face. She felt mesmerised, like a rabbit caught in the headlights of a car. Her lips parted and he raised his hand to trace the contours of her mouth.

'Stop it, please, Riccardo,' she mumbled weakly, and he gave a low, sexy laugh.

'Sure. But only because I can think of better places for my finger to be.' He removed her spectacles and placed them on the walnut dashboard, almost expecting her to pull away from him and not knowing what he would do if she did that. He didn't trust himself to behave like a perfect gentleman.

'Do you want to know where I want my hand to be?' he asked softly, and Julia shook her head dumbly and muttered,

'No.'

'Then you'll stop me, will you?' He slipped his hand under her shirt and hooked his finger under her bra, tugging gently until her breast popped out, and without taking his eyes from her face, he stroked her nipple, feeling his own arousal surge as his finger grated over the tightened bud.

Riccardo buried his face against the side of her neck, nipping her skin until Julia thought she would pass out from the twin sensations of his mouth against her skin while his finger rubbed her sensitised nipple.

She wanted to drag herself away from this madness, but her brain seemed to be wrapped in cotton wool.

He was taking advantage of her, proving a point, proving to them both that the craving she felt for him was beyond control, but she was powerless to resist. As soon as he laid one finger on her, her body went up in flames, and her hunger for him fanned the flames until the only consuming thing in her head was having him.

She arched back with a shuddering sigh, and he bent to lick her stomach while his hand slipped beneath her skirt and he felt the soft flesh of her parted thighs.

She was certain that he would be able to hear the furious hammering of her heart as he nuzzled upwards until he found her nipple with his mouth and he began pulling on it, sucking her breast into his mouth as she caressed his dark, bent head. His exploring finger had now insinuated itself down under her briefs and began rubbing erotically into her, drawing her feminine moisture up to dampen the throbbing bud of her womanhood.

Twisting to her side, Julia groped until she found the zipper of his trousers and tugged it down, grappling with the button on the waistband and feeling a surge of satisfaction as he groaned and helped her in her efforts towards his rigid manhood.

As her hand clasped around it he groaned again, his breathing as uncontrolled as her own.

Had Riccardo been right? Had she only ever sought out the gentle, unassuming men because deep down she had felt that they were all she could aspire to? Unthreatening men who politely kissed her and fumbled with her body as though embarrassed at being in female terrain? Had she steered clear of aggressive, dominant males, men like Riccardo, although she had never actually met anyone quite like him, because of her own lack of self-esteem in how she looked? Surely not… Yet here she was, turned on and utterly incapable of turning herself off!

She only removed her hand to wriggle out of her under-clothes, scarcely believing what she was doing, eager to resume her exploration of his body. With a little shove, she pushed his head away from where his mouth was fastened to her nipple, nipping it and licking, and with her free hand she shakily undid the buttons of his shirt and ran her hand over his taut stomach before she flicked her tongue over his flat brown nipples.

This couldn't be happening, yet it was. The windows were misty but she still felt her instinctive modesty kick in when he commanded her to sit on him.

'I can't! We're in a car park,' she gasped and he gave a low growl of amusement.

'So what? No one's around and God, I want you. Now!'

Julia wondered whether slightly built frames were fashioned for making love in small places. Or maybe her own frantic need was sufficient to expedite what he had demanded. Her skirt, twisted around her, barely hampered her lithe transference from her own seat to his and she felt the thrust of him in her with exquisite, searing pleasure. Every pore in her body was tingling for satisfaction and all modesty was thrown to the winds as he freed her of her jacket and ordered her to take off her camisole and bra for him so that he could see her as they made love.

She heard his sharp intake of breath as her breasts were exposed and felt a heady, dizzying wave of power as his eyes raked over her nakedness. She leant forward so that her breast dipped towards his mouth and slowly began to move on him, watching with heightened senses as his tongue flicked to capture her nipple in his eager mouth.

He slipped his hands around her waist and her movements quickened until they were soaring, beyond caring who might pass by and be curious at what was going on in the expensive Jaguar with the steamed-up windows.

Julia felt her shuddering peaks of excitement ebbing and rising once again, and then, drained, she fell against his broad chest, wanting nothing more than to snuggle into him and let her spent drowsiness take her away.

Riccardo stroked her hair. God, he had just had the most intense orgasm he could remember, and he could take her again. What the hell was this all about? He sighed, perplexed, and she straightened, her languid gaze focusing finally on his face.

'My God,' Julia whispered. She was suddenly aware of her state of undress and began to edge off him, but his big hands covered her hips, holding her firmly in place. He looked at her, then lowered his eyes to roam over her upper body. Her breasts were perfectly proportioned for her slight body, pert and upright, with big, rosy nipples. Just looking at them made Riccardo stir in automatic response. He reached out and inserted his finger under one, gently stroking, then he blew and watched her nipple tighten as it reacted to his breath.

'Riccardo, no.'

'You doubt that I could give a repeat performance?' he drawled, catching her eyes with his. 'Believe me, I could.'

She could believe him. Not only was he the epitome of virile man, but she could also feel him hardening inside her, filling her out. Julia could have stayed where she was, pleasuring herself in his rampant feasting of her body, but the niggling doubts that had been cast aside when passion took over were now making themselves felt.

They had just made love, but why was it, when she looked at him, that the last thing stamped on his face was love?

She slowly lifted herself from him and slipped back into her seat, reaching out for her spectacles, but instead of putting them on, she held them loosely on her lap.

'What is it?' he asked sharply, turning to her.

'Nothing.' Everything, she thought. She had just performed the most intimate act that could exist between a man and a woman but that was where the intimacy stopped.

He had seduced her with his tongue and with his body, but not because he loved her or even cared about her.

He had talked around her accusations, had tried to make her feel as though she had misjudged his intentions, but now, when Julia thought about it, she realised that he had not denied any of the things she had hurled at him. He had not denied his intent to seduce her as a payback.

She bent over and began putting on her top, all too aware of her vulnerability as she struggled into it, her breasts dancing and almost hurting as his eyes raked over them.

Then she gathered the rest of her garments, shamelessly thrown off in the heat of passion.

Riccardo watched and waited. For the first time in his life, he didn't know where this situation was leading. He knew where he wanted it to go. He also knew that to push his point would meet with a blank wall.

'We really should go, Riccardo,' Julia said.

'You're doing it again. Why don't you say what's on your mind instead of giving me your British reticence? We've just made love and—'

'It means nothing.' It hurt to say it, but she had to. She had given herself to a charmer, to someone whose intentions were questionable at the best and downright cruel at the worst. She had ignored her better instincts and had melted at his touch and she was not about to put herself in line for his eventual gloating.

'No, it means we gave in to a moment of curiosity…'

'A moment of curiosity?' Riccardo's voice was grimly cold and Julia flinched, but reminded herself of what she meant to him. She was the woman who had sided with the enemy and deprived him of his child, she was the mousy, brown-haired sparrow to whom, as he had casually informed her at their first meeting, he could never be attracted. Because he went for blondes. Blondes like

Caroline, like Helen, like heaven only knew how many other woman discarded somewhere along the way.

Blondes because maybe, for him, the only woman he had really ever loved had been blonde. Blonde, childlike Caroline, who had finally broken free of his invasive personality.

Julia felt a stab of jealousy and pain rip through her, leaving in its wake the shattering realisation that what she wanted from him was not just sex, but much more. Because what she felt for him was not simply physical attraction, but the dawning of an emotion that ran far deeper.

She steeled herself. 'Sure. You're a man of the world.' She shrugged and continued to stare blindly out of the window, not trusting herself to look in his direction. She had already discovered, to her cost, what he could do to her with just a glance. 'You know how powerful curiosity can be, and,' she continued lightly, 'you were curious about me. Angry as well, but curious too. Maybe because I am so different from the kind of women you're accustomed to dating.'

'And you?' he asked softly, giving nothing away. 'You seem to have explained my motives to yourself, so care to explain your motives to me? Or shall I follow your lead and just take a pot-shot?'

Julia would not succumb to arguing. He won every argument. He could twist her words into knots and leave her floundering.

'Me?' she mused, eyes still averted. 'I was curious too, believe it or not. You were right. All the men I've ever dated, not that there has been a long line of them, have been just the opposite of you. Perhaps I was just curious to discover what a man like you had to offer…'

'A man like me…'

'You know…tall, dark, handsome, powerful, the essence

of every teenage fantasy.' She sneaked a sideways glance at him from lowered lashes and shivered at the icy expression on his face.

But she had to do what she had to do. To protect herself. Or else she would find herself as putty in his hands, taken and then discarded, and she knew that she was just not sophisticated or world-weary enough to deal with the heartache that would inevitably follow. What ingrained expertise and control she possessed was reserved for her working side. Her emotional side, as she was fast learning, was full of holes.

'I see.'

'We're both adults, these things happen. I just think we should put it all down to experience.'

He could still feel the melting compliance of her body against his, could still taste the sweetness of her mouth on his own, and here she was, talking about *putting the whole thing down to experience*! Riccardo wanted to believe that fear and not reason was talking, fear at how he had made her feel, fear that she might find herself in the grip of a passion she could not control, but alongside that wish was a nasty seed of doubt. Julia Nash was not like the other women he had known. Of that she was absolutely right. He could not read her. He might guess at what went on in her head, but he could not be sure.

And he would certainly never run after a woman who spoke of curiosity and experience, even if his gut instinct was telling him to disbelieve what his ears heard and go only on what his eyes read.

His pride slammed into place and he turned on the engine, the tyres screeching as he manoeuvred his car out of its slot and headed towards the exit.

'So we've both had an experience,' he said mockingly, 'and now where does that leave us?'

Julia had not thought that far ahead. As always, he was one step in front of her. She remembered they were still playing a game, still hanging on to the pretence that they were dating, so that he could have easy, frequent access to Nicola, until the time was right for their relationship to assume its natural course.

Her mouth went dry with apprehension. It would mean seeing him, being in his company.

'Perhaps we should tell Nicola the truth now,' she said quietly. 'Tell her that you're her father, and that way we can forget about this farcical pretence about going out.'

Riccardo laughed sardonically. 'Oh, I see. The time is right now because it suits you, is that it? Now that your adolescent fantasies have been satisfied, you're happy to break the news to my daughter, even if she might not be emotionally ready to accept such a revelation.'

He braked at a traffic light and she could see the harsh set of his face.

'She knows you now. It's not as if she's seeing you for the first time,' Julia argued.

'She lost her mother only months ago, and the only man she ever regarded as a father figure. Suddenly, you intend to tell her that no, we weren't going out, because I have appeared on the scene and she's to accept me. And you think she won't go scurrying into her shell? You think the trust she's building with me won't evaporate overnight?'

'I'm doing you a favour!' Julia heard the plea in her voice and felt a rush of panic.

'You mean you're doing *yourself* a favour!' He glanced across at her, his black eyes glittering. 'Well, it won't work.'

'What do you mean?'

'I mean that *I* am calling the shots here and *I* don't think the time is right. Whether you like it or not, we're going to carry on playing the devoted couple.'

He sped off from the traffic lights, barely hesitating as he manoeuvred along the streets and around roundabouts.

'And how long do you think that is going to take?'

'How long is a piece of string?'

Julia stared, unseeing, through the window and tried to imagine the agony of being in his presence and having to laugh and chat as though he had not rocked her to the very foundations of her being. Ironic insofar as that had been his intention, she thought bitterly. If only he knew.

'In fact,' he said slowly, 'we can't be too far away from the Easter school holidays. When are they, exactly?'

Julia gave him the dates, wondering what he had in mind. She had no need to ask the question.

'It might be an ideal opportunity for her to get to know a bit of Italy. She could meet some of her relatives over there. Naturally, I would expect you to come along as well, to ease the ground, so to speak.'

'That's impossible.'

'Nothing in life is impossible. Haven't you grasped that that is my motto and one I have always stuck by?'

'And what if one of us finds another partner before then?' Julia threw at him. As far as she was concerned, it was a far-fetched notion but the only one she could think of that might put a spoke in the devil's wheel, but far from seeming disconcerted he simply gave a dry laugh.

'You mean, what if I bump into one of those blondes to whom I apparently have no resistance?'

'I mean, what if *I* meet someone?' Julia flung back at him, and a thick silence ensued, which she feverishly felt was laden with implied disbelief. God, he must have thought that he could snap his fingers and she would jump, because she was no stunner. And was it any wonder that he had felt that way? After the impression her mother had inadvertently given him? The impression of a retiring girl, housebound because of her duties to her five-year-old niece, who rarely left the house? No wonder he had taken her to a nightclub. He probably thought that he would show her a little action and perk her life up. In more ways than one! She gritted her teeth in frustration.

'Oh,' he said softly, 'but how easy is it going to be to go running back to your predictable line of sensitive, domesticated males? You yourself admitted that they are not the object of any woman's fantasy…'

'Why, you are so damned *conceited*…!' Julia spluttered. 'And that's not what I said at all!'

Riccardo shrugged dismissively. 'Besides, you are not at liberty to do anything with anyone at the moment. Your duty is at my side, holding my hand and putting on a very convincing performance for the sake of my child.'

She hadn't realised how much ground they had covered and how quickly until the car slowed down and she saw that they were pulling into the short drive that led to the house, which was in darkness. She looked at her watch and realised, with astonishment, that the hours had slipped by. It was now after one and, strangely enough, she was not in the least tired. In fact, she had never felt more wide awake.

'Which, I believe, will be tomorrow? To take *both* of you to the zoo? Where you will laugh and give every semblance of being thrilled to be in my company.' He leant across to open her door and in the process his arm brushed her breasts, which tingled at the brief contact. She was certain that he had done that deliberately but Julia wasn't going to argue the point. She pushed open the door and scuttled out of the car, almost tripping in her haste to get to the front door.

'You needn't see me in,' she muttered, rummaging in her bag for the key.

'I wouldn't dream of driving off and leaving you on your doorstep. What kind of man would I be?'

'The kind of man you've proven yourself to be,' Julia retorted.

'You've already admitted that you used me,' he said coolly, 'so perhaps, then, we're better suited than you think.'

'I doubt it.'

A flicker of something shadowed his face, but his voice was neutral when he next spoke, asking her what time he could come and collect them the following day.

'After lunch,' Julia told him, feeling hunted. 'Around one-thirty. That will give us time to eat.'

'In which case I shall join you for lunch. I'll see you at twelve.'

Julia could hardly concentrate the following morning. Everywhere she turned, she caught images of herself and Riccardo. She had had a very long bath the previous night, or rather early morning, when she had returned home, but nothing could wash away the musky scent on her, the scent of a satisfied woman. Her thoughts haunted her, teasing her with remembered pleasure and then admonishing her for her insanity. And the more insane her behaviour seemed, the more coolly calculating his own appeared.

She was a bag of nerves by the time he arrived promptly at twelve for lunch, but his behaviour was impeccable. There were no allusions, not even on the odd occasion when they found themselves in the same room without either Nicola or her mother around, to what had happened the night before.

Disconcertingly, his silence on the subject only served to reconfirm her impression that their lovemaking had been a spontaneous but miscalculated error of judgement, at least on his part. He had given in to the temptation of appeasing his sexual curiosity about her and was now content to play his part without batting an eyelid.

The same could not have been said of Julia. She was agonisingly aware of him, and even when they touched in passing she could feel her body react, as though it had a life of its own, quite independent of the workings of her brain.

Her fiery little outburst about finding someone else, said in the heat of the moment to scupper his smugness that she would fall in with whatever he had in mind, for however long it took, had obviously been dismissed as ridiculous.

It was an unutterable relief when they wearily made their way back to the house, with Nicola chatting happily between them in the taxi.

'You can relax now,' Riccardo said, following her into the house and closing the door behind him.

'I wasn't tense,' Julia lied, with her back to him. 'I suppose you must be getting on your way now.' She turned around and looked pointedly at the door.

Wasn't tense? Riccardo thought that he could have had quite an argument with her about that, but it would have been an argument going in circles. For every one step forward with her, he took five back, and the amazing thing was that he was still determined to put another foot in front. Why?

He was better equipped to understand his motives for revenge, dubious though they had been. Revenge was a violent, passionate emotion in tune with his soul. But he no longer wanted any kind of revenge and the truth was that he was no longer sure what he wanted.

Except he wanted Julia. And he was determined that he would have her again. This time, though, his approach would not be one of physical persuasion, but something far more subtle. He shook his head to clear it of the buzzing hornet's nest that was driving him mad.

'I'll have a cup of coffee before I go.'

'Is that one of your orders?'

'It's a request,' he told her, in a voice that matched hers. 'Look, we've had a good day. Why don't we call a truce?'

Julia didn't answer but preceded him into the kitchen, to find Nicola getting out her colouring book, one that had been bought for her from the souvenir shop at the zoo.

'I'll colour with you later, honey,' Julia said, nervously aware that Riccardo was watching her. She almost tipped hot water over her hand under the casual, brooding scrutiny.

'I don't know if you want to see Nicola during the week,' she began quietly, edging towards the far end of the kitchen, away from idle ears. 'If not, next weekend would be fine, although not on Saturday evening. I won't be around.'

'Won't you? Where are you going?'

'Out.' A friend had invited her to a birthday party and Julia was looking forward to it. She had not seen Elizabeth in nearly two months and there would be other mutual friends there as well. It would be blissfully relaxing not to have Riccardo around like a burr under her skin.

'Out where?' His voice was hard and Julia met his stare levelly.

'None of your business, Riccardo. I *have* got a private life, you know, even though you might not want to believe it.'

'Cancel whoever it is you are seeing. I want to take you both out to dinner on Saturday.'

'Forget it.' She could have told him the occasion, knew that he would understand because underneath his aggression she was all too familiar with a side of him that was scrupulously fair, even though it might not always pertain to her. But a sudden wicked urge incited her to keep him guessing. 'I'm not changing my plans.'

Riccardo watched the shuttered expression as she sipped her coffee and a cold, icy rage wafted through him. He couldn't believe it. She was going out with a man. No woman looked like that, expression veiled, unless she was holding a secret to herself, and the only secrets women did not share with their lovers, because lovers they had been and would be again, was the presence on the scene of another lover.

Jealousy ripped through him, leaving him shaken. A pulse in his jaw began to beat fiercely and he lowered his eyes.

'Why not? Are your plans that important?' The words were dragged out of him. He knew that he should stop now but he couldn't.

'Very important,' Julia answered truthfully. 'I haven't seen this particular friend for quite a while now and I'm very much looking forward to meeting up.' She drained her coffee and thought, Well, I have a life and you can put that in your pipe and smoke it.

And she could see that he didn't like it, didn't like not being obeyed.

Perhaps, she thought in a blinding flash, the time was coming for her to change. To stop driving in the slow lane while everyone else was in the fast.

'I have changed my mind,' Riccardo said abruptly as jealousy stroked his mind with icy fingers.

'Changed your mind? What about?'

He glanced at Nicola and then stared broodingly at the woman in front of him.

No more pretences, dammit. He wanted Julia and now he would pursue her without the dubious advantage of knowing that her hands were tied, that she was compelled to wear a smile to fuel the illusion of a relationship in the eyes of his unknowing daughter. All of that suddenly seemed like the cheap tactics of a coward and coward he most certainly was not.

The time had come for honesty to prevail.

'Nicola,' he said softly, squatting so that he was on her level as she approached him. 'There's something I have to say to you.'

'Riccardo!'

'No, Julia. No more pretence.'

'But I thought—'

'It's time.'

'Time for what?' Nicola looked at them, frowning and Riccardo smiled tenderly and absorbed one of her small hands in his.

'Time to tell you, my sweet, that you have at least three people that love you very much, Aunty Jules, and Grandma and...' His voice wavered and Julia laid her hand on his shoulder, knowing that their shared strength would be important for Nicola.

'And...me.'

'What do you mean?'

'I mean that I am your dad, my child.'

There was an agonisingly long silence, or so it seemed to Julia, then Nicola smiled, a little shadow of a smile that was tinged with shyness.

'My *real* dad?'

'Your real dad,' Riccardo said gravely, his heart bursting as the smile enfolded him.

'I knew...'

'You *knew*? That I was your dad?'

'That you would come back to find me.'

CHAPTER SEVEN

JULIA looked at her reflection in the full-length mirror in her bedroom and didn't know whether to be shocked, thrilled or just confused at what confronted her. Over the past week, she had worked on her self-image with the fast and furious pace of someone fleeing from the devil. Which just about summed it up as far as she was concerned. Riccardo Fabbrini was the devil and she was fleeing from him and straight into the arms of a damage-limitation exercise which would give her strength and propel her into the sort of life which she felt she needed desperately if she wasn't to fall deeper into the quagmire of her confused emotions.

She needed to prove to him, once and for all, that she was no walkover to be used and discarded at his pleasure. She refused to be the brown sparrow to his circling hawk. And more than that: his role was now complete. He had told Nicola of his true identity and her heart wrenched as she imagined her niece's gradual withdrawal from her life. She *needed* to move on now.

On the Monday she had gone to her optician's. Having always worn spectacles, she had listened to Nick Healey's sales patter on the convenience of contact lenses with scepticism, and was even more sceptical when informed that with soft contact lenses there would be little if any initial discomfort. She had returned for her lenses three days later and had overcome her queasiness at the thought of putting a foreign object into her eye by reminding herself that it was all for a greater purpose.

In between ordering her lenses and having them fitted, Julia took herself to the hairdresser's after work. Her usual unexciting wash, shampoo, trim and blow dry was replaced by a dramatic blunt bob that fell thickly to chin level, and a complete dye job, with highlights. She was now the proud possessor, for the first time in her life, of a hair colour that was not her own. Rich chestnut with golden auburn highlights.

Julia spent the remainder of the week shopping. She ignored the temptation to throw her money in the direction of the most background outfits with the least daring cuts and staunchly headed for the overpowering sales assistants who eyed her body knowingly and were only too overjoyed to clothe her in short, adventurous designs in striking colours.

Now, barely a week later, Julia stood in front of the mirror and looked at the completed job. She looked much taller and a lot more shapely than she had imagined herself to be. Her hair swung provocatively around her face, a riot of carefully blended colours and without spectacles her eyes were clearly visible for the first time. Large grey eyes, shadowed with a subtle application of eye make-up.

And, to complete the show, her new pale blue, very short skirt and matching jacket that was tailored to emphasise every line of her slender body. Under the jacket, a small, tight top clung to her like a second skin. Her shoes were black and high and undeniably sexy.

Julia did a twirl and thought that she looked the part, if she didn't exactly feel it.

But looking was good enough for her. Let Riccardo Fabbrini see that she was a force to be reckoned with, that she was not some sad, desperate woman who found it impossible not to respond to his polished, experienced charm and fabulous good looks.

Shame it was all about to be wasted on a girlfriend's birthday party, but then again, she thought wryly, a bit of practice might help when it came to the niggling technicalities of sitting in minuscule skirts and walking in three-inch heels.

She glanced at her delicate bracelet watch, a present from her parents when she was sixteen and the only item with which she had refused to part company. Her mother would be here in an hour to babysit, although Nicola was already in bed at a little after seven, and then she would launch herself into the world.

She had just peeked in to see Nicola and give her a final goodnight kiss, when the doorbell rang.

Now this, Julia thought with a grin, will take a little getting used to. Sashaying. Something she had never done before. She sashayed down the stairs, resisting the impulse to remove her shoes and run down the way she usually did, and pulled open the door with a wide smile, waiting for her mother's shocked reaction.

The expression froze on her face as she absorbed who was standing on the doorstep, his hands thrust into his pockets.

'What are *you* doing here?' Julia stood in front of him, barricading his entry, one hand on her hip, the other holding the door ajar.

Riccardo recovered quickly from the gut punch he had felt on seeing her. So he had been right, he thought savagely. Out on a date with a man and dressed to kill for the occasion. Looking every inch a knock-out. His black eyes travelled the length of her body, lingering on her legs and the jut of her breasts under the cling-film top she was wearing. When he finally met her eyes it was to find her looking at him coldly.

'I asked you what you were doing here,' Julia repeated.

Never had she been so blatantly stripped before and she was angry to find that the mental striptease had turned her cool confidence into heated arousal.

But her appearance, she thought fiercely, was now her armour, and she remained where she was, not flinching.

'I've come to babysit,' Riccardo answered, his mouth twisting. 'I have every right, considering I am Nicola's father and there are no flimsy pretences remaining between me and my child.'

'That's impossible. Mum's babysitting,' Julia replied. 'In fact, she should be here any minute now.'

'Should be but won't. Because I phoned to let her know that as I am free tonight, I would take over. Now, are you going to stand aside and let me in or do I have to push past you and let myself in?'

Julia stood aside, furious, and waited until he was in before slamming the door behind her. 'How dare you?' she said in a low, strangled voice. 'How dare you re-arrange my plans so that you can come here and *check up on me*?'

'Check up on you? I'm doing nothing of the sort. I'm helping out. Where is my daughter?'

'Upstairs. Asleep.'

'Very wise.'

'And what is *that* supposed to mean?'

His eyes did another indolent appraisal of her body and Julia felt another wave of heat wash over her.

'It means that you did the sensible thing in making sure that my daughter does not see her surrogate mother going out dressed like a tart!' He knew that every word he was saying was getting under her skin and that every lazy glance over her barely dressed body was enraging her, and he felt a vicious sense of satisfaction. Let her go out raging, let her spend her romantic evening furiously thinking about *him*.

'I am *not* dressed like a tart,' Julia hissed furiously. She glanced up the stairs and then pulled him by his jacket out of the hall and away from any possibility of being seen by Nicola should she just happen to wake up and stroll out of her bedroom at the wrong moment.

'That skirt barely covers you. And where are your spectacles? If you don't fall flat on your face in those heels then you'll trip over something, and how elegant are you going to look in front of your man?'

'I'm wearing contact lenses,' Julia said tersely. 'Not that it's any of your business.'

'It damn well *is* my business! I will not allow my daughter to see you in a get-up like the one you're wearing! What the hell sort of example do you imagine you are setting?' God, he sounded positively Victorian but, dammit, he wanted to strip her of those wickedly provocative clothes. Just the thought of some man looking at her, daring to let his gaze linger over the swell of her breasts and that ripely deep-pink mouth, wonder what the body was like under the cling film, was enough to make him clench his jaw in a possessive fury.

'I will wear what I like, Riccardo.' She strode across to pick up her jacket which she had draped over the banister and slung it on defiantly, then snatched her small clutch bag from the table in the hall.

'Not if I have anything to do with it,' he growled. What exactly he *could* do about it was beyond his comprehension, and his impotence only served to add tinder to the fire. 'This is not the sort of example I want to have set for my child!'

Julia looked at him in frank amazement. 'Since when did you have such a highly developed puritanical streak, Riccardo Fabbrini? From the look of your last girlfriend, it must be a very recently acquired trait!'

'Helen was my lover; my child was not in her care. If she had been then rest assured I would not have allowed her to dress like a wh—'

'Don't even think about saying it,' Julia said in an icy voice. 'I'm going now and I'll be back in a few hours' time. You know where everything is.'

She turned and as she was opening the door felt his hand descend on her arm, forcing her to turn and face him.

'Where are you going, anyway?' he demanded, his eyes clashing with hers. A man could lose himself in those eyes. Clever, suspicious, bruised eyes that could trap a man. *Who the hell was she going out with?*

'That's none of your business!'

'And what if I need to get in touch with you? What if Nicola wakes up and asks after you? She might be disoriented. What if she falls ill?'

'I have my mobile phone with me.' Julia glanced around for a piece of paper and a pencil, glared at him and then began sashaying towards the kitchen. The tightness of the skirt combined with the height of her heels made her feel headily provocative, even though she was steaming angry at his high-handed attitude. But there was nothing to be done. She had to give him her phone number despite the fact that it was extremely unlikely that it would be needed.

She could feel his eyes boring into her as he followed her and it seemed to take several hours covering ground between the hall and the kitchen. How on earth did women maintain this look all the time? Did they get used to the heels or did they just resign themselves to walking very, very slowly for the sake of their vanity?

'Here's my mobile number.' She handed him a piece of paper, which he didn't glance at, just shoved in his pocket while he continued to stare at her blackly. 'Though I don't think you'll need it,' Julia informed him, clicking her way out of the kitchen and back to the front door. 'Nicola was exhausted tonight and she very rarely wakes up once she goes to sleep. And you're her father! I don't think she'll be alarmed if she does get up and finds you here instead of her grandma.'

'And what time do you intend to be back?' If any woman had ever questioned his movements the way he was questioning hers, he knew that he would have hit the roof, but he didn't give a damn if he sounded like an inquisitor.

'I'll be back when I'm back,' Julia informed him. She was beginning to enjoy the sensation of watching him squirm in his own discomfort and had absolutely no inclination to disabuse him of the illusion that she was going out with a man. Not that she was strictly telling a lie, she thought. There *would* be men at the party, although probably all of the safely married variety. 'In other words,' she added sweetly, 'don't wait up for me. You could try watching a little telly. There's a very good period drama on you might enjoy. You'll be able to identify with some of the men. They're overbearing and unreasonable as well.'

'With a tongue like yours,' Riccardo told her, flushing darkly as the accuracy of her remark hit home, 'you'll be back within the hour. Men don't appreciate sarcasm in their women.'

'You mean *you* don't appreciate sarcasm in *your* women,' she amended, pausing with her hand on the door and looking up at him. The beautiful, tearful Helen certainly had not seemed to be the sort of woman who spoke back, and Caroline had been as meek as a lamb. No wonder she had spent her marriage in a state of nervous tension.

'And you're telling me that the man you're going to be seeing *does*?' Riccardo gave a crack of derisory laughter that set her teeth on edge. If he hadn't been so damned unreasonable she thought that she might just have told him the truth, but his remarks about her appearance had hurt. Not once had he said that she looked good. He had insulted her from the very minute he had walked through the door.

'I'll have to wait and see, won't I?'

'I thought you were only interested in *nice men*,' Riccardo sneered. 'You'll send your *nice man* running for cover within minutes!'

'I'm going now.' Julia turned the door knob and offered him a bright smile.

He ignored her. His dark brows met in a thunderous frown and Julia responded by gazing serenely back at him. He could have killed her. Men were men, he thought savagely, and it would be easy for any nice man to turn into a wolf, given the goods on offer. God, he could see every curve of her body under what she was wearing and the exposure of her legs was positively indecent.

'Before you go,' he said, lowering his voice, 'I'll just give you something to think about, shall I? You'll want to know how your nice little man holds up to the competition.' And he pulled her towards him, his mouth descending to crush against hers. It was a hot, brutal kiss that made every nerve in her body leap. For the most fleeting of seconds, she responded. She had to. Then she struggled against him and he released her immediately, but not without affording her a look of pure triumph.

'I'll see you soon,' he drawled mockingly.

Julia turned away and let herself out of the house in a blind rush. How could he manage to do that? How could he manage to overwhelm her when he hadn't even been *pleasant*? The minute his mouth had touched hers she had felt herself falling and it had taken all the strength she could muster to pull her back. How could she have fallen in love with a man whose arrogance knew no bounds and who could be ruthless and charming in equal measure? Love should be gentle, a soothing meeting of minds, not this mad, roller-coaster ride that left her spending half her time in a state of anguished giddiness!

And he had been right. The memory of his kiss had ruined her enjoyment of the evening because she found that she could hardly focus on what was going on around her. She was dimly aware of compliments being lavished on her and of several men who left her in no doubt that they liked what they saw. One in particular was so bowled over that he pressed his name and telephone number into her hand as she was leaving.

'Call me,' he urged, while her friend made funny faces behind his back and gave her the thumbs-up sign. 'I work in the City. It would be no problem meeting up after work, or even meeting for lunch. I can easily arrange to come to you.' He was fair, good-looking and undeniably *nice*. Just the sort of man Julia knew she should be cultivating. In her old get-up of plain skirts and concealing tops, it was doubtful whether he would have given her a second look, but his blue eyes had been on stalks every time he had looked at her during the course of the evening.

'Perhaps,' Julia answered vaguely, backing away from the eagerness in his expression.

'What about next week? Give me your phone number and I can call you; see if we can touch base.' He was so insistent, and Julia was so desperate to wriggle out of being forced into committing herself to anything, that she hurriedly rattled off her home number, hoping that his memory would fail him. Not that he couldn't find out where she was and her telephone number if he wanted. Elizabeth would be more than obliging. She had spent half the evening telling Julia about his eligibility! Brilliant job, no messy divorce behind him, kind to children and animals, thoroughly nice guy.

Unfortunately, Julia's mouth was still burning from the kiss of a thoroughly *un*-nice guy!

But it was lovely being the object of flattery, and she returned home at a little after midnight, far more cheerful than when she had set out.

The house, when she arrived, was in darkness, which surprised her. She hadn't thought that Riccardo was the sort of man who retired early to bed. Which left her in the uncomfortable position of knowing that if he was asleep she would either have to wake him up or else let him carry on sleeping, and if she allowed him to carry on sleeping she would spend the rest of the night tossing and turning in bed, knowing that he was under the same roof.

She threw her little clutch bag on the table in the hall, clicking her teeth in frustration, and went through the downstairs rooms, checking them one by one to make sure that he wasn't in any of them.

The last was the small sitting room where the television was, which, like the rest of the rooms, was in complete darkness. Julia was about to shut the door when his dark, velvety voice addressed her from the direction of one of the chairs.

'Don't do that!' she said, still shaking from the fright he had given her.

'Don't do what?'

'You made me jump. What are you doing sitting here in the dark, anyway?' She switched on the light and saw him sprawled comfortably on one of the deep chairs, his long legs extended in front of him.

Riccardo could have told her that he had found it suited his mood but he didn't. Anyway, he was in quite good humour now. In fact, feeling amazingly contented. So instead, he pointedly looked at his watch and then at her face.

'Has Nicola been all right?' Julia hovered in the doorway, not too sure what she should do. Throw him out? Hint that it was time to go? Chat politely and wait for him to leave of his own accord? Maybe, she considered, she should offer him the going rate for babysitting and see what he did. The thought made her grin.

'Nicola's been fine, and what's so funny? Care to share the joke with me?'

'Oh, I was just thinking about this evening…'

'Had a good time, did you?'

'I had a brilliant time.' She looked at him, giving him the opportunity to stand up and leave, and when he remained sitting she reluctantly enquired politely, 'What did you do?'

Riccardo shrugged and threw her a lazy smile. A lazy, *genuine* smile, which made her narrow her eyes suspiciously at him. He looked a little too much like the cat that had got the cream for her liking.

'Oh, watched a little television. Didn't think much of that period drama you recommended. Not enough action. There was a much better film on another channel so I looked at that. On and off.'

Julia remained standing, arms folded, taking full advantage of her one-off situation of looking down at *him* instead of the other way around.

'Oh, and I grabbed something to eat. Hope you don't mind. Just a sandwich.'

'That's fine.'

He gave her a dazzling smile and relaxed a little deeper into his chair, resting his head back against his clasped hands, seeming unperturbed by the wariness stamped on her face. On her eminently kissable face, he thought, not that she was aware of that. Her superficial change of plumage would never be able to eradicate her innate modesty, however much she tried to camouflage it.

'So…' he said, raising his eyebrows, 'where did you go…?'

'Oh, nowhere out of the ordinary. The company is what counts,' she added meaningfully, and he gave her another brilliant smile, nodding in agreement. 'Anyway, I guess you must be tired…so, if you don't mind…'

'Oh, I'm not tired. It's only twelve-thirty. I have a body clock that relishes the minimum amount of sleep.'

'Well, bully for you. I don't.'

'And I thought we might have a cosy little chat.'

'A cosy little chat? What about?'

'About where you *really* were tonight, of course.' Riccardo almost wanted to purr with satisfaction. The thought of her being with another man had driven him almost mad with rage. Male pride, he assumed. No one liked to be walked out on, least of all a man like him. Deplorable, but at least, he thought, he had had the honesty to admit to the trait. Rage over nothing, as it had turned out.

'Get to the point, Riccardo.'

'In between the action movie, the sandwich and two glasses of wine—I hope you don't mind my raiding your fridge—I found some time to call your mother…'

'You found some time *to do what*?' So much for her provocative subterfuge, intended to leave him in no doubt that he was dismissible at the click of her fingers because she had another man waiting in the wings. She sat down and looked at him, her cheeks pink with guilt at what she knew was coming.

'Oh, to telephone your mother. I couldn't remember where I had put that piece of paper with your mobile-phone number on it and, naturally, I had to find out how I could contact you just in case…' He threw her a pious smile. 'Your mother was most obliging. In fact, we had a pleasant little chat. Seems that your hot date with a mystery man was in fact a birthday party at your girlfriend's house…'

'I never said I was going on a hot date with anyone…' Julia denied hotly. '*You* jumped to the conclusion that I was and—'

'You let me go along with the misapprehension…the burning question is *why*…'

'It's time you left.' Julia sat forward, flicked open her little bag and extracted her bundle of keys. Her skin felt as though it was on fire, a tingling sensation induced by the fact that she felt cornered, and was all too aware of what further conclusions he might be leaping towards in answer to his own question.

She could see it written all over that smug, breathtakingly handsome face of his. He thought that she had deliberately lied to make him jealous, and why would she want to make him jealous? Because she was violently attracted to him. She dangled the keys from her fingers and stood up.

'It's late, Riccardo, and I'm tired. I don't need to sit here and answer any of your questions!'

'Scared?'

'Scared of what? Of you? You don't intimidate me in the slightest, Riccardo Fabbrini!'

'What about scared of owning up to the truth?'

Julia didn't dare ask him to clarify his remark. She had a sinking feeling that she wasn't going to like what else he had to say on the subject and she could already feel her own arguments ringing hollowly in the room as she tried to convince him otherwise.

'Now, why don't you go and get us both a cup of coffee and we can discuss this?'

'There's nothing to discuss!'

Riccardo shot her a politely incredulous smile and Julia

feverishly wondered what the punishment was for man-slaughter. 'Of course there is,' he said calmly. 'Now, shall I tell you the way I see it?'

Julia sat back down, heaved a huge sigh and rolled her eyes heavenwards. 'I would rather you didn't, but I don't suppose that will stop you.'

'Quite true.' He appeared to give the matter careful con-sideration. 'Well, the way I see it is like this. You want me. That much is obvious, and don't look at me as though you haven't got the faintest idea what I'm talking about. You know exactly what I'm talking about, although if you like I can always remind you of the last evening we spent together…? In the space of one week—in fact, since you met that last girlfriend of mine—you've undergone a few radical changes. Not, I might add, that you didn't turn me on before—'

'I never turned you on, Riccardo Fabbrini! You used me!'

Riccardo shook his head sadly, as if despairing of a child being wilfully obtuse. 'Men don't work like that. You can think what you like about my motives, but no man can pretend passion. Oh, I wanted you all right. You felt it.' His voice was a low, sexy murmur that had the blood rush-ing to her cheeks. 'I was big and hard for you and that's not something a man can summon to order…'

'Riccardo…' Julia heard the weak desperation in her voice and wanted to groan at her own lack of will power in the face of this fascinating, unbearably sexy man.

'You don't have to feel that you're in competition with Helen or any of the other blonde airheads I've dated in the past.'

'I don't feel anything of the sort!' Her eyes flashed at him. Water off a duck's back.

'Or that you have to pretend to be going out with another man so that you can fire me up…'

'You…You are so…'

'I know, I know. Arrogant, conceited et cetera, et cetera. But accurate, no? So, what do we do with this…shall we say…passion of ours…?'

Julia stared at him, open-mouthed. This must be how it felt to toss a boomerang into the air, only for it to return and hit you straight on the face. At the party she had been the essence of poise and self-control. She had been able to have conversations with men without even paying them the slightest bit of attention. Fifteen minutes in this man's company and it was all blown to smithereens! Could this really be love?

The only clear thought running through her chaotic brain now was not to let him see just how much she felt and how powerless she was to resist him. For all his talk about passion and wanting and whether he had used her for his own purposes or not, he was a man incapable of giving with his soul. He could give magnificently with his body, but in her heart Julia knew that that would never be enough for her.

'I don't want to talk about any of this,' she breathed.

'You mean talk about us sleeping together? Giving in to this craving we have to touch each other's bodies?' Just talking about this and looking at her as she sat forward, pink-faced and rapt, wanting so badly to run but held captive by his voice, was enough to make him go hard.

She stared at him in silence. Every exit seemed to be blocked. She *hadn't* been trying to rouse his jealousy…had she? she wondered wildly. She had been trying to build up her own confidence in herself, to prove to him that she was not the pushover she must have seemed to be when she had swooned in his arms like a mindless Victorian maiden. She had changed her image because, obscurely, she had wanted to change the disastrous direction her life appeared to have been taking. Straight into his bed! Leaving her heart in tattered pieces when he was through with her! *That* was what she had been trying to do, except pointing all that out to him would be like running in circles.

'Look,' he said with sudden fierceness, sitting forward and filling the spaces around her with his overpowering masculinity, 'do you imagine I want to feel this way too? You detonated a bombshell in my life; you're the last person in the world I should be wanting to take to my bed, but I feel the same thing that you do!'

'You're mistaken,' Julia said in a shaky voice, standing up. Her legs didn't feel as though they could support her suddenly leaden body, but she had to get out of the room. 'I just thought that the time had come for me to take control of my life, that's all.'

'Make us both some coffee and you can tell me all about it. You'll find that I am a very good listener.'

Any excuse. She scurried out of the room and into the kitchen, where she leaned against the counter and closed her eyes. Everything inside her was pounding, her heart, her brain, her whole body felt as though it could burst through its skin.

Want, want, want. He wanted her, wanted to sleep with her, make love. It was all that mattered to him. But it wasn't enough. She wearily put the kettle to boil, her movements automatic as she piled a teaspoon of instant coffee into each mug, poured the water over, but her hands were shaking when she went to lift the mugs and she had to set them down again while she caught herself and took a few deep breaths. She might deter him for the moment, but he was like a shark that had suddenly discovered a source of blood. Hers!

And now that Nicola knew who he was, he was under

no obligation to hang around. He would take what he *wanted* and then he would be gone, with his daughter.

She was leaning against the counter, thinking madly of how she could extricate herself from the situation in one piece, how she could resist the temptation to cave in to both their needs because caving in would be the fatal step towards heartbreak. She barely heard his approaching steps.

When he spoke his voice was deadly icy and her eyes flickered open to see him standing in front of her, a piece of paper in his hand.

'What is this?' He held the paper out to her, and without thinking Julia asked him whether he had finally discovered the whereabouts of the missing mobile-phone number. Not that she had believed for one minute that he had really misplaced it.

'Look at it.' He thrust the paper at her and Julia was dimly aware that he had found the piece of paper with Roger's telephone number on it. At the time, she had barely glanced at it, but now she could see that he had inscribed a rough heart under the phone number.

'Where did you find this?'

'Does it matter?' He folded his arms and waited. Waited till her eyes had finished scanning the paper for a second time. 'I found it.'

'You had no right to go prying in my bag,' she said quietly.

'The damn bag was open from when you got your keys out! I saw the edge of paper sticking out and yes, I took it out and now I want to know who the hell this Roger person is and why his telephone number is in your bag!'

'You have no right to question me on—'

'I have every right!'

Every right, Julia thought, to be furious because his idea of a few nights of passion before he tossed her aside had been thwarted. Through the murky light, she began to see a glimmer of hope, a way out of the mess which would put her beyond his reach. Not to seize it would be folly. She knew, they both did, that, however much she might try to run, his pursuit would be successful, but if he thought that there was another man he would be forced to leave her alone and that way she would be free to retreat, to lick her wounds in private and thank the lord that they were not more severe.

And she was as free now as he was. There was no longer any reason to pretend a relationship. She could do precisely as she pleased!

'I met him at the party.' Julia stole a defiant look at his thunderous face and her eyes skittered away nervously. 'I thought it was going to be a small do, but it turned out to be quite large. A lot of Elizabeth's husband's friends were there. Roger was one of them.' His cold silence was making her ramble on. 'He…he's a stockbroker in the City. He was very interesting and when I was l-lea…leaving he gave me his telephone number. I… Riccardo, stop looking at me like that! It's not a crime to chat to a man at a party, or to take his phone number, for that matter…'

'Was that the intention when you left this house this evening? In your short skirt and high heels? To chat up any man you came across?'

'I did not *chat him up*! He chatted me up! And that wasn't my intention! I'm not the sort of girl who goes to parties to see who they can pull!' The idea was so ridiculous that in another situation she would have burst out laughing at the image he was portraying of her as some kind of vamp who flirted her way round the men until she found a suitable candidate.

'So let me get this straight. You've changed your appearance. Now you wear clothes that barely cover your body, and in addition you're willing to offer yourself to the first man that comes along and gives you a line about wanting to get to know you.' His mouth twisted into a sardonic scowl, but before Julia could open her mouth to protest he had picked up the thread of his accusation and was hurtling forward with it, giving her no time to think, let alone speak.

'And you want me to believe that this is the sort of example I want my daughter to be set? I don't think so.'

'You're being ridiculous, Riccardo.' But her protest was thin, simply because he had a way of twisting things to suit his arguments. Twisting *her* until she didn't know what she was saying or doing or thinking!

'I am not being ridiculous. Nor am I being ridiculous when I inform you that there is only one way to deal with this.'

'Wh-what way…?'

'Well, put it this way…I won't disrupt Nicola so soon after telling her who I am by removing her from her familiar surroundings. So…'

'So…?'

'So I am going to move in here with you.'

CHAPTER EIGHT

RICCARDO gazed out of the massive floor-to-ceiling window in his office and stared down at the busy, teeming London streets eleven storeys below. It was a view which, in the past, had afforded him a great deal of pleasure. To be in his large, plush office with its black leather and thick-piled carpet, to know that the entire glass building in which he stood and which dominated everything else around it belonged to him.

His family had begged him to return to Italy, especially after he had married Caroline, but it had been the only thing she had ever refused to do and secretly he had been delighted by the get-out clause her adamant refusal had given him. Because he had loved the vast concrete jungle that was London, had revelled in his relentless and satisfying climb into the rarefied reaches of true power. And after their bitter split he had thrown himself into his work with even more gusto. Nothing and no one, none of the blondes who had nurtured hopes of taming the beast, had provided even the slightest breath of competition when it came to where his attention was focused.

He sighed now with frustration and raked his fingers through his black hair as he contemplated how much things had changed in the space of a few short weeks.

Nicola was the mainspring of that change and one he welcomed. Fatherhood, delayed as it had been, was a joyous addition to his life. But she was only part of the equation.

He scowled as his mind began its familiar and invasive

exploration of Julia. In a short while he would begin the process of collating vital files and computer discs that he would be transferring to her house. He had already arranged for a computer terminal, a separate telephone line and a fax machine to be set up there. She would return from school to find him fully installed. The heady thrill of power and the frantic pace of life within the cool, elegant confines of his superb office no longer held the allure they once had.

Just the thought of her with her new look and her new hair and her legs on view for all to see, just the thought of her stepping out into the London social scene with that extraordinary appeal of innocence and sexiness threw him into panicked rage and consumed his every waking moment. Not to mention the appearance of some man, some stockbroker with octopus hands and sticky fingers.

Riccardo's jaw clenched and he began prowling through the office, sifting through his files, selecting some, leaving the rest. By eleven o'clock he was ready to leave, only stopping *en route* to remind his secretary that he would be available via e-mail, phone or fax and would continue to come into the office, albeit with less regularity. He knew that she was utterly bewildered by his decision to work more from home but he offered no explanation. He had called an emergency board meeting the previous day and had announced the same decision and had met a similar barrier of utter incomprehension, but they had rallied around quickly, moving with speed and efficiency into their extended roles. He had always surrounded himself with quick thinking, ambitious men and they had risen to the occasion admirably. A fat bonus to accommodate any extra duties had helped.

It was with grim determination that he spent the remainder of the day seeing to the installation of an office in one of the downstairs rooms and getting his driver to bring his items of clothing from his own apartment to the house.

By four-fifteen he was ready and waiting for her arrival back home. The fact that she had no idea that he had chosen that day to move in, indeed had probably thought that he had dismissed the idea, having given her three days' reprieve during which nothing had been said on the subject, did not unduly bother him. He had, in fact, elected that particular day because he knew that Nicola would be having tea with one of her friends from school. It would leave him time to placate Julia without the presence of his daughter.

He had obtained a key for the house on the spurious excuse that as Nicola's father he had a right to have immediate access to her should the need arise, and had squashed every objection provided with a flat refusal to discuss the issue. Had behaved, in fact, in a manner that had infuriated Julia and disgusted himself, but his single-mindedness in getting what he wanted had been too great a spur.

He was in the sitting room, waiting, when he heard the sound of the key in the front door.

Very calmly he walked to the sitting-room door and lazily leaned against the door frame, arms folded, watching as Julia bustled in, head bent as she tried to prevent the stack of books in her hands from crashing to the floor as she fumbled to stuff the key back into her handbag.

'Need help?' he drawled from where he was standing, observing, and predictably the stack of exercise books fell to the ground in a tangled heap.

Julia's head shot up and she stared at the apparition in front of her, open-mouthed.

'What are you doing here?' The shock of seeing him when she had been thinking about him was surreal, and she blinked, wondering whether the powerful, dark vision in front of her was just a figment of her fevered imagination.

Riccardo pushed himself away from the door frame and strolled towards her, then he bent down at her feet and began collecting the books, stacking them into a haphazard pile that he held out for her.

When she continued to stare at him, flabbergasted and red-faced, he dumped the lot on the table and then stared back at her with his hands in his pockets.

'What are you *doing* here?' Julia repeated. Her voice was a few notches higher. 'And how did you get in?'

Riccardo dangled his key in front of her. 'I got a copy of the front-door key. Remember?'

Yes. She did. She snatched the key from him and dashed it onto the table alongside the books. 'To be used in emergencies only, you assured me!'

'Oh, yes. So I did. But this *is* an emergency.' He smiled very slowly at her. Julia had never managed to get accustomed to those smiles of his. They always seemed to go straight to the very heart of her, making her feel weak. She held on to the ledge of the table for support.

'Oh, it is, is it? And *where exactly* is the emergency?' Her brain began functioning again and she stood upright, glowering. 'I don't see any fire, or floods.'

'Well, perhaps emergency is the wrong word. Let's just say I needed to get in.'

'For what? Nicola is at her friend's house and won't be back until six.'

'I know.'

'You know.'

'Which, actually, is why I chose to come now. I've moved in.'

The three little words hung in the air between them as Julia attempted to absorb the full impact of them. 'You can't have,' she finally told him shakily. 'I told you that it was a ludicrous idea. I told you that under no circumstances would I entertain the thought of you moving into this house. If you recall, I said that you could see Nicola whenever you wanted but that this house was out of bounds as far as you were concerned!'

'Yes, so you did. But I moved in anyway.' He smiled again, unruffled. Had she any idea how edible she looked standing there, flustered, stammering and overwhelmed? He wanted to kiss her protesting mouth, devour her outburst with his tongue. 'Care to see where I've installed my office?' He began walking towards the seldom-used dining room, as much to put some distance between them as anything else. Harbouring erotic thoughts about her wasn't going to get him anywhere, and if her eyes happened to drift downwards she would probably run screaming through the front door.

'Your office?' she shrieked from behind him, flouncing in his wake. 'Your office? You already *have* an office! It's in the City! You go there every day to work!'

'Correction,' he called out, without looking around, 'I own the building in which my office happens to be located. And now you could say I have two.' He stood in front of the dining room, waiting for her to catch up, and, when she did, stood back so that she could view the efforts of the dozen or so men who had worked through lunch under his instructions to have the room up and running before mid-afternoon.

'I'm dreaming,' Julia said as she took in the dining-room table, now converted into a desk, on which rested his computer, phone, fax machine, and several files. 'This is all a dream. In a minute, I'll wake up.'

'No dream. But I could pinch you if you like.'

'Why?'

'I told you why.'

'Look at me,' Julia said, spreading her arms wide to indicate her very suitable outfit of deep-grey skirt, white blouse and matching jacket. She had maintained her working wardrobe, the only difference to her appearance being her hair and the visibility now of her luminous grey eyes. 'Do I look like an immoral woman setting a bad example for a child?'

This wasn't about how she looked, Riccardo thought in a blinding flash, or about any ridiculous idea that her dress code would somehow be unsuitable to be seen by a child; this was about him. *She* was why he had felt the compulsion to move in, why he had been given no choice in the matter. He turned away as a dark flush spread along his cheekbones.

'I've taken one of the guest rooms. And now, I've got work to do,' he said abruptly.

'We're not finished discussing this!' Julia snapped, walking straight into his line of vision so that he had to look at her.

'You might not be finished discussing this,' Riccardo said, sitting at one of the chairs and switching on his computer, 'but I am.'

'And where am *I* supposed to do my marking?' she demanded, walking to where he was seated with his face averted and staring down at him, hands on her hips. 'I don't like marking in the kitchen because it means having to clear it all away for tea, and, besides, that's where Nicola's accustomed to doing her drawing!'

'You can share the table with me,' he told her, busily clicking on icons on the computer so that he could access his work.

So much for discussion, Julia thought as she watched him frown at whatever it was he was viewing on the screen in front of him. Autocratic did not begin to cover his attitude. Nor did the word hopeless begin to cover hers. Because looking at him surreptitiously as he sat there, unaware of her existence, she was filled with a stupid feeling of elation. He had moved in lock, stock and barrel without bothering to consult her first, had laid down his orders like a master stating a decree, and instead of feeling enraged and resentful she felt excited and idiotically completed. Julia ground her teeth together in self-disgust and went out to the hall, gathering all the exercise books in her arms.

'Don't think we're finished with this one,' she informed him, sitting at the dining-room table and making a deal of spreading the books in front of her.

Riccardo grunted something in response but didn't look at her.

'Because I'm not. I just haven't got the time to say what I want to say if I'm to get these marked before I have to go and fetch Nicola.'

Another grunt. Riccardo looked at her from under his lashes, his eyes raking over her downbent head as she busily scanned the page in front of her, one hand poised with a red pen for marking. He had no idea what was on the computer screen in front of him. E-mails by the dozen. He would have to read them later. He couldn't think straight with her just within touching distance.

After a while, he abandoned the effort and idly picked up one of the exercise books lying between them and began reading. His lips began to twitch. When he gave a hoot of laughter Julia looked up from what she was doing and frowned.

'I thought you were supposed to be working,' she said crushingly, speaking to the top of his head, as the rest was hidden behind the exercise book.

'I was,' Riccardo said, lowering the book so that he

could look at her over the top of it. 'But this is a lot more interesting.

'It was snowing outside when suddenly the baby was born. It looks very big, said the mum. It had a green face and three legs because in fact it was a monster.

'What are you teaching these poor children?' he asked, pushing back the chair and stretching his legs onto the ta-ble-top.

'Do you mind removing your feet from the table? I al-ways tell Nicola that table-tops are not for sitting on or standing up on.'

'Do many of your pupils suffer from nightmares?' Riccardo asked idly.

'It was a project on adventures,' Julia said, glancing over to him and feeling a churning feeling in her stomach as he gazed back at her, with his hands behind his head. It was sinful that a man could be so good-looking, she thought. If he were plain and uninspiring she would never have found herself in this situation. 'Rory has a very active imagination and he seems to be fixated with monsters.'

And who are you fixated with? he wanted to know. Roger? The mystery stockbroker with the sweaty palms? She must be keen on him or else she would never have accepted his phone number. That deduction had been play-ing on his mind and he could not get rid of it. He knew her. If the man's advances had been unwelcome she would have put on that cool, closed expression of hers and politely turned him away. It was a good thing that he had decided to move in here, he thought restlessly. He could keep an eye on her. Make sure she didn't bring home strange men for his daughter to meet. In fact, a little voice whispered, make sure she didn't bring home *any* men at all.

'What?' he asked as he realised that she was saying something to him, and Julia frowned.

'I said, could I please have the exercise book back. I want to mark it.'

Riccardo scooted it towards her and reclined back in the chair, staring at the tips of his shoes. 'What are we going to do about dinner?'

'Ah, yes.' Julia stood up and walked across to the bay window, where she perched on the sill. 'Another reason why this arrangement is not going to work out. I have got neither the time nor the inclination to start preparing meals for you on those days you happen to be around...'

'I'll be around a lot,' Riccardo drawled. 'Naturally, I shall still attend meetings during the day, but I plan on working a lot from here and also spending a lot of my evenings here as well. Getting to know Nicola better.' He looked down, slightly embarrassed by the patent shortcomings of this statement.

'As well as making sure that I don't set a bad example,' Julia said shortly.

'You can understand my feelings. I won't have you bringing strange men back to this house.'

Julia looked around her for a bit of heavenly assistance. How was she ever going to withstand the impact of this man on her if he intended to be around all the time, getting under her skin? And what gave him the right to keep an eye on her? It was an insult. He didn't trust her with Nicola and she could have told him that she had been doing a very good job of it and since Caroline and Martin were no longer around. She had been diligent, compassionate, understanding. Had choked back her own feelings of loss at the death of her brother, so as to maintain the semblance of strength that Nicola had so desperately needed. Did he really think that a change of appearance was going to alter her personality?

It felt good for her anger to begin surfacing. Better than the stupid feeling of contentment that had treacherously slipped over her as she had sat marking exercise books, feeling his masculine presence wafting across to her, pushing her to do something really pathetic, like sidle over to him and curl up on his lap, let him take her against all reason.

'I have no intention of bringing *strange men* back to this house!'

'What about the stockbroker? He's hardly a lifelong friend of the family!'

'There's nothing strange about Roger,' Julia retorted. 'In fact, you're a thousand times stranger than he is!'

'Ah, so another of your sissy men. Why bother? You will just go off him eventually when you discover how deeply boring he is.' Riccardo could hear the biting jealousy in his voice and flinched. 'In the meanwhile, I forbid you to bring him here.'

'You forbid? *You* forbid *me* to bring a friend back to this house?'

'Not a friend, a *man*.' Every pore in his body was revolting against the irony of the stance he was now adopting. He, a man who had always professed to abhor possessiveness in people, who had always detested when any of his girlfriends had tried to pin him down. Here he was, doing his damnedest to pin this woman down as tightly as he could. She had admitted to using him, had waltzed into his life and exercised the sort of control no other woman had ever dared to. He should be removing himself as far from her as possible.

'Are you jealous?' Julia asked hesitantly, and he banged his fist on the table.

'Jealous? Me? I have never been jealous of anyone in my life!' He stood up and began prowling around the room, as if he could no longer contain the energy coursing through his veins. 'Do I look like the type of man who is ever jealous?' he demanded, stopping in front of her. 'Do I?'

'Weren't you jealous of Martin?'

'I was never jealous of your brother!' Riccardo snarled. 'Furious, yes. He had stolen what was mine! But jealous, never.'

'Stolen what was yours?'

'Perhaps I used the wrong expression,' he rasped irritably as she raised her eyebrows in disbelief of the sentiment he had unwittingly expressed.

'You must have loved her very much,' Julia said quietly. Just saying it aloud sent a stab of pain to her heart and it took all her strength not to wilt in the face of the big man towering over her, not to let him see how much it pained her to think of him loving another woman, hurting when she walked away from him, maybe even nursing that hurt through the years as woman after woman failed to live up to his original blonde.

'Why do you say that?'

'Because of your possessiveness towards her, because of the anger you still feel after all this time at the thought of Martin.'

'I am Italian. She was my wife. Of course I was possessive. It would have been unnatural not to be. And I am angry with her and with your brother for concealing my own child from me, for taking that decision into their hands and playing God! As for loving Caroline, yes, of course I loved her. I married her! I happen to be a man who takes the vows of marriage very seriously. I would never have proposed if I had not loved her. Or thought that I did.'

Julia's heart gave a little lurch at that qualifying remark and she feverishly reminded herself that even if he no longer loved his ex-wife, was no longer driven by the need to try and replace what he had lost by cultivating a line of girlfriends more or less in her mould, then it still meant nothing. Because he didn't love *her*.

She felt her eyes glaze over as she concentrated on trying to read what was scrawled on the paper in front of her.

'Are you not going to ask me what I mean by that?'

'I told you, I have to get these books marked before I pick up Nicola.' She carefully circled a grammatical error to prove to him that she was already focusing on something else.

'I thought you prided yourself on liking New Man?' Riccardo said. He had never discussed his marriage or its collapse with anyone before. Not even with his family. His only response to them had been a curt withdrawal and a quelling observation that the past was another country, and, as such, beyond discussion. The few girlfriends who had expressed an interest had not even gotten that far. He had simply looked at them with a shuttered expression and changed the subject, leaving them in no doubt that his private life was forbidden territory.

It irked him now to think that he was willing to talk to Julia—in fact, driven to talk to her—about his marriage.

Julia looked up from what she was doing. 'Are you trying to tell me that you've suddenly become a new man, Riccardo?' She couldn't stop herself from grinning at the incongruity of the image presented, of Riccardo, the epitome of everything potently and exclusively male, shedding tears, discussing feelings and tinkering with healthy-eating recipe books. 'Does this mean that you intend to share the cooking, the cleaning and the ironing with me?'

'Ah, so I take it you are no longer going to fight me on my decision to move in here with you and Nicola.' He shot her a smile of barely concealed triumph. 'Naturally, I shall share the cooking. As for the rest, I intend to employ someone to take over the irritating little chores of cleaning and ironing.'

'Just as I expected,' Julia said feebly. 'You've been here two minutes and already you're laying down laws.'

'In fact, I could probably get someone in to do the cooking as well,' he announced. 'I am sure Pierre would not object.'

'Pierre?'

'My chef.'

'You have a chef?' Julia had the giddy feeling that she was being swept along by a series of rapid decisions and all she could do was cling to the coat tails of the conversation in a desperate attempt to hang on.

'He cooks for me when I need him. Of course, I pay him handsomely for his efforts.'

'Of course,' Julia said drily. 'An interesting variation on the new man. Not so much cooking, cleaning and ironing, as hiring the appropriate staff. I'm not so sure that that approach will ever get you accepted at the new-man club.'

He grinned at her and she reluctantly grinned back, feeling the shaky ground shift under her feet as she was held captive by his lazy, pervasive charm.

'But I have no intention of allowing you to lay down laws and regulations,' she said sternly, trying not to break into another grin as he did a poor show of looking chastened.

'Just doing the best I can to help the household run smoothly. I don't want to be a nuisance.'

'And don't put on that pious face. It doesn't work with me.'

'No, of course not.' He lowered his eyes, exultant at his victory. Of course, he would have stayed even if she had packed his bags and thrown them out onto the drive. And from his advantageous position he would make sure that the stockbroker wimp didn't set foot under the roof. If Julia thought that she was going to try those new-found wings then she was sorely mistaken. He felt absolutely no shame or guilt in his intention to keep her movements firmly under check, and as his thought clarified he knew why. Because he still wanted her. She had backed away from him, she had taken the phone number of another man, but he still wanted her, and have her he would.

Like it or not, the woman pulsed in his veins like his own life blood. He felt a shadowy unease when he tried to figure out why, and shoved the thought to one side.

She's a challenge, he decided to himself, and challenges, in his eyes, were to be met. He wanted to feel her soft and yielding against him, wanted her to think of no other man but him, he wanted to dominate her thoughts and her dreams.

But to do so he would have to fit in with her. That in itself, he thought wryly, would be a challenge, taking into account his personality.

'I shall prepare something for us to eat when you go to fetch Nicola,' he said magnanimously, and she threw him a sceptical look.

'What?'

'There is no need for you to look so dubious, Julia,' he said with a slow smile. 'I spent my childhood surrounded by great cooks. Cooking is in my blood.'

'And you have a way of transferring all this wonderful knowledge from your blood onto a plate, have you?'

'Leave it to me. In fact, you stay here and carry on with your marking and I shall make inroads into a meal.' He strolled over to his computer and switched it off. E-mails would just have to wait until later.

How she had managed to finish doing any work at all, Julia thought later as she headed off to collect Nicola, was a miracle. Even though he was no longer in the room with her, just knowing that he was in the kitchen was enough to rattle her.

But she would not let him get to her, she decided firmly. She would maintain a detached and healthy distance. She certainly would not allow him to undermine her social life.

She thought of Roger and wondered what she would do if he called, because she had certainly no intention of calling him. Would she go on a date? The thought of doing that was not inviting, but she realised that giving in to the alternative of staying at home and falling into any kind of routine with Riccardo was just downright dangerous.

By the time she arrived back at the house she had explained to Nicola that her father had moved in, which had met with an excited, childish yelp. And as far as bonding went, she could see that his presence did have certain advantages. It would increase their familiarity with one another. She watched as he drew pictures with her and left him to have her shower sitting on the sofa with the cartoon channel switched on.

In no time at all, Riccardo and Nicola would have forged the necessary bond that would give them the strength to fly away together.

And then what? Julia thought as she slipped into a pair of faded jeans and one of her small white ribbed tops. He would vanish with his daughter, only keeping in touch occasionally so that Nicola and she could maintain links. He would no longer have any need to live under her roof, to keep his eye on her, as he seemed to think necessary. She would have to set in motion some kind of life that could support her just to fill the inevitable gaping void he would leave behind.

She settled Nicola, who had worked herself up into a state of excitement as she contemplated the long list of thrilling activities that would now begin with Riccardo living under the same roof, and then walked slowly down to the kitchen.

She paused in the doorway for a few seconds to watch him unobserved as he stirred something in a frying pan and then lifted the lid on a saucepan.

'Smells good,' Julia said, stepping into the kitchen, and he turned around to look at her. 'What is it?' She could feel his presence drugging her.

'An old Italian recipe handed down through the ages,' Riccardo drawled, his eyes covertly flicking over her, taking in the skimpy little top that left very little to the imagination while still managing to send it rocketing into fifth gear. 'I used everything I could lay my hands on in the fridge and added a delicate mixture of herbs and spices. Sit.' He poured her a glass of white wine and Julia obediently sat at the kitchen table, trying not to over-relish the sheer pleasure of being waited on by him. How the hell did he manage to look so sexy in front of a cooker? He had rolled up the sleeves of his shirt, displaying his muscled forearms, and the slight sheen of perspiration on his face only added to his raw sex appeal. Her nerves began to jump and she hastily swallowed a mouthful of wine.

'Nicola's very excited about your moving in,' she said as he ladled food into serving dishes and began bringing them to the table.

'I like to think so. She asked if she could call me Dad. She told me that all her friends have dads and that she has always dreamed of hers. Of me,' he said proudly, before resuming his clipped voice. 'At least,' he huffed, to cover the uneven softening in his voice when he had spoken about his daughter, 'one of you is.' He twirled spaghetti around a long fork and slid a generous helping onto her plate. Even that slight action delineated the muscles in his forearms. Relaxing was going to be a major feat in his presence. 'Now dig in,' he commanded, waiting so that he could hear her verdict.

'Very good.' Their eyes met and he smiled with satisfaction.

'Did I not tell you that cooking is in my blood?'

'I didn't know whether to believe you or not. You don't strike me as a very domesticated figure.'

'Perhaps I never met the right woman who could domesticate me,' he drawled, his black eyes watching her steadily as he twirled some spaghetti around his fork.

'Not even Caroline?' She had been itching to bring up the subject of his ex-wife and get him to explain his mysterious insinuation that he had only thought he had been in love with her.

'I wondered when you would get back to that,' Riccardo said.

'I'm just making conversation, Riccardo. If you don't want to talk about it, then don't. It's all the same to me.'

'Caroline never managed to domesticate me, no. I look back now, and perhaps I can say in all honesty that she tried. Tried and failed.' He thought of his ex-wife and realised that for the first time he was glad that she had found happiness with another man. She had deserved it. 'I wasn't open to making sacrifices,' he murmured, more to himself than to his rapt audience, 'and, of course, making sacrifices is what a good marriage is all about. I found her twittering around me irritating after a while. I also found it hard to conceal my irritation.'

'Which is why she became more and more withdrawn,' Julia pointed out softly.

'Yes, she did. And the more withdrawn she became, the more irritated and impatient I became. In the end, it was a vicious circle. We barely spoke, and when we did we never seemed to get anywhere with the conversations.' He shrugged and sighed. 'Two people who started out with the best of intentions and just came unstuck somewhere along the way. But that was no reason for her to keep Nicola a secret from me.'

'No, no, it wasn't,' Julia agreed, and he shot her a brooding look from under his lashes.

'You were in on the scheme. How can you sit there and calmly agree with me?'

'I was not *in on the scheme*,' Julia retorted, closing her fork and spoon on her empty plate and taking a sip of wine. 'You seem to think that I was living here and party to every little decision Caroline and Martin made. I wasn't. I was renting my own flat on the other side of town and, whilst I didn't agree with their decision to keep you in the dark about your daughter, I didn't feel there was much that I could do, and I suppose I had my own life to think about.'

'You had no opinions on me?'

'I didn't *know* you, Riccardo! I only knew you from what Caroline told me and I was too busy with my own life to become involved in what was going on in my brother's! When they died…' Julia's voice faltered '…I realised that I had to make a decision and I decided to do what I had always thought they should have done. I decided to get in touch with you.'

'And are you pleased that you did?'

Julia picked up the faintest, fleeting shadow of innuendo

in his question. He was referring to far more than whether she was pleased that Nicola now had contact with her real father. Or so she imagined.

He toyed with some pasta on his fork and looked at her with a darkly inscrutable expression.

'Of course I am,' she answered jumpily. 'Nicola deserves to know you and she always has, even if she was denied the chance. I can see that you'll make a wonderful father. You're kind and thoughtful with her, and caring...' Her words were drying up in her throat as he continued to watch her, his dark eyes not once straying from her face, which was getting pinker by the minute.

'And if we leave Nicola out of the equation,' he said softly, 'are you still pleased that you contacted me?'

'Well...I...it's always nice to get to know different people...' Julia said weakly.

'Because I am.'

'You are?' She could only give in to her fascinated trance.

'I am. When we first met, I told you that you weren't my type of woman. I was wrong. You are very much my type of woman.' He swallowed a mouthful of wine as he appraised her flustered face. 'I made love to you once and I intend to make love to you again. Because I still want you and that's why your Roger stockbroker will not be calling you and neither will you be calling him.' His voice was perfectly calm. Calm and reasonable, for all the world as though they were discussing the weather. 'Your body is for my enjoyment only.'

'*For your enjoyment!*' Julia gasped, ashamed to admit even to herself that his Italian possessiveness had turned her body to water and set in motion a thousand sweetly seductive images in her head. 'What we did was a mistake, Riccardo!' she said in a shaky voice. 'And I'm not after a casual affair!'

'Then tell me what you *are* after.'

CHAPTER NINE

JULIA stared at him, pinned to the chair by his dark, brooding gaze. This was a terrible mistake, but then she had known that it would be. They couldn't exist under the same roof, sharing meals and conversations, while he kept her movements under check and began a slow process of seduction. She was too weak when it came to dealing with him. She just wanted too much, much more than he was capable of giving, and surrendering to their mutual lust was not a good enough reason for her to yield.

But she could feel her body burning under his stare, quivering with desire.

'We should clear up,' she mumbled, pushing back her chair and stumbling to her feet. Her hair fell over her eyes and she feverishly brushed it away then picked up her dirty crockery and headed for the sink, making sure not to look at him.

So much for tactics, Riccardo thought, following her every movement across the kitchen and breathing in her discomfort. So much for the subtlety of the master seducer. He had barged right in like a bull in a china shop and left her dithering and withdrawing at a rate of knots.

But God, he couldn't stop himself! She made him behave like a schoolboy.

He swiftly cleared the remainder of the table, while she huddled protectively by the sink, washing dishes with her head lowered; then he picked up a tea towel and began drying.

The atmosphere between them was crackling with tension.

'Have you got around to telling your mother about my moving in?' Riccardo asked, and Julia looked at him with troubled eyes.

'What?'

'Your mother. Have you told her that I have moved in?'

'No. Ah, I didn't…I haven't had the opportunity as yet.' She returned to the fork in her hand, washing it more carefully than was required. She could smell the clean, tangy, masculine scent of him, filling her nostrils, and she edged a little away from his arm next to hers.

'How do you think she will react? It never occurred to me that mothers might be a bit protective about their daughters living with a man.'

'You're Nicola's father; it's an unusual situation but Riccardo, I don't think this situation…can…is going to work out. I…'

'Why not?'

'Because…' Her voice trailed away into silence and she could feel his eyes on her, running over her flustered face and along her body.

'Because I have told you that I still want you?' Riccardo asked silkily, abandoning all his efforts to put her at her ease and not charge in. He wanted her to admit her attraction to him. It wasn't enough seeing it in her eyes. He wanted to hear it as well, wanted her to break down and confess that she couldn't resist him. He wanted her to come to him and the only way that was going to happen was if she was truthful, with herself and him. 'Would you rather that I had not said anything? Even though you must have felt it, must have seen it in my eyes whenever I looked at you.' He could feel himself getting hot under his collar as she clung to her stubborn silence. Dammit! This was taking

English reticence too far! 'And you're going to have to deal with this because I'm here now and I won't be going away.'

'You'll go away if I tell you to!' Julia bit out, her grey eyes flashing as they met hers. 'This is *my* house, in case you've forgotten!'

'Your house in which *my* daughter lives!' He knew that it was a low trick, bringing Nicola into the equation whenever he needed a winning card, but not all things in life were fair and playing by the book had never been one of his strong points. 'If it had not been for you, your brother and my ex-wife, this situation would never have arisen! Like it or not, you will just have to accept some of the responsibility for my being here in the first place!' A more convoluted argument it would have been hard to find, but he stood his ground, challenging her with a hard, unyielding stare.

'I won't tolerate you being here if you're going to make things awkward for me,' Julia told him unsteadily. She slipped off the daffodil-yellow washing-up gloves and draped them over the side of the sink, then she dried her hands on the small towel on the counter and sidled away from him, still watching him from under her lashes as though afraid that he might strike unexpectedly.

'In other words,' Riccardo mocked, turning around to look at her and folding his arms across his broad chest, 'I should just go along with the pretence that we're no more than, what…acquaintances? Two people who happen to be accidentally living under the same roof because of a third party? Tell me, do we converse at all or should I abide by strict guidelines that I never get too personal?' There was biting sarcasm in his voice that made Julia cringe.

'Of course we can be polite to one another—'

'Polite!' He gave a crack of hard laughter and walked towards her. 'We made love and yet you expect us both to behave like polite strangers when we're in each other's presence?'

'I…I wish you wouldn't keep bringing that up,' Julia stammered.

'There are a lot of things you seem to wish.' He stopped in front of her. It took supreme will-power to fight down his natural urge to say what needed to be said and hang the consequences. 'Look,' he sighed and raked his long fingers through his hair, then stuck his hands in his pockets, 'we're standing here arguing. I do not want to argue with you. Why don't I make us both a cup of coffee and we can go into the sitting room and discuss this like two adults?'

'You mean you're prepared to stop bullying me?'

'Is that what you think I'm doing?'

Julia hated herself for melting whenever he came close to her, whenever he spoke, whenever he so much as glanced in her direction. How could she be rational and logical when he made her feel as if she was walking along the edge of a cliff in a strong wind?

'Isn't it?' Julia asked, sticking her chin out and refusing to go weak-kneed.

'I don't bully,' Riccardo said, briefly looking away.

'No, you just carry on shouting until you get your own way.'

'Now you make me sound like a toddler. Throwing a temper tantrum if he doesn't get some sweets.' His voice was so disarmingly rueful that Julia felt herself beginning to smile, only to dimly remember the cause of their argument.

He could move from rage to charm, from aggression to humour so seamlessly that he never failed to take her by surprise. Was that how she had so carelessly managed to fall in love with him? Because her defences couldn't withstand the complexity of his personality? Every other man she had ever met seemed one-dimensional in comparison.

'Now, you go and wait for me in the sitting room and I shall bring some coffee in. And you have my word that I won't raise my voice or bully you. Deal?'

'Why do I trust you even less when you're being nice, Riccardo?'

'Because you're suspicious.' He held his hands up in mock-surrender. 'I will be as good as gold.'

Julia headed for the sitting room, vaguely aware that she had somehow been manoeuvred, and then sat on the sofa, her legs curled up beneath her. God, he might drive her crazy, scare the hell out of her when she thought of the damage he could do to her heart, but every pore in her body felt alive when he was around. It just wasn't fair!

He came in a few minutes later, carrying a circular tray on which were two cups, the glass jug of percolated coffee and a small jug of milk. 'I waited tables when I was at university to earn some money,' he said, resting the tray on the table and sitting on the sofa. 'Are you impressed?'

'*You waited tables?* I'm not impressed, Riccardo, I'm surprised,' Julia said, diverted by this revelation. She watched as he poured her a cup of coffee and handed the cup to her.

He shot her a gleaming look over his shoulder as he leaned to pour himself a cup. 'Did you imagine that I would never do anything so menial as waiting tables?'

'I imagined that you would not have had to. Caroline said that—'

'I came from a lot of money? You and my ex-wife seem to have had quite a lot of conversations about me.'

'I guess there was a lot of stuff she needed to get off her chest.' Julia shrugged and hoped that this would not lead to another surge of anger over his ex-wife's dubious politics concerning their daughter, but he seemed relaxed.

'My family is very wealthy; I would be the first to admit it.' He sat back and stretched out his legs. 'But I never felt that I had the right to use their wealth when I was perfectly capable of supporting myself. I did a number of jobs when I was at university, including bartending and holiday work at a building company. Now, that is what I would call hard work. Lifting bags of cement and heaving bricks.'

Julia imagined him bare-backed under the summer sun, body glistening with sweat as he heaved bricks, and her cheeks pinkened at the violently erotic image her mind conjured up. He would have been the sort of workman that women paused to wolf-whistle rather than the other way around!

'I worked my way through university as well,' she admitted. 'Although that was largely from necessity.'

'What did you do?' There seemed no end to his curiosity. He wanted to find out everything he could about this woman, every little detail of her life.

'I worked at the check-out tills at the supermarket in the evenings. It was fun. The people were a good laugh. And I worked in shops.' She smiled at the memory and sipped her coffee.

'So we have more in common than you admit,' Riccardo murmured and he sensed her tense, but he would just have to break through that tension. Either that or remain politely distant until the time came for him to leave with his daughter. And he was not going to remain politely distant.

'We should be able to share this house quite amicably,' he continued.

'You know why we can't, Riccardo.'

'I know why we might not be able to…'

'It's the same thing.' Julia rested her cup on the table

and drew her knees up, circling them with her arms as she looked at him.

'It is very far from being the same thing,' he told her conversationally. 'If I thought we couldn't share this house because our personalities were incompatible then I would never have moved in. But I don't. The reason we might not be able to share this house is because I am honest about the way I feel, while you persist in holding on to a lie.' His voice was quite calm, as were the dark eyes resting on her flushed face. Persuasively calm.

'Why do you have to insist on reducing everything to a personal level?' Julia pleaded.

'Because, whether you want to admit it or not, the personal level exists between us. I can feel it throbbing in the air whenever we're in the same room, I can feel it down the end of the line whenever you're on the phone! Why pretend otherwise?' When she didn't answer he shook his head impatiently. 'You never answered my question.'

'What question?'

'The one I asked you earlier. You told me that you weren't after a casual affair. So what *are* you after, Julia? Love, marriage and fireworks? Romance with all the frills and a happy-ever-after ending?' His mouth twisted cynically and Julia blinked rapidly as tears tried to push their way through from under her eyelids.

This was why they had to be polite to one another! Because every time feelings entered the equation a Pandora's box was opened and they came up against the same, immovable brick wall.

'I thought you were immune to such dreams?' he pressed on ruthlessly. 'I thought you had rebelled against your mother's nagging for you to settle down, have two children and spend the rest of your life playing the housewife.'

'I'm just not interested in having a casual affair.' Her

mouth was set in a stubborn line and she began to stand up, to run away from the conversation, but his hand descended on her wrist, forcing her to remain where she was.

'You've had affairs in the past, haven't you? You're not a virgin!'

'I haven't *had affairs* in the past! You make it sound as though I've led a life of debauchery! I had a couple of boyfriends, yes, but that's it!'

'So why is it so different this time?' he asked, jerking her towards him, his eyes grim.

Because I'm in love with you, Julia wanted to throw at him. Because I can't just have uninvolved *fun* with you! I want too much.

'Maybe I'm just getting older,' she said, her breath catching painfully in her throat. 'I don't want to waste any more time with someone who isn't meant for me. So it doesn't matter about physical attraction or about whether you want me or I want you. I might want you, Riccardo…' Saying it hurt but she had to, or else he would pursue her. Challenges for a man like Riccardo were fine, just provided none of them got away. If they did then he would chase them to the ends of the earth and back, but if she mentioned commitment and marriage he would back off. She looked at him without flinching. 'I just don't want what you have to offer.'

'Are you sure about that?' he murmured lazily. He began to gently caress the tender back of her wrist with his thumb and Julia's eyes widened.

'Very sure,' she replied hoarsely.

'How can you say that,' he chided softly, 'when you haven't sampled all I have to offer? It is very small-minded to reject something when you haven't first tried it.'

'I don't think…tha…that that refers to sexual experimentation,' Julia whispered. He was no longer holding her wrist, yet still her arm refused to move. It lay there, leaden and impassive, inviting him to run his forefinger from elbow to wrist, making her shiver.

He mesmerised her, and the devil knew it. She could hear it in his smoky voice and see it in the slow smile.

'You want a routine courtship and a white wedding,' he drawled softly, 'but take it from me, there's more to life than marriage. What we have is bigger than both of us...why fight it?' He shifted until he was close to her, then he very gently smoothed her legs flat so that she was lying on the sofa and staring up at his darkly sexy face.

'I miss your spectacles,' he murmured wryly. 'There is something very erotic about removing a woman's glasses.'

'You've done a lot of that in the past, have you?'

'Never,' he admitted, tantalising her senses with another of those lingering smiles. 'I pride myself on being open for new experiences.'

'And that's what I am, isn't it, Riccardo? A new experience.'

He halted the fight she wanted by putting his finger on her lips. Then he held both her hands and raised them to the back of the sofa so that she was stretched out for his hungry eyes.

They could argue until the cows came home, he thought as his body reared up in response to the sight of her, she could preach about right and wrong and should and shouldn't, but they were drawn to each other like magnets.

He lowered his head and kissed her. It was a lingering kiss and he traced her lips delicately with his tongue, explored the softness of her mouth until she was gasping.

Then he kissed her neck, nibbling the slender white column, letting their anticipation mount while his thoughts played with images of her nakedness, milky white against his copper skin.

'Riccardo…'

'Ssh, don't talk.' She wasn't wearing a bra. He knew that much, had spotted it as soon as she had appeared after her shower. The top was not transparent and she probably wasn't even aware of how lovingly it shaped the contours of her breasts. He teased her collarbone with his mouth and with a little groan Julia curled her fingers into his hair.

This shouldn't be happening! But the minute he touched her she was lost. She didn't just want him, she was burning up with it! She wanted to taste him, that sweetly addictive masculine taste that dragged her into a vortex of desire.

She gave a little squeak when his mouth moved down to her breasts and he began sucking her nipple through her clinging top, dampening it until the outline of her nipple was evident.

'No bra,' he murmured, lifting his gaze to her.

'I hardly ever wear one when I'm in the house,' Julia panted unsteadily.

'Keep it that way,' he laughed huskily and resumed his tender nibbling of her breast, saving himself for the moment when he could lift her top and view the real thing.

One hand stroked the line of her thigh. Jeans had to be the most frustrating item in a woman's wardrobe, he thought. Now if she had been wearing a skirt he could have felt her skin under his, felt every little shudder.

He gently lifted the top and groaned as he looked at her pert nipples, aroused and dark. He flicked his tongue over one and she shifted on the sofa, releasing little sighs of contentment that went straight to the core of him, making him want to take her right there and right now, without the preliminaries of foreplay.

'If you don't want this, tell me now,' he ordered roughly.

'You know I don't want it,' Julia moaned, but when he

raised his head she pulled him back down. 'I don't want it, but I need it. Make love to me, Riccardo.'

The sweetest words ever uttered. He stood up, watching her watching him, and undid his belt, letting it slither to the ground, then he unzipped his trousers and stepped out of them.

Julia had never found anything remotely fascinating about male strippers. In fact, on the one occasion she had gone with a gang of friends to see some perform at a club for a hen party she had found the sight of men removing their clothes positively comical.

But this was mind-blowingly erotic. She knew that he was looking at her, maybe amused by her intent gaze, maybe turned on by it, but she couldn't help herself. She watched as he removed his clothing and then carried on watching when he stood in front of her, unashamedly masculine and very obviously turned on.

'Now it's your turn,' he said, standing proudly male while she slowly stood up and began fumbling with the button on her jeans. She might have changed her image and polished her exterior, but her newly acquired outward shine certainly did not penetrate below skin level. She had never been watched by a man before, not like this, not knowing that his eyes were focused on her every movement, and her hands were slippery with nerves.

'I wish you wouldn't stand watching me like that, Riccardo,' she said shyly, and he grinned.

'OK. I'll sit.' He sat down and watched. Not much better from her self-conscious point of view.

But it was a sight he would not have missed for the world. So gauche, so unrehearsed, so utterly, utterly feminine with it. He had a stab of painful regret that he had not been the one to gently lead her out of her virginity. Her fingers were trembling and he wanted to pull her towards him and bury her against his chest.

She modestly stood, nude, before him, her arms crossed and he beckoned her to him with the crook of one finger.

'You are beautiful,' he murmured throatily, tucking her alongside him on the sprawling sofa. She needed tenderness, and he made love tenderly, rousing her with his tongue, with his hands, with his fingers, tracing the outline of her body, revelling in her pliancy and bringing her to the point of orgasm, only to thrust inside her with an explosion of fulfilment when neither of them could hold out any longer.

Julia lay against him, her head on his chest, listening to the rhythm of his heartbeat.

When she stirred he gently pushed her head back into its resting position.

'Now tell me what we just did was a mistake,' he said softly and Julia sighed.

'You know it was. It won't happen again.'

'A one-off?' he said, lazily content. 'Like the last time? We are irresistibly drawn to one another. Now is the time for you to admit it.'

His words flowed around her, confusing her. Was he right? Should she just acquiesce and go with the flow, then sort out the consequences when they arose?

It took her a few seconds to register the distant trilling of the telephone.

'Let it ring,' he commanded as she struggled up. 'We have to talk.'

'I can't let it ring. It might be Mum. It might be important.' And she didn't want to talk. Not yet. She didn't know what she could say to him. She needed time. She hastily slung on her jeans and pulled the top over her head, leaving him sprawling on the sofa.

The house felt cold as she hurried through it, desperate to reach the phone before it wakened Nicola. Unlikely, but a possibility and one Julia could heartily do without.

'I was just about to ring off.'

'Who is it?' Julia was still breathing quickly from her race through the house. She had not buttoned the top of her jeans and she cradled the receiver between her head and her neck while she fumbled with them.

'Don't you recognise my voice?' There was an amused laugh down the end of the phone. 'So much for my unforgettable impact on the opposite sex.'

'Roger!'

'I've been thinking about you since the party, Julia. Would you like to come out with me? Movies? Theatre? A bite to eat afterwards?'

'Roger…I…'

She glanced furtively over her shoulder, half expecting to see Riccardo lounging indolently in the doorway. She had just had the most beautiful, meaningful experience in her entire life and he would be waiting for her, waiting to hear her tell him that she had caved in, was willing to have a fling with him and play at happy families until he decided the time was right to leave. He had spoken a lot about want and attraction but not one word had passed his lips, even in the depths of passion, about permanence or love or commitment.

Her jaw hardened. 'When were you thinking of going out?' she asked, blinking back tears and telling herself furiously that she was doing the right thing.

'Is tomorrow too soon?'

'Tomorrow's fine,' she heard herself say.

'Why don't you give me directions to your house? I can be there to pick you up at—'

'No! I mean, it would be a lot more convenient if I met you at…at wherever we're going.'

'OK.' He paused and she could hear him thinking down the end of the phone. 'There's an excellent Italian…'

'Not Italian. I'm…I don't care for Italian food.'

'How about French, then?' He sounded mildly surprised and Julia wondered whether he was cursing himself for arranging a date with a woman who sounded bizarre down the telephone.

'French is fine.' Julia closed her eyes and breathed deeply. 'What's it called and how do I get there?'

He gave her detailed directions, getting her to repeat them so that he could make sure that she knew where she would be going and then she said, 'I'll meet you there about seven-forty-five. Is that all right?'

'Better than all right. See you tomorrow.'

Julia walked slowly back to the sitting room to find Riccardo semi-dressed, with his trousers on, standing by the window, waiting.

'Important phone call?' he queried laconically, testing the water, but he knew, with a knot of anger and desperation in his gut, that he had lost her. She had that closed look on her face that spoke volumes. How? *How, dammit?* He wanted to break things, but he remained where he was, rigidly poised, looking at her.

Julia shrugged. 'I'm going to bed now.'

'We have to talk,' he grated and she gazed at him distantly.

'What about?'

'About us.'

'There *is* no us, Riccardo. Yes, we're attracted to one another, but there's no us and I'm not willing to have a fling.'

'And you've had time to make your mind up about that in the time it took for you to answer the telephone?'

Julia bravely met his eyes. God, how easily she could move over to him, run her hands over the hard, muscled chest and lift her mouth to his.

'That's right.'

'Why don't you stop hovering by the door and step inside the room?' He knew that if she did she would come to him, but he realised, suddenly, that it would be an empty victory and he flushed darkly. 'No, forget I said that,' he told her roughly. His pride kicked into gear. She had turned him down. Twice. No more. He was finished running behind her. Women were a dime a dozen, he thought viciously. He didn't need to pursue this one, whatever she did for him and however much of a challenge she was.

Julia looked at him hesitantly until he said coldly, 'I get the message loud and clear, Julia. So why don't you go to bed and we'll both be adult about this and pretend that nothing ever happened?' His mouth twisted cynically as he turned away to stare out of the window, his back to her.

It's for the best, Julia thought as she headed up to her bedroom. So why did she feel so hollow? Tomorrow she would begin the dating game. She would be going out with a perfectly nice man, a nice, *predictable* man who did not swing from one mood to the next in a matter of seconds. And if Roger wasn't the man for her then there would be another, and another, until she found one.

The following morning she awoke at her usual time to find that Riccardo had already left for work. His car was not in the drive and the half-empty cup of coffee on the kitchen counter showed that he had been up and out long before seven-thirty, which was when she and Nicola had come downstairs.

At lunchtime, still feeling peculiarly empty inside, Julia

called him at the office and was surprised when she was
put through to him.

'I just want to find out whether you'll be in tonight,' she
said, playing with the cord of the phone and talking quietly
into the receiver because the staff room was full, with most
of the teachers choosing to have their lunch at their desks.

'Why?'

'Because I'm going out tonight and I want to know
whether I should ask Mum over to babysit.' In fact, she
would have to get in touch with her mother later that day
and explain the arrangement of Riccardo living in the
house. At least she would be able to say, with her hand on
her heart, that there was absolutely nothing going on between them, that Nicola now knew who he really was and
so any so-called pretend relationship had ceased. The proof
of that would be the presence of another man on the scene.

'I'll be home. What time are you leaving?'

'Around seven.'

'I'll be back.'

And that was the end of the conversation. She had demanded politeness from him and she had got exactly what
she had wanted. His voice had been coolly courteous and
Julia knew that his behaviour, when she saw him, would
be as well.

She spent the remainder of the day at school operating
on automatic, teaching her classes without really being
aware of what was going on around her. She collected
Nicola from kindergarten at a little after three-thirty and,
instead of returning to the house, took her to the shopping
mall for a treat and then to a fast-food restaurant, where
Nicola chattered on relentlessly about everything under the
sun, asking thousands of questions about her father which
Julia had to answer as brightly and normally as she possibly
could. How long had this child been waiting for the missing

jigsaw piece of her father to be slotted in? Forever, it now seemed!

The house was in darkness when they returned at a little before six. So he wasn't back from work yet. Julia was unutterably relieved. She went through the motions, bathed Nicola, and then, with Nicola lying on her bed watching television, Julia got dressed, feeling all the while as though she were heading for her doom instead of preparing herself for a date, an exciting date, she told herself, with a good-looking, pleasant, eligible man.

And soon it would be the holidays. Nicola would be taken to Italy, without the necessity of needing a chaperon, and there she would see the sprawling family of which she was now a member and by whom she would be lovingly embraced.

But there would be no void because she would be dating, dating, dating.

She chose a sober but figure-hugging wool dress, short-sleeved with a scooped neckline, and the high heels, then she stood back and looked at herself. She looked glamorous rather than sexy and she was pleased with her reflection.

'Where are you going?' Nicola asked idly from the bed and Julia caught her eye in the mirror.

'Oh, just for a meal out, honey.'

'Who with?'

'A friend.'

'What friend?'

'Father Christmas.' Which evoked a response of thrilled excitement, and by the time they strolled downstairs Julia, at least, was smiling.

The sound of the key in the door and the sight of Riccardo entering almost eradicated the smile from her face, but she staunchly maintained it as their eyes met. He was in his working clothes, a dark, impeccably tailored suit that he wore with easy panache. Julia stifled the flutter of awareness as she looked at him and kept the remnants of the smile on her face.

'Nicola's eaten,' she said brightly, relieved when Nicola began describing their adventurous after-school activities of a shopping mall and burger.

'And I'll be back later,' she threw in, edging towards the door with her jacket slung over her arm and her bag in her hand.

'And where are you going?'

'I have the telephone number here and my mobile number.' She handed him a slip of paper and began opening the door, almost expecting him to try and stop her, but he was already turning away with uninterest, and his indifference sent an arrow of pain shooting through her.

'Have a good time.' With his back to her, he held out his hand for his daughter and Julia watched as the both of them left her standing by the door and headed towards the kitchen, with Nicola offering a cheery wave over her shoulder.

It already felt like the final goodbye.

CHAPTER TEN

THE French restaurant was just off the King's Road and, aside from its name discreetly etched on a gilt plaque on the wrought-iron railings, it could have been a private residence. It breathed good taste. Just the sort of restaurant to appeal to a stockbroker. Nothing flashy, nothing ostentatious. Very English.

Riccardo stood outside for a few moments, letting the cold air cool him down.

He had had no intention of being here. He had watched Julia leave the house and thought that he had been superbly self-contained. Indifferent even. He had turned his back on her, signalling that he did not give a damn where she was going or who she was going with.

He had put Nicola to sleep and had then proceeded to spend an hour in front of a stack of files, tapping his fountain pen on the table and frowning at the blur of writing in front of him.

Who had he been kidding?

He walked down the four concrete steps to the front of the restaurant and pushed open the door to find himself towering over a diminutive, smartly dressed waiter. His eyes quickly scanned the room which was loosely sectioned off into three eating areas, pausing when he saw the object of his search. She was sitting at a table in the corner, her face propped on the palm of her hand and looking at the man who was with her and who was talking animatedly about something.

'You have a reservation, sir?'

'No.' Riccardo did not even bother to look at the man who was giving him an ingratiatingly apologetic smile.

'Then I'm afraid—'

'I'm joining those two people over there.' He indicated Julia and her date with a jerk of his head.

'We were not told that there would be a third party.'

'Well, I'm telling you now.'

'I'm afraid…' The poor man's sentence remained unfinished as Riccardo began closing the distance between himself and Julia.

There was no lull in the low conversations as he strode past tables. The clientele were too well-bred to stare. He reached the table and only then did Julia look up, as he leaned forward and placed his hands firmly on the tabletop, his body looming over them both intimidatingly.

'Riccardo!'

'Sir! I must ask you to leave at once. This is most unorthodox!'

'Bring me a chair,' was Riccardo's growling response and at the risk of causing an even greater stir, the waiter scurried off and returned with a chair.

'What are you d-doing here?' Julia stammered. 'Roger, this is…Riccardo. He's…he's babysitting for me. You haven't left Nicola in the house on her own, have you?'

'Your mother is with her.' He turned to Roger and bared his teeth into a menacing smile. 'Why don't you go, *old boy*? I'm taking over from here.'

'What's this all about, Julia?' enquired a confused Roger.

'Riccardo, please. *What are you doing here?*' One or two of the well-bred eyes were slanting in their direction and she sank into her chair.

'Yes, what the heck are you doing here? Julia, who *is* this man?'

'Why don't you tell him, Julia, *darling*?'

'I say, this simply isn't on.' Roger signalled to the waiter. 'This man is being a nuisance. Have him removed, please.'

The waiter hovered uncertainly behind Riccardo who ignored his presence. 'If you want me removed, *Roger*,' he drawled, pushing his face further forward so that the sheer force of his powerful personality became a thinly veiled threat, 'then I suggest you attempt to do so yourself.'

'I don't indulge in scraps.'

'Then why don't you either clear off or shut up?'

'Riccardo, this is *enough*! You're creating a scene and…and embarrassing everyone!' Julia licked her lips nervously and felt a tremor of wild awareness as his black eyes met hers with burning intensity.

He didn't answer. Instead he sat in the chair, leaned back with his eyes narrowed on Roger's blustering face and signalled a waiter over.

'A whisky.'

'This man is *not* joining us!'

'Julia…?' His black eyes swept over her flushed face, and in her moment of hesitation he smiled with tigerish satisfaction. 'Your date is at an end,' he said to Roger and Julia reddened as both men stared at her. Now was the time to firmly send Riccardo on his way, but she couldn't. She couldn't choose Roger because she knew with weary resignation that he was second best.

'Roger, perhaps you'd better leave. I'm very sorry, but if you don't we'll all probably end up being thrown out.'

'But—'

'But you heard the lady. Go.' His whisky had been brought to him and he sipped it, casually dismissing the hapless Roger, who stumbled to his feet, dropping the starched linen serviette on the table in front of him.

'Don't expect to hear from me again,' he told Julia, who

smiled weakly at him, and as soon as he had walked off she leaned forward and said in a low, angry voice,

'What do you mean by barging in here? How dare you interrupt my date?'

'Have you eaten?'

'Yes! No! We've had our starters. We *were* looking forward to enjoying our main course before you stormed in!' She looked at that dark, handsome face and felt a wave of irrational love wash over her, leaving her weak.

'Good. In that case, let's get out of here and go somewhere a little less...' he looked around him condescendingly '...stuffy.'

'I'm not going anywhere with you!'

'Oh, yes, you are.'

'Because you say so?'

'Because you want to.' He stood up while Julia gaped at his sheer arrogance, clumsily following suit when he tossed some notes on the table and beckoned their confused waiter across. 'This should cover the cost of the meal, with a very generous tip.'

'I do apologise...' Julia began, but he was already taking her arm in his vice-like grip and steering her towards the door. The well-bred clientele had given up on their etiquette and were now openly staring as she was ushered through the restaurant.

'You...*you*...*you caveman*!' she spluttered as soon as they were out of the restaurant.

'I'd rather be a caveman than a wimp. I didn't notice your knight in shining armour jumping in to your rescue.' He hailed a taxi and ensured that she was left no choice in the matter of climbing in by blocking the open door with his big, muscular body, then he slid in after her and gave the driver an address.

'Where are we going?'

'To my apartment.'

'There is no way under the sun that I am going to your apartment, Riccardo!' The prospect of being somewhere with him on her own, without the protection of other people around, sent her nervous system skittering into mad overdrive.

'Oh, yes, you are.' He shot her a sideways glance and said unevenly, 'We need to talk.'

'We've already done that!'

Why should she be interested in going over old ground? How many more times did she have to hear that he wanted her and that she should capitulate? How many more times did she have to listen to him tell her that the physical attraction that burned through their bodies like hot lava was just too big to resist?

'No, we haven't. At least, I haven't.'

There was something uneven in his voice that made her stare at him, but he wasn't looking at her and her heart was slamming against her ribcage as they completed the remainder of the short drive in tense silence.

'I won't lay a finger on you, Julia,' he said as they took the lift up to his apartment. Surprisingly, he still wasn't looking at her and she felt a little flutter of dreaded excitement stirring in her blood. 'I just want to…talk.'

She followed him docilely into his apartment, only vaguely registering the classic minimalist styling of the confirmed bachelor. A bachelor wealthy enough to have the best of everything, but without the desire to improve on any of it. The entire apartment was wooden-floored, with a sunken sitting area to one side that was lavishly furnished with a black leather sofa and two chairs. The kitchen was open-plan and looked brand-new, as though the various appliances had never been touched.

He was walking now towards a bar area that was an

exquisite blend of various woods, so smoothly joined together that it appeared as if they were all from the same
tree.

'Well, now that you've got me here, what do you want
to talk to me about?' She dared not go any closer to him,
so she remained where she was in the middle of the vast,
open-plan room, clutching her little black handbag in both
hands.

He poured himself another whisky, offering her a drink,
which she refused with a shake of her head, and then
moved to the leather sofa, where he sat down, leaning forward with his arms resting on his thighs and his head lowered.

He couldn't remember a time when he had been nervous.
Not even when he had sat his exams in his youth, or taken
his driving test. Certainly never in the company of a
woman. He was nervous now. He could feel it racing
through his veins like deadly adrenaline and his breathing
was shallow and laboured.

He was only aware that she had approached him when
he saw the black high-heeled shoes out of the corner of his
eye. He waited until she had hesitantly sat on the sofa next
to him, and even then he didn't dare look her in the face.

'What's the matter?' she asked in a hushed voice. She
was so accustomed to his towering self-control, his confident assumption that other people were born to fall in line
with his wishes, that to see him like this now was throwing
her into a state of inner turmoil.

'Why did you come to the restaurant, Riccardo?
What…what have you got to talk to me about?'

He finally looked at her, his black eyes shorn of their
self-assurance. Julia felt her heart flip over and shakily told
herself that this was all just another ploy to get her into his
bed. He wasn't ready to forgo his challenge, he had simply

decided to switch tactics, to get her to somehow feel sorry for him so that he could move in on her vulnerability. It didn't quite ring true, but she braked at the possibility of speculating further.

'I came to the restaurant because I had to. I had no option. I told myself that you could see whoever you wanted to see, that you were free to do whatever you wanted, but I realised that I do not want you to be free. I do not want you to see other men, to talk to other men or even to think about other men. I sat down in front of my work papers and all I could see was you and that man, laughing, talking, going back to his place, making love. I came because I was torn apart with jealousy.' He raked his fingers through his hair and then pressed the palms of his hands tightly against his eyelids.

Julia felt herself begin to melt. If this was a ploy then it was working. She could never be without this man and to have him for only a short while would be worth the lifetime of heartache that would follow. She tentatively reached out and placed her hand on his thigh and he covered it with his hand, squeezing it gently.

'Riccardo.' She sighed and edged closer to him. 'I give up. I know you want me and I want you and I just…give up. I'll be your little fling.'

'It's not good enough.' He turned to face her fully and for a few dazzling seconds Julia was caught between bewilderment that her offer had just been refused and hope that the tender expression in his eyes would give her the answers she desperately yearned to hear. 'I don't just want your body. Oh, I fooled myself that that was all there was, but I want your soul as well.'

'What are you saying?' Julia whispered as the little seed of hope began to shoot up, swarming through her entire body until she was engulfed with it.

'I'm saying that I love you.'

'You love me?' Her eyelashes glimmered with the sheen of tears and he pulled her roughly towards him, burying his head in her hair so that his words were muffled.

'I love you,' he confirmed in a shaking voice. 'I don't know how and when it happened but you went from being the source of my rage to the object of more emotions I ever thought it was possible to have. I told myself that it was all about lust because I knew that I could control lust, that lust was transitory and did not involve the heart. I believed that one failed marriage had made me jaded towards the whole concept of love except…except when I thought about that I realised that what I felt for Caroline had never been love. I had fallen for the concept of the ideal woman. The truth was that Caroline left me cold, even before I finally admitted to myself that my marriage was dead and due a decent burial service. I clung on because of pride but now I realise that the best thing she ever did was to find someone else, someone who could restore her faith in human nature. But still, I stupidly tried to convince myself that there was no such thing as love. Then I told myself that I would seduce you as some warped form of punishment for dropping a bombshell in my life, and when that didn't work I said that I was just doing it because you were a challenge. But I wasn't. I wanted you because somewhere along the line I fell in love with you.'

'Oh, Riccardo.' Her voice broke then and she tilted her face to his and gently kissed his lips. 'Do you mean it? Mean it all?'

'Every word,' he said in a choked voice.

'I could never understand how you could possibly be attracted to me when all your ex-girlfriends had looked like Helen Scott…'

'Because love runs deeper than looks. You are not just

beautiful on the outside, my dearest darling, you are beautiful on the inside as well. Why do you think that when I was in your company I could never tear my eyes away from you, and when you were not around my mind was filled with you? You made every emotion I ever felt pale into insignificance...

'I know you have doubts about me,' he continued gruffly, 'but—'

'No doubts.' Julia smiled, filled with bliss and wonder that this big, dark, powerful man cradling her against his chest could actually love her. 'You have no idea how much I've wanted you to tell me what you just did. I fell in love with you and it hit me like a bolt from the blue. When you kept talking about want I felt that I had to run away because I wanted so much more from you.'

'And that's why you accepted a date with that wimp...'

'Roger is not a wimp!' Julia smiled with unconcealed pleasure into his chest. 'Although I did find my attention straying quite a bit when I was sitting at that table with him.'

'Straying to me, I take it?'

Julia moved sinuously against him, curling into his body, and he groaned. 'Carry on like that and my little talk for the night is finished,' he growled, bending to kiss her with a fierceness that was returned.

'Oh, good.' She began unbuttoning his shirt, running her hands over his broad chest and teasing the flat brown nipple with her finger. 'Just so long as you take it up again later.'

'Later,' he promised solemnly, 'and tomorrow and the day after, right into forever...'

EPILOGUE

'APPARENTLY you're the woman for me,' Riccardo said, his arm around Julia's shoulders as they both sat on a swinging chair on the wooden deck, staring out into the velvet moonlit darkness. She could hear the sound of the surf, gently lapping against the beach ahead of them, although the sea was just a black lake, fringed with sand and the swaying trees.

'It would seem that I need a woman who can keep me on my toes.' He tilted his bottle of beer, swallowed a mouthful and leant to nuzzle the neck of the woman he adored.

'And I thought your daughter was the one who could do that,' Julia murmured with a smile on her face. Nicola was absorbed with her father, but she would never forget her mother. Neither she, Julia, nor Riccardo would allow that to happen.

'Oh, that child of mine can keep anyone on their toes. I needn't tell you that my family think the world of her. The first granddaughter among four grandsons. She will be spoilt rotten.'

They had been in Italy for two weeks now and Julia had met most of his family and it was as vibrant and closely knit as he had promised. She had been afraid that her mother might have been put off by the sheer volume and effervescence of them all, but she had taken to them like a duck to water.

'And what about the next child?' She patted her stomach which was only now beginning to show the signs of the baby she was carrying, the baby that had been conceived when love had still been an unmentionable word and passion had driven caution to the winds.

'A son,' Riccardo said firmly and he laughed that sexy, low laugh of his that never failed to make the hairs on the back of her neck stand on end. 'I shall need all the help I can get to support me with my women…'

He placed his hand over hers on her stomach and then began stroking her belly in slow, circular movements until her body went limp and she moaned softly under her breath.

'I absolutely refuse to make love out here,' she said, hooking her finger around his thumb. 'Nicola might be sound asleep, but mothers have a tendency to hear the smallest of sounds. My mum would have a heart attack if she came out here and found us…'

'In flagrante delecto…?' He chuckled. 'Your mum would discreetly disappear with a smile on her face. You know I can do nothing wrong in her eyes.'

'Poor, deluded woman…' Julia turned to kiss him, holding his beautiful face between her hands. 'However, there is the beach, and it is rather warm tonight…'

'You're a wicked woman.'

'My darling, you taught me everything I know…'

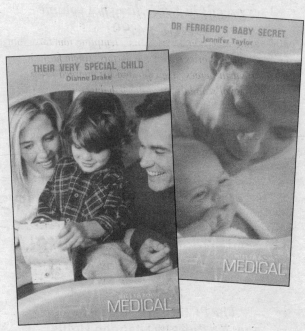

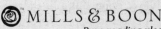

Celebrate 100 years of pure reading pleasure with Mills & Boon®

To mark our centenary, each month we're publishing a special 100th Birthday Edition. These celebratory editions are packed with extra features and include a FREE bonus story.

Plus, starting in February you'll have the chance to enter a fabulous monthly prize draw. See 100th Birthday Edition books for details.

Now that's worth celebrating!

15th February 2008

Raintree: Inferno by Linda Howard
Includes FREE bonus story Loving Evangeline
*A double dose of Linda Howard's heady mix
of passion and adventure*

4th April 2008

The Guardian's Forbidden Mistress by Miranda Lee
Includes FREE bonus story The Magnate's Mistress
*Two glamorous and sensual reads from favourite
author Miranda Lee!*

2nd May 2008

The Last Rake in London by Nicola Cornick
Includes FREE bonus story The Notorious Lord
*Lose yourself in two tales of high society and
rakish seduction!*

Look for Mills & Boon 100th Birthday Editions at
your favourite bookseller or visit
www.millsandboon.co.uk